THE
RESURRECTIONIST

A. R. MEYERING

MONTAG

Montag Press
ISBN: 978-1-940233-72-7
Cover design © Mateus Roberts
Editor - John Rak
Managing Director - Charlie Franco

A Montag Press Book
www.montagpress.com
Montag Press
1066 47th Ave. Unit #9
Oakland CA 94601 USA

Montag Press, the burning book with the hatchet cover, the skewed word mark and the portrayal of the long-suffering fireman mascot are trademarks of Montag Press.

Printed & Digitally Originated in the United States of America
10 9 8 7 6 5 4 3 2 1

"A.R. Meyering's *The Resurrectionist* is a thriller firing on all cylinders. Lit by gaslights, haunted by the past and the long dead, the witchcraft, the protagonists, not to mention Scotland's turn of the century setting, will delight readers. Part high Romance, part supernatural thriller, The Resurrectionist dives into a rabbit hole of magic and secrecy that will keep readers flipping pages long into the night."

> — Stephen Scott Whitaker, member of the National Book Critics Circle, author, and managing editor for *The Broadkill Review*

"The raw beauty of the Resurrectionist is more than the intricate world of hidden magic Meyering builds, or the complex characters, both good and bad, so easy to bond to and commiserate with. It's the very real and frightening possibility that such chaos can come of a single decision made in anger by an individual. At its heart, *The Resurrectionist* is about the power of choice and consequence, and the very real horror one can inadvertently unleash upon the world."

> — Author Lisa Gail Green, author of *The Gallows House*

"The real-life story of the infamous body snatchers, Burke and Hare, is the inspiration for A.R. Meyering's *The Resurrectionist*, a sophisticated, lush, and engaging fantasy novel. It offers the perfect touch of Gothic horror, along with thought-provoking ideas, an elegant use of fantasy, and well-drawn characters whose humanity is the perfect counterpoint to the evil of their adversaries."

> — Victoria Gilbert, author of the Blue Ridge Library Mystery series and the "Mirror of Immortality" series

Meyering's world fluctuates between Barker-esque scenes and Dostoyevskian guilt-complexes with such ease that one wonders whether the 'The Resurrectionist' can function as a concise, thoughtful novel – but it does, and it's a bloody good time.

> — Walker Zupp, Author of *Martha*

For Angela,
who led me to the kingdom

What Became of the Thief

On a skinny, forgotten road in Edinburgh stood a shop without a name—a shop that could be found only if one had previously been led to its door.

The blind man shuffled down the road, his fingers bouncing on the elbow of the information broker who had first told him of the peculiar establishment. His eyes, calloused over with thick white tissue, rolled around in his head as if he were regarding something that hovered nearby. With a bony hand, he covered the deep crevices and wrinkles of his face, but his expression remained troubled.

"Here, William." The broker stopped, roughly grabbing the blind man's wrist and leading his fingers to a metal sign on the wall. "Here's where ye'll find it. Now the payment, if ye dinnae mind."

William snarled, not bothering to hide his distaste as he dug around in the grimy, frayed pockets of a coat that had once fit him so smartly. The way the Scots rolled over their words was enough to make his lip curl. Ignoring his dislike of the broker, the Irishman slapped a heavy envelope into his hand, keeping himself anchored to the wall with the other. His eyes continued to swim and twitch about; he tended to keep them from hanging in one place for too long, even though they were completely sightless.

"It's all here. Careful in there, I suppose," William's companion offered with a halfhearted grunt before clomping away.

William waited until the noise of footsteps faded, then turned his attention to the sign. His fingers searched out the letters:

EST. 1790

He pawed the wall on either side of the gnarled wooden door but found nothing else. Taking a deep, rattling breath and hanging his head, William paused for a moment before knocking. He removed a flask from his pocket and took a great, gulping swig of whiskey that burned all the way down his throat.

William rapped his knuckles on the door, took an instinctive step backward, and pulled his cap farther down his head. Everything seemed so still, save for the roaring and churning of a distant factory belching a foul-smelling vapor into the sky. Then William heard something slide open.

"What's your business?"

The voice was female, youthful, and not Scottish. Each of these qualities surprised him, making him stutter.

"I-I was told I could find help in this place."

"There's no help here, not for anyone. Now—"

"Services then. I wish to commission some rather *particular* services," William interrupted, his tone desperate. The possibility of letting this opportunity slip away due to poor phrasing was unthinkable. There was only silence from the girl.

"I have money. I can give you almost ten pounds now, and I've got more back home—"

"I've no interest in money. What is it you need? Be quick about it," she hissed. William now realized her accent sounded vaguely Germanic.

"It's not the sort of business a man might be comfortable discussing out in broad daylight or in the company of a lady," he began, but when he heard the sliding of the wooden panel again, he cried out, "A curse! I need a curse dealt with."

For a moment, William heard only his own aggravated breathing. Clutching his chest, he winced as if enduring a wave of agony and tried to keep his face from contorting.

"Please, miss, please let me in. Just let me speak to the master."

The panel slid shut with a snap. William stood with his old, aching knees threatening to buckle as he stifled a scream with his hand. Despair threatened to devour him, and he leaned over with his head against the rain-slickened stone as he tried to swallow the anguish. When the heavy door unlatched and swung open, William let out a thin, whining sound of relief.

"Get in," the girl commanded, and with shaking hands, William felt his way through the doorway. The heavy sound of the door slamming behind him let him know he was sealed within the walls of the shop. A pungent, choking odor, like that of peat and lye, hung heavily the air. Stumbling forward, William wrinkled his nose and coughed.

"Stay there, old man. Don't move or touch a thing," the girl said.

William froze in place. He heard a bubbling sound, as well as a fire crackling somewhere at the end of the room, though it was as chilly as a crypt inside. More sounds of footsteps, the rustling of a curtain, and the clatter of a chair on stone cut through the near silence.

"I recognize you now," the woman murmured. Shuffling and clinking noises came, and William guessed she might be gathering materials from where she sat. "You're the thief from the song the children sing. You're the one that slithered away while your partner swung by his neck." She laughed as she spoke, a sound that was at once amused and mocking. William's lip curled up again, and he let out a guttural snarl. Clearly this girl had no idea what kind of person she was dealing with, even if she did recognize his face. His fingers flexed, and he sighed through his nose.

"The master, if you please, miss," came his reply.

The sound of her standing up from her chair cracked through the shop. "*I am the master!*" Her voice rang out shrill and infinitely more petrifying, as if a different person had screamed through her throat. William's aggravation immediately gave way to fright. Something in that wild, wicked tone told him this woman wouldn't hesitate to harm him if the mood struck her.

"B-begging your pardon, mistress," William breathed. "I only meant—"

"Silence. I know why you're here; I can smell it on you… and I can…" Her voice trailed off as she shuffled some papers and a small powdery burst puffed up. "Yes, I can see it. You got what you deserved, and now you want a way out."

"I beg of you. Set me free, if you can, mistress. I know I've done wrong. I know I can't make up for my actions, but I beseech you all the same. I've been denied a chief liberty—the only true liberty a man can have. I've suffered enough in this life. Won't you help me get back the rights to my own death?"

The mistress laughed again, this time sardonically. She tutted to herself, toying with his plea. "You should know here and now that in its current state, your curse cannot be broken—"

"No! That's—"

"*It cannot be* broken, but it can be displaced. The woman who cast it on you truly knew what she was doing. It's deep magic and dark magic, but I'd wager that if it ever found a proper victim, it was you." The response came hissed through clenched teeth, at once both vengeful and indulgent.

"You don't know what you're saying," William said, shuddering.

"Oh, believe you me, Mr. Hare. I know exactly what I'm saying," she continued poisonously, then cleared her throat with a curt cough. "Now, I have one question to ask you that will determine whether we shall do business."

William gave an urgent sigh. "Anything, Mistress."

"Is your death so precious to you that you would destroy one more innocent life to get it? The life of your own child?"

The Incision

The Great Northern Hospital, London, 1895

Edgar's hand trembled as he gazed at the silver pocket watch.

"Time of death: seven thirty-five p.m.," he said weakly, and recorded it into his log as he tried to avoid looking at the woman's corpse. Edgar sat at her bedside with his elbows on his knees, replaying the events that had led up to her demise, trying to find the flaw. The pallor of death had already blanched the supple curves of her face and neck. The dead woman lay as if carved of white stone, her pale hair pooling around her shoulders, a ghastly vision of fading loveliness corrupted by a stitched wound of black-and-ochre blood.

The operation had gone perfectly—even better than Edgar had anticipated. He had expected his nerves to hinder him, but Edgar felt only perfect confidence and control from the moment he cut into Mrs. Sheehy's neck, removing the tumor with the utmost care and precision. He had not overlooked the use of carbolic acid to disinfect the operation room and his tools; he always insisted on meticulous caution with hygiene. Edgar himself had administered the chloroform to sedate the young wife and mother, refusing to cede that simple yet risky task to a nurse. The tumor had come out with little resistance, and no other structures had been significantly damaged in the process. Now, inspecting the stitches on her throat, he repeated the steps in his mind incessantly.

The cause of death was clear: blood poisoning from a septic wound. Somewhere in the series of events, something had infected his patient and caused her untimely death.

Edgar snapped his watch closed and carefully slid it into his coat pocket. He formed a list of duties in his mind to complete before he told Mrs. Sheehy's family the news. Mechanically, he completed the tasks of cleaning and disposing of waste. Somewhere behind him, a nurse murmured words of assurance, but Edgar could hardly hear or be comforted by her promises that he was not to blame. He desperately wanted for her to leave and felt a momentary flood of relief when she quit the room at last. However, the longer he remained in there with the corpse, the more uncomfortable he grew with his thoughts; they threatened to fall out of order and give way to a dreaded storm of emotions.

After lining up the sparkling instruments, now wiped clean of blood and tissue, and disinfected yet again, he turned his gaze to her still form. Edgar had seen perhaps a hundred cadavers or more during his education. He had watched them being cut into, peeled apart, flayed, unpacked, and thoroughly dissected—sometimes to the point where they didn't even look remotely human afterward. Never once had such sights bothered him. They were simply specimens, subjects devoid of life or spirit. Although Edgar had known those bodies on the operating table had once belonged to vibrant souls from all ranges of existence, somehow he had not truly made the connection in his mind until now. He did not know any of those poor souls whose final destination had been the anatomy theater at Cambridge University. Mrs. Sheehy, however, had trusted him with her husband's money and with her own life, both of which he had confidently taken. She had been his third surgical patient at his first appointed position at the Great Northern Hospital. The operations had killed all three of his patients.

As Edgar rose and made his way toward the door in a daze, he tried to steady himself. Making lists in his head always helped—finding priorities, executing the most important action, following through until he had seen to all responsibilities—but as Edgar walked steadily down the hall to where Mrs. Sheehy's husband and son were waiting, his ritual offered him no relief.

Edgar jarred to an unexpected halt as he caught sight of his face in the reflective surface of a window. Perhaps it was just a trick of the cloudy sky behind the glass, but his complexion looked whiter and more sterile than the walls of the hospital. It shocked him to discover that he found Mrs. Sheehy's deathly countenance less disturbing than his own. He studied his image, repulsed that his eyes, which were black and usually appeared alert and curious, looked like two empty pits. The image discomfited him so much that he went on to straighten his coat and flatten his dark hair against his head in hopes of appearing more astute. The effect, however, was that he looked even younger and more naïve than his true age of twenty-eight.

Edgar couldn't bear to look at himself a moment longer. Rushing away from the window and down the hall, he passed the hospital staff and patients with a brisk step that he hoped seemed natural.

All too soon he saw the two of them at the corner of the room: a tall, reedy gentleman with sunken cheekbones, and a smaller version of the man standing at his elbow. Breathless for a word of news, the father gripped the edges of his waistcoat. Edgar faltered, reaching into his coat pocket to touch his watch.

As father and son approached him, hope showed in their expectant, nervous smiles. Words would not rise to Edgar's lips. Conveying the news seemed utterly impossible for the surgeon, until his glance connected with the young boy's eyes. The look on the child's face made his stomach clench with a keen familiarity.

"Mr. Sheehy. I'm afraid I have some terrible news," Edgar whispered, clutching his pocket watch. He couldn't stand to keep his eyes on the boy's face after his look of optimism had turned ashen. The father licked his lips, his eyes darting around Edgar's face.

"Did everything not go as we hoped, Mr. Price?" asked the dead woman's husband.

"The operation was completed according to plan," he said, "but the incision became infected shortly after. Your wife ran a high fever, and we administered drugs. I am greatly saddened to have to report this, but we couldn't help her. We did everything we could, Mr. Sheehy."

Edgar's chest ached as shock spread over them. The man sunk into a nearby chair, his face drained of color. His boy merely stared off into the distance, gripping his shirt and trying to form words.

"I know this isn't much comfort, but I can assure you she didn't suffer," Edgar continued. "She didn't wake after the procedure, and she felt no pain."

There was nothing more in the way of consolation that he could conjure, save for a few words of condolence and direction to more hospital personnel. After a short farewell, he dashed out of the room. Edgar remained in the hospital for half an hour longer, hurrying to finish his work and saying a tight-lipped goodbye to his superiors. He left the hospital, his footsteps echoing in the corridors and mingling with the distant sounds of hacking coughs. Even with the frequent cleanings of the operating and holding rooms, the miasma of pestilence and medical powders hung faintly in the air.

***

Edgar's two-mile walk back to his home in Dartmouth Park felt longer than it ever had. He traversed the winding streets in something that resembled a sprint, feeling somewhere in the back of his mind that if he moved quickly enough, the grim reality of today's events wouldn't catch up with him.

When he unlocked the door, Edgar expected his small but comfortable home to provide some feeling of solace or, at the very least, safety. However, the crowded space with its towering bookshelves and scholarly clutter only pressed in on him, grim and unwelcoming.

After removing his coat, folding it neatly, and loosening his tie only a fraction, Edgar moved through the sitting area and into the kitchen. There, in the cramped space of brick and dingy wallpaper, he set about making himself a cup of tea, taking it as he usually did without sugar or milk. The kettle's shriek made him flinch, and the burn of the aromatic drink on his tongue felt harsher than usual. He carried the cup back to the sitting area and sat in front of the cheerless hearth. Leaving the curtains drawn closed, he lit a lamp against the dark and sat in silence among his books, medical models, and unloved furniture.

During his time at Cambridge, Edgar had studied under Professor Aleister Douglas, a man who had taken a particular liking to him. He always had urged Edgar in a gruff, rumbling voice to "better thyself, young man." It was a mantra that Professor Douglas had repeated every time any one of his students had made a mistake. Edgar, out of admiration, had adopted the professor's maxim as a personal truth. Every time life didn't go as planned, he heard the old man's voice echoing in his head, and Edgar would heed that voice and study or practice or revise or improve himself in any possible, measurable way.

That night, as Edgar stared into the depths of his teacup, Professor Douglas' rebuke in his mind pushed him to study his anatomy books. He approached the small writing desk which bore his carefully ordered stack of papers, notes, and texts. After a quick glance at the cover of a book atop the pile, Edgar was overcome by an unshakable urge to wash up first.

He bathed, scrubbing every part of himself until his skin felt raw and tingly. He scoured his mouth with antiseptic and scraped his teeth clean until his gums bled. Still not satisfied, Edgar went over his fingernails, hair, and feet until they too were raw. Frightened that he might open a wound—he still saw flashes of the dark-purple veins under Mrs. Sheehy's neck—he returned to his desk and forced himself to study next to his now-cold cup of tea.

Edgar turned the pages, sweeping through black-and-white illustrations of human heads, bereft of their skin. The muscles of the throat distracted him briefly as he mentally recited the anatomical terms to himself, but anxiety proved itself inexorable. It took several deep breaths before Edgar could steady himself.

He turned another page to reveal an inked image of the human eye, scanning the collection of beautifully complex natural structures that worked in tandem to give creatures the gift of sight. Delving into how the body worked usually stirred the same emotion Edgar felt as when he looked up at the stars. It was the marvel of smallness and humility in the face of an intricate scientific system that he considered himself privileged to be a part of. But as Edgar studied the ocular diagram, he couldn't banish the memory of staring into Mrs. Sheehy's eyes as they drooped and closed for the very last time—how her awareness seemed to have left before they'd even shut. Her last conscious moment.

Fighting off another wave of sickness, Edgar shut the book and rose from his desk. Chancing a look back down at the mostly untouched cup of tea, he decided he was in need of something much stronger. His first instinct was to seek a companion who might be interested in accompanying him to a public house and sharing a drink, but his heart sank even further when cold reality washed over him: there was no such person he could call upon. Although Edgar was respected among his peers and praised by his professors, the only person he could imagine sharing his poisonous musings with lived far beyond his immediate reach in Scotland.

So he located the decanter of fine brandy given to him by the man who had raised him from boyhood. Taking a seat in an armchair in front of the empty fireplace, Edgar poured himself a generous amount of the amber liquid. The heady scent tickled his nose as he raised the glass to sip at it. After letting it hover before him for a moment, he instead downed it in a single gulp.

Edgar refilled his tumbler. As his head grew foggier, the barriers that kept his thoughts contained eroded. When he'd emptied his third glass, Edgar leaned back in the chair, still trying to discover a flaw in his methods, though now the timeline stretched much further backward.

Did I not follow every instruction properly? he wondered. *Did I not complete my apprenticeship with outstanding results? I was top of my class. I was the pride of my professors. I lectured the other students, for God's sake. I did everything right. I was perfect.*

All at once, as Edgar considered the life he'd led, he was suddenly revolted by his own arrogance. Instead of relieving the overpowering shame he felt, the brandy only exacerbated his mood, and he stowed the decanter back in the cupboard. The mere idea of showing his face at the hospital in the morning made him cringe.

Edgar bit down hard on his tongue. *How did I dare do any of this? How could I have been so unprepared for this? It shouldn't have affected me this deeply; I shouldn't have let it.*

He moved restlessly from the armchair back to the desk. As he paced, the images of the woman's eyes closing again filled his mind and were overlaid with different pairs of eyes—first the two men who'd died on his operating table before, then those of his sister, Ella. For the sharpest of moments, long-suppressed grief tore through him. At once, truth flowed through him, leaving his knees feeling unsteady. Edgar had arrived at a conclusion. Though he knew it was a drastic one, he fully intended to follow through. He grabbed a piece of paper from the drawer and dipped his fountain pen in the ink bottle.

Edgar had only managed to write "Dear Gregory" at the top of the page before more images from the past stayed his hand: a man sprawled and broken in a courtyard; mother and daughter lying in a bed as if asleep; light fading as a pair of hands rushed nearer. Unable to face those memories on this night, he paused, then went to his bag and sought out his bottle of laudanum, which he used most nights to produce sleep, and took a heavy dose of the bitter substance.

He could write the letter in the morning. While Edgar undressed and crawled into bed, Mrs. Sheehy's last words haunted him. As she lay in the operating chair, her breathing labored under the tumor's weight on her throat, Mrs. Sheehy had spoken to him about herself, and he'd found it distracting. The details of her day-to-day life and her child's unimpressive achievements had tried his concentration as he prepared for the procedure. Edgar had raised the sponge soaked with chloroform in his gloved hand, businesslike and silent, when she'd asked him a disarming question.

"Will it—will it be anything like dreaming?" Her voice had trembled, and she'd swallowed with difficulty.

Edgar had hesitated, drawing a short breath. "It'll be even quicker," he'd replied. Her expression softened with hope, and Edgar's nerves spiked. At once, he'd been afraid of failing her and simultaneously eager to assure her further. "You'll hardly feel that you've slept at all, and...I'll be here when you wake up."

Rabbit Stew

Even before Ainsley entered the clearing, she could tell she'd caught something. The tall woman loped over the hill of moss and ferns, batting a branch away from hair so red it glowed like an ember. Quietly she followed the sounds of small claws struggling against wood.

She spotted it skittering about within the trap she'd built earlier that morning: a fat, healthy-looking rabbit with wide, panicked eyes. It grew more agitated as Ainsley approached, stood over it, and watched it squirm inside her homemade prison. After tossing her wild hair back and fastening it behind her neck, she knelt beside the creature, examining it. The stout little coney would make a nice stew, mixed in with the mushrooms her sister, Elspeth, had collected and the fresh carrots and potatoes Colleen had picked yesterday. The three of them would share a lovely meal tomorrow night, after it had slow-cooked in a pot over the fire in their cottage.

Ainsley's mouth watered at the distant hope of the delicate combinations of herbs and spices that would turn this quivering rabbit into a savory treat. After hitching back the sleeves of her frock and drawing the knife from her belt, she reached inside the trap and yanked out the animal by the scruff of its neck. With a hum of satisfaction, she noted the unusual softness of the fur; the makings of a fine pelt. Winter was not far off, after all.

Winter...how could I have forgotten?

Ainsley took a long breath, watching the rabbit struggle in her hand. The thrashing was of no use, though. Life in the forest had made her grip strong. She raised the knife, prepared to kill as she had done nearly every day of her life, but something in the rabbit's flailing made her hesitate.

It does have such nice fur. Perhaps I'd better break its neck instead. It would be a shame to bloody it.

Ainsley sheathed her knife, still firmly keeping the rabbit trapped while it kicked frantically, its tiny eyes bulging out of its skull, its gasps audible. She grabbed its skull with her other hand and tensed her muscles, preparing to twist. However, she stopped a second time. The creature felt so alive and warm in her fingers. She felt its eyes rolling around under the lids, the nose and mouth working madly to try to get free. Ainsley hardly winced when it bit into her.

Colleen would like the pelt for when it gets cold. And I...

Her eyes fell on her hand and the brown-red marks that decorated her skin as if they were drawn onto it. However, the tattoos that traced the back of her hand hadn't been put there by ink or needle. She became distracted by the two knots and their ancient designs woven into each other, stretching out for another that most likely never would appear beside them.

Before Ainsley could stop herself, her grip on the rabbit relaxed. The animal's eyes opened once more, staring up at her in terror. Then it stopped thrashing, as if transfixed by her gaze. With a sigh, Ainsley hung her head.

The vegetables probably will be enough on their own.

She laid the rabbit on the ground, where it already clawed at the dirt. When she released it, it rocketed off faster than she could track it, and soon the clearing fell quiet again. Ainsley collected the trap, wondering what she would tell Elspeth and Colleen when she returned home later that day.

Before leaving the clearing, she glanced up at the ring of sighing hazel trees. The leaves already had begun to grow dry, and the forest was changing from the vibrant, saturated shade of summer green to dustings of pale gold. Fallen leaves carpeted the ground in a patchwork of burnt orange and dark crimson. When a breeze drifted by, it carried a chill that blew right through Ainsley's dress and burrowed under her skin.

So this is it then…the last autumn I'll see. The last season of the last part of my life.

Shallow breaths passed through her as a melancholy pang spread out in her chest. For the first time since she was a small child, she felt as if she were going to cry. The urge piqued and threatened to win out over her resolve to keep a straight face, even in the solitude of the woods, but the sound of hooves on dead leaves made her stand up straighter. A small start rocked her, and she fled the clearing moments before a doe peeked over the hill.

Passengers

Edgar's eyes fluttered open as the train car bumped around a sharp turn. He took a shallow breath and bleared through the window, noting that twilight had started to gather at the edges of the sky. The great metal serpent of a steam engine thundered through the countryside, throwing a line of thick white vapor toward the heavens. He removed his pocket watch to check the time: it was a little past five o'clock.

For perhaps the tenth time that day, Edgar suffered a rush of acute anxiety. He resolved once again that when the train pulled to its shrieking stop in Edinburgh's Waverley Station, he would locate the first ride back to London.

The image of the hospital superintendent's face twisting in shock recurred to him. Edgar heard his words over and over in his mind whenever he let his thoughts wander.

"You wish to...*resign?*" The superintendent had echoed Edgar's statement as he sat across from him, dumbstruck. Edgar nodded, stone-faced. "But you've only just started!" the man had protested, his pince-nez wobbling on the bridge of his nose.

"I understand, but I fear I am..." Edgar's voice wavered, and he took control of it. "...insufficiently skilled and underprepared." He wasn't able to force himself to say any more. He couldn't relate the depths of his horror and panic at the mere thought of ever taking up a scalpel again: that he couldn't bear to take one more life or that his confidence had been irreparably broken. However, the stern expression on the superintendent's face demanded more of an explanation.

"I'm so deeply remorseful for what I've done," Edgar went on. "I've failed you. I had no business, no right to play at this job. I—"

The superintendent studied him. "You're too fine a surgeon to walk away this soon. You've worked too hard to simply forfeit," he stressed, and let his words ring. Edgar's brow knit. "Take a leave of absence, if you must, but come back to us when you're ready. I won't have talent such as yours squandered."

Edgar had thanked him profusely and left the office, fully intending never to return. He'd spent the rest of the week hiding in his flat and awaiting Gregory's reply. After it had come, Edgar had set off for Edinburgh as soon as he could.

The long journey had sobered him and put his irrational behavior into perspective. As soon as he returned to London, he would march back into the hospital and reclaim his position. He would put this whole mess behind him. Then, once again, this plan was dissolved by his shame, and Edgar exhaled. He glanced around the empty sleeper car for a moment before sliding out his black leather bag from under the seat. The silver writing emblazoned on the satchel showed his full name, "Edgar Winston Price." He undid the clasp with a careful motion and withdrew the novel *Bleak House*, which he'd been skimming through yesterday.

From between the worn pages—the book was one of Edgar's favorites—he pulled the slip of paper on which he'd scrawled Gregory's new address and read it again. Almost a year had passed since he'd last seen him, and he wondered what had become of the man whom he'd called his brother since childhood.

Edgar knew Gregory had recently married, but he hadn't been able to attend the wedding. He sensed that Gregory had never truly forgiven him, judging from the silence that had followed his preemptive letter of apology. Edgar looked forward to the chance for reconciliation or at least an understanding. Judging from Gregory's last letter, which welcomed him into the new home he shared with his bride, it was within the realm of possibility.

Edgar stared at the cover of *Bleak House* for a long while, trying to muster the motivation to read more of it, but it merely hovered in his vision. Too many other things occupied his mind during the long trip to Edinburgh. While he looked out the windows and into the pastoral scenes that rolled by, all Edgar could see were the faces of countless men and women who had lain upon his dissection table.

Until a week ago, all of it had been science. Brilliantly woven tissue waiting to be explored, defined, touched, prodded, understood. The human body was a puzzle to be solved—a near-perfect machine crafted by the most inspired accidents of the universe. Nothing about it had disturbed Edgar in the slightest, even as he folded back the skin of the human face to reveal the bald, unseeing eyes of murderers and the vestiges of souls claimed by the river. The causes of death could be rooted out, explained, then controlled.

Yet as Edgar sat musing in his sleeper car, sealed off from the chattering, carefree world of people, a throbbing shame twisted his insides, reminding him that he'd been a fool all along to think he'd understood any of it. Edgar had invaded the most sacred, private areas of human beings and sliced them to pieces.

For what? To satisfy my own curiosity? For profit? To prove something to people, to the world? Because it was fascinating?

He looked up at the window again and, with effort, studied his pale, angular face, with its sunken, dark-ringed eyes, as if looking for an answer there.

Because I wanted to help people. Wasn't that it? Yes, I wanted to help people.

Feeling sick all over again, Edgar loosened his cravat. Flashes came to him—of organs split wide open, of rib cages cracked, of his own hands slicked in the long-congealed blood of victims of every variety of misfortune, of those same hands lifting out lengths of intestines and explaining them to a roomful of rapt students and encouraging professors. He was not able to stop these flashes any longer. A man with his legs detached to better reveal a cross-section of the spine. A woman with the skin peeled away from her hand so he could explain the relationship of muscles. An elderly chap with a hideously overgrown goiter, hacked into and displayed to gaping, scribbling young men. Blood. Bones. Bile.

Edgar's chest tightened, and for a moment he was incapable of stopping himself from imagining how he might look unfolded and spread apart on a table. It wasn't until then that he realized he was gripping the novel so tightly that the binding was crackling. At once he released it with a tiny exhalation and hastily stowed it back inside the bag, where it was safe from his practiced, destructive hands.

He decided in an instant that he could no longer be alone and stood up stiffly, tightened his cravat, smoothed his coat, and marched into the corridor.

If I remember correctly, the bar car is to the left. Edgar turned and proceeded through the cars with his back and face as straight as he could keep them.

He found it with little trouble, and with his chin pointed upward, he entered, still focusing on keeping his posture impeccable. The car was beautifully crafted with mahogany paneling, soft-burning lamps, and a carpet that evoked images of wine. Past several sets of tables and chairs stood a bar with a sleepy man working behind it. Only a few of the tables were occupied by other passengers, most of whom were sitting and reading newspapers, some cradling drinks and staring out the window.

In front of the polished wood bar stood three red stools, the leftmost of which was taken by a man in a long frock coat. Edgar took a seat, leaving a space between him and the stranger.

He then scanned bottles of amber, deep-green, and cobalt on the shelves behind the bartender, looking for anything that might tempt him. He decided on whiskey, and soon after reporting this to the bartender, he sat sipping his selection with tight lips.

Edgar had dispatched with his first glass before he noticed the man to his left was peering at him from over his shoulder, sniffing audibly. Edgar caught a glimpse of two bright-blue eyes under a mop of unkempt white hair but turned back to his empty glass with haste. The man shot him an inquisitive glance, clearly aware that Edgar had noticed him.

"Another, if you please, sir," Edgar requested, embarrassed to hear that his usual crisp tone sounded ever so slurred to his ears.

The bartender poured a healthy splash into the glass then stepped away to serve a man at the far end of the car. After raising the glass to his lips, Edgar chanced another look at his neighbor. The man had swiveled all the way around and was now looking at him directly, his piercing blue eyes shocking. The man smiled in a meek sort of way, but with eyes a bit too still and wide to be of any comfort.

"It's you," the man finally spoke, his accent Irish.

Edgar set his glass down without drinking from it. "Beg pardon?" he replied, and the man laughed. Now that Edgar had gotten a proper look at his face, he noticed something peculiar about the man's skin. It looked waxy and discolored, as if slick with fever. However, despite his white hair, the man retained a look of youth. His face had no deep wrinkles, yet Edgar couldn't discern what age he might be. He could have been in his middle twenties, or just as easily his late forties.

"That smell...that funny smell. I've been trying to figure out where it's coming from, and I think it's you. Smells like...like metal. Or something out of a chemist's or—"

Edgar gave a short mirthless laugh, reached into his pocket, and produced a vial filled with a dark, yellowish liquid.

"Tincture of iodine," he told the man. "A disinfectant. I apply it to my hands periodically throughout the day."

The man cocked his head to the side a bit and gave Edgar a smile as if he'd said something absurd. "Now you don't really take any of that nonsense to heart, do you?"

"I assure you, sir, I take this matter quite seriously. Hygiene is not to be overlooked. Medical professionals and laymen alike vastly underestimate its importance."

"What are you? Some kind of physician?" Even through the fogginess of Edgar's head, he could tell his neighbor was also well on his way to intoxication.

Edgar took another heavy sip and sighed. "A surgeon," he told him, then stopped. A strange urge led him to tell the man more. "Well, I was, up until quite recently. I left my position."

"And why'd you do that?" The Irishman moved over to sit beside Edgar. As he got closer, Edgar became truly discomfited at the state of the man's skin. He mentally shuffled through his knowledge of dermatological conditions, but nothing answered the question of what would give the fellow such a waxy, sallow look.

"I, ah," he began thickly, and took another drink. "I made some rather unfortunate mistakes."

"Somebody died?"

"Yes. Somebody…somebody died."

They were both quiet after Edgar spoke, and for a long time, the only sound was the train jostling down the tracks at full speed.

The Irishman hung his head and heaved a sigh. "Well, that's just…" he dropped off in midsentence, staring a corner of the train compartment as if shocked by something. Edgar followed his disturbed gaze, but found that nothing was there. When Edgar turned back, the man recouped with a little shake of his head, then looked directly into the surgeon's eyes.

"…that's just bloody terrible, isn't it?" the stranger said this in such a way that Edgar guessed might actually be sincere but he just raised his eyebrows in response and quaffed the rest of his drink. The Irishman seemed to want to say something more, since he kept opening and closing his mouth and raising a finger. Finally he laid some money out on the counter and slid it over to the end.

"Get another whiskey for my friend, Mr...." He looked over to Edgar, waiting for him to supply his name.

"Price. Thank you kindly. I appreciate the gesture," he replied, as the whiskey flowed back into his glass.

"Anything I can do to lift some of that weight. Name's Jacob, by the way. Jacob Hare." He took Edgar's hand in his calloused fingers and shook it vigorously.

"Like a rabbit," Edgar mumbled, hating himself for only having something so vapid to say in response. However, Hare seemed pleased with this for some reason, and a broad smile spread over his face, stretching back that rubbery skin. Edgar noticed that his teeth were rotten. A short laugh rattled out from between them.

"Like a rabbit."

Edgar and Hare talked for hours more, finishing off most of the bottle of whiskey between them. They discussed the world's problems as if they could likely fix them, as if they alone had all the best ideas. Hare told him in a rapturous, heartsick voice about the cottage he'd grown up in as a child in Ireland, and about his mother, whom he dearly missed.

Edgar grew so comfortable with his new companion—in large part thanks to the drink—that he even went so far as to joke with the man. Although none of his quips were any good, Hare laughed nonetheless. Edgar's head was muddled, but through that haze he revived aloud his days at boarding school with Gregory, going on at length about Gregory's father, who had adopted Edgar when he was young. At times, Hare clutched at his chest or looked over his shoulder as if checking on something, but mainly stayed focused on the conversation. Edgar, however, tried to ignore this, judging it to be a tic of some sort.

Talking about such personal things with a stranger was a harsh reminder that it had been years since he'd revealed anything of substance about himself to any living soul. It made him feel vulnerable and nervous but also relieved in a way, almost as if the disclosure validated his existence.

As the hour neared midnight, the car emptied of all passengers aside from Edgar, Hare, and a lone woman at the far end whose face was buried in a book. The bartender was asking for pay or he'd threaten to cut them off. Edgar dug inside his pocket and overpaid him by a staggering amount.

"There you are, my good man," he slurred. "That should cover the cost and then some. Please do keep it coming, for both me and Mr. Hare."

"What a kind soul you are, Mr. Price." Hare hiccupped, raising his glass in a toast that Edgar completed.

"Not kindness, my friend. I simply have an ample sum in savings and nearly nothing to spend it on. I'd wager that if I didn't work a day more, I should still be able to live comfortably for the rest of my life. Perhaps I ought to be more generous," Edgar huffed, so drunk that he remained unbothered by how arrogant and improper he sounded at that moment. Prior to the last few days, he'd never had much experience with drinking, and the churning threat of nausea already crept up on him.

"And how'd you get such an *ample* sum, you lucky son of a bitch?"

"Not lucky, dear man. Terribly *unlucky*." Edgar's breath came heavy now as he dabbed sweat from his brow with a handkerchief. He nervously removed the iodine tincture from his pocket and spread some over his hands. How long had it been since he'd washed? He wouldn't arrive in Edinburgh until tomorrow. And then he had to have tea with Gregory. A bath seemed so painfully far away. Edgar shut his eyes and leaned onto his arm.

"You know, Mr. Hare," he said, "nothing...nothing is *ever* as good as it used to be." Edgar heaved a sigh, and Hare grew quiet and stared into his shallow, swirling whiskey. "My boyhood is still so clear to me, before I went to boarding school with Gregory. The sensation of being young and being happy—feeling that the world was new and exciting; feeling so small, yet not even close to as helpless as I feel now. It's all so fresh in my head."

"I remember," he continued, not really caring whether Hare was listening but just yearning to say the words out loud. "A fond memory of mine is one where my father took our family to the river on our property...and when my sister and mother were playing off across the field. He'd pull me up onto his lap and speak so kindly to me—not at all like his usual taciturn self. He'd say, 'Look, Edgar. Look at all that world out there. You can have a piece of that—whichever piece you like the best. There are so many things waiting for you in this life, and you were born lucky enough to see them all.' It was always something along those lines, at any rate."

"Fathers...to hell with them," Hare gurgled, his pale cheeks taking on the very lightest shade of pink.

"He always, *always* reminded me that I was *lucky*. And the grand irony is that I've been so ferociously *unlucky*, which is something no one I meet can seem to sympathize with. Every time the merest hint of something good enters my life, it's destroyed before my eyes. It makes a man not want to care anymore. And this *isn't* the way they told us the world was going to be—our fathers promised it would be filled with beautiful things, but they lied. All they did was make a massive mess, and they expected their children to clean it up for them." Edgar moaned and nuzzled back into his arm, his head starting to pound.

Hare didn't respond, but when Edgar chanced another glance upward to see how his emotional vomit had been received, he found his drinking companion was staring at him.

Edgar tried to read what Hare was feeling from his expression, but it was hard to decipher—the man's eyes were so constantly wide and restless. For a moment it looked as if Hare was trying to form an acceptable response. At length, he laid his hand on Edgar's shoulder and gripped it, perhaps a bit too forcefully.

"That's the world, my friend. Bad things happen to people who don't deserve it. They happen more than you'd think. All we can do is…" Hare trailed off, then picked up the bottle from behind the counter without waiting for the bartender and grabbed Edgar's glass. He filled it then pushed it back into Edgar's wobbly grip.

Hare raised his glass high and waited for Edgar to meet his hand. Their glasses clinked, and completely against Edgar's better judgment—what was left of it, anyway—they both downed their glasses in a single gulp.

Edgar passed out in less than a minute.

Venom

Nausea assailed Edgar the moment he awoke. Panic shortly followed.

Edgar's hands were tightly bound, and a blindfold covered his eyes. He struggled, only to feel through his still-drunk haze that fabric rubbed against his bare skin. His jacket, waistcoat, and shirt had been removed. He was lying face-up on something long and flat—something that felt like his cramped bed in the sleeper car. When he forced himself to focus against the alcohol that remained in his veins, he heard the chugging of the train as it sped across the tracks.

As he cried out and flailed about in shock, two strong hands clamped to his shoulders, pinning him down.

"He's awake." It was Hare's voice.

"Please don't do this. Please stop. Whatever you need, I'll give it to you—"

"Shut him up, quick," hissed another voice, this one female.

A dirty rag pressed against Edgar's lips, and after a short struggle, his jaw was wrenched open and the rag shoved inside. A cord wrapped around his head and mouth, securing it in place. All Edgar could do was to try to sit up and escape, but the struggle proved useless. Edgar's hands were tethered to the rail behind him, keeping him rooted to the bed. Bolts of terror shook through him, coming in pulses. That this could be reality seemed impossible, even as he felt cords bind his ankles together.

With a loud intake of breath through his nose, Edgar started as two hands pressed down on his bare chest: tiny and thin, like a petite woman's, but strong beyond comprehension.

"Bring it to me, Jacob, and I'll get started," her voice purred, tinged with an Austrian accent. The tone was cold, but quietly satisfied with Edgar's fear. Edgar tried to scream desperate pleas through the rag in his mouth, but nothing came through. The inflamed suspense at what they were planning to do with him ripped at him. Urgently he tried to make sense of the rummaging sounds in the corner of the room and Hare's quiet but harrowed breathing.

What are they gaining from this? Is it a way to take my money— didn't I mention my money? You absolute idiot, Edgar...

...No, it can't be the money. They'd have strangled me while I slept. This is different—they're doing this for the thrill. I'm the entertainment. There's no bargaining my way out of this.

Anguish swept through his stomach, and his breathing sped up even more. The woman was dragging a thin, cool finger up and down his chest, along his breastbone, as if impatient.

"*Bring it here,* Hare!" she cried in a harsh whisper. "This is the last opportunity we have to get it right. I'm not leaving anything to chance."

"I'm trying—it's tricky. This thing scares me. I don't want it to touch me."

No, wait, Edgar told himself. *They're trying to accomplish something. They're pressed for time, and they're trying to be quiet—that means people are still around. I've got to make as much noise as possible.*

Edgar wriggled against the ropes that bound him, trying to knock against the walls or floor. He screamed as loudly as he could against the foul-tasting rag in his mouth, but his voice came out muffled. Though he thrashed his head, a pillow stopped it from making any noise. The woman pinned him down even more tightly. Her surprising strength overpowered him, and Edgar could soon do little else than squirm in place.

"Hare, *now!*" the woman snarled, and Hare responded with some irritated scoffs. Edgar heard his footsteps getting closer.

Good Lord, what is it? What is he afraid of?

"Here it is. Take it. I'll hold him." Hare touched his calloused palms to Edgar's shoulders, but the woman slapped his hands away.

"You can't touch him while it's happening, you halfwit. It won't work. Now, give me your hand." Edgar's entire body began to suffer violent tremors. The quiet grew in heaviness until it was broken by the sound of Hare wincing as if in pain.

The woman's fingers crept over him, undoing the tie that held Edgar's gag in place. As she pulled out the cloth in one hasty movement, he took a great breath with the intention of screaming. However, as his mouth opened wide, Hare jammed his finger between his teeth and pushed it along Edgar's tongue. The metallic taste of blood filled his mouth, and his already-sickened stomach clenched as if to expel its contents. As Hare withdrew his finger, leaving Edgar retching, he heard a tiny metal creak, and something was tossed onto his chest.

Edgar whined a long, petrified sound as he felt the armored, prickly belly of a creature about the size of his palm crawl up from his navel. Itchy, pointed legs—perhaps six of them—scuttled up his ribs. He managed to emit a loud, dire sound before the woman clamped his jaw shut with her impossible grip.

No coherent thought possessed him—only a fierce, blind terror. Then the little gripping legs found their way up onto his left breast, where it stopped in place. With shocking suddenness, a single, sharp appendage dug into his skin and drove deeply into the muscle. Edgar screamed once more against the woman's hands, the violent fear and excruciating pain forcing his entire body to seize up. There was venom in that sting—he felt its burn—and it was spreading quickly with a sensation that was both numbing and unbearable.

"It's done," the woman said. "Grab it."

"I told you I'm not touching that thing."

"Step aside then." The woman sounded as if her patience were being tried. The creature was plucked off Edgar's body, and even though he was free to scream again, all that escaped from his throat was a broken whimper. While he tried to stop the whirling panic, he only barely noticed his body growing cold with pain from the wound. In the very farthest edges of his consciousness, there came the soft, almost imperceptible sound of a child sobbing and begging for something—salvation perhaps.

"P-please..." Edgar said, his heart's thump going slower and slower. The cries grew louder.

They have a child with them too? They're going to harm a child?

"Please don't hurt him...let him go. I'm enough. Don't... not a child..." His own voice seemed miles away; consciousness was fading fast.

"What the hell is he talking about?" Hare growled. "What's he on about, Mag?"

"It worked."

Catching Crows

Magdalena undid the last of the stranger's bonds and laid his hands over his chest. She leaned back against the train-car wall. Their new friend looked peaceful at last. Briefly, she caressed his cheek, taking in the warmth of his flesh. With the blindfold removed, she saw he was a rather handsome man, if not a bit peaky. Though his cheeks and eyes were sunken, and his body thin, there was something rather romantic about the sharpness of his face and the dark, glossy hair that clung to his forehead with sweat. All at once, Magdalena's throat burned and ached, and her tongue went dry. She pulled her eyes away from him.

"Dress him," she told Hare, who sat gazing at the unconscious form of their final victim. "We don't want to attract any more unwanted attention than we can afford."

"You do it, why don't you?" Hare glowered at her. "I spent all night drinking with him, didn't I? I was the one who caught him for us and my head's splitting."

"I'm going to the roof for a bit; I'm famished and in need of a refreshment. And I'm doing all this for *you*, if you recall. Pull your weight," she snapped, with punctuated timing, then rustled over to the washbasin.

"You're getting something in return. Don't forget that," Hare griped as he massaged his temples, but dutifully rose and collected the man's crumpled cravat, shirt, and waistcoat from the corner of the train compartment.

Sighing, Magdalena washed her hands and face in the basin. In the looking glass, she caught a quick glimpse of her face, ghostly white and delicately youthful as ever. She sighed again. There was nothing to be done—no matter how she dressed, she never looked old enough to truly pass as an adult. Her short stature didn't help in this regard either. Magdalena took a moment to comb her fingers through her inky black hair, which always was short, wildly messy, and stuck out around her chin. Her bangs covered her eyebrows, making her blue eyes pop out even more from under them. She smoothed out her exquisite charcoal-colored gown, then teased out the shoulders and bosom of the taffeta dress to give the illusion of maturity to her skinny frame.

After she forfeited that losing battle, Magdalena made her way to the door, looking askance at Hare as she went. The oaf was battling with the limp form of the unconscious man, trying to get his shirt back on and button it. Resisting the urge to comment, Magdalena ran her tongue across her teeth; the way they almost cut into her tongue provided a strange relief. The spot on the man's chest where the scorpion had stung him already showed a purplish tinge. How nice it was to see her plan proceeding so well.

Magdalena's throat prickling with an uncomfortable sandiness. "I shall return shortly."

"Ah, you've no idea how good it feels to be rid of the last one—and you know, I think it's a bit funny that this bloke was a surgeon." Hare gave a wheezing laugh as he took the man's face in his hands and pinched his cheeks for Magdalena. He wiggled the man's head around and laughed even more, baring his yellow teeth as he did.

Magdalena's lips pulled back ever so slightly. "Yes, a very amusing coincidence." she said flatly.

Hare sneered at her condescension. "See here, though. Here's his things. His bag's got his name on it: 'Edgar Winston Price.' Phoo, how's that for snooty? And let's see what he's reading..."

Dickens. Never liked him much—ah, here's where he was going. Not too far from Westport actually. Now *there's* a coincidence," Hare cackled as he dug through the surgeon's bag.

"Just make sure he stays asleep. Drug him if you have to. I don't care much about who he is. He's not going to last very long. When we're approaching Waverley, stuff him in the trunk," Magdalena ordered, then grabbed the doorknob. Hare tutted as if something in her behavior upset him, and she turned back to challenge him on this.

"When you're up there...do you *have* to torment the poor creatures?" Hare said with a shudder. "Can't you just kill them first? I hate the way they scream. Gives me the collywobbles."

"What, the birds?" Magdalena laughed. "Would you prefer it if I chose something else to eat? I'm sure I could manage with the passengers in the next car over. They'd be much easier to keep quiet, I assure you, and far more nourishing," Magdalena smiled, revealing every one of her keen, ivory teeth. Hare lowered his eyes and sniffed.

"No, Magdalena. Let them be. Just stick to catching crows for now," Hare conceded before shifting his gaze to the body before him.

Flight

Edgar understood that his survival was based on keeping quiet and entirely still, yet the urge to scream and tear out of the train car had never been stronger. However, he forced himself to remain motionless, his hands folded atop his chest, where his heart crashed against his ribs. When the woman called Magdalena had unbound him, it had pulled him from his shallow sleep. For an instant, his eyes had eased open, but he quickly shut them again.

Now he waited and listened as Hare sighed and picked through Edgar's bag. At frequent intervals, Edgar's stomach threatened to betray him—the copious amount of whiskey he'd consumed carried the very real possibility of producing violent illness. Every time his abdomen seized, he clenched his jaw as tightly as he could and breathed through his nose to control the response.

Keep the poison in, he told himself. *It'll save your life.*

With each breath, the pain from the wound in his chest bloomed, growing into a heavy pulsing that demanded a reaction. Eventually it sounded as though Hare had grown bored with rifling through Edgar's bag, and he tossed it onto the surgeon's legs. The shock of it nearly made him flinch, but he mastered the urge and kept his breath steady and his face still.

You will get through this. You will not let these criminals win. You will see the streets of Edinburgh. You will have tea with Gregory and his wife today. *You will survive this.*

Hare sounded as if he were settling into his seat only a few feet from where Edgar lay. After the longest thirty minutes of his life, Edgar heard snoring. With his heart rate increasing by the second, he chanced a peek. Lifting one eyelid, he saw Hare slumped up against the wall with his cap over his eyes; the whiskey finally having beaten him. A breeze of relief hit him when he saw that he was still in his own sleeper car.

Taking the utmost caution, he opened both eyes and stared at Hare. Sleep held total sway over the man, his head nodding forward on his chest, his breath rattling in his throat. Hardly allowing himself to breathe, Edgar began to sit up. However, when he shifted his pectoral muscles, blinding pain sliced through him, and he gasped. Clapping a hand over his mouth, he stared back up at Hare, who remained lost in his dreams.

Trying again, Edgar sat up, this time expecting the pain and gritting his teeth through it. With an agonizingly slow pace, he moved his legs over the side of the bed. After his feet touched the floor, he looked directly across the small, enclosed space at Hare. Edgar guessed he could still fight him off even with the chest wound, but he dreaded to think what would happen if he caught the attention of the Magdalena woman. Not wanting to take any chances, he lifted himself up off the bed and took his bag in his hands, keeping his eyes moving between the door to where Hare slept near the desk. From the light streaming in from behind the curtains, he guessed that it was a little past dawn. Only a few more hours until they arrived at Waverley.

Edgar stood up, almost gasping when dizziness threw off his balance. He still expected he might be sick at any moment, and his throat felt parched, but he kept himself focused. In three long, tiptoeing strides, he crossed the compartment and laid his hand on the door.

With the utmost control, he slid open the door, hoping to escape without making a sound. At that very moment, the train car gave a lurch and the sliding door hurtled forward and clattered against the wall with a resounding bang. Edgar went faint with fear and froze again as Hare grumbled in his sleep. He didn't wait to see what would happen next.

Despite the pain radiating from his chest, Edgar flew from the room, his footsteps pounding the floor and the door slamming behind him. From the commotion that rang up after him, it was apparent Hare had woken up and was scrambling to his feet. Edgar whipped down the corridor and into the next train car, holding his satchel tightly against his stomach.

"Help! Help me! I'm being attacked!" he cried, hoping to rouse any nearby support. He continued to holler even though he felt Hare thundering closer to him. His chest stung, and his knees were giving out. Soon people surrounded him—men pushed their way out of compartments, frightened ladies peeked out from behind doors, others called for the conductor. As Edgar began to hope for salvation, he turned to see Hare stop in his tracks at the end of the corridor.

"There he is! Restrain him!" Edgar pointed at Hare, whose face turned a petrifying shade of white. As his assailant snarled at him, the pain in Edgar's chest flared up to a fiery crescendo, and he doubled over, moaning and struggling to take a breath. His windpipe seemed to be blocked, and he kneeled on the floor, gasping and reeling in pain. Several of the men around him lunged for Hare, but he was too quick.

Through streaming eyes, Edgar watched as Hare evaded them. The man had nowhere to run, his pursuers would eventually get a hold of him.

Running farther down the car and out of their grasp, Hare slammed himself against the wall and attacked the window with shivering hands. He elbowed the pane of glass; it shattered just as the men reaching for him caught up. Everyone watching the scene sounded with fright as the white-haired man hauled himself up and leapt from the window in one fleet movement.

A woman behind Edgar screamed, and he lurched back up to his feet to press his face against the nearest window. In the distance—and getting farther away—lay the crumpled form of a man in the lonely heather, his head twisted nearly all the way around.

Misplaced

Magdalena's lips cupped around the wound that she'd hewn between the dark feathers. The crow's wings flapped as she sucked at it, a low moan humming in the back of her throat as its still-warm blood sated her. She suppressed the urge to take a bite, knowing the creature would die too quickly. Crows had a tolerable flavor and they were easy to lure in. All she needed to do was whisper, and they'd flutter willingly into her hands, not realizing they were flying to their doom; this was only one of the many benefits of working with her master. Magdalena suckled at the wound until the bird's screams turned weak and the blood pumped less furiously between her teeth. After licking at it a few more times, she took an enormous bite out of the neck, spitting out feathers as she tried to separate them from the living sinew.

Soon, however, the bird was dead, and the taste of the flesh and blood began to sour. Having fed on it too long after its death, Magdalena smacked her lips, trying to rid her mouth of the unpleasant aftertaste. She tossed the used-up crow over her shoulder, where it bounced off the top of the train and into the grass on the side of the tracks. When the burning in her throat subsided, she cleaned her mouth as daintily as she could with a handkerchief and picked off the feathers from the front of her gown. Just as she was taking a moment to enjoy the fierce wind atop the train, a clamorous noise from below disturbed her.

She looked around wildly for the source of the sound. It took her only a moment to locate it: there in the grass, speeding farther away by the second, was Hare. He rebounded off the ground headfirst, his neck snapping and his head swiveling backward. The man's chest caved in from the blow against the ground, and after a few more violent flips, he lay still in the grass, a heap of broken bones and open wounds.

Cursing, Magdalena scurried to the edge of the train car, took a moment to aim her landing, and leapt off the moving locomotive. For a moment, she soared through the air, her gown flapping riotously around her thighs and her hair whipping about. The feeling of absolute freedom in the face of her rage consumed her for an instant before she hit the ground feet first. Both of Magdalena's left and right ankle bones snapped as they absorbed most of the massive shock, but she felt only a sufferable splintering sensation. Enduring it, she remained standing, though she teetered a bit while she waited for her body to repair itself. She stayed standing, tolerating the pulsing and rushing sensation in her legs as her broken bones mended. Casting a quick glance around, Magdalena noted that they were quite alone out here—nothing but heather, hills, and fog. No chance that they would be seen.

Once her legs were in working order, she set off at full speed toward Hare. With neat bounds over the tall grasses that grew on either side of the tracks, Magdalena bore forward until she stood above him, pouting down at the mess he had become.

Sighing with frustration, she knelt beside the quivering, fractured mass and started the process of resetting his bones. She knew he could manage it on his own, but without her help it would only waste precious time. Magdalena threw him over onto his back, turned his head around so that it faced forward, then stretched out his arms. When she was about three minutes into her work, Hare's eyes began to roll around again, and he took a long, tortured breath. Groaning, he blinked madly until the hemorrhaging in his eyeballs faded and he could see again. She stopped her mending to give him a stern look.

"Care to explain this?" The quiver in her voice betrayed she was expending every effort not to fly into a fury. It was a few more minutes before Hare's lungs re-inflated, and a bit longer still for him to get past his coughing fit. When his airway began to operate again, he let out hoarse screams in Magdalena's direction.

"The bastard got away from me!" he rasped, shaking as he lurched into a sitting position. He groaned after his paroxysm of anger passed. "He tricked me...I was just resting my eyes for a moment, and he escaped and raised hell, so—"

"Forgive me, I must have misheard you." Magdalena slowly simmered over each word as rage welled inside her. To keep control over herself, she dug her razor-edged fingernails into her hand, the sharp pain keeping her mind clear. "Do you mean to say that you fell asleep? Is it...is it actually possible that you're as stupid as your father was?"

"You shut up, Mag. It was only for a moment! I was only resting my ey—"

Magdalena lost her hold over herself, grabbing Hare's throat and tearing out a huge hunk of flesh. The thought that she mustn't be too furious with him sobered her. She'd been making such progress with keeping her anger in check—why throw it all away over this? Still fuming, she pulled in breath after heavy breath through her nose. Blood streamed down Hare's front and he gurgled and gasped. He stood up in consternation as more of the lustrous substance issued from the gaping hole in his neck. Hare's foot stamped against the ground. Magdalena's lengthy history with Hare often involved teaching him plenty of lessons about respect, so there was no chance that he might try to strike her. Hare would be facing the loss of his arm if he even threatened it. As she had many times before, Magdalena merely waited for his throat to patch itself up, teetering on impatience, a tooth biting at her lip and her gown pooling around her as Hare wrestled with his tantrum.

"You...bitch. I...*hate* you...for doing that to me so often." Hare took sharp breaths, his face growing pink. "*It's torture! Every single time!*"

Magdalena caught him by his bloodied, shredded shirt. She pulled him close enough so he'd feel the fierce pulse of air that streamed from her nose.

"I'm aware of that. That's why I keep hoping you'll learn from your mistakes, but it seems the only punishment that gets through to you is pain." She took several more deep breaths before continuing. "I believe I expressed myself *very* clearly when I told you there was no more room for error in this operation."

"Of course I know that, you vicious little c—"

Magdalena jammed her hand into Hare's mouth and seized his tongue. She pinched it until the man whimpered, then released him.

"You'd do well to remember you're in the presence of a lady. I won't tolerate that kind of language." She wiped his saliva onto his shirt then took a step away from him, showing her back to him. Folding her fingers before her, Magdalena regained enough control over herself to stop her voice from shaking.

"Allow me to explain this to you...*once* again. If I don't get that last revenant, it means you won't have paid me for my services. I took a risk doing this in the first place, and I fully intend to be paid for my work. Because of your past blunders, we don't have any more souls left to work with. I could only recover the anchoring items for eight of them. I need *seven* revenants, but I only find myself with *six* and a cursed man on the loose."

"Hey, it weren't my fault that bastard in Aberdeen offed himself before he could get properly transformed," Hare was defending himself, eyes wide with indignant warning.

"That isn't my concern. You employed me to complete a task for you, which I've done. I detached eight of the original sixteen for you. As payment for releasing all of the souls, I was to receive the remaining eight connected to the anchoring coffins— the only ones that could become viable revenants. All of them were to be my property. One has already been lost due to your mishandling. My patience is wearing very thin," Magdalena rumbled lowly, keeping her fingers laced. Her anger and contempt had cooled to a low smolder.

"Well, what the hell do you want me to do about it? He's gone—he's on his way to Edinburgh right now. Do you have any idea how many people there are in Edinburgh?" He was desperate and wailing, gesturing in wild movements.

Magdalena turned, irate. "I *live* in Edinburgh, Jacob."

"You know what I'm trying to say. It's impossible! You can do with six. You—"

"No. Six *is not* enough..." Magdalena's teeth peeked out from behind her lips, and her huge eyes narrowed to slits. "I will not sink to your level—you know quite well I am not a woman who takes insults lightly."

"You're not a woman at all," he sneered under his breath, but Magdalena heard him all the same. The urge to tear Hare's innards out and scatter them about, leaving him to hunt for them across the lowlands of Scotland, tempted her. With tremendous effort, she kept her face straight.

"It upsets me to be treated thus," Magdalena started, deeply affected. "I'm very sensitive when it comes to these matters. I can't get the thoughts out of my head—the awful things people have said and done to me...they never leave me. I give a great many chances to a great many people. I run a fair business. My clients are treated with respect, until some misguided soul gets the idea in their head that the promises they made to me aren't as important as they were on the day they made them. Like you, Jacob, they took what they wanted from me. They were desperate for help, and I gave it to them. Don't you think it's only fair that they hold up their ends of the bargains? Isn't that common sense?"

"But this is—"

"No one deserves to be cheated out of something they earned. Don't you agree?" she pressed the issue, and Hare settled down slightly, the bitter look still on his face.

"Of course."

"You came to me—miserable, tormented, willing to do anything to remove your curse. You got your wish. But have you paid me?" Magdalena persisted, her tone brisk.

Hare stood quiet for a long while. "No," he finally allowed, his brow deeply furrowed.

"Have you met my friends? The ones I keep in the cellar? Have you heard them down there? Do they sound happy?"

Hare's face turned grim, and he swallowed, his newly repaired throat still flimsy. The serious nature of his situation seemed to dawn on him.

"No," he repeated, eyes swimming in their sockets.

"I truly would prefer it if we remained on good terms." Magdalena strode over and took Hare's clammy hands in hers, squeezing them with an affection that made him shiver with terror, but also with something softer. "It's what I always prefer. But there are so many disappointments...people are so painfully selfish. And I'm not going to let anyone get away with that. You're no exception, Jacob. I'm sorry."

"Will you help me? Please? I'm scared I won't be able to do this, Mag. I'm scared of you too," Hare whispered, abandoning his pride.

As Magdalena looked over his face, taking in his pathetic, pleading expression, her heart, tired and numbed as it was, clenched with the memory of what pity used to feel like. Despite everything that had happened between them, she couldn't help caring for Hare. She supposed—in her own way—she loved all the people who had come into her life. Even the ones who'd hurt her, even the ones she'd had to hurt. She hung her head and breathed through her teeth, pulling in the chilly, humid air, and knowing she couldn't refuse him.

Sylvia's Stone

Ainsley stomped into the cottage, throwing her scarf off as she did. She tossed a trio of dead pheasants onto the table where Colleen sat, skinning potatoes. Colleen jumped at the sight of the defeated birds and the smudge of blood that now smeared the wood.

Collapsing into a chair, Ainsley let her head roll back as she gave an almighty sigh and kicked off her boots. "Meat," she stated without looking at Colleen, then shut her eyes.

Ainsley heard a gentle click as Colleen set down her knife, and quiet footfalls as she crossed the room to where she sat, putting her hands on the red-haired woman's shoulders. When Ainsley opened her eyes, she saw Colleen smiling down at her, blonde hair falling in curtains around her face and tickling the tips of her cheeks.

"Now, is that really the kind of greeting I get?" Colleen asked playfully, her summer-blue eyes mischievous.

Ainsley laughed a bit sheepishly then returned Colleen's grin. "Ah, I suppose not." She softened, feeling a bit more like her old self, then sat up and kissed Colleen, her fingers weaving through her hair. Colleen leaned into the kiss—Ainsley could feel her smiling, which made her weary heart brighten with warmth. Colleen broke away, let out a soft laugh, and headed back to her peeling. Ainsley's eyes stayed glued to her.

"So I guess that means you'll want to pluck and clean those, then, to make up for your beastly manners," Colleen's voice brimmed with spirit.

"I should've known—always a scheme, with you." Ainsley sighed contentedly and leaned back again. "Why can't Elspeth do it? I'm knackered."

"She's indisposed..." Colleen gestured with her knife down the hall to Elspeth's room.

Ainsley got up with a groan, clomped down the hall, and peeked in to see her sister laying on the bed with her hands crossing her chest. Elspeth, whose silver-blonde hair spread out behind her, was completely still, her eternally youthful face peaceful, her chest barely rising as she dreamt. Ainsley tutted, knowing nothing could reach her in this state. Elspeth's familiar had guided her spirit far away from their world, yet again. She would remain there for at least several hours more.

"She's been going to the other side more and more these days. It worries me," Ainsley said, as she dutifully returned to kitchen and began to yank out the feathers of the pheasants. She never liked to see Colleen work more than she had to.

"She's depressed. It's hard for her to be in the Wood right now. She's happier up there, with her familiar. She can be at peace for a little while," Colleen said delicately, as she dumped skinned potatoes into a dish.

Raising her eyebrows, Ainsley pulled out the feathers with a mite more aggression. "You mean it's hard for her to be around *me*." Colleen grew silent. Ainsley sensed Colleen didn't want to start another fight. There had been a great many of them recently. This troubled her—the three years they'd spent together had hardly seen anything besides the occasional tiff.

"Cold out there, isn't it? This October is going to be a chilly one." Colleen tried to change the subject as Ainsley chopped the head off one of the birds in a clean stroke. Ainsley couldn't decide what she hated more: dealing with the subject or ignoring the subject. Both options made her chest burn with frustration.

I'm the one who's dying. They could at least have some sympathy instead of trying to make this harder for me.

One bird cleaned, two to go. Colleen's chopping of vegetables slowed and eventually stopped, noticing Ainsley's lack of reply. Ainsley felt Colleen's eyes on her but refused to look up from her work. To distract herself, she peered about the room.

Their cottage was cozy and smelled of fragrant herbs. Other odors hung in the air as well—Colleen's fresh bread and residuals from the potions Elspeth brewed. On one side of the room was a cluttered kitchen overflowing with dried meats, mushrooms, plants, and ingredients for spells and concoctions. A painted ceramic oven smoked with the merry scent of burning wood. The windows were colored with fanciful hues that stained the entire room with fiery, jewel-bright light in the evenings. In the middle of the room sat a large, well-loved oak table, covered in a splendid mess that consisted of every sort of wonderful, terrible oddment that could be found in the woods—animal bones, wildflowers, medicinal roots, and moth wings among them. At the other end of the room was a trio of armchairs upholstered with fur and animal skins; a worktable with Colleen's books in various stages of binding; a soot-caked hearth with a heavy, large-mouthed iron pot; and a massive stack of assorted weapons, hunting gear, and handmade wards, most of which belonged to Ainsley.

"Ainsley…" Colleen started but was jarringly interrupted when Ainsley slammed her butcher knife onto the table.

"Can we please not discuss this right now? Can I just have one day where I don't have to talk about it?" Ainsley was exasperated, and Colleen fixed a melancholy stare on her.

"There's still time! You've given up too early. You can—"

"Colleen!" Ainsley barked a little too sharply and instantly regretted it. She hated herself when she was short with Colleen.

Sighing, she wiped off her hands, undid the tie in her hair and let her wild, red curls hang all over her face as she tried to think of which words could possibly make anything better. After a moment, Ainsley realized there weren't any.

"I'm…I'm going out to the shed for a little bit to find that, erm, satchel that belonged to my mum. I needed it today. I'll be back, and I'll clean those." She pointed two the other two pheasants. "Don't bother yourself."

Ainsley stood up, pulled her boots back on, and made for the door. She ensured that her pace was quick enough so that Colleen couldn't get in any words that might draw her back into the impossible discussion.

Outside in the gloaming, the air was brisk. To Ainsley, October always smelled like the combination of all the finest things in the world—in a single sniff, she picked up the aroma of the fallen leaves, wood fires puffing out from chimneys, damp soil from the frequent rains, baking from far-off ovens with traces of precious cinnamon and cloves, and the rich scent of ripe turnips and pumpkins from the neighbors' vegetable patch. Their own garden was filled with dewy plants, all glowing green with nourishment from the fertile earth.

Flowers grew in bright patches of purple, orange, and yellow, their petals catching the light of the failing sun, and their perfumes riding on the autumn gusts. Ainsley meandered through the flower patch and around the gardens, which were abundant with produce yet to be gathered, past the ring of mushrooms and the sacred stones, until she reached the shed. It needed no lock—it had been enchanted to keep any unwanted hands out of its contents by one of the most powerful witches ever to live in the Wood: Ainsley and Elspeth's mother.

Every witch in the Wood's coven remembered the remarkable ferocity and kindness of Sylvia Allaway, and they awarded the same respect to her daughters, even if they might have acted otherwise had the girls come from different lineage. These thoughts rattled around in Ainsley's head as she flung the door open and rummaged through the long-forgotten, dusty belongings. She resented the careful dishonesty with which people treated her, though this was not a special feeling. Ainsley harbored at least some resentment for most imperfect human behaviors.

Why am I even here? I should go back inside and apologize to Colleen, she thought bitterly as she dug through the mountain of broken, discarded things. She still managed to smile with nostalgia at toys she remembered from her childhood, as well as some photographs and drawings of her mother. That was the only way she had ever known Sylvia—through images and stories.

Usually uncovering the lost treasures in the shed soothed Ainsley and gave her perspective in times when her temper fixed her mind on trivial matters. This evening, however, it only deepened her misery. She picked up a fabric doll Elspeth had sewn for her in her early years and turned it over in her hands. The workmanship was far from skilled, but Ainsley had loved it without giving that a second thought. Elspeth had been forced to assume the role of both mother and sister for Ainsley almost twenty years ago when Sylvia had returned covertly to the Wood with an infant in tow. Sylvia had risked her life and left Ainsley in her only living daughter's care, insisting that her child be raised in the Wood and not the outside world.

Though Elspeth was well over fifty years old at the time, she was unaccustomed to motherhood and not ready to care for a child as untamed as Ainsley. It had taken the combined effort and education of the entire community of witches and their mortal sons and husbands to raise the hellion that she had been. Ainsley gave a doleful smile as she ran her thumb over the shoddy embroidery that depicted the doll's face. All her memories sat before her in a small, cluttered pile. This was all she had amounted to. Her entire life would be over before she turned twenty.

And what a sad, short life it turned out to be. All these years— wasted. I've been so selfish. But it's a vicious world. I'm not entirely sorry to be leaving it or its barbaric inhabitants.

Ainsley set the doll on top of a box and huffed, anger welling up again as she recounted the injustices she'd been told of the world beyond the Witches' Wood—the world that had claimed her mother.

I've been selfish, but at least I've never been that *selfish. I've never harmed another person for my own gain. The only real disservice was to myself. The outsiders never did anything to deserve my love, so why should I be forced to help them? I really would rather die.*

When Ainsley no longer could convince herself that there was something of importance to be found in the shed, she stepped outside to shut the door, but was jarred when a loud crack rang out from the shed's depths. Perplexed, she swung the door back and tried to identify the source of the sound.

A thin trail of smoke leaked out from the box she'd set the doll atop only moments before. Pushing the poppet aside, Ainsley lifted the lid. Inside the box, on a bed of animal skin, was a gray stone with a crack splitting it down the middle.

The smoke was leaking out from the tiny fissure, and when Ainsley tried to pick the stone up, her fingers met searing heat. Wincing, she squinted at it, her mind racing with possible explanations. It appeared to be a perfectly normal rock that anyone might pluck from the riverside. It took her a few moments to connect a memory with the object, and when she did, Ainsley nearly tossed the box aside in surprise.

It was the anchoring stone her mother had made. The object to which Sylvia's most wicked spell was still attached, and which kept her curse in place and operating—the only curse she ever laid upon another living being. This was why Sylvia had been banished from the Witches' Wood for eternity, by law of their society. This curse was the reason that Ainsley never had known her mother.

With old feelings of betrayal dredged up, Ainsley allowed herself to stew in her unpleasant thoughts before more disturbing questions dispelled them.

She wasn't such a scholar of magic that she could outdo Elspeth or even half the witches in the Wood, but one thing had become apparent to her. The only reason an anchoring stone would begin to crack was that someone was trying, and succeeding, to break the curse connected to it.

So…there's one last thing to take care of before I go.

Caledonian

Edgar leaned against the side of Chemist Campbell's Drugs, wondering how a person could possibly be this tired. Since the instant Hare had jumped off the train, he hadn't had a moment's rest. He was interrogated, taken into police custody for questioning, and examined by the first physician he could find. However, through all the madcap responsibilities that needed attending to after the catastrophe, nothing yet had made a modicum of sense.

The wound on his chest had been cleansed, inspected, and puzzled over a great deal by a Dr. Franklin Roberts of Edinburgh and by Edgar himself, but neither of them could discern what was wrong from the sickly purple welt and spreading coloration. Antidotes were administered, tonics prescribed, and remedies recommended. Edgar followed through on all of them, not bothering to rest at all. It was well past noon now, and he found himself in a peculiar state of mind—a place beyond exhaustion and terror that felt as placid as it did otherworldly.

Nothing seemed to be wrong, aside from a constant ache in his breast. He had no fever or any indications of poisoning or infirmity. It made no sense to stay under medical care or with the city police, who had begun a hunt for either the body of the madman Hare or his wicked female accomplice.

Even after everything he'd been through, the thing Edgar craved most now was a bath. He yearned for the hot water, for a chance to scrub himself and to apply soap and disinfectant liberally. It had been ages since he'd felt this filthy, and it caused him prodigious anxiety. However, he knew that in only ten minutes he would be late for his teatime appointment with Gregory and his missus at the Caledonian Hotel, which was quite a way out from the chemist's shop against which he now reposed. The sore temptation to abandon this appointment altogether and instead search for a place to wash up and rest would not let Edgar move from the spot. Would Gregory understand if Edgar did not come? Would he still allow Edgar to stay with him afterward? Something in Edgar's stomach nagged at him—their friendship might be irreparably broken if he did not make it to tea. After his dismissal of the wedding, he feared this might be the only chance at reconciliation.

So, with strained effort, Edgar pushed himself off from the side of the building, pocketed the medicines and salves the establishment had sold him, and beseeched his tired legs to transport him safely to the Caledonian Hotel.

Edinburgh stretched out before him in a shining array of slate and emerald green that stretched under a crisp sky. Edgar blinked at the majesty of the ancient towers and steeples, with their many windows and the myriad lives sheltered behind them. Wide streets bustled with life, shifting in the constant movement of proud ladies in elaborate gowns, of salespeople calling out to passersby to examine trinkets and produce, of beggar boys streaming past in lines, of the clacking of horses' hooves upon the cobbled roads, and all varieties of human emotion zipping by. Lush gardens lay between the hallowed Gothic structures, looming high into a sky that was astoundingly blue when it was not blanketed with clouds. Rain came and went in sheets of brief moisture, and a brisk chill bounced through the lanes and the people who coursed through them.

Edgar sensed that the very stones that paved the roadways could still remember the stories, woeful and wonderful, of all the feet that had passed over them; even so, they refused to share more than hints of their secrets. The rain gradually ceased as he made his way down Princes Street. Though it was his first time in the city, he couldn't help feeling the slightest bit nostalgic—a sensation that both unnerved and enchanted him.

In the posh areas, the tantalizing smell of roasting coffee beans hovered on the breeze, as did the seductive scents of whiskey and sizzling sausage from the open doors of boisterous taverns. Far off in the distance, a churning, filthy smog cloud issued from the domineering smokestacks of factories. Shop fronts gleamed: pawnbrokers, public houses, haberdasheries, carved faces of churches, butcher shops, a department store, clothiers, cobblers, toy stores, and restaurants, all packed side by side along the narrow lanes and stacked high with apartments.

As Edgar approached the grand hotel where he was to meet Gregory and his wife, he stopped in awe of Edinburgh Castle on its glorious green hill, a wise old patriarch watching over the rest of the city. He gazed on the sight of the steadfast structure, drinking in every last sublime detail. When at last his eyes had supped to their fill of the austere beauty, Edgar turned to seek out their meeting place, eager to see Gregory and unload the tale of what he had experienced upon a sympathetic ear.

The lobby of the Caledonian Hotel was adorned with crystal chandeliers that sparkled so brightly they looked to be carved of ice. Edgar left his bag with the elderly man behind the front desk and ascended a magnificent staircase on his way to the tearoom.

After a short walk through the halls, he stepped into a room alive with chattering and merriment. Soft light poured in from the arched windows, dusting the exquisite gold trimming around creamy white walls. He couldn't stop his attention from getting lost in the sight of powder-blue panels painted with heavenly images of flowers and rare birds. Scented tea flowed from clinking teapots into china cups that looked as if they'd been crafted by fairies. Edgar picked up on the steamy aromas of Earl Grey, jasmine, bittersweet matcha, Scottish breakfast, and fragrant herbs. These coalesced with the bell-like laughter of a group of elegant ladies, all swimming in gowns with buoyant, puffed sleeves. The gentlemen who joined them spoke in tender tones and smiled with urbane goodness at their friends and partners, all of them nibbling on savory sandwiches, smoked salmon, scones with fluffy clotted cream, and dainty sweets piled high on tiered plates.

In his hazy state of mind, Edgar stood ensnared by the softness, which seemed to him so simultaneously absurd and inviting after his being the victim of such cruelty. No longer able to police himself to appear strict and proud, he cleared his throat. He tried to pick Gregory's face out amid the carefree, gay visages that crowded the room and was shocked to find he'd already passed over it several times without recognizing his old friend.

Gregory had always had something of a robust frame, but he had perhaps doubled in size since he and Edgar had said farewell in London some two years prior. As Gregory rose upon seeing Edgar, the buttons on his green silk waistcoat complained against the pressure his belly put upon them. Edgar's heart warmed when his friend's ruddy face split into a smile hidden underneath his bushy mustache. As Gregory got closer and spread his pudgy arms out to either side, Edgar noticed that much of his friend's hair had begun to disappear from the crown of his head, even though he was newly thirty.

"My dear man." Edgar greeted him with a relieved grin and allowed himself to be crushed by Gregory's spongy girth and tight embrace. Though Edgar's flesh usually crawled under the slightest human contact, there was something about the familiarity of those hands that offset the unpleasantness. Edgar looked down at him—Gregory stood an entire head shorter than Edgar, who was not of any extraordinary height—with affection and relief.

"Good God, Edgar, you'd think a surgeon could afford a meal every now and then!" Gregory's unapologetically loud, cheerful voice boomed as he slapped Edgar on the arm. "I've seen matchsticks with more substance to them. Ah, don't worry yourself, though. We'll fatten you up some. Lord, it is good to see you. Come! Come meet Genevieve!"

As Gregory ushered him to the table where he'd risen from, Edgar caught sight of a woman whose look of repugnance shifted cleanly into a transparent smile. She offered him a limp hand, the back of it facing upward, and simpered up at him.

"So nice to meet you at long last, Mrs. Farrow." Edgar took the woman's hand gently within his, unsure whether she meant it to be kissed or shaken. He looked her over, searching for something in her appearance that he could perhaps make a courteous remark about to win her favor.

The woman wore a gown that was a size too small, giving her an appearance that said she was being squeezed. Her ample bosom threatened to violate the seams of the dress, which was a rude shade of pink. The sleeves were so puffed, it was as if she had attached two balloons to either side of her shoulders and they were keeping her substantial self afloat. The hat that covered her sandy hair was a world unto itself, decorated with such twee adornments as silk flowers and fake birds. She tilted her nose upward, facing Edgar with two gaping nostrils that he found incapable of avoiding with his gaze. Lost for words, he simply offered, "Gregory has written such wonderful things about you."

"And yet you are something of a mystery to me, Mr. Price. There's so much I'm eager to learn," she drawled in a heavily affected accent Edgar supposed was meant to imitate upper-class London society. He was at once disheartened. Clearly, Gregory hadn't mentioned much about him to Genevieve. Edgar smiled politely, despite his depressing supposition, and took a careful seat beside her. Their table was littered with stacks of empty plates that bore the remains of a large meal; evidently the main event of teatime had come and gone without him.

Gregory lowered himself into the seat with a sound like that of a sputtering steam engine. After Edgar settled, the ache in his chest pulsed more painfully than ever, this time accompanied by a sharp twinge in the middle of his back.

Gregory looked to Edgar as if expecting something from him. Edgar began to grow tense as well, unsure of what he wanted, and became even more uncomfortable when Gregory gestured in his wife's direction.

"Ah..." Gregory started softly, mopping at his forehead with a napkin and chuckling. "Ah, Edgar. I believe—erm, perhaps it would behoove you to..." Edgar remained nonplussed. "I mean, you are rather late, old chap."

"Oh!" Edgar felt heat rush to his face as he flushed. "Yes, I'm terribly sorry about my tardiness. I had the most dreadful time getting here. If you can believe me, I was att—"

"Well, that's quite all right, but I should hope it won't happen again," Genevieve huffed with a look that portrayed self-satisfied benevolence. "I believe Gregory might've told you so, but my time is so often occupied by social engagements, I consider it very precious. I do hope you understand, Mr. Price."

"Oh, er, yes, of course, Mrs. Farrow," Edgar stammered.

"Oh, *do* call me Jenny, won't you? We should be fast friends. Gregory told me this morning that the two of you once were quite close, is that right?" She smiled indulgently at her husband, who tried to hide a look of guilt behind a quivering grin.

Edgar blinked. "Gregory and I...we were raised together. His father, Samuel, he was my guardian from the time I was a boy. We attended boarding school together." Edgar couldn't quite conceal his wounded feelings but tried his best to remain cheerful in the face of Gregory's whining laughs. He always had regarded himself as Gregory's brother, and the shock of discovering that perhaps his feelings had been incongruent to Gregory's all along disturbed him.

As boys, they had bonded after Samuel Farrow, who had been a business associate of his father's, took Edgar in. Though Gregory was a few years older than him, he had welcomed Edgar into his life, looking after him as he recovered from the trauma of loss and violence. It had been a difficult time, but it was hard to keep up a somber mood when one was in the presence of a boy as mirthful and boisterous as Gregory Farrow.

While Edgar had been a small boy with a nature that was prone to nervousness, Gregory was always rife with health and spirits. At boarding school, he'd been wildly popular due to his brazen, outgoing nature, and Edgar believed he himself would've endured far more attention from bullies if not for Gregory's loyal friendship. They'd been as close as family until recently, when Gregory had married. His courtship with Genevieve had been hurried, lasting only three months before Gregory had proposed. The wedding invitation had come with little time to plan, and Edgar already had agreed to give a lecture at the anatomy theater on the very same day. Although Edgar knew Gregory had been affronted by his absence at the wedding, it pained him to think that his closest friend had failed to mention him almost completely to his new wife.

"Ah, what was that you were saying about your journey?" Gregory scrambled to change the subject as he picked up a teapot and filled Edgar's cup with the remaining lukewarm liquid.

"Oh, heavens, look at you—how tired you seem," Genevieve told Edgar. "You know, my dearest," she said, addressing Gregory, "have I told you that Mrs. Wensleydale once…" She launched into what would become a fifteen-minute lecture about the flaws of the transportation system and how harrowing it was, but not before asking Edgar if he wouldn't mind if she might have the last of the cucumber sandwiches.

In her soliloquy, Genevieve provided numerous examples of how the ladies in her social circle were forced to travel alongside those of the lower classes and how being exposed to what she referred to as "less refined beings" endangered not only their health and safety but also their morality. Her stories were punctuated by peals of a terrible, shrieking laugh that grated against the ears as it shot up and down in pitch. Edgar soon learned to loathe this sound and made a note to himself to avoid humor at all costs.

Neither of the men could get in a word until she had exhausted every last sprawling anecdote she knew that had even the remotest connection to railways. Edgar took the opportunity to scavenge what was left of the meal, all the while wondering if it was really his tardiness that caused Genevieve to act so abrasively toward him, or if she was simply predisposed to unpleasantness.

"Oh, dear!" She let loose a whirlwind of laughter that made the grandmotherly lady behind her wince. "Oh, silly me, but I've talked too long! My Greggy darling always jokes that I'm *ka-wiiite* the chatterbox, doesn't he?" She smiled, her pink cheeks bulging outward as she rubbed Gregory's arm sensually. Edgar blushed as Gregory returned this affectionate gesture with a devilish grin.

"Please do tell us what happened, Edgar," Gregory implored him, at last showing something of the caring side Edgar remembered.

"It was nightmarish," Edgar began, thirsty for the chance to bleed his tired mind of some of the poisonous memories that refused to let him relax. At once Genevieve and Gregory were both looking at him, only now aware that he had been through something unspeakable. Edgar recounted the night as it had happened, editing out, of course, the part about his disgraceful drunkenness and bragging. When he finished, Gregory's face was stony, and Genevieve's mouth hung open in disgust. Neither of them knew how to respond until Edgar mentioned that he was feeling exhausted to the point of delirium and desperately wanted a bath.

Edgar handed money to Gregory, who then rose to settle the bill while Genevieve remained silent in her ruffled state. Something in her expression suggested that she held Edgar accountable for what had befallen him.

Gregory ushered both of them out of the tearoom under the shadow of his frowning wife, who also vastly overtook his height. They took a short carriage ride to Gregory and Genevieve's town home, where Gregory helped Edgar with his bag. The outside of the building was stately yet cramped, with a steep set of brick steps leading up to the narrow front door. The interior and furnishings spoke of newly acquired wealth and a strong urge to appear impressive—Edgar guessed this to be the result of Gregory's recent promotion to head bank clerk. There was a short tour, and after the niceties had passed, Edgar made straight for the washroom.

The hot water felt rejuvenating on his aching body. As he lay soaking and trying to keep awake, he inspected the wound on his chest—the color had darkened, and the sickly purple looked to be seeping into the surrounding veins. Edgar washed it fervently, applied more of the prescribed salves, and took an extra dose of the medicine he'd purchased. The rest of his muscles began to loosen in the bathwater, but the longer he lay there, the more his back hurt. Knowing now that sleep was imperative, he dried himself quickly, said a quick thank-you to Gregory and Genevieve, who continued to wear her trademark sneering grin, and excused himself to the guestroom for a nap.

Edgar parted the curtains surrounding the four-post bed, and after throwing himself onto the mattress, lost himself to sleep in an instant.

***

Hours later, he was drawn from a deep pool of unconsciousness by a sharp pain in his spine. As he jerked awake, breath flowed into him then caught in his lungs as he endured the wave of torment in paralyzed silence. Certain he had accidently lain upon an errant knife or letter opener, Edgar forced himself to flip onto his belly and clawed at his back, only to find nothing there. Once his ability to breathe had returned, he took great gasps and stared down at his pillow as sweat beaded on his forehead and rolled down his nose.

Then, as quickly as it had come, the pain subsided to only a dull ache. Edgar lay sprawled, listening to the cannon-like booming of his heart and feeling a kind of panicked joy that the agony had ended. As he began to get a hold over himself, a shuffling sound from the carpet beyond the curtains of the bed stirred him.

"Gregory?" he mumbled, and the alarm that had just started to ease began to rise again. "Is that you?" he said a bit louder as the noise intensified. Something dragged itself across the floor. Edgar righted himself and stared at the end of the bed. He jumped when a slight breeze teased at the curtains. Then the dragging sound stopped.

Edgar froze, unable to react. Normally he would have risen briskly to investigate without the slightest worry, but an oppressive, heavy tenor to the moment warded him away. It communicated that whatever was beyond that sheet of fabric threatened something more dangerous than death or bodily harm. It was corrupted...unearthly.

The crying began so softly that Edgar could hardly identify it. Several sniffs and a low anguished moan evolved into shuddering breaths and stifled sobs. Soon the sounds were loud enough that he realized they belonged to a child. The weeping sounded eerily familiar to him—not the crying of a boy who had lost sight of his mother or the sound a youngster might make when he scraped his knee after playing too roughly. No, this was the sound a child made when exposed to a horror that shattered all innocence and illusions of safety. It was the cry of a mind that had been temporarily broken—a place where pain had become channeled only into sound because words and concepts had stopped making sense.

Immediately, alongside his fright, Edgar felt a rush of sympathy and protectiveness. He crawled forward and tore the curtains apart, looking about frantically for the suffering child, but as soon as he did, the room was again plunged into ringing silence.

He pulled in harsh breaths, leaning backward and sitting on the bed as he tried to order his thoughts. *This could be a dream. Am I dreaming?* He pinched his arm to test this theory, finding the sensation to be quite in keeping with waking life. Just to make sure, he stood up and crossed the room, which was just barely lit in the dim purple glow of the last light of sunset, to the looking glass in the corner. His reflection was there, and he became certain he was awake—this did not, however, prove comforting. As he stared at the sweaty pallor of his face and watched his eyes dart about, something in the reflection caught his attention.

Cowering on the other side of the room near the bed was a small boy. He lay on the floor, clutching his body. Edgar saw that his spine bent off at an odd angle so that his body was curved backward into a C shape. At once his fear quieted and years of medical training, bolstered by a doctor's instinctual compassion, spurred Edgar to action. Desperate to attend to the broken boy's injuries, he hurried to the side of the gasping child but stopped several feet from the wretched creature. Everything from his hollow eye sockets to his grimy clothes warned of danger. The boy's skin resembled the flesh of the cadavers Edgar had worked on in the anatomy room— just beginning to rot and looking as if it might peel straight off the bones if one yanked hard enough. Edgar stumbled backward, the hideous stench of decay filling his nostrils.

As he retreated in fear, the boy lurched upward, moving like a marionette, his broken backbone causing the upper part of his torso to swivel about on an unnatural, unjointed axis. The smell of rot grew stronger than anything Edgar had experienced in his studies, and he clamped his hand over his mouth. The boy flopped onto his distended belly and crawled forward, throwing one hand forward then the other as he pulled himself along, his two eyes fixed on Edgar with what could only be murderous intent.

The child pulled himself up over Edgar's legs, his clammy hands dragging their way across his chest. He tried to plead with the unholy thing but found he couldn't make a sound as the boy wormed his way on top of him. Soon his fetid palms were slithering over Edgar's shoulders, and the boy's jaw unhinged to reveal a reeking, gaping esophagus and teeth riddled with rot and decay. Before Edgar could find his voice, the boy tore back the collar of Edgar's shirt and sunk his teeth into his chest. He took an enormous bite of flesh, yanking it away with a splatter of blood and torn sinew.

Edgar's scream rang throughout the house, and as he threw his head back while howling, his chest felt as though it were splitting apart. As he rolled over, the weight from the boy on his chest at once dissipated. There was nothing but air above him, and the pain that had racked him only a second before lessened to the now familiar pulsing ache. Edgar's cry of torment died in his throat, and he lay on the floor, immobilized by shock and panting as he searched his torso for injury. He was astounded to see that he was utterly unharmed.

Pounding footsteps in the hall heralded Gregory's entrance into the room. He burst in, looked about wildly for any sign of something wrong, then grew silent and confused when he caught sight of Edgar lying gasping and terrified on the floor. Edgar did his best to wipe the heavy film of sweat from his forehead then stood up on untrustworthy legs. Certain there was no way of shrugging this moment off as ordinary, he had to say something to Gregory, anything. Shame and the need for decorum prevented Edgar from allowing his old friend to witness him in such a vulnerable state.

"I heard—you sounded like—"

"Awful nightmare. F-fell straight out of bed." Edgar tried to force a laugh, but the sound of his false voice made him cringe.

Gregory blinked as Edgar braced himself against one of the bedposts and caught his breath. For one long, strained moment, Edgar marveled at how a person with whom he used to converse so easily—a man who had once listened to and shared the most intimate of thoughts and secrets—could seem like a complete stranger.

Gregory cleared his throat. "Well, I…I expect you're hungry at any rate. Dinner should be served in about half an hour. Do join us, won't you?" he requested, and Edgar quickly nodded, grateful for the shift of attention: "of course, gladly." Gregory nodded once more and left Edgar by himself in the room.

Every hint of twilight had disappeared, ushering in the night. Edgar lit the gas lamps in the room, finding that the light made him feel safer. Still reeling from shock and confusion, he sat on the bed. During his medical studies, Edgar had read about the phenomenon of waking dreams. The idea didn't seem very credible at the time, but it was a believable, rational explanation for what he'd just experienced. Edgar went over the chilling episode several more times in his head and convinced himself of this possibility.

Dreaming while awake—this state can be brought about by heightened stress and sleep deprivation, according to testimonies. Both of these conditions were met. I remember reading that these visions can be quite intricate and vivid. This is the most plausible explanation.

With his mind spinning, Edgar stood and dressed himself in a fresh waistcoat, ascot, and jacket, then attended to the shadow that had crept in around his chin. In no time, he resembled his usual, proper self. Though his back and chest still ached, and his thoughts were heavy with recollections of the abominable waking dream, he took a steadying breath and prepared to rejoin his party. As Edgar reached for the doorknob, dread accosted him once more as he was taken by the oppressive suspicion that the sobbing boy still watched him from the corner of the room. Edgar's neck prickled at the very thought. Unable to restrain himself, he jerked around, only to find the room quite empty.

Nostalgia

Edgar found Gregory and Genevieve sitting at a long, polished table made from fine oak. An array of china and silverware gleamed before them, and they looked up expectantly as Edgar crossed through the archway into the dining room. The paneled walls were decorated with ornate deep-red wallpaper. No small amount of clutter and curios were set amid the paintings and vases, and though the adornments were mostly elegant in nature, the entire display seemed to Edgar to have been arranged without much sense of style.

"Oh, Mr. Price. We thought you weren't coming. How good to see you so revived." Genevieve hung her trademark toothy grin on her face. She had donned an evening gown that was suffocating in faux flowers and clashing patterns. The sleeves were so disastrously puffed that Edgar was struck by the notion, in his delirious, half-awake state, that she might begin to balloon away at any moment.

He nodded politely in her direction before sitting down. "Thank you, Mrs. Farrow, for this kind welcome into your home and to your table." Although he tried to portray his gratitude, the memory of what he'd seen upstairs clawed at his attention.

"Please, as I've said, 'Jenny' will do." She batted her hand in his direction with a saccharine giggle then raised her eyebrows as if waiting for something more from Edgar. She stayed that way, with Gregory flashing his eyes at Edgar as if to defend her.

"Ah, of course…Jenny," he muttered, flicking his napkin out and spreading it over his lap. Her eyes lingered, and suddenly it was clear to Edgar what she desired from him. Swallowing his irritation, he bowed his head once more and added, "My sincerest apologies for holding up dinner."

This concession made Gregory deflate slightly, and he too unfolded his napkin and placed it across his lap. Genevieve finally gave orders to a serving man who stood quietly behind her, awaiting a command after listening to her chatter on about their honeymoon in Prague and boasting about all the expensive gifts Gregory had showered upon her.

As a team of domestic workers brought a feast out to them, Edgar wondered how Gregory planned to maintain such an extravagant lifestyle. Surely his salary, ample as it was, could not withstand this for long. After a creamy potato, onion, and haddock soup, they were served a roasted quail swimming in a sweet orange sauce and garnished with shallots. A luscious wine was paired with the meal, and between the three of them, the bottle was soon drained.

With each sip of wine, Edgar relaxed a bit more, and the incessant, insipid babbling that streamed from Genevieve's mouth seemed almost tolerable at points. After Gregory swallowed the last of his drink, she snapped in the direction of the man in the corner and jabbed her sausage-like fingers at the empty wine bottle.

"Another bottle, madam?" the man inquired gently, and Genevieve laughed incredulously.

"Of course, you dolt!" she squawked, then looked at Gregory with a kind of ruffled disbelief as if to ask, *Is this really the best man you could find?* Gregory shrugged it off by lifting his glass to his lips and trying to drain the drops that still lingered at the bottom. Genevieve frowned and mumbled, "I shouldn't even have to ask" under her breath.

The stiff atmosphere overseen by the lady of the house was finally disrupted when the second bottle had been halfway demolished.

"So I said to Miss Conway, 'Honestly, what time did you *expect* me to arrive?'" Genevieve shouted, then let loose her howl of laughter. Edgar was feeling so woozy from the wine that he couldn't stop himself.

"Ten sharp, lads. Ten sharp..." Edgar looked at his mostly clean plate as he said it and couldn't help smiling. Gregory looked up as if waking from a dream, then boomed his old, familiar laugh, which Edgar so dearly missed.

Genevieve looked between them, head snapping back and forth, at once avian-like. "What's so funny?" she demanded.

"What time was that, sir?" Gregory played along.

"Ten sharp. Ten sharp, Farrow!" Edgar couldn't contain himself, and for the first time in what felt like decades, he laughed freely until he was giddy.

"What sort of nonsense is this?" Genevieve seemed alarmed at how little the topic involved her.

As Gregory dabbed at his eyes, he tried to explain. "Oh, darling, it was from our school days. We had this *decrepit* professor—his name was..."

"Bloomsburg," Edgar reminded him, then picked up the story. "He taught Latin, and the man was so old and doddery he would remind us of things six or seven times a day—especially our church meetings on Sunday, which began at *ten sharp*, and Gregory would incessantly ask, two or three times during each class at least, what time the service began. Poor old thing, you did torment him so."

"Do you still remember the time we found that crawlspace that led up into the ceiling? We were going to hide up there until classes were over for the day," Gregory said with a laugh.

"How could I possibly forget? We came crashing through the roof straight onto Professor Harding's desk. We had detention for ages." The merriment and daringness of their youth was all at once fresh to Edgar.

"Oh, and the day you challenged that oaf Malcolm Gibbons to a fight to defend Charlie's honor, and we had to concoct an elaborate scheme to avoid getting your head bashed in?"

"Poor chap was locked in the toilets for two days."

"Or when we stole the trombone and tuba and kept the staff awake all night trying to find us? God, we were monstrous."

"The day of the snowstorm when we pretended to be explorers on an expedition to Everest. Shocking that neither of us ended up dead."

"Oh, I still remember when you argued with the headmaster about that math equation he'd done wrong, and you persisted so much until he was screaming at you, his face all ruddy and bulging with veins. Then, when you proved him wrong in front of the entire class, he got so furious he hurled the textbook through the window."

"My finest hour."

They continued on this way, becoming more and more intoxicated with wine and with golden, warm nostalgia in equal amounts. Edgar's spirit lightened by the moment as he and Gregory wove through bouts of hilarity and recalled problems that once had seemed so enormous but were now bittersweet from age and simplicity. Summers spent in Mr. Farrow's home were reborn to them—boating and picnics at the river, Mr. Farrow's wild stories, walks in the woods, and the magnificent automaton toy of a skipping dog all became real again. Gregory's father had been the kindest and most generous of men, treating Edgar no different than if he truly had been his son, warmer and more attentive than his own father had been. Life before Gregory and Mr. Farrow had been quiet, strained, studious, and full of tiptoeing around a neurotic, ailing mother and a stern father. In five short years, his sister, Ella, had quickly learned to keep her voice down and often shadowed Edgar wherever he went. Though it had been a bit of a strain, he'd never objected to her constant nearness, in a display of comforting protection and solidarity. Life with Gregory, on the other hand, had been everything Edgar had always dreamed of, although he could never truly experience it with as much abandon and presence of mind as his adopted brother had. There always seemed to have been a shadow over nearly everything in those days, but this didn't make them any less precious to Edgar.

The longer they talked and the more they tried to include Genevieve in their fond memories, the more she became sullen and refused to say more than a few pointed words. Every so often, her eyes flashed in Edgar's direction, burning with anger as she seemed to wonder how he dared to be so chummy with Gregory when she was sitting right there, withering from the lack of attention.

Edgar noticed that the more stories they shared and memories they uncovered from the dusty corners of their minds, the more Genevieve actually began to look disturbed. He sensed that it was as if their friendship threatened her, and the longer she stewed, her glances grew increasingly more hateful. When the man in the corner instinctively brought another bottle of wine for them after the second had been done away with, Genevieve's eyes went wide.

"What do you think you're *doing?* You wait for me to request it—you don't just pull out refreshments as you please!" she sharply reprimanded him, and Edgar, through the haze of wine and mirth, was struck by the blatant contradiction to her prior remarks. "I'm beginning to suspect everyone working in my home is a degenerate. Now take it away before I decide to replace you. Be quick about it."

Edgar raised his eyebrows at her. Perhaps it was his unusually light mood, or the wine in his blood, or even the fact that he had experienced so much unpleasantness recently and his spirit had been emboldened by the danger, but for the second time that day, he spoke before he could think. "You might treat that fellow with more kindness and respect, *Jenny*. He's a good man, doing the best he can for you," he said calmly.

Genevieve instantly turned a fabulous shade of purple and straightened up. Gregory's mood soured at once, and they both stared Edgar down. "*What...did you say to me?*" she snapped, her face contorted with rage.

Gregory frowned deeply, his manner becoming stormy. "You're out of line, old man. I demand you give Jenny an apology. At once."

"Are you really one to approve of this, Gregory?" Edgar was shocked by his own determination, but he simply could not let it go. "You never used to stand idly by while a person treated anyone from any station of life with so much disdain. Why has that been compromised?"

Genevieve made a noise like a chicken being strangled and held a hand up in disgust.

"Edgar, watch yourself. You've no right to comment on how we treat our servants. Now apologize to Genevieve at once." Gregory was snorting through his wide, flat nose—his nostrils flaring as he took each breath.

The tension in the room sobered Edgar, and after a moment of deliberating, he decided it was best to defuse the situation and keep the peace, even if it meant glutting the overblown egos of husband and wife.

"You're right. I sincerely apologize. I've no right to make judgments," Edgar recited.

Genevieve retained her look of distaste a moment longer; then a smile spread over her lips. She knew she had defeated Edgar and made him look the fool, which clearly pleased her.

"It's quite all right, Mr. Price. We all make mistakes." Her voice dripped with false forgiveness. "Now, if you'll excuse me, I'm off to bed. Won't you join me, Greggy darling?"

"I'll be up in a moment," her husband replied with a sigh.

She gave him a noisy, wet kiss on the cheek; beamed a venomous smile at Edgar; then bobbed out of the room. Edgar and Gregory sat avoiding each other's eyes.

After a few minutes that might've passed as hours if not for the clock on the mantel, Gregory lifted his head. "Join me in the sitting room for a nightcap?"

"Yes. Yes, that sounds lovely," Edgar replied briskly, getting up from the chair perhaps a bit too quickly as Gregory's mouth sloped. As they were leaving, the man in the corner gave Edgar a grateful nod, and he smiled back. Gregory led Edgar through the house until they reached a cozy little chamber on the opposite side. Two large, overstuffed chairs were positioned in front of a fireplace roaring with a blaze. Gregory poured Edgar a glass of cognac, and they sat down beside each other, letting the awkwardness fade.

"So, what's this all about, Edgar?" Gregory said at last over the crackling of the wood. Too tired to play games, Edgar let the confusion show on his face. Gregory swirled his drink, his posture slumped. "You seem troubled—more than usual, I should say." He attempted a laugh, and Edgar dropped his gaze and sighed.

"I suppose things aren't quite the same as they used to be. This last year has been a lonely one." He tried to think of an explanation that would satisfy Gregory then added, "You're not exactly the same man I remember either, for what it's worth."

"Marriage will change a man, but all for the better, I believe. I was getting older. It was time to settle down," Gregory let the firelight filter through the crystal snifter and illuminate the pale-gold liquid until it shone like an alchemist's solution. "But I'm happy now. I'm very *happy*, Edgar. Very." He repeated it so many times while staring into the fire's hypnotic flickering that Edgar wondered whom exactly Gregory was trying to convince. Behind his old friend's slurred words lay an awful sort of emptiness. Edgar squinted through the haze of drunkenness as the sad understanding washed over him; Gregory believed his own lie. His sorrow deepened as he peered over his glass in the orange lowlight and realized he no longer knew the man sitting across from him.

"I've killed someone, Gregory." The words tumbled out of Edgar's mouth. He kept his eyes on the man who wore his friend's face, watching as it rippled with shock and morbid curiosity. "Several people, in fact. I failed. Everything went perfectly. I was confident; I completed each of the procedures properly, but they still died."

Some of Gregory's shock faded when the context of the deaths in question was revealed, but Edgar did not relent.

"Everything became so clear afterward. I've been wrong about myself the whole time. I was passionate, and I thought was skilled, but I was wrong. This isn't the life I wanted. It's not even close."

"Well…" Gregory smacked his lips in thought then took another swig. "You're still young; you have money; you're an intelligent man. You can do whatever you like."

"That's just it, though. I have no idea what I want—and it makes me sick to admit it, but I never did. I held on to a falsehood in hopes that this career would bring my life meaning—that it would soothe some of my pain. But I'm starting to understand that I didn't study medicine to help others. I always believed it started out as a mission to help people like my mother—if someone could've treated her properly before her affliction overwhelmed her, then perhaps…but no, I was wrong about that too. I didn't really do it for her, or for anyone else. I did it for myself. As if healing others might help me in some ludicrous, roundabout way." Hardly knowing what he was saying, he lay his head against the side of the armchair.

"And all this business with the madman aboard the train," he whispered, clutching at his chest. His head grew dizzier and his words further away from his control. "I'm terrified. I'm terrified of the world; I'm terrified of myself. It's as if this last decade I've been acting under an outside influence—like a sort of drugged numbness—and I'm only just starting to wake up. Why did my patients' deaths have to be the catalyst, though? How could I have let things get so out of control?"

Gregory stared at Edgar with a look of pity and utter confusion, as if Edgar were speaking a foreign language he'd only briefly studied. He smacked his lips again and set his glass on the table between them.

"It wasn't fair—what happened to you, I mean." He spoke with a gruff form of sympathy to Edgar, who was taken aback. "No child deserves to endure what you went through. And I've always tried to be understanding about that."

"How could you possibly understand, Gregory?" Edgar snapped, inexplicably furious. "Your father loved you. You were loved, wholly and selflessly, until the day he died."

"He loved you too, Edgar," Gregory volleyed, incensed.

"It didn't change what happened."

Gregory's eyebrows drew inward. "You have to let that go. It's been years—nearly *decades*."

"Let it go?" Edgar echoed. He was shaking now, gripping the armchair as he stared at Gregory. "You have no idea what you're talking about."

"Because you've never told me!" Gregory shot back, sitting up and staring him down. "All these years and you've never been able to talk to me about it. I had to hear the story from my father, and—"

"You truly want to know?" Edgar hissed, half furious and half repelled by the mere memory. Gregory stared at him, still slumped in his chair and challenging him to continue. On any other day, Edgar might've kept his silence, but he'd been pushed too far. The combination of wine and weariness had overpowered his self-control. Edgar marshalled himself and continued.

"My mother was always frail and given to long bouts of illness and malaise. After my sister's birth, she became more and more consumed with melancholy, and then began to suffer elaborate hallucinations. By the time Ella was five, Mother could hardly rise from bed. No physician could figure out what was wrong with her, and it only grew worse—I suppose it..." Edgar's voice cracked as the memory of their pallid forms, blanched further in the sunlight from the bedroom window, streamed through his mind. The image of his final patient Mrs. Sheehy, taken by death, overlaid itself onto the memory, and Edgar's throat grew tighter. "I suppose it all became too much. I returned one day after school to find my mother and sister dead. They were lying on the bed, still—as if they were only asleep."

"I drew nearer and found them cold," he continued. "I backed away—I couldn't believe they were gone, and then...I saw him. My father was sitting in the corner, his face in his hands. I went to him and begged to know what had happened. He only kept repeating, 'I had to do it' and 'She drowned Ella. I had to.'"

"He killed your mother?" Gregory breathed, his eyes wide. He didn't look nearly as brazen as he had moments ago. Edgar gave a grim nod then took a long draw on his drink, needing to be even less aware of the moment. "My father never told me that. I just assumed she...did herself in. H-how did he...?"

Edgar looked at his own hands and weakly clenched his fingers. He hadn't the heart to say it out loud, but Gregory gathered the meaning all the same.

"How did you know?" Gregory asked.

"Because he tried to do the same to me," Edgar said, struggling to keep his voice steady. "After I realized what had happened, I collapsed beside him. I could hardly do anything but force myself to breathe. He got up and staggered to the door. When I heard the sound of the lock, I knew I...but I couldn't get away. He was beside himself the entire time, apologizing. He said it was for the best, that I shouldn't have to live with it. I tried to get away, but the door was locked and he was too fast."

Edgar put his face in his hands, and he could see it, fresh in his mind. His father's hands closing around his throat, the look of utter despair in his eyes as he stared down at him, Edgar's small hands prying at his fingers, helpless against his strength.

"How did you stop him?" Gregory asked, transfixed.

"I didn't. Just as I was fading, he seemed to realize what he was doing. He let go then stumbled away, staggering around as though trying to escape his own misery. I was just starting to catch my breath when—it happened so fast. He flung open the window and leapt out. I didn't even have enough air in my lungs to scream. I looked out and saw him there, in the courtyard. He'd landed on his head." The image of splintered bone, uncoiled brain, and pooling blood filled Edgar's mind. He drew in on himself, setting his drink aside. He didn't think he could stomach the rest of it.

"Happy now? Did you get all the details you wanted? Or would you like to hear all about how their corpses looked?" Edgar growled, staring daggers at Gregory. His friend appeared affronted and looked as though he were scrambling for words. "Well, then, do tell me, Gregory. How exactly do you suggest I simply *let* that go?"

"I didn't know. I didn't mean—"

"What *did* you mean? I sat there for hours with their bodies before our neighbors found me—trapped, calling for help, not knowing what to do or where to go." Edgar's voice was low and dangerous, though it never rose above a murmur. "But how could you understand…"

"See here, stop this. I'm only trying to say you can't let it define who you are." Gregory fought back at last.

"How easy it must be. To sit back, guarded by your creature comforts, your thriving career, and your *fine* wife, and hand out precious jewels of advice. What noble sentiments," Edgar said, and Gregory stood up in rage.

"That's enough. If you want devote your life to feeling sorry for yourself, I suppose you're entitled, but don't expect me to give you any more sympathy. You can go ahead and continue throwing away your opportunities for success, and bring misfortune on yourself for all I'm concerned, but I'll not be a part of it. It's

just this kind of attitude that makes people turn away from you."
Gregory puffed up, and now Edgar got to his feet in retaliation.

"What exactly are you insinuating?" Edgar's voice was hardly a whisper. His head was swimming with alcohol and anger. Their combined force was so overwhelming that he found himself unable to speak.

"All I'm trying to say…is that I see a pattern in your life," Gregory grumbled, red-faced and slurring.

Edgar opened his mouth in a gaping, indignant sneer, but he never got a chance to reply. Someone was pounding on the front door. Both men turned in the direction of the entranceway as three more resounding booms hammered against the wood. Then all was silent.

Feast

Edgar looked immediately to Gregory. His stoic visage was tinged with fear; like Edgar, Gregory was terrified but too proud, and residually angered from their heated discussion, to admit to his apprehension. Yet the tension between them was quickly shouldered as Gregory marched forward to answer the door, glancing at the grandfather clock in the corner as he went. It was well past midnight.

"Who could it be at this bloody hour...?" he grumbled, but before he reached the doorknob, Edgar cried out to stop him.

"Wait!" He held his hand out in a warning motion. Then, after Gregory halted in confusion, he scrambled to order his words. "It...what if...I mean, those people I met on the train. That wicked woman could still be on the loose."

Before Gregory could answer, a flurry of footsteps on the stairs announced Genevieve's arrival. She stopped halfway down the staircase, her substantial figure wrapped in a flowing white nightgown, her long sandy hair streaming down her back.

"What in the world is happening down here?" she demanded in a loud squawk.

Gregory turned toward Genevieve, set his shoulders, and charged toward the door, his hands swinging apelike at his sides in a pantomime of masculinity, as if he couldn't abide being timid in the presence of his wife. Edgar took an instinctive step back as Gregory wrenched the door open.

Nothing was on the other side but the empty street. Rain fell mercilessly upon the roadways and rooftops of Edinburgh, the gas lamps barely cutting through the billows of fog and moisture that rolled by.

"Gregory, what do you think you're you doing?" Genevieve chided. "Close that door and come up to bed at once!"

"Rotten brats playing jokes in the night. I'll have them for this—they won't come back to this porch again," Gregory boomed, and took several pounding steps onto the porch, where he peered about for children hiding in nearby bushes or behind the streetlights.

"*Gregory!*" Genevieve stomped her way down the stairs and hollered at him from the doorway, but he wouldn't stop his prowling. When she saw that she couldn't force him to heed her, she turned on Edgar. "What is the meaning of this?"

"Someone knocked on the door," Edgar offered meekly, but she blustered up to him, her beady eyes glittering as she stared him down. "I advised him not to answer it. I was worried it would be the maniacs from the tra—"

"*You led those monsters to my home?*" she whispered furiously.

"No, madam. I was only suggesting caution."

"You...you have been nothing but trouble since you arrived, Mr. Price. You've treated me with deep disrespect when I've been *nothing* but kind to you. And now you've put me and my husband in danger. You must leave here immediately." The woman put her foot down—literally and figuratively—sneering at Edgar all the while. Gregory appeared in the doorway, likely drawn by his wife's venomous timbre, and she repeated herself when he was within earshot. "Your friend must leave. At once."

"What's he done to you, darling?" Gregory immediately went to her defense and took his place at his wife's side. Edgar tossed up his hands in a gesture that was meant to quiet their anger but only succeeded in incensing Genevieve.

"He's been rude beyond measure to me. I demand you ask him to leave, Gregory. He must never come to call on us again," she warbled, sounding like a sullen child. Gregory faltered, looking at Edgar as if actually considering this. When Genevieve saw him hesitate, she cried out again. "He said he might've led those maniacs here—to *our home!*"

"But dearest, there was no one outside."

"*Gregory!*" she blasted, her face livid.

His hesitation vanished in an instant. "Yes, Edgar…I…I believe you must leave us, come morning," Gregory said in a hushed voice.

Edgar could hardly register what he was saying. He blinked for a moment, feeling numb, until Genevieve stopped taking snorting puffs through her nostrils long enough to speak again.

"Greggy, darling, I don't feel safe with him in the house. It's upsetting me." She opened her eyes wide and clutched at his chest.

Gregory sighed and lowered his head as if in thought. "Tonight then. Please get your things, Edgar." Gregory gruffly waved to the staircase.

Edgar was dumbfounded. "Please let me see if I understand you properly," he began softly. "You're asking me to leave late at night, in the pouring rain, with no ticket back to London, the day after I was attacked. Is that what you're saying? Am I never to see you again?" he finished emphatically, his voice cracking.

Gregory remained firm. "I'm sorry, Edgar. Perhaps in a few years, once you prove to us you have a better handle over your emotions and—"

"We…we're practically *brothers*. Have you forgotten that?" Edgar said hoarsely, but Gregory's frown only deepened.

"You're disrupting the happiness of this family. You must leave," Gregory stated, and just out of his view, a victorious smile spread over Genevieve's face.

Edgar, ever the pragmatic scientist, didn't have a single thing to say to any person who didn't look at the world with reason. Letting his anger drop, he turned to head up the stairs and gather his belongings but stopped halfway as a cold shock ran through him. The man who once was Edgar's brother and his repugnant spouse observed the change in his complexion, and soon all eyes were fixed on the dining room.

A girl in a black gown was seated at the table, looking placidly about the room as if patiently waiting for them to finish their argument. Genevieve's eyes popped, and she opened and closed her mouth, reminiscent of a fish exposed to the air. Gregory's masculine bluster and sense of danger flared up at once, and he gave a great shout to get the girl's attention.

"I say, miss! What the devil do you think you're doing in here?" He crashed through the entranceway into the dining room without a shade of fear for the stranger, who appeared much smaller, and many years his junior. "You are breaking and entering—if you do not leave immediately, I will phone the police and—"

The room fell into an eerie silence as she turned her head and faced Gregory. Edgar knew, instantly that this woman was not human. She had the features of a young woman of about fourteen, but warped, as if trying to disguise a visage of something unearthly as normal. Her hair was the color of soot and cropped short in a fashion that Edgar couldn't recognize from any other lady he'd ever encountered. It looked as though she had attempted to make her hair sleek, but it was unruly and didn't like to be told what to do. Bony, delicate hands the color of frost sat folded in her lap; Edgar saw that the fingernails had been manicured into cruelly sharp points. A fringe covered her eyebrows, making it look as though she were peeking out of a dark place. Great blue eyes beamed out of her face, impossibly large and ringed by spiderlike eyelashes. She kept them opened very wide, while the irises darted around either too quickly or remained chillingly still. She never seemed to blink.

The girl rose, her sumptuous black gown rippling around her feet, a striking juxtaposition to the pallor of her skin, which jarringly reminded Edgar of a particular body that had ended up on his dissecting table—a man who had frozen to death in the snow.

Edgar and his former compatriots were struck dumb by the young woman's deathly pallor and inhumanly large, unblinking eyes, which seemed to amuse her. Her face broke into a smile that momentarily stopped Edgar's heart. Each tooth was a touch longer and sharper than normal.

"My, I thought you'd never notice me. So caught up in your silly, bullying games," she said with a chuckle, her voice was beautiful, but deeply unnerving, like music sung just slightly off-key.

Something in her dissonant tone teased at the back of Edgar's mind and sent adrenaline rushing through him. It was familiar. As she laughed, Genevieve seemed to overcome her initial dread. With several long, deliberate steps, Genevieve approached the intruder and pointed authoritatively at the front door.

"*Get...out,*" she ordered with snapping enunciation, holding her position while the young woman continued to shift her weight and look about the room.

"You know, I've been watching you all day." She maintained a conversational manner, then, from a credenza, picked up a photo of Gregory and Genevieve on their wedding day, made a small noise of interest, and set it back down.

"Young lady, we will not warn you again. The door is this way," Gregory bellowed, having found something of his courage along with his wife. He strode to the door, exuding a false bravado, and opened it wide. The rain thundered down outside, but the girl merely looked up at Genevieve.

"Originally I was only here for business," she demurred, as if sharing a rather interesting fact she'd read in the newspaper that morning, "to recover misplaced goods. But I've come to a conclusion after observing you for a day's time."

"Gregory, the police. Hurry," Genevieve yelped, her courage dissipating as fast as it come when the girl faced her.

"You really are a wretched person. Do you know that?" The young woman seemed almost sad now. Genevieve's face contorted in response.

Suddenly a pump of panic rocked Edgar so that his knees almost buckled. A stark realization cut through his fear born of the woman's unnatural form. He suddenly knew why her voice bothered him so. He recognized it at last—the cold hiss, the light Austrian accent. It was Magdalena, the woman from the train.

"Genevieve, get away from her!" he cried, lunging to grab her while Gregory rushed to get between Genevieve and Magdalena. Casually, Magdalena sidestepped away from Genevieve and met Edgar and Gregory head on. Moments before they were about to collide with her, she smacked them both away with the back of her hand, connecting with Gregory first, then Edgar on the follow-through. The force was so strong that it knocked them both backward and onto the polished hardwood floor.

Genevieve screamed and made to rush to Gregory's side, but Magdalena caught her by the hair. She gave a wicked cackle and yanked the wailing Genevieve backward. As the men struggled to get back up and gasped for air, Magdalena knelt beside the sobbing woman, beaming her blood-freezing smile.

"The thing is," she said in a mock whisper as Genevieve whimpered and tried to worm out of her grasp, "I really hate wretched people. I can stand broken people—they're fine, in a tiresome way—and truthfully I'm rather fond of good people. But wretched people...no...no, no. I cannot suffer them, no matter how much I try."

Gregory was on his feet again and smashed his way toward Magdalena, his face red and a rage and fear filled bellow resonating from his lungs. Mildly irritated, she rolled her eyes, let go of Genevieve for a moment, and stood up. As the sniveling woman tried to crawl away, Magdalena brought her foot down on her back, pinning her solidly to the floor. She looked quite bored as she caught Gregory by the throat and lifted him into the air, his squat legs kicking madly. Even when they connected with Magdalena, she didn't flinch.

"Do you mind?" she asked, her voice thick with vexation, then flung Gregory aside again, who hit the far wall with resonating thud and remained still. Edgar shivered to his feet and ran to his friend's side. With a hasty check of breathing and pulse, Edgar determined that Gregory was alive, but unconscious. While there was certainly a possibility of internal damage, the strength of his pulse suggested any such injuries were minor.

Magdalena kicked Genevieve onto her back then grabbed the folds of her nightgown and wrenched her to her feet. With a push, she shoved her against the wall, where Genevieve continued to hiccup and sob hysterically. In the struggle, their wedding photograph was knocked to the floor, where it shattered at Magdalena's feet.

Knowing better than to challenge Magdalena, Edgar instead reached into his pocket, where he kept a bottle of smelling salts. He pulled it out, uncorked it, and brought it to Gregory's nose. Instantly he began to stir.

Magdalena tossed Genevieve's hair out of the way, exposing her throat, as a predatory look passed over her face.

"W-what are you doing...? No, please! I-I'll give you anything. I'll...*no!*" Genevieve let out a piercing scream as Magdalena leaned forward, her jaws widening beyond should have been possible given the limits of anatomy. Edgar stood, paralyzed and disbelieving, as Magdalena sank her teeth into the soft flesh of Genevieve's neck. As she flopped about in her grasp, gurgling and squealing, Magdalena moaned with an almost carnal pleasure. She gnawed and chewed until a massive chunk of the woman's neck came loose and stained the front of her black gown with fresh red blood.

Gregory howled in abject anguish as his wife sank to her knees, blood pooling on the floor and wall around her. Magdalena continued to tear of hunks of flesh from around the open wound and bolt them down. She slurped the blood, appearing to savor the taste of each bite like a revolting parody of a gourmand.

Edgar, who had long been desensitized to the sight of gore, was able to snap out of his initial revulsion and made a mad dash for the telephone at the other side of the room, grimly happy that his ostentatious friend had installed one. Gregory sat against the wall, weeping, eyes hollow with horror and grief. His hand clawed in Genevieve's direction. He knew she was already dead, but her eyes were open—staring and glassy. Soon Magdalena's gnawing slowed, and she stopped chewing. She stood up with a noticeable spring in her step and used a linen napkin from the dinner table to wipe the blood off her hands and face, licking her lips in satisfaction.

"Hello? Operator? I need help! There's been a murder. We're being—"

Magdalena was at Edgar's side in an instant. She took the telephone box in her hands and ripped it out from the wall in a swift motion. Then she turned her smile on Edgar, whose stomach clenched at the stringy pieces of muscle and skin caught between her teeth.

He stood less than arm's length away from Magdalena, whose eyes were still so full of the delight that death apparently had given her that they nearly gave off sparks. Gregory sputtered and gasped, crawling his way over to Genevieve's corpse, while Edgar stood stock-still, taking slow breaths through his nose. He watched Magdalena as if she were a feral creature that might pounce at any moment rather than a wan, short-statured waif.

"What will it be? Will you come quietly?"

"What are you going to do to me?" Edgar asked in a husky, quavering tone.

Magdalena cocked her head in vague interest. "Is that a no?" She sounded almost playful.

At the other end of the room, the plaintive, guttural sounds Gregory made were verging on inhuman. He cradled the gashed body of Genevieve, weeping into her stained nightgown. Magdalena head swiveled sharply in his direction.

"Will you please *shut up?*" she scolded, then turned back to Edgar and continued on in her atonal purr. "You won't get very far. I'll catch you. My master helped me find you here—I can find you elsewhere too, even if you *are* able to slip away. And I believe you're smart enough to know that fighting me isn't an option."

Gregory threw his head back and screamed at the ceiling so loudly and for so long that Edgar actually heard the moment when his vocal chords became damaged. Magdalena's lips grew tighter, and she gave another warning glance in Gregory's direction.

"If I go, will you let him be?" Edgar whispered.

Magdalena rolled her eyes toward the ceiling, paused, then shrugged. "I suppose. He means nothing to me, and I'm already satisfied. Eating such rich fare always does satiate the appetite so quickly. Let us depart. Mr. Hare's waiting for us outside."

She took Edgar by the arm and led him toward the open door. Edgar followed, hoping to lead Magdalena away from the house and the charnel pit inside. As they walked toward the downpour, Gregory stood and gave a snort and a growl.

"You bitch, you murdering bitch!" he snarled, dashing forward until he was right behind her.

Magdalena turned, looking deeply insulted. Gregory grabbed her by the shoulders and shook her violently. "You killed her! Monster! Demon! You murdered her, and I can't live without her. You—"

In a motion so swift Edgar could barely track it, Magdalena took ahold of Gregory's round head and twisted it violently, snapping his neck. His deadweight collapsed to the floor without so much as a trace of the life that had flowed through him seconds before.

"Well, then. Now you won't have to," Magdalena said matter-of-factly.

Edgar made a strangled noise; he found that he couldn't breathe. Gathering his wits, he lunged instinctively for Gregory, but Magdalena caught him by the arm. His heart thumped against his ribs as he looked up to face her odd, patient smile. Her touch was deceptively gentle on his arm. She nodded toward the door, her eyes alight with a mischievous invitation that sent ice-cold horror rushing down Edgar's spine. Magdalena led him out of the dining room, her arm linked with his, like a guest at some hellish ball. Outside, as the curtain of rain hit Edgar and began to soak him through, the first of many tears shed for his lost friend began to fall.

Famine

The rhythmic churning of the wooden cart over cobblestones distracted Hare; it helped take his mind off the live cargo they towed. He whipped at the horse for it to hurry along faster, but Mag touched him on the leg in a quiet request to stop. Irritated by her constant urge to control his every action, Hare gave her a look of reproach, which she matched.

"We don't need anyone thinking we have something to hide or that we're on the run," she said under her breath as another carriage passed them. "Proceed slowly, and we'll get there without any trouble."

"Maybe I'm not as good at this sort of thing as you are, but I think the sooner we get off the streets, the better. It won't be long until someone finds those bodies. Then the police will be swarming down these lanes." Hare gave an anxious mutter, and Mag leaned back in the seat, letting the rain crash down on her as if it were nothing but a drizzle.

"Patience, Jacob. Trust me," she said through the side of her mouth as they turned a corner past several unfortunate folk who were spending the night crouched against the wall of a general store. Hare tipped his hat to them, then dug a coin out of his pocket and flipped it in their direction. Although they weren't too far from Mag's shop, he kept craning his head over his shoulder to look at the wooden chest in back of the cart.

"Why does he have to be locked up like that? What if it suffocates him?" Hare's nerves jangled aloud in the form of the question, and Mag released another sigh.

"I told you, I'm not taking any more chances with this one. It's bad enough we almost lost him the once. We'll make him comfortable when we get settled back at the shop," she assured him, as the rain fell so hard that it drowned out the sound of the horse's hooves on the stones.

Everything had to go as planned, Hare knew there was no escaping Mag. Her strange connection to an unseen master guaranteed that. If he ever tried to flee from her, Mag's master would lead her back to him.

They turned several more misty corners and rolled past gas lamps with their lonely lights. Soon the cart had veered from the main streets and was twisting down a narrow road, when they found their way to that forgotten street that hardly anyone bothered to walk down. To the left was the doorway that wouldn't appear unless the traveler seeking it had stood in its shadow once before.

Mag and Hare got down from the cart, tethered the horse, and got to work unloading the chest. Mag did most of the lifting—even after years spent in her company, Hare was still baffled that her thin, childlike arms possessed so much power.

They dragged the locked chest across the rain-slicked stones. The man inside made no noise at all, so Hare could only imagine he might be quivering in terror or too distraught to make a sound. The idea brought him no satisfaction—grief and its emotional companions were no strangers to him. Hare's sympathy for the surgeon was fleeting, however, because the man's impending death would mean the end to his own pain. Hare's relief was far from complete; his suffering might continue for much longer—if not indefinitely, considering Mag's fierce accounting—if anything went awry.

No, this will all be over soon, he halfheartedly reassured himself. *Once he's dead, I'll be free.*

They lugged the chest inside, then shut the door behind them with a clank, plunging them into darkness. Mag muttered a brief, quiet incantation, and instantly several fires burning in eldritch hues of purple, dark rose, and acid green crackled to life in braziers set around the shop. With the light came the pungent, oily smells of black magic.

The entire shop was set up at a crooked angle, narrowing until it reached a door that led into the back rooms. From the ceiling hung a set of bones that had belonged to a marine creature that Hare had no name for. He suspected most scholars wouldn't either. Huge ceramic jars of viscous substances were pushed up into corners. Bizarre earthy-toned tapestries woven with powerful magical symbols lined the walls. On tables scattered about in the disorder stood dried animal parts, human organs preserved in bottles, broken mirrors, cages full of scuttling insects, tools for divination, crystals with cracks through them, and an assortment of cruel weapons and medieval implements of torture.

On a desk of black, gnarled wood near the back of the shop, a line of silver ampoules sat arranged in a neat line, the care of their placement standing out amidst the chaos. Hare's eyes fixed on them for a moment, and his breathing grew short. He didn't know whether it was his imagination, but he thought he heard all-too-familiar whisperings coming from those tightly sealed glass containers. Lying in front of them was a collection of eight miniature wooden coffins, each about an inch in length, with a carved figure inside. Hare quickly and deliberately averted his gaze; he couldn't bear the sight of them for very long.

Mag approached the chest warily, poised herself, then unlocked it and lifted the lid. The surgeon lay curled up in the fetal position, his red-ringed eyes darting upward. Damp with sweat, he recoiled from her, pressing his back to the corner of the box and trembling.

"Stand up," Mag ordered, and the surgeon got to his feet, quivering. He stepped out of the trunk without waiting for permission, taking in his surroundings with an analytical, almost scholarly curiosity that was quickly overtaken by an expression of mounting dread, but the surgeon did not dare to look away from Mag for long. This brought a crooked smile to her lips. Clearly his destination wasn't what he'd expected.

"What is this place? Why are we here?"

"You'll stay for a week or so," Mag answered, still tensed to spring if he should decide to make a sudden attempt to escape.

"And what happens after that?" Edgar swallowed, his black hair stuck to his forehead.

"After that you won't be around anymore," she explained, sauntering away from his side and standing protectively in front of the ampoules.

A look of horror crossed over Edgar's face, and his skin turned the color of milk. "Do you mean to say you're going to kill me?" he asked, his voice controlled but verging on breaking.

"No. I killed you last night on the train." Mag pointed to the spot where the cursed scorpion had stung him. His hand shot upward and he grasped his chest. "That curse will eat away at you until it consumes your body and soul. You'll be gone soon enough. Until then, I'll make you comfortable here, as long as you're willing to behave."

"I only have a week or so until I'm…dead?"

"Well, yes, in a manner of speaking." Mag leaned back against the table, sounding as if her patience were being tried. "However, you'll lose more than just your life, I'm sorry to say. When most people die, their soul gets repurposed and reborn. *Your* soul will be eaten by the parasite I've attached to you and will cease to exist."

Edgar's breathing became aggravated, and it looked as though he might fall forward. Hare wondered whether he should help him steady himself when Edgar looked straight at him with an expression of pure anguish. Hare endured a stab of guilt, suddenly feeling the urge to apologize to the man who had so briefly been his drinking companion, but he reminded himself that this was the only option he had.

"Why?" He directed the question at Hare as he blinked away tears. "Why are you doing this? Why are you doing do this to *me?*"

Hare licked his lips as he thought then finally gave a noncommittal shrug, his guilt deepening somewhat. The other seven victims had only screamed or raged or begged. They hadn't faced him like this, demanding an answer with quiet plaintiveness.

"You were...there at the right time. It could've been anyone really, but...but you made it so easy. You were just...*there.*" Hare knew his answer would give the condemned man no comfort, but he took a little solace in the fact that he was honest with him.

To his surprise, Edgar returned this with a cynical, caustic laugh. "So. More bad luck then." He buried his face in his hands and took a shuddering breath.

"Sorry, mate." Hare shrugged again, unsure how to explain himself and not certain he actually owed the man an explanation in the first place.

Mag interrupted their discussion, her patience for explanations clearly exhausted. "You'll be treated kindly here until it's over—if you agree to be civil, that is. I'll ensure that you want for nothing. Now come along. I'll show you to your room."

She beckoned Edgar to the door at the end of the shop. As he stepped forward in a haze, she watched him carefully, obviously more relaxed now that the surgeon didn't seem to be struggling against his fate. Hare's worry began to loosen at the sight of Mag's coolness, and his attention wandered as she slowly drew Edgar into her lair. He had no desire to follow them—the images of what she kept back there still haunted him each night as he tried to fall asleep.

The surgeon turned back to Hare, his lips parted as if he was formulating a final remark. Hare looked to him, expectant, but before the man could speak, Hare's gaze flashed nervously down to the line of ampoules. The surgeon's proximity disturbed him. The man's face underwent a quiet change as he followed Hare's glance; eyes narrowed and calculating, he took a quick, single step in the ampoules' direction. Mag tensed and Hare gave a soft yelp, reaching out to stop him. Hare's stomach dropped as a steely look of victory flashed in the man's eye.

"No!" he gave a strangled cry to stop him, and Mag, eyes popping, began to lunge, but it was too late.

Everything shifted in an instant. The surgeon threw his arm out violently at the line of ampoules on the table, sending them flying. In one abysmal moment, everything Mag and Hare had spent years building had shattered in so many shining pieces on the floor.

An unholy wail escaped from Mag's lips as the containers smashed, and she tore so fervently at her face that Hare thought her skin would come loose.

From the shattered remains of the ampoules, a blackish-purple light shone—a type of radiance that swallowed up the brightness around it as it gathered. Mag wouldn't stop screaming, and she sank to her knees in despair as a tremor shook her lair. Bursts of power that felt like forceful gusts of fetid wind emanated from around the shattered glass and spread out farther. Things that got in the way of the bursts were thrown about, torn apart, or destroyed in an instant. Hare backed away from the mayhem, self-preservation his only concern. Edgar darted by him, shoving him as he went, Hare toppled off his feet into a pile of wooden crates. The blasts of energy, now feeling almost magnetic in nature, struck a nearby cage. In seconds, the floor was crawling with spiders, centipedes, beetles, and scorpions.

Edgar had fled, leaving the door to the shop swinging wide open. Hare had no intention of following him now—his only present goal was to make it through the next few minutes without being torn apart.

"Stop them! We've got to stop them! Trap them, Hare! Find a mirror!" Mag's voice was a mere whine over the whirring hurricane of sound filling the room. However, even with her unnatural strength, she wouldn't dare approach the circle of radiating energy that was coagulating above the pile of glass shards. Figures formed out of the purple-black light—six of them in a ring, their faces starting to come into shape. They were warped with rage and agony, howling at Hare. Words from these coalescing voices whistled by him, some incomprehensible, others pleas or threats. The luminous figures then broke free of their ring and swooped, wraith-like, around the ceiling. Both Mag and Hare took cover, their clothes and skin torn in the massive churning of wind and energy. The noise grew to an unbearable cacophony as each of the figures went flying out through the open door and into the torrential rain.

The silence that followed was one of the most oppressive things Hare ever had to bear in his life. He got to his feet, shaking uncontrollably, and looked about at the wreckage that had once been Mag's store. No amount of weeping would relieve the feeling that welled inside him now—everything had been lost in a matter of seconds, and Mag would no doubt blame him.

"Oh, Lord, help me. Help me, dear, sweet Lord Jesus. What...what do we do?" he finally ventured to say, unable to look at Mag. When she didn't reply, he dared to glance in her direction.

She was kneeling in front of the pile of shards that had remained undisturbed through the storm. Her hands shivered as she picked them up, cradling them between her fingers. After a moment of beholding them with utter heartbreak, she let the delicate slivers fall between her fingers and back onto the pile. She collapsed onto the mound like a building imploding from within. When Mag finally wept, she did so softly, like the meager voice of wind whistling through a crack in a window.

Splintered

It had been the first good day in a very long time. Not a single argument had arisen in the cottage. Ainsley had stayed home to work alongside Colleen in the garden. It was uncharacteristically warm for October, and the other witches and their families in the Wood were filled with merriness as they made their preparations for the Samhain celebrations, which were only a few days away. Today felt like the old times—the days when there was only fresh, young love between Ainsley and Colleen and enough time that hope was abundant. After a long walk in the woods, they returned to see that Elspeth had cooked for the evening. They enjoyed a hearty meal of pumpkin soup, fried potatoes, fresh salmon, and greens, talking and laughing like they had in years past. No one seemed eager to break the spell of peace and serenity that had been cast on the cozy autumn evening.

Just as they were getting comfortable around the fireplace and talking in sleepy, contented voices about old stories, a loud noise disturbed them, like a large branch snapping off a tree. All three women turned their heads toward the window, in the direction of the sound. It rang out again, this time louder and more pronounced. Elspeth rose and drifted over to the window. She peered out, her dreamy eyes searching about the gardens for anything unusual.

As she looked, Colleen glanced at Ainsley, her pale face orange in the firelight. Ainsley was suddenly moved by her beauty, the way she so frequently had been when they'd first met. She reached out and brushed her hair back gently. Colleen smiled at this and rested her head on Ainsley's shoulder. The tranquility lasted only seconds, before Elspeth interrupted with a dazed mumble. "I think the shed's on fire."

"What?" Ainsley's voice was sharp, angry that her brief repose was shattered, as she rose from her seat by the fireplace and hurried to the window.

"It might just be one of my visions, though. Check and see, won't you?" Elspeth's voice rose with concern, and she rubbed at her eyes.

As Ainsley peered through the glass, her heart leapt to see that the shed was, in fact, consumed by flames. She didn't waste a moment before she rushed out into the yard and tromped through the gardens. It had begun to rain after sunset, and Ainsley's feet were soon slick with mud. She slid to a halt in front of the flaming shed and pulled a piece of paper from her frock's pocket. With hasty resolve, she nipped at the very end of her fingertip, broke the skin to draw blood, and wrote a runic symbol with the ichor on the paper. Though the rain splattered the lines, the spell survived, and the paper glowed with the witch's ethereal light.

She threw it into the fire then quickly muttered, *"Spirits of the wind and rain, I beseech you. Bless me with your favor."* Water began to fall down in torrents upon the shed, and soon the blaze was diminished. Ainsley didn't allow herself to relax, though, because a bluish glow still burned from within the charred wood. Unknown, possibly unfettered magic was dangerous, even to the person who may have cast the original spell. As she picked at the door with tentative fingers, she heard Colleen run up from behind her, calling out to inquire what was wrong with the shed.

"Stay back," Ainsley warned. Inside the confines of the shack, many of the precious items that had been long preserved with magic were now damaged beyond repair. However, buried underneath a board was the very box that had caught Ainsley's attention yesterday.

The entire frame of the box was wreathed in a ghostly blue flame. Ainsley knew that to touch that fire meant to go to the grave in a matter of moments. So she produced another slip of paper and used her bleeding finger to trace another spell onto it—an older and more complicated one. Ainsley spared a quick glance at Colleen, who was watching her intently as she tried to reproduce the symbols from memory. After failing on the first attempt, Ainsley threw the stained paper to the ground then fished in her pocket for another sheet. The second time proved more fruitful—the hairs on the back of her neck stood up the moment she finished drawing the last line.

With a careful toss, she fed the paper to the unholy, cerulean flames. They rippled, licked up, then died away. After waiting a few moments out of extreme caution, Ainsley took the box in hand and opened it with careful fingers. Inside was the anchoring stone. Colleen peered into the box, confused. Not having been born a witch, and despite her role as the coven historian, she wasn't privy to the more secretive bits of magic.

"What is that?" she whispered.

"The reason my mother was banished," Ainsley murmured, then called toward the house for Elspeth to come outside. She would know more about this than Ainsley. "You remember that she was expelled from our Wood for casting a spell of revenge? Well, this is the stone that curse was anchored to."

Ainsley's chest tightened as she took in the sight of the splintered stone. Yesterday she'd assumed that there would be time to puzzle over it before the spell had been completely broken. She now regretted keeping the knowledge to herself.

Suddenly a flash of light split the thickness of the clouds above. Ainsley paid little attention to it, thinking it to be lightning, her vision locked on to the shattered curse anchor. However, when the light failed to fade or flicker, her eyes were drawn sky-ward. What she saw hovering above the treetops made her heart sink in abhorrence. Colleen clung to her arm with a little gasp, and Ainsley took hold of her.

In the sky hovered three spectral lights, each one in the vague form of a human being. They seemed to be watching the Wood and the souls who took refuge there. Ainsley's hand twitched to-ward her pocket, ready to protect herself and Colleen, but stopped halfway. She knew she could do nothing to them.

Colleen quivered. "A-ainsley...what are those?"

A voice from beside her—deep, foreboding, and con-trolled—answered.

"Revenants," said Elspeth, her pale-blue eyes huge, her white-blonde hair streaked with rainwater as she strode up to join them.

Elspeth clutched her willowy frame as she gaped at the hid-eous sight. Ainsley took in Elspeth's look of dread, praying to the Goddess that her sister was mistaken, but knowing in her heart that she was not.

The Mentalist

Keep running. Just keep running. Don't stop, not for anything, Edgar told himself as a stitch in his side screamed with pain. The streets were pitch-black and almost completely devoid of movement at such a dark hour. Rain fell relentlessly, but Edgar could hardly be bothered by it. He had encountered something this night that would remain with him for the rest of his life, however limited that might be. The breaking of Magdalena's vials had permanently altered his mind. As Edgar tried to make sense of the phenomenon, the only thing he could liken it to was pestilence. He had seen men and women in hospitals, dying of the most horrific of afflictions. There had been a look on the faces of these terminal patients—a look of otherness that couldn't be truly understood by any person other than the victim. It was a solemn awareness that there was no going back to the life that was once theirs. And whatever Edgar had sensed coming out of those shattered containers had infected him with a malevolent knowledge, and he never would be himself again.

The sureness of this realization was what rattled him the most as he fled down the streets into the wilder parts of Edinburgh. The streets weren't so clean here, and the public houses and apartments weren't as inviting as they had been on the other side of town. Men, women, and children huddled in filthy masses under overhangs, sleeping and shivering together. For the first time in his life, Edgar recognized their pain on a human level instead of an intellectual one, and he fought off the urge to howl up at the clouds.

Gregory was dead. The man who had been his steadfast companion through most of his childhood and all of his adult life was dead. Murdered before his eyes in less than a minute. Edgar couldn't even approach this as a reality, even though he'd witnessed it firsthand.

Such a pointless end to such a complicated life. And will the same end come for me? Can that dreadful woman be believed? If she's telling the truth, then running will get me nowhere. My fate already has seeped into my bones.

Then he had to stop. It was the first moment he was able to truly think since he'd escaped Magdalena's clutches and felt the devilish force hatch from the silver ampoules. It seemed ludicrous to him, all at once. His perception had to have been distorted by terror. That had to explain it. Just because she'd said that he was doomed didn't make it true.

She said I was going to be consumed, but she only mentioned the culprit as being a...a parasite. But no, this is impossible. This is... The more Edgar tried to deny it, the more panicked he became, and he frenetically ripped open his soggy shirt. The wound had grown, spreading across his breast and onto his sternum, the veins bulging with the black-purple substance.

It was too much for his fractured mind to handle. Surging from the adrenaline and the will to flee even farther from Magdalena's clutches, Edgar burst off down the street. The buildings were becoming dilapidated now, squeezed together and crowded. A choking stench of human waste and factory sludge lay so thick in the air that even the rain couldn't wash it away. Everywhere he looked, there was a frightened pair of eyes, a gaunt quivering body, a still form lying in an alleyway unattended. The sky was silhouetted with the spires from the factories that churned out the choking, burning odor. Hacking coughs mingled with the wailing of throngs of children squeezed into tiny rooms. The sights, smells, and sounds were enough to drive Edgar mad. The suffering was unimaginable.

I must already be in hell was his last cogent thought before his foot slipped on the cobblestones. He tumbled over, landing hard on his jaw. The burst of pain snapped his resolve, and he simply lay on the ground, letting his face bleed freely and the rain pound his aching body. Finally he screamed—a long, high, visceral sound—over and over until he thought his throat might be bleeding too. But he didn't care. All that mattered was the corruption he felt within him, the reality he could no longer deny. In his state, it seemed the only way to get it out was to bleed it out.

Suddenly he felt a pair of hands on his shoulders, and he grew silent and afraid. Thinking Magdalena had caught him again, he whipped around to see a completely unfamiliar face. It was a thin woman, distressed at his appearance, but with kind eyes. She looked to be in her early forties and wore a shawl over her long, dark hair.

"What's happened to you?" she asked, her voice kind and, her accent Punjab. Her manner was soft and welcoming, and soon Edgar's terror subsided a bit.

Edgar collected himself and addressed the woman politely. "I...I...I'm sorry to alarm you," he said, pulling a handkerchief from his pocket and dabbing at the wound on his face before standing up. "I've just lost a dear friend—he's been murdered. I'm lost, and I'm trying to escape." Edgar looked around, trying to get his bearings. *There must be a train station somewhere around*, he thought.

"Come inside for a minute," she offered, her eyes watering, moved by his desperate state of affairs. This surprised Edgar—he'd never expected strangers to be caring, particularly those found in such destitute environs.

"That's very kind of you, madam, but I cannot endanger you. Someone is after me, you see, and I—"

"If that's true, no one will find you in the home of a stranger. I can't leave you out here like this. At least wait until the rain stops. We don't have much room, but you're welcome to stay for a while. Please," she beckoned with genuine concern.

Edgar was truly upset and profoundly disoriented, and the woman's invitation was so compassionate that he couldn't turn her down. She led him into a building nearby. Inside a narrow doorway was a room crammed so tightly with people that Edgar's heart gave a twinge. At least seven others, most of them children, were shoved into a room not much bigger than Edgar's washroom. Dirty pots and clothes were piled up in corners, and a feeble log smoked in a stove to the side of the room. The air was humid and thick with the inevitable odor of close human occupation. In one of the rickety beds lay a small child, coughing herself hoarse and shivering.

Edgar was appalled that anyone should be forced to live in such inhospitable conditions and instantly was deeply ashamed for himself and the people he knew. Through stories and newspapers, he had heard of the lives of the unfortunate, but seeing it firsthand was enough to make him want to begin weeping all over again. Slowly it dawned on him that every apartment in this unkempt, beaten-down area of Edinburgh had a family like this inside it.

To two men who were still awake, Edgar murmured a humiliated hello, keeping his voice low so as not to disturb those who were sleeping. One of the men was older, bearing a gray mustache and suspicious glance. The other was closer to Edgar's age, with a beautiful ochre complexion and two dark, shining eyes that exuded warmth. While the older man's robes were careworn and dingy, the younger's clothes were of a richer quality. After studying his face, there was no doubt that he was the son of the woman who had invited Edgar inside. In the bed nearest to them, the tiny girl continued to cough in sharp, hacking breaths then gave a pained moan. The woman went to the child's side and stroked her hair.

"Your daughter?" Edgar asked gently, taking a few cautious steps in her direction. The anxious man kept his eyes glued to Edgar, bristling protectively.

"My niece," she whispered. "She has been very ill as of late."

"May I take a look at her? I'm a surgeon. I might be able to do something."

"I thought you looked lost." The younger man spoke up suddenly, a wry grin on his face.

The woman stared up at Edgar and shook her head. "Oh, sir, we…we could not afford such a service."

Edgar shook his head vehemently. "I wouldn't dream of charging you, my dear woman. I merely want to assure her well-being. Permit me?" he asked again, another pang of shame flowing through him. He thought of the many operations he had assisted with during his apprenticeship and the exorbitant fees the hospital had requested to save lives. Many of the patients had been wealthy, and Edgar had only ever thought of his own salary during the procedures. The reality of how misguided he had been made his stomach lurch again.

The woman looked to the older man in the corner, as if asking permission. At last he nodded, and Edgar knelt to examine the child.

"What's her name?" he asked softly, as he pushed her hair aside and checked her forehead for a fever. Her skin was hot and clammy under his touch.

"Anisa," the woman replied.

"Has she complained of aches? A sore throat?"

"Yes, both," she said, her voice cracking slightly as Edgar felt for and found swollen lymph nodes in the child's neck. After a few minutes of inspecting her and asking about her symptoms, he had a probable diagnosis.

"She most likely has influenza. It's not as bad as it could be, but without proper care, she could die. These conditions"—he gestured around the squalid room—"could cause the spread of it too," he told them soberly, and the older man's eyes burned, angered by Edgar's remark. However, Edgar continued, eager to see the best possible solution come to reality. "Anisa must be brought to a hospital immediately."

"Sir, we cannot…" The woman seemed tormented by the news, but Edgar held his hand to stop her. An idea had occurred to him, and he patted the front of his coat. A rush of joy filled him when he felt that his cheque book was still in his pocket. Edgar withdrew the pen he kept alongside it in a small box and scribbled on the note. The family grew tense at the sight of this and exchanged worried looks.

"Here. Take this. Take as much money as you need—take more than you need. Share it with others who could benefit. I've left the sum blank. I have several thousand pounds in that bank. I'm not going to need it anymore—I'm not long for this world. Please. Take it all. I have no family to leave it to. Please. Get the child to safety. Get your whole family out of this place." Edgar had to plead with them for a long while. They were so shocked by his offer that they didn't reach out to take the cheque. At last he laid it on the nearest surface and left the home without another word, reaching instinctively for the iodine to cleanse his hands.

Edgar trudged through the rain, still lost and unsure where to go. He had enough cash in his pocket to get home to London. He supposed, if he was going to die, he had better set his affairs in order, but the idea of returning to England seemed an almost impossible task. For a long time, he stood in the road, devoid of all priorities and prerogatives for the first time in many years. He took a peculiar comfort in just letting himself be rained upon.

The sound of footsteps behind him broke his meditative state, and he turned to see the young man from the woman's home rush toward him.

"What kind of game do you think you're playing?" he asked, his black eyes flashing, his elegant hair dampening with rain.

Edgar stared back at him, feeling distant and confused. "I don't view this as a game at all. I was completely serious. I want you and your family to have it." He shrugged. When the man continued to eye him suspiciously, he offered the same explanation as before. "I meant what I said. I'm done for; I have no family or friends to give it to. I'd rather the money help someone than have it seized by greedy, impersonal hands."

"You're—you're actually serious? You're giving it all away to my family?" The man breathed deeply, holding his hand to his forehead as if trying not to faint.

"Why shouldn't I? I'll have no use for it." Edgar shook his head, thinking of his imminent doom with a cynical helplessness. It still seemed impossible to fathom, yet he knew from the pain in his back, the things he had witnessed, and the dark gnawing at the edges of his awareness that Magdalena hadn't lied to him.

"I..." The man faced him, his black eyes looking deeply into Edgar's, as if trying to spot a lie somewhere within them. He gave a short laugh then shook his head. "You're telling the truth. You actually are a surgeon. You're from London. The posh part of town...and you've just lost a friend. You've seen something awful, something that has deeply frightened you...and..."

"Did your mother tell you that just now?" Edgar guessed, but the man continued anyway.

"You're not sick. No, that's not what's threatening you. But you are on the run."

"How are you doing this?" Edgar asked, alarmed.

"Ah, yes. You don't like being read. You're a secretive man. A serious man. You keep to yourself and take pride in perfection and excellence and austerity. Probably because…something very unpleasant happened to you at a young age, I'm thinking." He smiled broadly, seeing that his guesses were making Edgar uncomfortable.

"I say, what's going on here?" Edgar demanded, thoroughly perturbed, but the man laughed his attitude off. "I've had enough to do with black magic." Edgar hardly believed he was using the term in conversation at all. None of this fit in with his ordered, pragmatic view of the universe, and it would take all his remaining time to try and reconcile with it.

Looking impish, the man chuckled to himself. "It's not magic, I assure you. It's called mentalism—just a trick. More for performance, but it does help me get to know people a bit quicker. There's something I can't figure out, though… What's going to kill you? That fear in your eyes is real," he continued, as if fascinated by Edgar, who raised his eyebrows at this.

"If I tell you, it will sound preposterous." Edgar remained hesitant to say anything else to the stranger. "You won't believe me."

"Preposterous is perfectly fine. I work in a business where strange things are common," the man continued, his spirit seemingly unshakeable.

"I was told…I was told it's a curse. And not the sort of hokum nonsense. I've seen things tonight that have inspired a belief of the unearthly. I saw my…my *brother* murdered." Edgar shuddered.

The man squinted at him a while longer, perhaps scrutinizing him further. Eager to get out of the rain, he beckoned to Edgar to follow him to the awning of a nearby cobbler's shop, and he followed. "And you're sure there's nothing you can do?"

"What *could* I possibly do? March up to a physician and complain that I've got a nasty case of soul consumption? That I'm haunted by a murderous, parasitical demon? I'd be institutionalized." Edgar noted the wild, panicked sound of his own laughter.

In response to this, the man's eyes sparkled with a hidden knowing. "How very like a well-to-do London gentleman. I don't know what I expected, though." He gave a nonchalant chuckle. "You never think of going beyond what you know—what is tested and true. How would you respond if I told you there might be a chance to break the curse? Would you venture beyond the boundaries you've spent years constructing?"

Edgar needed to stop and think for a moment. This man's eagerness to believe what yesterday he himself would have deemed raving madness was cause for concern. But when he remembered that he didn't have much left to lose, he sighed then nodded.

The man slapped him gently on the shoulder and squeezed. "Good. I want to help you for what you did for my family. Come this way." He gestured for Edgar to follow. "First I'll take you to my place of business, and from there I'll tell you where we'll go next."

"Ah, just one question." Edgar stopped him, and the man looked back over his shoulder. "What is your name?"

"Oh!" He gave another little chuckle as if comically aware of his forgetfulness. "I'm Rahul. Come along now. Haste is in order."

Rahul took Edgar away from the slums and down the neighboring roads. Edgar was glad to be away from that place of rampant suffering, though he sensed that the images wouldn't leave him, no matter how far they went. Edgar wasn't surprised in the slightest when Rahul pointed to a painted carnival wagon at the end of an out-of-the-way road called Robin Street. The painted letters on the side of the cart read, THE AMAZING DEVARAJA beneath an exaggerated image of a man with impossibly huge eyes peering into a crystal ball.

Rahul waved at it with mock showmanship, and Edgar raised a questioning brow. "It's all about the image—it attracts fools, and there's nothing I love more than a fool with full pockets. Put on a costume, speak in a dramatic voice, and they're yours." The young man leapt up onto the front of the coach after tethering his two dappled gray horses to it. "Jump in the back—we'll be there by morning. Sleep if you can."

At first Edgar hesitated, wondering whether he should trust Rahul. After giving it a moment's thought, he decided the idea of getting out of the rain and away from the city was too tempting to pass up. After thanking him for his offer to assist, Edgar did as he was told.

The inside of the cart was decorated with gaudy trappings and ornaments such as crystal orbs, mystical cards, sparkling curtains, and various wands that Rahul no doubt convinced his clientele were enchanted. Having recently seen actual enchanted items, and the trappings of true dark magic, Edgar found the fakery quaint yet almost sad.

Numb with grief and fear, Edgar soon fell into an uneasy rest on the sofa at the back of the wagon. Though he didn't dream during his brief sleep, he kept coming out of the shallow slumber, convinced he heard far-off weeping. Every time he opened his eyes, however, the sensation faded, and his heavy emotions dragged him back down into the oblivion of sleep.

Several hours later, Rahul shook Edgar awake. He blearily looked about, trying to make sense of where he was. It took a moment to remember why he felt so harried. As he rose, feeling empty, he noticed the pain in the middle of his back had sharpened.

"How are you feeling, my friend?" Rahul inquired, the kindness in his voice identical to his mother's.

Edgar groaned and rubbed his hair. Every inch of his body complained for a bath, and the urge was maddening, but he shouldered it long enough to formulate an answer. "Like I've been filled with lead. Where are we?" he croaked, looking through the window of the carnival wagon. Huge, striped tents, bustling food stalls, flashing lights, exotic animals, and bright costumes swirled by in a kaleidoscope of color and motion that blazed in the late-afternoon sun.

"The All Souls' Fair—my home, for all intents and purposes. But we'll only be here a few hours. We'll get some food and rest, and then I'll take you onward," Rahul said cheerfully, apparently still unfazed by Edgar's morbid situation.

"Onward to where?" Edgar pressed as Rahul started to exit the wagon.

The young man stopped and craned his neck back with a gleam in his dark eyes. "You shall see. Now kindly wait here." He sprang from the wagon and into the singing madness of the fair.

Rahul returned more swiftly than Edgar had expected, carrying two bowls of steaming vegetable stew and flat bread. Edgar had to restrain himself from boorishly wolfing down the entire meal. Rahul watched him with distant curiosity, taking gentlemanly spoonfuls from his own bowl. It was some of the most nourishing, savory food Edgar had ever tasted, and when he was at last finished, he thanked Rahul for it. Rahul nodded back, still watching Edgar carefully—perhaps using his keen abilities to gather more facts about him without having to ask. Once Edgar's stomach stopped aching with hunger and his head felt clearer, he asked for their destination once again.

"What sort of place are we going to anyway?"

"I couldn't really tell you," Rahul said. "I've never stepped foot inside. The stories I hear say that it's full of deep, ancient magic. Real magic, not the sort of thing I play at in this wagon. Sometimes the women who live there venture outward—sometimes they pass through the fair. We always offer them safe room and board whenever they do. They do good for this world—they stand up for those who cannot help themselves."

"They're all...women?" Edgar asked curiously.

"The ones who travel away from the place are. I cannot speak for the settlement itself," Rahul said, and Edgar's brow pinched as he tried to make sense of the man's words.

"You will most likely face many things there to which you are not accustomed," Rahul continued. "There are people there who will not meet your standards of...ah...*polite society*." His normally cheery voice carrying a hint of derision. "I suggest that you treat them all with respect if you know what's good for you," he warned, and Edgar nodded, fully intending to comply.

After their meal was complete, Rahul blew out the candle in the lantern above them, and they got a few hours of sleep. Rahul woke him again once night had fallen, and they both climbed onto the front of the wagon. The horses prepared, they set off through the fair, which was roaring in the height of its activity. From where he sat, Edgar gazed at the marvels that surrounded him: electric lights blazed; children swarmed at game booths; a jet of fire streamed from a man's jaws. In the distance, overgrown shadows danced behind the striped cloth of a massive tent. As Rahul stopped to purchase a bag of roasted nuts for the journey, Edgar caught a glimpse of a twirling carousel. He found the blankly staring eyes of the wooden horses and beasts unsettling. Rahul climbed back up onto the seat and they set off.

When the madness of the fair was behind them, they traveled down a treelined dirt road for what seemed hours. It was bitingly cold, and it rained on and off. All the while, Edgar's back pained him more and more. During the journey through the increasingly wild, misty territory, he and Rahul conversed, if only to pass the time, and Edgar learned about the circumstances that had brought him to Scotland in the first place.

Rahul's father, Sudesh, had earned a reputation as a prominent scholar of psychology in Bombay. Through his father's work, Rahul became acquainted with a visiting English scholar who practiced mentalism as a hobby. The scholar taught Rahul much of his performance techniques throughout his teenage years. Sudesh's reputation grew, and he was eventually offered a prominent research position in Edinburgh. His extended family agreed to accompany him on the journey to Scotland a few months later. In Edinburgh, the family prospered until Sudesh, after venturing to the market one night after work, never returned home. Rahul's family had been left completely without answers as to what became of him, but Rahul suspected that his father had perished in some way. The family's funds soon dwindled, they lost their new home, and were forced to take jobs as factory workers at a textile company. Rahul put his own unique talents to work, earning money by telling fortunes and pretending to read minds. Business was best for him at the fair, and he had been saving to help his family return to India for more than three years.

"But you have fixed all that, my friend," Rahul said. "My cousin will recover, and soon we will all be home again. You've saved us from this nightmare. I hope I can help save you from yours in return." He smiled gratefully, and Edgar couldn't help smile as well.

They seemed to be delving farther and farther into the most desolate region of nowhere. Tangled copses of dark woods obscured the view, and thick clouds of mist enveloped their cart at intervals. Huge craggy rocks loomed around every turn, and every so often the glint of moonlight on black water twinkled in the murky distance. While they rode, Edgar withheld his questions, not wanting to perturb Rahul. So many thoughts were tumbling around in his head that he simply focused on sifting through them.

Gregory's father always had professed optimism, a trait that, through years of exposure, had become somewhat hybridized with Edgar's natural sense of pragmatic objectivity. It made sense to him in way—a positive attitude often led to productivity and affability among others, and therefore yielded more favorable results. When faced with truly difficult situations, he sometimes thought of Samuel Farrow's bright outlook and attempted to mimic it. But as Edgar sat jostling up and down on the wagon, wincing from the pain in his back, mourning the loss of the only man whom he had ever called a true friend, and anticipating his own destruction, it seemed impossible to mimic his adopted father's assurance.

As the night wore on, the trail grew bumpier, and the sharp turns, overgrown pathways, and patches of forest became more frequent. Edgar sat in a constant state of awe that Rahul could navigate through this landscape at all. The moon had risen and was high in the sky, and a strange silence had come over the surrounding woods. Even the animals and birds stayed hushed, as if disturbing the tranquility of this secret place was an offense against nature.

After Rahul ascended a forested hill, the woods ceased abruptly, and the wagon rolled across a wide-open plain that seemed to stretch on forever. They passed mounds of heather and wild plants, moving ever closer to a line of pines and oaks that grew unnaturally high and wide. Edgar didn't have to ask or wonder—this was certainly their destination. As they approached the thick of those foreboding, primordial arbors, he tensed. A stone wall, about as high as his chest, soon became visible, and eventually the form of a stone arch materialized out of the curling mists.

The horses seemed unwilling to get closer. Their pace slowed, and their nervous whinnies cut through the heavy silence. About fifty feet from the wall and its otherworldly archway, the horses stopped altogether, refusing to go another step, no matter how much Rahul urged them.

"This is it, then, my friend," Rahul said softly, staring into the black mass of whispering woods. Though Edgar already had begun to digest the fact that his destruction was imminent, the sight of those trees still scared him.

"So, I just…" Edgar murmured, not wanting to leave the comfort of Rahul's companionship just yet.

"Just keep walking. Someone will find you." He touched Edgar's shoulder in a moment of solidarity then nodded, willing him to venture forth.

"I'll never forget that you did this for me, Rahul. I only wish we could have been friends a while longer," Edgar said with an unexpected lurch of emotion. Somehow unadulterated honesty was easier for him to manage now.

Rahul, who was quite apt at recognizing the truth, seemed quietly moved by his words, and they shared a final, lengthy gaze.

There was no more stalling to be had, so Edgar bade him a final goodbye and dismounted from the wagon seat. Feeling awkward without a bag, or any real possessions to speak of, he took his first timid steps toward the archway.

He hesitated for a while longer as he watched Rahul turn around and ride away into the fog. It felt easier to face the future when the option to turn back was no longer present. Taking a deep breath and steadying himself, Edgar mimed his usual proud posture. His head held high, he crossed under the ancient threshold and into the wilds.

Sand Castles

Magdalena sat with the bow in her hand as she stared at the patterns on the wallpaper. Closing her eyes and letting a wave of rage and despair come and go, she put the bow to the strings of the cello and drew a long, resonating note that filled her tiny living space. The sound of it made her heart ache, and the enchantment of the song captured her. The rest of it flowed, tumbling from her deft hands like a perfectly coordinated avalanche. The swelling notes of the song vibrated in her chest, making her feel as if she were properly alive once more. Music was one of the few things that allowed her to feel human again, even if it was only ephemeral.

She pulled the bow into producing a sweet, high crescendo, feeling the instrument resonate between her legs as her finger pulsed over the string. She let the note die away, and at once she could not continue. A stab of stinging bitterness pierced her heart. She held her position a while longer then sighed and stood up to put her cello back in its case.

I was so close. All these years...all that work. I almost had it. One wrong move. If only I hadn't been so foolhardy. If only I hadn't taken pity on him. She let her face fall into her hands as she choked back her tears. She was in a place beyond fury or sorrow—there was only a futile numbness that permeated all the way into her bones.

Magdalena wandered in circles around her apartment. The entire space was decorated with a gorgeous assortment of furniture. In the corner of the room, a massive wooden bed, hung with embroidered silk curtains and laden with the softest of pillows and blankets, loomed over all else. Magdalena went and sat upon it, staring at the bookshelves that lined the walls, all of them stuffed full with an assortment of texts. An entire shelf was dedicated to works of scientific mastery, ranging from the year 1679 to the very latest publications. Volumes that unpacked world-altering discoveries in mathematics, technology, anthropology, chemistry, biology, and nearly every other prominent field of interest were their neighbors. Novels, poetry, and fairy tales lined the shelves on the far side of the room. The whole circular compartment gleamed with trophies and memories that Magdalena had won or stolen throughout the journey of her exceedingly long, exceedingly violent life. She peered about at fine oil paintings of victims she had painstakingly sought, jewelry pilfered from extravagant ladies, and a stack of yellowed love letters purloined from around the world—none of them addressed to her. On the table beside them stood the line of eight tiny coffins she had recovered from the wreckage of her shop. Each time she glanced upon them, she felt a rush of gratitude that they had survived the chaos.

From the ceiling of her bedchamber hung a massive chandelier that looked fiercely out of place, as it dominated most of the space above. Magdalena had claimed it as her own after a particularly memorable night: she had been discovered just before trying to assassinate one of her bitterest enemies in Russia and had single-handedly fought her way out of a ballroom full of people trying to decapitate her. No one besides her had lived to see the dawn, and as a reward to herself, Magdalena had snatched the chandelier that bore witness to her triumph. It tinkled whenever a gust of air breathed by, and Magdalena liked to imagine she could still hear the dying screams of her victims from that exhilarating night. Her entire room, to an outsider, would have looked like a magpie's nest—crowded with a patchwork of treasures and memories. To Magdalena it was the only place in the world where she felt truly at ease.

However, even her sanctuary, with all her precious belongings, couldn't bring Magdalena peace that night. The devastation of losing every single one of her revenants was all encompassing. She had wanted to blame Hare directly, but she couldn't. He hadn't done anything wrong—it was her fault. Her fault for trusting the surgeon.

Every time. Every time I try to employ kindness in my actions, I'm punished for it. And Hare constantly asks me why I'm so harsh. The filth of this world deserves no scruples. I must do my best to remember that.

She lay back, clutching the pillow for a moment, then was moved to rise from the bed. She prowled the room until she came to a halt in front of the gold-framed mirror beside the door. When she caught sight of herself, her pacing was forgotten.

She drifted toward the mirror, slowly reaching her hand out to touch the reflection of her fingertip. Her appearance always brought her equal amounts of pain and felicity. Her eyes traced her face—a face that would never grow old. She would be eternally fourteen. She would never become a woman. For the rest of her time, that cursed bud of youth would define her. As she stared at herself, she struggled to look past the frightful features that had warped her face after the transformation. When she squinted, her vision blurred, and she could almost remember what she had looked like before her life had been halted for eternity.

Magdalena closed her eyes now, trying to draw upon that far-off memory. She searched back through the centuries of things she had lived through and fought for, traveling even further back to a time when life had seemed simple.

I was so close to escaping. If only the fever had been a little stronger...if only father had been a bit less hasty...

Her mind flashed over the torturous night that had resulted in her eternal punishment, to the hazy time of sickness, to the time when her mother's neck had swollen with dark nodes and eventually burst, leaking black blood onto her sheets and depriving Magdalena of an innocence she would never recover. She pushed her thoughts beyond the day when the schism from her humanity first had occurred, back to the time when her mother had been a healthy, vibrant, loving being. Although time and turmoil had eaten away most of the memories from Magdalena's early life, a particular one lingered in her mind—one in which she often found refuge when things seemed the most hopeless.

She remembered a time when her family had ventured from their estate in Austria to a lakeside hidden deep in the woods. That excursion had been among the happiest times in her life. One day stood out in particular, when she'd made forts and castles out of sand on the lakeshore all afternoon. She recalled the feelings of wonderment, pure creativity, and power; she had ruled numerous kingdoms, if only for a sunset. She often wished that after she'd fallen asleep that night so many centuries ago, she would have died peacefully, lost to her childlike dreams forever.

Magdalena lamented the loss of the life that had been promised to her at that time, even if it would have been a short one. Although hundreds of tiresome years had passed, that particular ache hadn't faded—and neither had the urge to hurt the people who had done this to her. As she thought about them, a notion in the depths of her misery simmered and grew to a rolling boil.

They will not have a moment's peace. Not ever. Magdalena thrust herself away from the mirror, detesting everything as her throat burned with hunger. She wouldn't feed on flesh tonight, however; she had more pressing matters to attend to. She thundered out of her room and down the windy spiral staircase. Hare called to her from the shop side of the door as she stamped past it, but she didn't answer.

This isn't over. I haven't lost. I'll find that surgeon, and Hare and I will track down every last one of those souls and put them back where they belong. And once I have them, none of my prisoners will have a moment's peace ever again.

Magdalena was at the vault door now and pulled a ring of keys from the spot where it hung. In a fury, she undid all the locks one by one then threw open the heavy oak door. The dark, subterranean room stretched out before her. Seven pits had been bored into the ground, and from the moment the door scraped open, seven voices wailed in terror. Magdalena grinned and let the sounds ring for a moment, enjoying how the very hint of her presence induced such horror.

Walking between her rusty, sharp sets of toys, she peered into the first pit to see her favorite plaything cowering at the sight of her. He had long since stopped trying to beg. He looked up at her, the same too-large eyes, lengths of dark hair, and sharp teeth glaring out from the dingy blackness of the oubliette. She edged to the side of the pit, smiling down as her sorrow already began to ebb into a sense of confident power.

"Guten abend, Ulrich," she greeted him. He shut his eyes and hid his face in his quivering, emaciated hands.

Things were going to get better soon.

The Witches' Wood

Mist embraced Edgar as he moved toward the tree line. Feeling as though he were stepping into another world altogether, he melted into the fog. He was blind to nearly everything except the dim grayness around him. Moisture clung to his skin, and uncertain rustlings surrounded him. With every breath drawn, the fog and scent of soil seeped into Edgar's lungs, and with each step, his back ached more. By the time he'd gone half a mile, he was shaking with cold and wincing from the pain. Edgar had a vague sense that the path was wide and clear; the forest felt oppressive enough even with it. After ages of wandering in the fog with nothing around him save trees and cloudy, wet vapor, a faint shape began to emerge. Warily he inched closer to it, then relaxed somewhat when the form of a signpost became clear. It was ancient, covered in moss, and he could hardly make out the carving on its surface. Edgar squinted, trying to decipher it.

"Ahead lies...the Witches' Wood. Come only...with friendship in your heart," he read aloud, then frowned. Edgar supposed he had a reasonable amount of friendship to spare and decided he was under no violation of this law, so he pushed forward.

After about a mile more, the fog began to subside, and the way was lined by two dizzyingly high rows of trees. The black silhouettes loomed ominously on either side of him, lightly silvered by the light of the moon, yet Edgar didn't find them as threatening as the ramshackle buildings he'd seen in Edinburgh. Stopping for a moment to rest his back, he took the opportunity to check his wound—he wasn't surprised to see the discoloration had spread even further. The dark-purple veins beneath the skin stretched to just under his collarbone, and the entire area was splotchy with bruises.

As Edgar dug into his pocket for his vial of disinfectant, an unexpected change in emotion overtook him. He had been slightly wary moments before, but now a rapidly growing sense of dread filled him. Without his knowing why, Edgar's instincts screamed that something was behind him, and he leapt off the path and stared into the trees. At first he heard nothing but the rustling of the wind through the needles on the trees and his own breath, but soon his ears picked up the sound of something crawling through the underbrush.

"I...I'm a friend. I mean no harm!" Edgar shouted, and put his arms up, praying this was one of the mysterious women Rahul had mentioned coming to find him. But he knew in the depths of his subconscious that it was not.

The child apparition that had haunted him in Gregory's guest bedchamber came crawling out on his belly, his spine loose where it had been snapped. Tears splattered his rotting face, which had turned a purplish hue and was beginning to burst open in places. The eyes moved roughly in his head, looking dry and calloused over.

Edgar's balance was thrown off, and he found himself on the ground, his mind reeling as the pain in his back grew so intense that he could only gasp for breath. The child was on top of him again, emitting small hiccupping cries. Edgar managed to take a breath that sent a hot knife of pain digging into his chest, and though he tried to scream, he produced only a low moan. The child positioned himself above Edgar's midsection then ripped Edgar's shirt aside and took a bite out of his abdomen.

"Get off! Stop—someone—hel—" Edgar stammered as he tried to push the child's head away from his stomach. The boy, however, would not be deterred from feasting on his innards. The pain encompassed him, searing away any form of rational thought. Edgar frantically pushed at the child, and his pale hair came away in clumps.

"What in the hell d'ya think you're doin'?" called a voice from a few feet away.

Edgar sprang up, reaching out in a desperate plea for help from the stranger, and as he did, the nightmarish scene melted away without a trace. He panted wildly, dripping with sweat while panic coursed through him like molten iron. At the edge of the trail stood a tall woman with high cheekbones and sharp, searching gray eyes. Her hair, the color of a dying flame, whipped around in the wind, and Edgar got the distinct sense that she would kill with judicious swiftness should the right mood strike her.

"I...I...I'm a..."

"You're a what?" she demanded, putting her hand on the hilt of a dirk that was hitched to her muscular thigh.

"A friend...I'm a friend," Edgar gasped, trying to get a hold over himself and pointing in the vague direction of the signpost.

The woman looked at it for a moment, drew her dirk, then gave a smile that was as sharp as its blade. "Funny. You don't look like any friend of mine," she murmured as she toyed with the dagger. "In fact, you look sort of dangerous, and you've caught me prowling around, looking for dangerous things to exterminate. Strangely enough, we don't take kindly to outsiders threatening our home."

"No, madam, I assure you"—Edgar got to his feet and dusted himself off with quavering hands—"I need help. That's why I came here. I'm looking for...some witches, if I'm not badly mistaken. Rahul sent me," he protested, trying to come off as polite and informed. The woman leaned closer but kept her distance.

"Madam?" she scoffed. "Look here. I don't know any Rahul, and I don't know *you*—which means you could pose a threat. You look like one of them rich, snooty, pompous, greedy, soul-sucking insects that live in their grand mansions and crush weaker people into powder. You're a dead ringer for one of those folks, I'd reckon."

"Truthfully, *miss*," he corrected himself with no small amount of irritation, "I haven't got more than a few pounds to my name, anymore. And I'm dying. And I would *truly* appreciate it if you would stop threatening me. If you don't wish to help me, I'll happily leave you be," he huffed, Edgar could not curtail his rising emotion, and was sure some of his former arrogance was showing on his face.

The woman's eyebrows rose, and for a moment her expression betrayed something like begrudging surprise. "Did you say you're dying?" she asked, sounding strangely hopeful.

Edgar chose to ignore her tone. "In a manner of speaking. Certainly I haven't got much time left. I was told there might be a chance to stop it," he ventured, and the woman stopped to consider him. She seemed to be possessed of some sudden prospects, and Edgar waited for her to respond, though he felt his remaining restraint fluttering away.

"Come with me." She turned her back to him, sheathed her dirk, and gestured with her head for him to follow.

A Way Out

Though Ainsley faced forward and purposely affected an aura of practiced nonchalance, she kept herself prepared for anything. The man couldn't be trusted, no matter how he seemed. Trying to gather more information about his character, she stole glances at him as they walked on. Although she fully expected him to either try to sidle up and remark on her appearance or say something antagonizing about witches in general, he just seemed to be getting more distant.

The man was pale, as if he spent a great deal of time indoors, and the near black of his hair accentuated this effect. His frame was thin, and his cheeks and eyes had a somewhat hollow appearance. He was, however, handsome—but in a sort of fragile way that Ainsley wasn't altogether impressed by. He also seemed miserably frightened in the moments when he thought Ainsley wasn't watching him, but when she let her gaze fall upon him, he immediately straightened up and took on an analytical expression. After about ten minutes of hiking up the path with its carpet of fallen leaves, she was almost convinced he posed no danger.

She became completely certain of this when he collapsed without warning moments later. Ainsley turned and gaped at him, a strangled laugh escaping her throat. Approaching him with a little caution, she gently kicked him onto his back. The man had fainted dead away. With another, more pronounced laugh, she hoisted him upward, slung him over her shoulder with ease, and continued onward.

"Pathetic." Ainsley chuckled to herself, not laboring at all under his weight, though he matched her height. It took almost half an hour to get to where the village lay nestled in the dark alders and oaks, hidden safely away from the rest of the chaotic world. As she walked through the overgrown lanes and trails to her cottage, however, Ainsley didn't feel the same sense of security as usual. The Wood had changed since the spectral lights had come. The waters that usually ran fresh, cold, and clear had turned murky. The streams and creeks had taken on a brownish, sickly color, and a smell of rot suffocated the air around them. All around the banks, dead creatures lay, poisoned from drinking it. Vegetables in the gardens around the community had wilted overnight, and in the skies, birds were flying in erratic, confused patterns, screeching as an unseen terror drove them wild.

It was clear to Ainsley that something had corrupted the very heart of the forest; the wellspring that was the home of the fair lady of the woods had been defiled. She was certain the coming of the ghastly, luminescent figures—the revenants—was the cause.

Mind troubled by these notions, Ainsley flung open the cottage door, trudged in, and tossed the man unceremoniously onto the floor by the fireplace. Elspeth and Colleen, who were chatting at the table over tea, stood up in shock and rushed to her side.

"Oh, Ainsley...I wasn't aware we'd started to eat human meat," Elspeth joked, her whitish-blonde brows raised as she looked the man over. "It's a bit barbaric, don't you think?"

"Are you daft?" Ainsley gave her an incredulous glare, missing her humor entirely. "He's not something I hunted. And he's only fainted, not dead."

"Oh, the poor thing's in quite an awful state." Colleen knelt at the man's side while Ainsley frowned in disapproval. A protective urge came over her, and she wanted to shoo Colleen away from him, but she kept her mouth shut. Colleen attended to the man as Ainsley sat down in the nearest chair, scowling over the scene.

"What's he doing here then?" Elspeth sat beside her sister, her heavy-lidded gaze roaming over the stranger.

Ainsley hesitated before speaking, not sure if she wanted to give them a false sense of hope. She hardly dared believe it herself. "He...said he was dying. He was looking for something here that might save his life," she muttered. Just as she suspected, Colleen looked up with dire attention, her eyes growing wide and watery. Even Elspeth's awareness became uncharacteristically focused, and she kept her eyes fixed on Ainsley. An ache started in Ainsley's chest as she observed their eagerness to believe that tragedy could be avoided.

"Ainsley, it's a sign. It's—" Colleen was already breathless, but Ainsley's gloominess wouldn't allow her to get carried away.

"Don't go riding away on your dreams just yet. I've no idea what he needs or wants, or even if he's telling the truth. We have no reason to trust him—he's an outsider. I just thought he might be worth a second glance," she grumbled, keeping her arms across her chest.

"I'll wake him up right away." Elspeth drifted up from her seat, stood over the man, and drawled an incantation in a sleepy voice.

"*Slumber, lift. Find your eyes. Spirits of the dream time, dispel the veil of sleep.*"

Moments later came a sharp intake of breath, and the man's darkened eyelids flitted open. A fit of disorientation gripped him for a few seconds as he looked between the two unfamiliar faces; when he found Ainsley's disapproving glare, he relaxed. He creaked upward until he was sitting up, taking in his new surroundings.

"Are you feeling all right, sir?" Colleen asked him, and Ainsley was again possessed by the urge to remove her from the room. Colleen was so trusting of strangers and gave too freely of her kindness.

"Y-yes, I think so." He sighed, bracing his forehead against his hand. "Where am I?"

"The Witches' Wood, just like you wanted. I've brought you to my home." Out of agitation, Ainsley got to her feet and stepped between Colleen and the man. "Now I want you to state your business, and be hasty about it. If you're of no use to me, I'll send you right back where I found you."

"Oh, at least give him a moment, Ainsley," Colleen protested, turning to face her with an irritated glance.

"No, he talks now or he leaves." She remained firm and gave the stranger a hard stare. He returned it with a look of aloof disdain.

"Oh, he doesn't have to explain it really," Elspeth hummed, then turned her head to the side with a sphinx-like smile. "My familiar can see what's wrong. He told me—this man's got a spirit attached to him. A rather nasty one too. Just like the ones we saw in the sky yesterday, sister. Or was it last week? Or…early this morning?"

"A spirit?" Ainsley nearly coughed, looking at the fellow with growing interest. If there was a chance that he was connected to the apparitions that were befouling her woods, she needed him more than she originally had anticipated. "What's your name, outsider?"

"Edgar…Edgar Price," he stammered, holding out his hand for her to shake.

She would not take it but gave their names in return and kept her eyes fixed on him, silently demanding an explanation. Over the space of half an hour, the two witches and Colleen became acquainted with Edgar's tale, and he finished telling them about his capture and narrow escape with a shivering sigh. The three of them watched him in silence, digesting this new information.

"These ampoules that you smashed…you said a force erupted from them?" Elspeth asked, anxiety creeping into her voice.

"Yes, enough to demolish some of the items in the room. I didn't know what was in them; I was just looking for a distraction. I ran as soon as I could, but—"

"And did you see any figures come out of them? Anything at all?" Ainsley pressed the matter, dread growing in her. She expected Elspeth was already drawing the same conclusions as she was, judging from her unusual alertness. Edgar thought for a moment, putting his hands to his lips as his eyes flashed downward.

"There was a curious set of lights in the sky as I fled. They streaked off. A bit like comets, really," he murmured, and Ainsley let out a long breath. Her eyes connected with Elspeth's, and at once she knew that her fear was not without base.

Edgar picked up on their anxiety almost instantly. "What? What is it?" he asked, looking between the sisters. "Is it incurable? Have I come here in vain?"

"There's nothing *we* can do to help you," Elspeth said uneasily, and Edgar's expectant expression diminished.

Ainsley couldn't help but empathize with him. She was all too well acquainted with the dread of a quickly encroaching end, but she refused to let her face shift to show this.

"However, we could always ask—"

"No." Ainsley bristled, sensing what Elspeth was about to suggest. Her heart filling with ire, she turned to face her sister. "No outsiders are to go anywhere near her. I won't stand for it."

"It used to be that anyone could visit her," Elspeth countered.

Ainsley glared at her. "I won't hear of it. Even if we allowed it, the woods are too dangerous right now. We could end up like him"—she gestured to Edgar—"or worse."

"I don't understand. Have I missed something?" Edgar inquired.

"It's just that, very recently, there was..." Colleen started, but Ainsley lifted a hand to stop her.

Colleen's face grew serious, and she stared Ainsley down. Being of an agreeable nature, Colleen rarely stood up to Ainsley, but when she did, Ainsley wouldn't even attempt to stop her. The woman was downright frightening when angered.

"He has a right to know. It sounds to me that the same person who put the curse on him is responsible for the state of the other revenants too," Colleen reasoned, and Ainsley reluctantly bowed her head.

"Revenants?" Edgar questioned.

"They're vengeful spirits. As it happens, that's what you've got fixed to you at this very moment, though it's not yet fully matured." Elspeth answered and, upon seeing Edgar's look of fascinated alarm, continued. "Those who have passed on generally go to a very quiet end and slip into the next life without so much as a whisper. Others have unfinished business and become ghosts or perhaps poltergeists. Then there are revenants. The spirit that's clinging to your soul, along with the spirits that I suspect your captor kept in the ampoules, can be called by this name. They're of a very particular and violent nature," she said, then hung her silvery-blonde head. "And if my assumptions are correct, I'm sorry to say that, because of a curse our mother cast, these spirits remain earthbound."

"Our mother is a witch." Ainsley took control of the story, wanting Sylvia to be properly represented in front of the stranger. "She's a damn good one too. Around half a century ago, she made what *some of the coven*"—she narrowed her eyes at the window—"might refer to as a 'transgression,' but she did it in the name of justice." She paused before asking, "Tell me, have you heard of Burke and Hare?"

The Abominable Pair

"Burke and Hare?" Edgar repeated, his mind tingling with the recent memory. "Those names, well one of them at least, sounds familiar. Hare was the name of the man from the train, but aside from that..."

"Oh, Goddess be good. You said you came from London? What? Do you know nothing of the world? We here in the *Wood* know about it," Ainsley griped.

Edgar bristled. "I'm a very focused man. My attention hardly strays from my work. Do *deign* to enlighten me, won't you?"

"Almost seventy years ago in Edinburgh, two Irishmen and the women who took up with them committed a series of heinous crimes," Elspeth said gravely, then took Edgar's hand in hers. As she grabbed it, his sight of the room faded, and he saw the stone towers of a younger Edinburgh as clear as if he were standing before them. The harrowed visages of two men, one of whom looked uncannily familiar, appeared in the shadows of these towers. He hardly had time to reel from the shock of this vision and its scientific impossibility—the swirling mixture of Elspeth's voice and the images had completely captured him.

"William Burke and William Hare were poor, desperate, and of a monstrous nature," she continued, and impressions of years spent suffering in filthy, unkind conditions swept through Edgar. He cringed as the memories of the two dead men flowed through him. "In those times, anatomy theaters urgently needed subjects for public dissections—as such, the bodies of the recently deceased were in high demand. Many people desperate for money became resurrectionists—grave robbers who pillaged fresh earth for those who'd been laid to rest within—and sold their corpses off to surgeons. However, this wasn't the case for these two."

Edgar swallowed as a wave of guilt crashed through him. He knew that through their connection, Elspeth was aware of his profession. She ignored it, and the images of an antique Edinburgh became clear to him again.

"Burke and Hare weren't grave robbers—they were killers. They lured innocent souls to a boardinghouse, addled their minds with drink, and suffocated them in the night. Sixteen victims fell to their hands, and each found their way to the dissection table. Burke and Hare were paid well for their *work* by a doctor, Robert Knox, who turned a blind eye to their deeds. They might've gotten wealthier too, but the police caught wind, and eventually their spree came to an end."

Edgar's mind was bombarded with images of helpless, struggling women gasping for air as a pair of cruel hands squeezed their lives away from them. Swarms of guilt, anxiety, and the sick intoxication of power seeped into him no matter how much he tried to resist the emotions. Elspeth wanted him to feel everything firsthand.

"In prison the partners turned on each other. Hare gave a full confession, condemning Burke to the gallows. That man hanged for his crimes, and his corpse was dissected in front of an audience for good measure. His skeleton is on display in a museum, from what I know," Elspeth said with a bite in her voice. "Burke paid the price for both of them, and because of Hare's eagerness to sell any soul for his own profit, he was free to go. He ran back to Ireland, thinking he had escaped a miserable fate. But he was wrong. Wherever he went, people knew him. They hunted him, furious that this man could so easily get away with murder with the sanction of a court of law. He lived in constant fear of being caught and torn apart by angry mobs, even with a sea separating him from his wicked past.

"Hare had heard of this place—the Witches' Wood—when he lived in Edinburgh. Having grown up on ignorant folktales and gutter legends, he foolishly thought witches to be as vile in deed as he was. He'd also heard that our home offered safety to the lost and unfairly persecuted souls of this world. So Hare traveled here in search of amnesty, still thinking himself worthy of it."

Elspeth's voice hummed with quiet anger. Edgar saw the drunken, miserable face of William Hare chancing nervously down the very path he himself had walked hours earlier. Another image of Hare talking to a woman who possessed Ainsley and Elspeth's high cheekbones and intimidating beauty flashed before his eyes.

"The Witches' Wood was where Hare met my mother. He told her of his crimes and begged for safety from the world, hoping she would be merciful." Elspeth paused for a long moment then said, "She was not."

The image of the witch grew frightening and warped by an unearthly black light. Her eyes widened, and her limbs seemed to lengthen as she stretched upward. With her hands extended like the grasping talons of an eagle, a din as loud as a squall burst around her. The echoes of forbidden chants ripped at Edgar's ears, and he found it almost impossible to draw a breath.

"She cursed the man with the darkest of incantations. She summoned each of his victims' souls from the grave to follow him for all eternity, torturing the man with the very pain he had inflicted upon them. Through this curse, their spirits became the very revenants that haunt us now. To those sorry ghosts, she gave a second chance at life by fixing them to Hare—though it was a tormented half life at best. To the murderer, she also gave life, but as a punishment. He could not die; he could not rest. Forever, he would suffer the same agony of the people his avarice destroyed."

Edgar saw a ring of unholy lights closing in on the cowering form of the murderer William Hare.

"And so he was cast from the Witches' Wood, doomed to wander the earth for all time, bearing the weight of his crimes. Last I heard, he threw himself into a lime pit. He tried to blind himself in order to stop seeing the horrors, but they continued to visit him even in the darkness," Elspeth finished, then finally let go of Edgar's hand.

He took a moment to acclimate to reality, mulling over what he'd just experienced. "And your mother?" Edgar finally said, with a tremble in his voice. "What became of her?"

"She was banished from the Witches' Wood," Ainsley answered with distaste. "Witches who use black magic aren't permitted to live here. I assume she's made a life for herself, somewhere. If you ask me, it was what the evil piece of filth deserved—Mother acted in the name of justice. Those who do wrong should be held accountable for their actions."

"We thought this tale had been set to rest," Elspeth said. "Sadly, we were mistaken. Last night three revenants appeared in the sky, and since that moment they've begun to infect these woods and the creatures that live here. The animals are mad with fear and rage. The soil has become fallow, poisoning the plants and trees. Our waters turned foul and noxious overnight.

"Something has altered our mother's curse, and I believe this *other* Hare and the woman you mentioned are to blame. It sounds to me as if she's been trying to set Hare free from the revenants, and to do so, lives must be sacrificed. She might have been holding the spirits in those ampoules after detaching them from Hare...and when you smashed them, they were set free on the world." She looked to Edgar, the corners of her mouth sloping downward.

"Do you see now? You put our home and the people who live here in danger by breaking those ampoules," Ainsley growled. "All to save yourself. If the curse keeps spreading to the entire Wood, soon all the plants and animals will perish, and our way of life—"

"Ainsley, it's that woman's fault for tinkering with the curse. Edgar's just as much a victim as we are. Do try to see reason from time to time," Colleen argued, but Ainsley still looked as if she wanted to scold Edgar.

"Colleen is right, sister. We might have use for him yet, if he can help us find and remove the other revenants. We should take him to Fana. She'll know what to make of this, and she can tell us if there's any way to help him," Elspeth suggested gently.

Edgar didn't have any idea who Fana was, but a small glimmer of hope ignited in his chest once again.

"He's not fit to look on her," Ainsley retorted. "He has no love for these woods...he has no respect for this land. He comes from a people who destroy everything and everyone they touch. It would be a crime to let an outsider into the Well. I could never forgive myself." The mere thought appeared to be a violation to her, which in turn made Edgar feel further ashamed and frustrated with himself.

"Ainsley, have you forgotten that I was an outsider once too?" Colleen touched her arm, and the witch's look softened. She sighed through her nose, staring long and hard at Edgar.

"Please," Edgar tried to appeal to Ainsley's innate kindness, which he sensed despite her strains to deny it. "I couldn't see it before, but this...this *curse* has changed a great deal about how I view the world. I've wasted a good deal of my life being miserable and feeling sorry for myself, and now that I'm dying—well, I want another chance to remedy that. I will only do as you tell me. Please."

After a long few minutes of deliberation, Ainsley's face fell into a defeated yet understanding expression. "Aye. I'll give you this chance. I'll take you to the Well, Edgar Price. But if you give me cause to regret this, just know that you will pay."

The Poisoned Well

Ainsley rushed between the house and the shed, picking up tools she might need. Taking chances while the revenants' presence seeped further into the heart of the Wood was out of the question. She knew well that even though her life might be ending soon, there were things in this world that could make death seem like a privilege. To underestimate them would be a foolish error.

She stuffed her satchel full of invocation paper then slid a peculiar ring over a finger on her left hand. It was an ugly thing made of iron, but if she pressed a button on the side, two latches would swing up, revealing a needle. After she had sufficiently stocked up on protective amulets, bandages, and spell books, she went inside and roused Edgar from his spot by the fire. As he got to his feet, she glared at him.

"You going to faint again? I can't have that nonsense happening if something serious arises" Ainsley bore a secret hope that he might so she could have the chance to preserve his life. She wondered if it would even be effective if she saved him—how much was a condemned man's life worth to the magic of the Goddess?

"That was...that was highly irregular. I was suffering from fatigue, and I'd endured several great shocks, and..." he said in a restrained panic, his face going pink.

Ainsley rolled her eyes and started toward the door. As she placed her hand on the handle, she hoped Colleen would stop her, and her heart surged slightly when she saw her rise and come toward her.

"Ainsley..." She gave her an unwavering look. "Be careful out there. I'll not tolerate losing you—not yet, anyway," she murmured.

Ainsley took Colleen's hand in hers for a moment and squeezed it. "That's why I'm going, love." She stared at Colleen, her chest beginning to ache. She wanted so badly to kiss her good-bye but felt Edgar's uncomfortable presence behind her. Then, in a moment, she decided she didn't care what he thought and pressed her lips gently to hers. After they broke apart, their eyes remained locked for a moment.

"All right, outsider, let's go," she said, then opened the door and marched out, shouting a vague farewell to Elspeth, who might already have begun to dream again.

Edgar followed Ainsley's powerful stride, keeping up with a ragged breath. She silently anticipated that he might say anything unpleasant about her and Colleen. However, he remained quiet, aside from his heavy breathing; he seemed more focused on his own discomfort than on causing any for her.

"Where are we going exactly?" he finally asked.

"To the Clootie Well. You know what that is?"

"N—"

"Of course you don't," she said. "A Clootie Well is a sacred spring. It's very important to our Wood—our guardian spirit lives there." She looked back at him to gauge his reaction, and he gave her a curious look. "People tie bits of cloth to the trees there and ask the spirit to heal them or grant wishes. Do you ken what I mean by this?"

"I think so."

"Do you really? Think of your churches. Think about how respectful you'd act there. Try to do that," she advised.

"I'm not a churchgoing man. Sorry to disappoint." Edgar seemed to be getting testy with her. "I'm a man of science."

She laughed, a sound like a fox's bark. "Right. Now try and keep quiet. We don't want to be caught unaware by anything unpleasant."

"What do you mean by 'unpleasant' exactly?"

"Hush."

They left the safety of the cluster of cottages, with their abundant gardens and flowers that perfumed the misty night air, and made for the edge of the trees. As they progressed, Ainsley felt an oppressive force growing. The gloom seemed thicker, the air heavier, the breeze fainter. Whenever Ainsley took a breath, she thought she detected a smell she likened to rotting flesh, but when she breathed deeper to try to locate the source, it was gone. None of the comforting sounds of the animals on their nightly prowls greeted them—only frantic skittering and far-off, mournful howls. A way into their hike, the moonlight stained the trees and soil purple in a foreboding light. Ainsley bristled under the fell atmosphere of that place. She turned to look at Edgar and his face plainly indicated that he felt it as well.

"Something's wrong here. My back's starting to hurt again, but the pain isn't entirely physical. I feel...I feel..." He grasped huskily for the right word as his eyes darted about.

"It's the dead. You feel the dead. I feel them too. Press on," Ainsley's voice was hushed, knowing their conversation might stir up the intruding presence and draw it near to them.

After a moment more, anxiety started to eat at her, though it wasn't herself she was concerned about. As they drew nearer to the Well, it was fast becoming more apparent how deeply this blight ran. The trees had turned black and were showing signs of decomposition, their leaves dropping heavily to the forest floor. In a nearby stream, a mass of dead fish blocked the waterways, their eyes dull white like tarnished pearls. Beneath Ainsley's feet, swarms of insects surged through the damp soil, attacking one another; a wave of ants slowly pulled a dragonfly apart as its legs and wings thrashed. In the treetops, spiders frantically spun webs in erratic, asymmetrical patterns.

Fana never would allow this to happen; Fana protected the Wood—she *was* the Wood. If something had done this much damage to her trees, then something might've done equal damage to her.

I was a fool not to go to her earlier. I went hunting for the source of this corruption myself, but I never thought to check on Fana. Ainsley chewed her lip in guilt. As she lay her foot down, she was surprised to find that the soil gave way with a wet squelch. When she lifted her boot, a syrupy red substance dripped from it.

Blood?

Ainsley looked around in a panic. The forest was swamped with the fluid. Abandoning all caution, she propelled herself down the muddy trail. Edgar followed, keeping silent, though she sensed his palpable fright. When she burst over a hill and into a wide, tree-circled meadow, she couldn't prevent a moan from floating past her lips.

The Well had been utterly violated. The ferns around the spring were all dead, dried up, and covered in thick blood that dribbled down from the purpled leaves of the trees. The deep pond itself was polluted with reddish-black water and bubbled thickly. The ring of mushrooms that separated it from the meadow was covered in ghastly, warped appendages and smelled like an opened grave. A dried black crust was all that remained of the moss that usually covered the ancient stones.

Ainsley stumbled forward as if wading through a nightmare, approaching the Well while clutching at her collarbone. As she looked upon the desecrated pieces of cloth that people had left as offerings, tears of profound despair filled her eyes. Edgar wandered down the path behind her, aghast at the sight of the ruined land and recoiling from the stench, though he couldn't fully comprehend what had befallen it. With trembling hands, he fumbled in his pocket, produced a small tincture bottle, and began to feverishly apply the contents to his hands. He opened his mouth to speak but was silenced when the ominous sound of something large moved toward them through the brush. A dark shape as tall as many of the younger trees and covered in shaggy hair was lumbering through the shadows toward the meadow.

"What's that? What's happening?" Edgar whispered in a strangled breath, and Ainsley hissed at him to be silent. She grabbed a piece of invocation paper and opened the latch on her ring in preparation.

The creature shifted through the ferns, grasses, and withered flowers, lurching through the tree line until its begrimed head came through. Edgar gasped and almost stumbled back into the bloody muck, but Ainsley reached out and grabbed him. They both stood frozen, a wave of revulsion and fright washing over them as the creature emerged into the clearing.

The beast stood almost eight feet tall and was covered in matted brown hair that crawled with maggots and fetid plant life. Its hooves looked afflicted with rot and were caked with the same black moss as that of the nearby stones. It took Ainsley a moment to realize the creature was shaped like a deer but wildly deformed. The eyes were unfocused, bulging, and oozed a yellow mucus between the sores that ringed them. As Ainsley's eyes followed up its head to look upon the antlers, another wave of despair struck her like a strong breath of wind in a blizzard.

The antlers looked like tree branches, and the leaves and flowers that sprouted from them were falling off at an alarming rate, raining onto its fur and the forest floor. Ainsley covered her mouth, her eyes watering.

"No…no," she wailed, drawing closer to the creature as it bellowed in pain. "What's happened to you?"

"Help me…" The words echoed from the beast's open mouth, sounding like a gust of air. It groaned into the night. "Help me, Ainsley."

"What is that thing?" Edgar cried out from behind her. Ainsley ignored him and went to lay her hand on the beast, but it shook violently.

"Don't touch me!" The words rang through the meadow, now like wind whistling through a crack in a window, and Ainsley drew back. "If you do, it'll corrupt you too."

"What can I do? Please tell me...tell me." Ainsley was tearful, clutching at her chest as the beast lowered itself with labor onto its knees. It let its head drop into the dry grass and heaved a tortured sigh that sent a miasmic stench flowing through the meadow. Ainsley and Edgar covered their noses and choked.

"Go deeper into the woods. The poison starts...at the wellspring. Follow the spring. Please...help me..." The beast let out another ragged breath and closed its festering eyes.

"Yes, dear one. I'll do anything I can," Ainsley promised, her voice warbling. She looked back at Edgar, her eyes urging him to follow. "Come with me. I might need you."

"I...it said it's contagious..." He faltered while gaping at the cursed Well and the perversion of life that shuddered in the grass. "Perhaps there's some way to help it...medicine or...?"

Ainsley's eyebrows pinched together, daring him to run away. "There's no medicine in this world that can heal this. The source of the affliction runs deeper than the body," she stated. Edgar's look of horror turned into one of tremulous resolve, and he nodded.

"Understood."

Carefully they walked around the beast's quaking body then climbed over the rocks at the edge of the meadow. After they'd scaled the small waterfall, they found the trickling stream and wound up between the boulders. They farther they went, the more the odor of death and decay filled the air, and the blacker the stream's water became.

"What is happening to this place?" Edgar asked.

"The revenants have corrupted it. This is the center of life and magic of these woods. They're feeding off the living things here, absorbing their energy. You were the one who loosed them on the world, even if it was an accident. You owe it to us to help me exorcise them. You owe it to *her*." Ainsley pointed back in the direction of the ailing creature.

Edgar was taken aback. "It's a *her?*"

"Keep your head focused. Things are about to get worse," Ainsley warned, feeling as if the oppressive force in the air were crushing her. The rocks became larger and more difficult to scale, and soon the black, bloodied water soiled their clothes. Eventually the trail evened out, and the ground became flat, but the spring seemed to disappear into the ground and went no farther.

Ainsley searched the area, clawing through brush as she listened for the trickle of water. The night was pitch-black, and the trees blotted out the moon, but still she kept hunting. Edgar watched her, seemingly unsure what to do. She trekked about in circles, her frustration becoming maddening, with no evident signs of a way forward.

"Ah, Ainsley…" Edgar began, and her rage flared up. She expected him to say something about her going in circles, and she was too distraught to deal with him.

"Quiet. I'm trying to find out where to go next." She dug into her frock pocket, pulled out a strip of invocation paper, and opened up the ring to prick her finger. Once the sharp sting of pain had come and gone, she traced out a locating spell on the paper with her blood then tossed it into the air. The paper ignited and burned away with a blue flame, but no flash of clarity or knowledge came to her. She growled in frustration, setting off in one direction in hopes it would lead her somewhere.

"Ainsley, pardon my interruption, but—"

"What did I *just* say?"

Her trail went cold, and she turned back to try another way, but Edgar stepped in front of her. He opened his mouth once more, and she had to restrain herself from grabbing his shirt in anger.

"Look, I know you're confused, but this is *very* complicated. So could you please, for one moment, let me—"

"Ainsley, there's a sort of odd light *right there.*" He pointed to the other side of the stream to what looked like a weed patch.

Ainsley blinked at it, then at him. "You're mad. There's nothing there but brambles," she snapped.

Edgar's brow knitted, and he broke away from where they stood, heading confidently toward the patch.

"Where do you think you're going? I told you to stay put," she protested.

He reached the rough patch and wove his way between the weeds. Just as he stepped over a line of dead plants, he disappeared entirely from view.

Pearl, Cage, and Candlelight

Edgar passed through the wall of black light and Ainsley's complaining voice faded to naught. As he crossed the barrier, the pain in his back flared up so powerfully that he fell to his knees. It was a moment before he could get to his feet again, and when he did, he saw Ainsley step through the threshold with another slip of paper in her hand. Immediately she cringed under the ominous atmosphere of the place, her eyes going wide.

"Feel free to apologize whenever you're ready," he groaned at her, massaging his aching back. She was apparently too distracted to acknowledge this.

"This...this is the spot," she whispered, her eyes locked with Edgar's. "I've got to find the revenant and put a stop to it." They held their gaze as Edgar steeled himself. "There's a very good chance we could both be destroyed here. If you aren't willing to risk that, go back to the Well. I'll do what I can."

"No. As you mentioned, I *am* partially responsible for this. I'll do whatever I can to bring this to rights," he told her. She nodded at him, and he caught a flicker of approval in her face. Moments later she broke their gaze to begin her search.

"I can't see much of anything. It just looks dark," she whispered, holding a bleeding finger over the paper, ready to draw a spell.

Edgar walked in a circle, peering at their surroundings. At first glance, it looked to be the same overgrown forest path, only darker than it had been moments ago. As he squinted around, Edgar spotted a soft glow emanating from a trio of lights hovering above the earth in the distance.

"There. Those lights." He pointed toward the phenomenon and carefully set off toward it.

Ainsley blinked again. "I still can't see anything. You'll have to lead the way," she said, grabbing the back of his shirt. They fought their way through the overgrowth, tripping in the darkness until Edgar began to perceive the shapes of the lights more clearly. He could see they were orbs floating and spinning round one another. One was a ghostly blue and flickered like a flame; the next was a pale-purple sphere of diffused radiance; and the last pulsed sea green and rippled, as if underwater.

"Ainsley...your sister said there were three apparitions in the sky, yes?" Edgar whispered as he led her forward.

"Yes, three," she said.

"I believe they're all here. All in this place."

They drew close now, and Edgar spotted a curtain of the thinnest, shimmering gossamer surrounding the three lights. It fed up into the boughs of the trees, its origin obscured by the leaves.

At the sight of this, Ainsley exhaled, taken with fright. "It'll be a miracle if we get out of this alive. You know that, right?"

"What have I got to lose really? My soul is already forfeit. That poor creature back there is suffering. I might as well do something useful with the time I've got left," Edgar reasoned aloud, speaking to himself more than to Ainsley. He could hardly believe how calm he felt, though the danger ahead of them was obvious. Ainsley's hand let go of his shirt, and she stopped walking.

"You're right...I haven't got much of anything to lose either," she said softly.

Edgar turned back, watching as she collected her thoughts. Her eyes flicked upward, and in that moment the two reached a silent understanding. Ainsley nodded to Edgar, and he led her onward, taking her to the very edge of the curtain. It swayed as though it were submerged in a pond.

After he halted, Ainsley glanced around. "Why have we stopped?"

As she tried to continue, Edgar extended his arm to stop her before she could come into contact with the curtain.

"There's a kind of shroud here," he said. "I can only just make it out. The lights are on the other side."

Ainsley's expression darkened. She was still and silent for a moment, and then her lips parted. "Just there?" She pointed ahead, and Edgar followed her gesture, nodding his affirmation. Ainsley pushed his arm out of her path and reached forward with outstretched fingers, despite his stammered protests.

The moment her fingers came in contact with the ghostly fibers, a gale-force wind struck without warning, knocking them backward into the mud. They screamed and clutched each other as the wind tore by. When at last they were able to open their eyes and sit up, an unreal vision appeared in the thicket.

About fifty feet away, a crooked tree stood in the center of a deep, green pool. Candles flickered among its gnarled branches, their wicks alight with dancing blue flames. At the point in the center where all the branches converged, the largest candle of the bunch stood rooted. Below this, in the tree's trunk, gaped a knot-hole two feet in diameter. Inside it was a birdcage, and behind its bars a tiny, crystal bird sat perched upon a wooden swing. Purple light refracted from its icelike wings as it twittered and fluttered against the grate.

As Edgar's eyes followed the trunk downward, he noticed a tangled collection of plants, all of which sprouted out of the murky waters of the pool. Beneath the surface at the rocky bottom, many discarded treasures lay forgotten. Among them he counted a rocking horse, bits of tarnished jewelry, music boxes, a china doll with a broken face, and a book of fairy tales. In the very center of the pile sat a scallop shell made of porcelain. At intervals, the current teased it open to reveal a misty green light within.

"Do you see this?" Edgar whispered, gripped with an overwhelming fear that was yet tinged with a slight fascination.

"I do," Ainsley replied, her visage awestruck by the tree and its myriad haunting lights.

Neither of them knew what to do, so they merely sat side by side, quivering and transfixed by the sublime beauty. A minute passed before they were able to get to their feet and proceed.

Step by trembling step, they approached the sloping sides of the pond. As Edgar stared at its rippling waters, he felt the distinct sensation that it was pulling him in. It seemed the world was tilting forward in hopes that he might lose his footing.

"What should we do?" he asked, not daring to speak above a whisper.

"How should I know that?" Ainsley answered a bit testily.

"You're a witch, aren't you?"

"Yes, but that doesn't mean I know everything. I don't deal in black magic," she said, her whisper growing pettish.

Suddenly the pool's surface was disturbed. Ainsley and Edgar drew back as a few bubbles rose from the bottom, followed by the furious rippling of water. Whatever was in the shadowed pool moved in peculiar rings of motion, creating waves upon the pearly shore. At once, Edgar's back felt as if it were being cleaved apart, and he screamed as that now-familiar tortured weeping filled his head. He fell to the ground, head in his hands, groaning while Ainsley frantically tried to quiet him.

Something was rising out of the water. From the tendrils of seaweed and the pile of sunken memories, three heads emerged. Their long, tangled hair covered their faces and floated in the green water like trails of ink. Edgar opened his watering eyes just long enough to see three bedraggled maidens rise from the pool, each of them clinging to one another as they kept their heads together. The trio ascended from the depths until their torsos appeared, and then they came to a gradual stop, dripping wet and shivering in one another's arms.

"Get back, Edgar," Ainsley said hoarsely.

She wrenched him to his feet and forced him behind her with her arm. Faster than his eyes could track, she scribbled out wards with a quaking, bloody finger. Edgar couldn't tell whether the magic was working, but each time the paper flared away in a burst of firelight, the three maidens in the spring didn't seem to mind in the slightest.

"Ainsley, I don't think that's accomplishing anyth—ah!" Pain roared through Edgar's spine, and he tried to keep his balance. Everything seemed as though it were rocking back and forth, as if he were on the deck of an ocean liner rather than solid ground.

"Well, then why don't you come up with a plan?" she cried, growing frustrated with her useless wards.

"I don't think weapons will work. Use bottles or jars if you have any. The woman, Magdalena, she kept them in ampoules," Edgar said through clenched teeth.

As Ainsley's hand reached for her satchel, the three spirits raised their heads to gaze at her. Tears streamed down each of their faces, each one showing a fear of the fiery-haired witch. Her face softened slightly.

"Can't we help them?" Edgar said, at once transfixed and gripped with compassion for the apparitions.

"Spirits, begone from these woods. You are not welcome here," Ainsley declared in an unwavering voice.

The revenants stared up at her, still clinging to one another. As Ainsley tried to speak again, the three specters opened their mouths, and a single unholy shriek filled the air, knocking her to the ground. Edgar cried out too, but his voice was lost in the cacophony; all he could do was double forward with his hands over his ears. He heard the voices of the tormented spirits ringing inside his head, rather than in the air.

It's your fault—you took everything. You'll pay; you'll suffer. How dare you disturb us? Ann, Mary, run away...I'll get her...I'll tear her apart!

The blonde girl in the middle swam forward through the green water to where Ainsley had fallen and was struggling to sit up on the edge of the water. The other two—one with black hair and one with brown—scrambled up the trunk of the tree. One took refuge within the birdcage, shrinking and crawling, spider-like. After she squeezed inside, the door shut behind her and she melted away into nothingness. The other climbed the tree and disappeared into the candle flame at the top. Just as the shrill wailing faded away, Edgar caught sight of the blonde maiden grabbing Ainsley's heels and trying to drag her into the pool.

Get her, Effie. Drown her, the two other spirits whispered, urging her on, their voices ethereal. Ainsley yelled, scrambling away as her hands dug feebly through the sand. She couldn't get a hold on the bank, and the spirit succeeded in dragging her downward.

Edgar launched forward and caught Ainsley's hand. She was pulled back and forth between the two of them, crying out all the time. Where the spirit touched her bare flesh on her arms, Ainsley's skin began to grow loose and rub away as if melted by lye.

"Hold on, Ainsley!" Edgar shouted, his heart sick at the sight.

With a powerful heave, he yanked her out of Effie's grasp. As she came free, Edgar fell onto his back, and before he could right himself, Effie crawled forward and seized his ankles with an iron grip. Edgar had no time to react. He only caught a glimpse of a pallid face with soft features and hollowed blue eyes before he was drawn into the icy pool. All the air in his lungs escaped in the first few seconds. Choking, he was numb with cold almost instantly. The sight of blue candle flames became mere ripples beyond the surface.

Effie caught hold of his shoulders and pulled him deeper into the pool's green water. Her hands gripped him ever more tightly, and the longer they remained in contact, the more he understood about her. Memories of her lost life bloomed in his head, and her thoughts became known to him, just as they had with Elspeth. However, whereas the witch's connection felt illuminating, the revenant's felt infectious. Images of the green pearl within the scallop shell burned in his mind like the pulsing of an electric light. It was precious to her.

They were now floating in a churning shaft of dully gleaming treasures, all of which Edgar now knew belonged to Effie. His lungs felt as if they were threatening to explode as the waifish spirit swam up to look him in the face, fascinated by the fact he was dying. As she ran a finger down his cheek, he expected his flesh to become loose as Ainsley's had, but he felt only a slight pressure.

His consciousness was fast fading, and the cold was closing in on him, making his arms feel as if they weighed hundreds of pounds each. No longer able to kick his legs, he focused on the swirling keepsakes embedded in the blackness around him.

You're not a bad person. You'll be safe here. I won't let anyone hurt you. I won't let them hurt you like they hurt me, Effie's voice rang in his mind.

Sounds grew farther away, distorted by the water in his ears. Edgar looked around and saw broken violins, satin dresses, pocket watches, letter openers, a silk ribbon…and, in the center, a pulsing green light guarded by a large scallop shell.

As Edgar's eyelids began to close on their own accord, he summoned the remnants of his energy and kicked out to propel himself upward. As he did, his foot connected with the top of the shell, and at once Effie flinched as if she'd been struck. She released him, and Edgar flailed upward until his face broke the freezing surface of the pond. Air stung him, but the water in his airway prevented him from drawing breath.

"Edgar! I'm coming!" Ainsley's voice called, and in moments she was at the edge of the pond with a paper in her hand.

As it ignited into a purple flame, all the water in Edgar's lungs issued forth from his mouth, and he could breathe freely again. As he struggled toward the shore, Effie's hands clamped down on his ankles once more and pulled him under again.

This time he'd taken a breath and was better prepared. Effie clearly didn't expect him to fight, and he took her by surprise by swimming downward and out of her grasp. She dove for his shoulders and missed. Edgar swam down past her collection, keeping his eyes fixed on the shell at the bottom. He was making progress, flowing past her sunken treasures in sweeping bursts, when he noticed the items were drifting toward him. They floated up, attempting to block his way to the scallop shell, further encouraging him of its importance. Just as he shoved a broken clock out of the way, he felt her fingers tug at the hems of his trousers.

Just get there, he told himself, keeping his eyes locked on the shell and the green pearl that glowed within. It was an arm's length away, but she'd caught him and pulled him out of reach of the shell. In his shock of being yanked away, his breath was shaken from his mouth, and water again rushed in.

The surface broke violently as Ainsley dove into the pool. Edgar saw her face, cast in eerie aquatic light, moving closer to him. Her bright-red hair looked even more like a flame as it flowed in the water's currents. She was beside him in seconds, grabbing Effie's face with the intention of pulling her off Edgar. When her hands connected with Effie's skin, blood instantly clouded the water, and Ainsley pulled her hands away as if she'd touched the side of a hot kettle.

Effie let go of Edgar, and reached out towards Ainsley. Seizing the chance, Edgar pushed off her with his legs and grabbed the scallop shell. It started to snap shut just as he took hold of it, but he wedged his fingers inside before it closed. As it clamped down, crushing his hand, the coldness of the water and the aching in his lungs were the only things keeping him focused. No matter how hard he pulled against it, it wouldn't budge.

Every time he applied force to the shell, Effie thrashed about in the middle of the pool like a hooked fish. Ainsley kicked her way up to the surface and out of harm's way. As Edgar's alertness began to ebb, his lungs filled again with a mysterious burst of oxygen, and the water forced its way out through his mouth and nose. Evidently, Ainsley's witchery had bought him a little more time.

His heart sank in terror when he saw that Effie was coming straight for him, her tattered white gown billowing around her like mist, her wan face set in a vengeful sneer. She caught him around the neck and throttled him as her collection of keepsakes pressed in from all sides. They forced Edgar and Effie together, sealing them in a sort of cocoon. The dull-green illumination from the pearl was the only source of light as they became entombed in the shell of discarded treasures. Edgar could hardly move due to all the pressure, while Effie clenched at his throat, her deep-blue eyes blazing spots of color on her white face.

How dare you...how dare you? Don't take my life from me; I can't bear it. I don't want to die again. Let me be. Let me live.

Edgar heard her thoughts loud and clear. Her very spirit overflowed with misery, her face contorting in anguish as she stared beseechingly at Edgar. Shutting his eyes, he focused all his energy on prying the shell apart. It was giving way, even if just a little.

You're no longer alive. Nothing can change that. I'm trying to set you free, Effie, he thought, hoping his voice would reach her. Her eyes opened wide in reaction to this, and the shell loosened even more. Her eyebrows pinched together in confusion.

No! You're trying to fool me. You're—

Hare has done harm to me as well. See for yourself. Edgar used his free hand to tear open his shirt and expose the sickly purple wound on his chest. Effie drew back at the sight of it, and the fearsome clamping of the shell let up. Acting quickly, Edgar lifted the top back and plucked the pearl from inside. As soon as he took hold of it, a rushing sensation shot up his arm and a bolt of awareness seized him. At once, he understood that the pearl was not simply Effie's vulnerable point, but it was indeed her entire being. Her soul was housed within the pulsing sphere. It was both her prison and the source of her power, allowing her to create and control her treasures, as well as her apparition. Each element was a part of her soul, all built up to protect the source.

Effie's scream filled the underwater cavern, echoing off the sides as the current swept up with such a fierce strength that Edgar felt he was at sea in a storm.

He held tightly to the pearl, feeling Effie's agony flow through him. Objects from the enclosure around them began to drift away, and soon small patches of murky light showed through the spaces between the items. Using one arm, Edgar ripped a cracked vase aside then pried a candlestick away. He created a hole just large enough to wriggle through then wormed his way upward and out. As soon as he was free, he was tossed about so viciously in the water that he had no clue which way was up. By some miracle, he felt air on his face and opened his eyes.

"Edgar!" Ainsley cried.

There was a splash, and moments later he felt her hands on his back. She towed him to the shore as his head reeled and his vision started to refocus. Against his hand, the pearl felt as though it had a tiny heartbeat. Both Edgar and Ainsley crawled out of the churning water and back on land, but there was hardly time to rest.

Effie! Effie! What have you done to her? the spirits cried.

Fire rained down from the tree, and Ainsley and Edgar rolled out of the way just in time to avoid getting scorched. As they did, the pearl slipped from Edgar's hands and bounced toward the pool. As he scrambled to reclaim it, it was caught beneath his knee. It crumpled under his weight like a Christmas bauble, and he leapt back from the broken mess, sharing a look of horror with

Ainsley. From the broken shards, a green flame arose and flared up in the shape of Effie, just as another shower of flames floated down from the tree in an assault.

Ainsley sprang to her feet and scrawled a bloody symbol on a strip of paper. It rose from her hand, creating a small vortex of wind that extinguished the flames before they could get near her. The shield of wind remained around them in a dome, protecting them from assault.

In this brief moment of safety, Ainsley reached into her pack, pulled out a bottle, and placed it on the ground before the spout of light that was Effie's soul. She got to her knees, opened the satchel at her side, and produced a bundle of strong-smelling dried herbs. In a flash of light, she ignited them with a spell, and the perfumed smoke caused Effie's soul to shrink and the other revenants to cry out in aversion. The smoke continued to reduce Effie's soul fire until it was tiny enough to be trapped in the bottle.

When the flame was inside, Ainsley shoved the cork into the neck of the bottle, then quickly wrote another runic seal and laid it over the top. With her hand clasped over the bottle, she shut her eyes and muttered under her breath.

"*Be at peace. Rest within. This will be your cage; these walls cannot be breached,*" she said in a soft incantation, and her hair fluttered around her face as if caught by a strong breeze. With a flare of light, the paper ignited and burned away, and the oppressive force surrounding Effie's soul diminished. She was sealed.

"You've done it!" Edgar cheered as the other two revenants cried out in distress.

"We're not safe yet." Ainsley stowed the bottle in her bag then pulled out two empty ones as more fire from the tree rained down against the shield of wind. Their eyes turned to the tree where the other two spirits had taken refuge, shrieking at Edgar and Ainsley to stay back. Both faced the grim task ahead with resolve.

"You're the only one who can touch them," Ainsley told Edgar. She lifted her raw, bleeding hands and showed them to him; some of the flesh on her palms had melted where she had touched Effie. Edgar's gaze narrowed as he reached out instinctively to begin attending to her.

"Those wounds need treatment at once. They'll need to be disinfe—" Ainsley stayed his hand as he reached for the iodine in his pocket.

"Now's not the time. If you can retrieve them, I can seal them. Hurry!" She directed another strip at the sky, renewing the energy of the wind shield. "I'm running out of invocation paper. If that happens, we're better off dead."

Edgar gave her a nod then turned to the tree. His eyes fixed on the glittering bird in the cage the brown-haired girl had crawled into. There was no longer any trace of her, but the bird fluttered madly against the bars as his gaze fell on it. A strange purple gleam akin to the radiance of Effie's pearl flashed when the light hit its crystal body at an angle. Following his intuition, Edgar plunged back into the freezing water and swam across the pond to the tree trunk.

Stay back! Stay away from me! the voice from the birdcage cried shrilly as he reached the trunk of the tree and leapt for the nearest notch. Shivering and numb with cold, he began his climb. Edgar's swollen fingers found a groove, and he pulled himself upward with great strain. As the bird's screaming pitched into a crescendo, a spasm of pain shot through Edgar's back. He nearly let go but held on, focusing on Ainsley's shouts of encouragement.

His hand reached up to the birdcage's door, and he could just peer inside, seeing the crystal bird with its refracting colors fluttering about in a panic behind the bars. As he opened the tiny door, to his great surprise, hundreds of bird-shaped shadows exploded outward, throwing him off the trunk and lifting him into the air.

Thousands of beaks and tiny, sharp talons ripped and tore at his flesh as he remained suspended in air, caught in a tornado of feathers. The needlelike appendages dug into his wrists, ankles, and neck.

"Edgar!" Ainsley screamed, tossing two bloodied strips of paper skyward, rocking him with bursts of air and knocking some of the birds away from him. With another shout, she tossed another one in his direction; it stretched out with a rustling whoosh and created a suspended pathway of paper that led straight to the birdcage's knothole.

"The bridge will be gone in a couple of minutes! Make haste!" she shouted up hoarsely, and Edgar fought off the last of the shadows and dropped onto the paper walkway. He ran across it, watching blood stream from his wounds onto the paper, weakening the magic where it blotted the markings. When he was halfway across, the bird's voice echoed in his head as Effie's had.

I know your kind. You're just another man with creeping hands, another man who'll pluck and pry at me. In life they tried to buy me; they kept me in cage, used me how they wanted. Isn't that what you want? Am I something to be kept, something to be caged? Mary, Mary, quite contrary, show me just how your garden grows. Pig—you pig! Don't touch me with those filthy hands. Don't you dare!

Edgar stumbled as this voice ripped through him like arrows. He lost his balance mere feet before he reached the cage, his stomach clenching with revulsion. A feeling of deep violation crept into him, filling him with the sensation that he was crumpling inward. Edgar found himself unable to get any closer to the cage and instead hung his head, reeling from his state of oppressive helplessness and overwhelming pain.

"Don't you dare stop!" Ainsley called out.

He tried to stand up, but the shadow birds landed on his shoulders, head, legs. With each one roosting on him, he felt more crushed and powerless. Their weight was immense. When they touched him, he felt understanding creeping into his mind. The revenant Mary was in that cage, both protected and trapped by it, her soul housed within the little bird. The weight from the birds on his shoulders was growing unbearable, and Edgar found himself sinking downward, wanting to escape from the pain that Mary's soul emanated.

Go to sleep. They can't get to you there, she coaxed softly, and Edgar's head drooped under the pressure. He urged himself to keep going, even under the weight of the birds, and trudged forward a few feet, reaching out with his torn, bloody hands toward the latch of the cage. The crystal bird was still now, staring at him with its diamond eyes. It looked so fragile. The very idea of hurting it made his chest clench.

With all his might, he lifted the latch and reached into the cage.

How will you live with yourself? Am I nothing to you?

Soon he would collapse; soon the paper bridge beneath him would tear. As tears rolled down his face, his hand shot into the cage and took hold of the crystal bird. It was warm and delicate in his fingers.

"I'm sorry," Edgar breathed, feeling as if he too were trapped by an insurmountably strong grip. The creature struggled in his hand, screeching madly, its wings twitching feebly behind his fingers. Shutting his eyes and gritting his teeth, he clenched his fingers around the bird. He felt the sensation of bones breaking in his hand, snapping under the pressure. His heart strained with pity as the bird grew still.

With silver bells...and cockleshells...and pretty maids...all in a row...

He felt the weight lifting as he squeezed the broken thing in his hands. The shadowy birds on his shoulders took flight, one by one, drifting upward—still, silent, and lifeless as they melted away into nothingness. His wits returning to him, Edgar turned to Ainsley, took careful aim, and tossed the corpse of the little crystal bird down to the lakeshore. When it hit the ground, it shattered, leaving a fountain of purplish fire. Edgar leapt up to the nearest branch of the tree as the rest of the remaining shadow birds flew away, rising with limp wings into nothingness.

Ainsley rushed forward and began her sealing ritual for Mary's spirit as Edgar sat upon the branch, wiping away the last of his tears. Above, the branches looked like a halo of stars, the cluster of blue-flamed candles flickering menacingly as he climbed toward them. The leaves glinted with the specter's fire, and at the center of these was a single massive candle. Edgar's eyes were fixed on that strange blue flame, and he became certain that the soul of the last girl, Ann, was hidden within it. The revenant's flame burned high as he climbed nearer, challenging Edgar to try to claim it.

It was eerily silent. The rain of fire from the candles had stopped, as if the spirit were too disturbed by what she'd just seen to react. Drops of wax struck Edgar's forehead as he stared up at the top, preparing to scale the tree. He glanced back down at Ainsley, who had finished trapping Mary's soul, and she nodded as if urging him to move forward.

Cautiously Edgar began his ascent, keeping his eyes fixed on the largest candle and its dancing blue flame. As he hoisted himself up, branch by branch, the heat of the flames made him overheated and exhausted. The wood felt waxy under his gashed fingers, and he almost lost his footing several times.

Say, mister...mister...

Edgar told himself to keep going, but he couldn't ignore the coaxing tone of the voice.

Mister, wouldn't you like to hear a story? Wouldn't you like to hear my story? It's such a very sad story. Don't you like sad stories, mister?

Ann's voice was so sorrowful and sweet that Edgar stopped his climb for a moment, distracted by the hypnotic effects of the flames around him. Inside the flames was an image of a pretty young woman wearing a bonnet and dancing. Her hair was black and kempt, and her face was pleasant, with rounded cheeks and inviting eyes. The vision was so hauntingly beautiful that Edgar stared, his eyes transfixed on it, while the wax dripped onto his hands. The mournful voice of a flute played in the background, lulling him as the girl danced.

Kýrie, eléison…kýrie, eléison…

Edgar slumped against a large branch. Somewhere Ainsley was yelling his name, but it no longer seemed important. The lovely, melancholy sounds of Ann's requiem were all he cared to hear. He wanted to give her the attention she deserved and make sure her sadness and suffering would not go forgotten. As her dancing became more fluid, Edgar continued to watch.

Don't let them forget about me. Lux aeterna luceat eis, Domine.

A great wind blew by and put out several of the candles, including the one Edgar was staring at. Ainsley had summoned a gust from below, breaking Ann's spell. He blinked, coming out of the dreamlike state. At once he became aware that his arms were covered in wax, fixing him to the tree, and the edges of his trousers were aflame. Feeling pain come back in agonizing clarity, he cracked free of the wax coating and frantically patted out the flames on his legs as Ainsley sent more gusts upward, blowing out many more of the candle flames.

"Get to the top!" she shouted up to Edgar, who groaned under his many burns and wounds. "Don't pay her any attention!"

No! Look at me! Don't let me fade away! Please, I'm begging you! Don't let me have died in vain. Don't forget—lux perpetua luceat me!

Edgar kept his eyes pointed to the sky, just to the side of the largest candle. The wax scalded him as he ascended to the top of the great tree, each of the smoking candle flames trying to sputter back to life with hissing sparks. He scaled his way to the center and firmly grabbed the base of the queen candle with both hands, attempting to pry it free.

At once, fire licked up his arms. Edgar's scream split the night, mingling with Ann's malicious, delighted laughter. He was burning alive; the fabric on his sleeves already had been charred away. Soon he would be consumed by flames; they wouldn't stop spreading. As the flames ate away at his clothes and reached his skin, Ann's memories seared into his flesh, flooding his mind. He bore witness to a lifetime full of dreams and aspirations that never had come to pass, but he would live within them forever. He would die; he would stay with her so she would not be forgotten.

In one last effort, Ainsley produced a final burst of wind that disturbed the flames. The force of the gale blew Edgar off balance. As he fell from the branch, he hung on to the candle, his weight enough to break it free from the branch. He plummeted from the height of the treetop, wreathed in the blue flames. The rushing air pulled the flames away from his body, and in the moments before impact, the fire took the shape of Ann. She clung to him as they fell, refusing to let go.

Dona me requiem sempiternam.

When they struck the icy surface of the water, Ann's form was extinguished in a plume of smoke. Edgar sank first, then bobbed back up, clutching the diminished, sodden candle in his ruined hands. Racked with pain, he fought his way to the shore, set the candle at Ainsley's feet, then collapsed nearby. He forced himself to stay awake, to watch the wax melt away to reveal the blue spirit flame and observe Ainsley seal it away safely inside the final bottle she'd brought.

After she laid the paper over the top and repeated the incantation, the haunted tree shifted in appearance. Slowly the haunted arbor rippled, as if seen through a heavy mist, and then it disappeared altogether. Light filled the space around them and the disenchanted trees of the Witches' Wood. The nearby pool was all that remained of the revenants' grim tableau. The water's surface reflected the light of the periwinkle sky above, while soft shades of yellow and pink crept up from the deep-blue mountains in the distance. Dawn was breaking.

Ainsley and Edgar stared at each other, each grateful to have another person nearby to comfort them in their moment of exhaustive pain.

"Is it over?" Edgar dared to ask, looking at the collection of bottled lights Ainsley clutched to her chest. She swallowed and gave a trembling nod.

"I believe so. For now."

Edgar threw his head back and allowed himself to breathe at last as the glowing orange crescent of the sun crept up over the horizon, bathing them in light and blessed relief.

The Cold Voice

Water slid over silver as Magdalena poured out the contents of the pitcher. As the liquid filled the dark stone basin, her heart swelled with dread and anticipation. She was careful not to let her expression betray this, and she prepared herself; Hare watched from the corner of the room. She stole a glance at him as the last of the water left the pitcher. Breathless, he couldn't hide his eagerness.

As Magdalena bent her head over the surface of the water and shut her eyes, she felt a brief spike of panic.

Will this awaken his wrath? Am I going too far? She drew a long breath, held the air within her throat and lungs, and focused on reaching her master.

As she whispered in a plea for his attention, more in a hiss rather than speech, the air that passed her lips stung with cold. When she exhaled, a cloud billowed forth, and the water in the basin whitened with frost. Lips still parted, Magdalena stared into the basin, willing herself to continue.

At last she mastered her trepidation and plunged her face into the bitter cold. Moments after it struck her, darkness flooded her vision like unraveling ink. In the silence and the darkness, she sent forth her plea.

I've lost them. I need you.

For an instant all remained still. Then like a thunderclap, a fierce concussive wave exploded inside her skull. Magdalena's bones rattled with the sound as it ripped through her. She felt a sensation of rushing downward at an impossible speed, through the deepest black water, through wind and ice.

She at last felt the Cold Voice's overwhelming presence. As it loomed forward, a void amid the blackness, powerful and vast as a star, Magdalena cowered. Now she was certain of its fury.

Master, I have failed. I am weak. Grant me strength and wisdom, she begged. Another crash split her consciousness, shaking the very roots of the realm that they shared. When the torture passed, silence filled the space between them. Magdalena wouldn't yet let herself feel a thing as the quivering stretched on and on. The longer it lasted, the more courage she gained. It was considering her, and that meant that some hope yet remained.

The Woman of the Woods

Edgar reveled in the experience of having eluded death. However, as he and Ainsley eased over the boulders toward the place she called the Clootie Well, he guessed he might succumb to his injuries before they could get back to Ainsley's cottage. As they walked on, Ainsley suddenly stopped. She inspected her raw hands for a moment then examined the back of her hand, where a tattoo was emblazoned onto her skin. For a long time she stared at it. Her eyes grew red, and she blinked tears away before continuing her hike alongside the stream.

As they went along, Edgar watched the stream that fed the Well. Fresh, clear water flowed past now, washing away the filth that had turned it bloody and black the night before. A clean wind smelling of pine and wet earth blew past them, banishing the stench of rot. As they passed, Edgar saw the corpses of the fallen creatures decay rapidly before his eyes, returning to pearly-white bones, their flesh nourishing the earth. The forest was transforming—recovering impossibly fast before his eyes. Edgar assumed this was what true magic looked like, and he felt humbled that he was able to witness it.

"The meadow...it's back to normal." Ainsley stopped in midstep as she caught sight of the valley below. With an energy Edgar couldn't believe she could produce after everything she'd been through, she raced forward, vaulted over the waterfall, and darted across the restored meadow. "Fana! Fana!" she cried.

Edgar followed her but with far less energy. He felt miles away from the world. His vision was bleary, and when he slid clumsily over the waterfall and into the meadow, he had to blink frantically to make sure that what he saw was real.

In his childhood, before the destruction of his family, Edgar had believed in God. His mother had told him comforting stories about heaven and rewards for the just and kind of heart. Before he went to sleep, she had asked him to say his prayers so that one day he would gain entrance to heaven. After the mumbling of many holy words—words he could hardly understand—he was tucked in bed, and he'd ask his mother questions about what this fabled place would be like. Edgar's mother had painted a picture of the eternal kingdom as a wooded field, overflowing with life and love.

As he gazed out at the Well, it was as if those lingering childhood memories had come to life and were spread out before him. The grass grew thick and lush and smelled like the first day of spring. Flowers of every color and variety grew in abundance and perfumed the air with their unearthly fragrances. Edgar bent down to touch the delicate petals, mentally naming the ones he recognized: Queen Anne's lace, lily of the valley, baby's breath, violets, posies, foxgloves, snapdragons. Lightfalls, dancing with pollen, cascaded from the treetops, looking like golden veils. A pleasant chorus of bees hummed, and lights from iridescent wings shimmered here and there between the plants.

Ancient stones were scattered about, each one seeming to vibrate with a forgotten magic. In reverence, Edgar placed his hand on one of the weatherworn, mossy faces. Ainsley stood beside the Well, which now was as clear as glass and smelled richly of minerals. Strips of cloth tied to the tree branches around it swung dreamily in the breeze. At her feet was a mossy mound, surrounded by a long, elliptical ring of mushrooms, flowers, and ferns. In the center of this lay a sleeping deer that was so lovely and fragile in the morning light that Edgar's eyes stung with tears at the very sight of it.

The animal had the body of a doe but also two antlers atop its sleeping head. After a moment, he saw they weren't antlers at all but two tree branches. Pink apple blossoms and spring-green leaves sprouted from them.

Edgar sat on the ground next to a nearby ash tree and watched the deer as it lifted its head and opened its eyes to see Ainsley. It watched her as she spoke softly to it, its liquid eyes too understanding and its body too still to be any mundane creature. Edgar slipped further from the moment, closing his eyes and drawn toward sleep by the gentle buzzing of bees and breath of wind. He couldn't stop himself from falling into a slumber that felt as deep and encompassing as death. It was impossible to tell whether moments or hours passed when he opened his eyes again in response to Ainsley calling his name.

She waded through the grass toward him, the miraculous doe at her side. Edgar was so captivated by the creature and its ethereal beauty that Ainsley's words didn't reach him. As it approached him, he yearned to reach out for it, to stroke the fur on its neck and feel its warm breath on his cheek. However, he remained frozen, feeling it would be sacrilegious to even consider such a deed. As the creature came within feet of him, he was mesmerized by the sweet scent its flowered antlers gave off. Edgar knew, with an understanding more profound than anything he had learned during years of study, that this being was holy.

"Edgar, stand up," Ainsley said gently.

He struggled to get to his feet but couldn't, so Ainsley offered him one of her injured hands. They both winced, but Edgar finally stood up, though he had to lean against the ash tree for support. The doe looked at him with eerily intelligent eyes and took a cautionary sniff. Then it bowed its head and stepped several paces backward. Its eyes slid shut, and the flowers that decorated its tree-branch antlers bloomed larger. From its fur and out of its head, plant life burst forth, all over its body. Edgar gave a start and reached out in a protective gesture. Ainsley touched him briefly on the shoulder to calm him.

All at once, the creature became consumed by flowers, leaves, and vines. They grew into an upright shape then dispersed like so many butterflies. As the flowers and leaves blew away, they took root in the grass and slowly revealed a woman standing where the doe had been.

For the first few moments after Edgar laid eyes on her, he forgot all else. The entire story of his life had been unwritten in moments, and his mind felt empty and light. This woman was perfect in the way that mountains were perfect: full of vitality and mystery, earthy and uncharted. She was simultaneously raw and refined—effortlessly, naturally flawless, like an uncut ruby. Her hair was the color of new bark, the same gentle brown that her doe's fur coat had been. A crown of meadow flowers and berries adorned her head, where the two antler-like appendages still protruded. Her eyes, dew bright and deep brown, blinked back at Edgar. A light dusting of freckles painted her creamy, pale cheeks. She wore a mantle of brown fur, silky and spotted white. Beneath this were layered many robes that looked as if they'd been sewn by elfin hands, the stitching delicate and the fabric woven finely with threads that shimmered like faint starlight when the sun hit them just so. They were all the colors of the forest; some gray like river water in the winter morning, others as green and soft as moss, and still more in harmonious hues of mulberry, silver, and ochre. Her feet were bare and clean, and as she took her first step toward Edgar, the grass appeared to grow upward incrementally.

"Ainsley told me how you came to arrive here and what you've done for these woods." The woman's voice was as melodious and melancholy as birdsong in the fading light of day. "You may call me Fana, stranger. I am the guardian of this Well, and of the Witches' Wood."

Edgar opened his mouth to speak to the sublime woman, but his words were caught in his throat.

"Thank you...both of you." Fana smiled, and a gust of air swept through the meadow, blowing the intoxicating smell around. She held out her hands, one to Ainsley and the other to Edgar. Without knowing why, he took her hand in his both of his. Both Fana and Ainsley looked to him, quietly startled, and Edgar suddenly withdrew his hands, blushing crimson and hating every inch of himself.

"I do beg your pardon...I'm...so...I don't know what came over me, I..." he stuttered, wishing for the second time that hour that he was already dead.

Ainsley gave him a hard look before taking hold of her shawl, tearing off a bit of cloth, and handing it to the woman. "She needs an offering," she explained.

Edgar murmured some indistinct words to try to account for his behavior and gestured incomprehensibly before deciding just to move forward. He tore off a bit of his ruined shirtsleeve and handed it to Fana, taking care not to make physical contact with her again. She closed both of the strips of fabric in her hands, and then, when she opened them again, they had disappeared.

"Come, come," she said, beckoning them to the Well.

When they arrived at the water, Edgar and Ainsley both knelt at her direction, and then Fana dipped her hands into the pool. First she went to Ainsley, letting the water drip over her wounds. Ainsley gritted her teeth as the liquid soothed the rawness of her hands, healing them until they had scabbed over. Fana continued to pour the water over Ainsley's body until she was rejuvenated.

While she tended to Ainsley, Edgar's heart pumped madly in his chest. Even though he was on his knees, he was frightened he would lose his balance again, and when Fana turned with her hands dripping wet to soothe his wounds, he couldn't hide that he was slightly quivering.

Up until the fateful train ride to Edinburgh, he had lived a very serious life in the company of very serious men. In his youth, he had attended a boarding school that was strictly home to men and boys. During his apprenticeship and later education, the only expertise he'd accumulated regarding the female body was how to treat it for illness and operate upon it if necessary. There had been no moonlit dances, no flights of fancy that occupied his young mind, no love poems he yearned to write. He never had been compelled to delve into the complicated, secretive world of women, and even if he had, he wouldn't have known the first thing about doing so. He'd always thought of women as lovely works of art in a museum; he strolled past, took a quiet studying look, appreciated for a moment the work that had gone into creating such an image—and perhaps, if he was feeling roguish, let his mind expand upon the scene—then continued along his way. Pictures were just pictures; they couldn't be interacted with. So it was with women, Edgar had always thought.

Thus, the emotions and sensations that overtook him at that moment were, at best, alarming and addling to his mind, which already had been pushed to the breaking point from last night's events. He couldn't look at Fana as she touched his hands and undid the cruel burns and lacerations inflicted upon them. The stinging pain from his injuries soon faded as the water rolled over them, and after a minute or so, there was only the wonderful, dreadful feeling of her skin on his, which he both craved and could not stand.

Fana, who seemed to sense his ruffled nature as she went about mending him, raised her eyebrows in curiosity. "Does it hurt very badly?" she asked, and he felt a rush of relief that she didn't suspect the true source of his distress.

"N-no. I'm...I'm Edgar. I mean—I'm fine! I'm also Edgar, as it turns out, but—oh, good Lord," he stammered.

Ainsley's mouth was slightly agape, and Edgar stared at the dirt in order to avoid both of their glances. Fana laughed in a musical, carefree way—a sound that made Edgar's face uncomfortably hot.

"Are the revenants sufficiently contained, Ainsley?" Fana asked after she was finished healing Edgar.

Ainsley pulled the three bottles out of her bag and showed them to her. The ghostly lights of green, purple, and blue swam around within each glass prison. "What would you have me do with them?"

Fana looked into the bottles, her eyes clouding with a sadness that ran fathoms deep.

"Poor, miserable creatures," she whispered. "There's nothing we can do for them. They're doomed to the half life—they'll never stop yearning to feed on life. Eternally hungry, eternally lost..."

"Is that what they were doing to the forest? Feeding off it?" Edgar asked.

Fana nodded. "Precisely. They desire nothing more than to return to life, but they cannot. They deplete the life-force of other things, destroying them and poisoning the world around them to get the merest taste of what they've lost. They grow more powerful with each thing they consume, until their influence results in ruination, such as what you witnessed here last night. Their hunger won't stop spreading if left to its own devices, and it can never be sated."

"Is there no way to send them on?" Ainsley asked, crestfallen. Edgar did not need to be an alienist to deduce that her discomfort was born of the fact that her mother was the one who'd created these tortured beings. "I'd hoped...I'd hoped you would know of a solution. One of them has been fixed to Edgar—he'll be lost to it soon. Can anything be done?"

"I'm not certain." Fana stared at the bottles in Ainsley's hands for a long time. "I never had the opportunity to ask Sylvia about the details of the curse. She was cast out of the Wood before I could speak to her. Edgar"—she turned to face him, and he stood up straight with attention—"could you tell me anything more about who did this to you?"

"The man...he's got the same name as the murderer Sylvia cursed. He looks to be his son or perhaps his grandson. I'm not certain. And the woman, she clearly isn't...human, but if I recall correctly, he called her Magdalena and—"

As Edgar spoke, Fana's eyes darkened, and a look of frightful revulsion crept over her face. "Ah, yes, I see now. The Lunatic Magdalena," her voice was hushed. "I know of whom you speak. She's known to many as the 'Blight of the Ophiuchans' or simply 'The Lunatic' among immortals and spirits. She's feared and reviled on this continent and only spoken of in whispers on the others."

"I'm...I'm sorry, Miss Fana..." She smiled at the word *Miss* as if it amused her, and Edgar's voice warbled momentarily. "Erm, I apologize, but I'm rather ignorant of these matters. What is an Ophiuchan?"

"They are an ancient race of creatures that came into being during the lost ages—they are those who have partaken of the blood of the Divine Serpent. Ophiuchans are killed and reborn from its venom, forever nourished and poisoned by it. They're powerful and fearsome beings, and live eternally by consuming living beings. Nothing with dead flesh will sustain them, and they feel an almost unrelenting hunger for that which lives. These creatures usually keep to themselves and form communities within their own race, feeding discreetly and dedicating their time to scholarly pursuits. However, just as there are monsters among men, there exist evil anomalies in all."

Fana's face took on a stony look, and her eyes strayed to the Well.

"The Lunatic Magdalena is one such case. She is cursed not only with eternal life but also with madness. She lives to destroy her own race—hers is a bloody and cruel legacy, and she is as vindictive as she is lethal. To date she slaughtered more than half the remaining Ophiuchans and is thought to be responsible for many more disappearances. Whatever purpose she has designed for revenants is of a fell nature. Of this we can be certain."

"She chose me at random," Edgar said, clutching at his chest. "She and Hare simply alighted on me, and now I am to be consumed alive by this...*demon*. I cannot allow this to happen—my life is yet unlived, I've accomplished nothing. Please...I beg of you, tell me you can lift this curse. Tell me you can exorcise the spirit from my body. If this forest could be repaired by their removal, then is there hope for my soul?"

Fana's eyes searched him for a long time, as if trying to translate what he had said, word for word. The woman narrowed her eyes in consideration, seemingly moved by the earnestness of his plea.

"I will do for you what I can," she acquiesced, then turned to Ainsley. "Leave us, dear one. Return at sunset—I would like to speak with you then."

"Fana, is it really wise?" Ainsley protested, looking at Edgar with distrust.

Fana shook her head. "Be restful and keep peace in your heart, child. Don't worry yourself on my behalf—I will act as I see fit. Go now. You have my gratitude and blessings," she said with a loving light in her eyes.

Ainsley's look of wariness softened, and she turned to face Edgar. "You can find your way back, I take it?"

"I—"

She didn't wait for a response. "Good. Be respectful," she said, before turning and climbing the hill that led away from the sacred meadow. After the sound of her footfalls faded, Fana touched Edgar's arm lightly, and he tried his hardest not to shiver.

"Come back to the spring, please...Tell me, where was the entry point of the curse?" she asked as Edgar followed her to the edge of the Well.

"Here, I think," he laid a hand over his breast. Even that glancing touch ailed him. "It felt like an insect stung me. Afterward, a wound appeared that no balm or ointment can mend. My back pains me a great deal too."

"There's a chance you may be spared." Fana waded into the Well, staying perfectly balanced and still, even when her feet no longer touched the bottom. Upon seeing this marvel, Edgar felt a rush of joy that was soon disrupted when Fana said, "Remove your shirts and walk into the spring."

"I say! Pardon me, miss, b-but," he stuttered, his face burning once again, but he fell silent when he saw her unfazed expression. With shaking fingers and the ache of shame, Edgar loosed the buttons on his ruined jacket and shirt, taking care not to catch her eye as he pulled them off. With the cold morning air stinging his bare skin, he started toward the water with the sound of blood rushing in his ears. A pang of humiliation struck him as Fana took on a revolted expression: the dark-purple wound had grown in size once again, reaching across his shoulder.

"It is in an advanced state," she commented as he entered the pool and waded over to her until they stood only a few feet apart.

When Fana's finger touched his chest, Edgar shuddered and broke out in gooseflesh. He shut his eyes, trying to order his thoughts from most pure to least, then focused on the start of the list. After several moments, her touch began to seem less arresting, and Edgar relaxed somewhat. As he'd been craving a bath since the moment the danger had passed, he welcomed the cold, clean water.

"Are you frightened?" Fana asked suddenly, drawing her hand away from him.

Edgar opened his eyes. "Of dying?" he asked, guessing at her meaning.

"Of me. You're trembling," she noted, though this didn't seem to perturb her. Edgar blinked and shook his head, perhaps a bit too vigorously. This didn't convince her, and her airy laugh showed so. "Would you permit me? I'd like to understand you better."

Although he didn't quite know what she wanted of him, he nodded on the impulse of wanting to do as she said. Fana put her hands atop his shoulders and shut her eyes. The peculiar sensation of another mind delving into his thoughts and memories bloomed in his head—though the feeling completely overwhelmed Edgar all at once, unlike the shallower connection Elspeth had forged before. It was as if his life were racing past him in a series of colored photographs flashing out of the darkness, each one carrying the emotional weight of the circumstances. The rushing stopped when the progression of events led up to this very moment. He gasped as the intensity of the experience faded.

"What…what did you do?"

"I only wanted to see what sort of life you've lived until now—as I said, to understand you better," Fana told him, ever serene and pensive. She was smiling, perhaps almost coy, which made her appear flattered. At that point, the reality dawned on him.

"You've…you've seen everything I've done? *Everything I've ever done? B-but—*"

"And thought all your thoughts too. You needn't be worried…I've collected many people's life stories," Fana hummed with quiet happiness. "I can't leave this forest for more than a few days at a time, so I experience the outside world in this manner."

"I am…so terribly ashamed and…what an indecent man I've been…and for you to—"

"Please, do not be distressed. You've no reason to be embarrassed. Your life hasn't been one of indecency. *Restrained* and a touch lonesome, yes. A life of ignorance perhaps, but not indecency. And a great deal more time spent in the company of the dead, digging through intestines, than is to be expected."

Although Edgar couldn't help laugh at this, his pride smarted a bit. With his panic somewhat abated, Fana put her hand to his chest again.

"Now, allow me to attempt to remove this spirit. It might yet be weak enough that it can be dispelled. If it does come free, be ready for anything," she warned in lilt. Her accent sounded undefinable and strange, and Edgar wished she would continue to speak so he could study it longer. Fana took a breath in, and his chest felt as if it were being tugged at by a hook. He winced, leaning inward under the pain, but the discomfort in his chest remained. It continued for a while, until Fana released her breath and drew her hands back.

"It's taken root inside you. I can't rend it from you without destroying you also in the process," she said, with an aggrieved look in her eyes.

Edgar's brief license to hope was stolen from him, and he could do nothing but stare forward. He wondered dully whether this was perhaps how the patients in the hospital felt when they learned that the most drastic of operations wouldn't change their fate.

"So that's it, then? This is the end?"

"It's a cruel fate. You didn't deserve this…but so few ever truly deserve what befalls them." The kindness that overflowed from Fana comforted Edgar, but not enough to stop a lump from rising in his throat.

"I cannot bear it. God help me, I am afraid. I'm not ready for this," he said, his voice quavering. Somehow, in that instant, he felt he could be vulnerable in front of Fana. She had, only moments ago, shared his every memory and passing thought. It struck him as tragic that no one had ever understood him half as well as she did, and no one ever would.

And I've known her for less than an hour. Wasted…I've wasted this life.

Fana's expression clouded at the sight of him. "Though I can't save you, I can offer you the gift of a little time, should you want it. A week more of life, maybe less. Would you like that?" she offered.

"Yes!" Edgar answered at once. A week more might as well have been an eternity to him. It was seven more sunsets, more chances to taste food, more opportunities to connect with other human souls before his was extinguished.

"There is a price, be warned. I need time to grant time. You'll have to trade me your old experiences if you wish to buy new ones," Fana said, and Edgar considered this.

"You mean, you'll need…"

"I'll need your memories. Memories of a particular thing—something important to you. A time in your life, a place you loved, a person you knew…and once I take them, they'll be gone forever. They'll live inside me—inside the woods. Do you still wish it?" she asked him, looking almost eager.

Edgar weighed the decision carefully, allowing the lapping waters of the Well to soothe him. The trees above whispered in the early-morning winds, and the heady scents of life and decay made him dizzy.

I suppose it's better that some part of my story survives, even if it's tucked away from the world.

"Yes, it is what I wish. Please grant me this request, Miss Fana," he finally said, and she nodded, the flowers on her antlers bobbing as she did.

"What will you have me take?"

A heavy part of my heart, so that these last few days might be lighter. He shuffled through his recent memories, and the choice became apparent to him soon. He was reluctant to let go, but the desire to purge the pain was stronger. *Yes, take him from me. Without my memories of him, there'll be no grief. No ache when I remember that he's no longer part of this world. No sting of betrayal, no cruel reality where I loved him like a brother and he barely mentioned my name to his wife. I want him completely gone.*

"Take Gregory. Take all of him," Edgar said to Fana, hardly wanting to listen to his own voice.

Fana let his words echo away then nodded. As she waded closer to him, Edgar knew this was final. In the moments before she took his shivering body in her arms and prepared to perform her own particular type of operation, Edgar relived each moment of Gregory in a hurried, panicked rush. He pried memories open wherever he could find them—the last time he'd heard Gregory laugh and loved the sound, late nights spent talking in his flat, schooldays when the world was still new to them. Meaningless conversations, moments spent in comfortable togetherness when no words were spoken at all, discoveries shared, jokes only they could understand.

Fana held him tightly, and as if intoxicated by her presence, Edgar leaned into her and released his hold over Gregory and all the countless hours in which they'd changed each other's lives. As he tried to cling to the single image of Gregory's smile, so drunk with life, so present in every moment, he felt it slipping away. Fana was absorbing it, drawing it from his very skin and claiming it as her own.

Edgar experienced only an instant of great terror as she pilfered sections of his mind—he was half aware that he knew Gregory, but he couldn't remember meeting him. He looked skyward, almost breaking his embrace with Fana in a dire attempt to hold on to any one thing to remind him that he'd had a man he once had called "brother"—anything at all. And then every maddening, confusing wisp of the flurry of memories was gone.

Edgar stared upward briefly, aware he had lost something but uncertain what it was. It danced on the very edge of his mind, like the details of an intricate dream that remain only minutes after waking.

He couldn't comprehend why, but he felt lighter. The world had brightened slightly, and in the hazy feeling of corrupt euphoria, he stole a moment longer, reveling in Fana's embrace.

How long has it been since another person felt welcome in my arms?

"Edgar…" Her voice reminded him that his proximity was no longer needed, and he broke away abruptly. Bit by bit, his bashful, strict nature reassembled itself. Somehow, though, as he collected his thoughts and thanked Fana, he was unable to remember exactly why it was so important to act so proud and distant. "How do you feel?"

"Odd," he replied, as he inspected the wound on his chest. It had shrunk significantly, and the pain was marginally reduced. "I feel…I feel *younger*."

Fana laughed again, seemingly more amused by him with each outlandish utterance. "Then I believe we were successful. Please, I beseech you, stay with Ainsley at her cottage tonight. I must consult with her on the morrow—but she'll need rest, for now, and I'll have need of further discussion with you soon after. Would you please do that for me?"

I would do almost anything you asked of me, spirit, blared the most foolish, underfed part of himself. The older, wiser part of his mind crushed that impetuous notion immediately. *Silence. I'll have absolutely none of that. You're verging on complete idiocy.*

"Yes, Miss Fana. I shall take leave now. Thank you—thank you for the time," he said with deep gratitude for her gift. He briefly felt the pang of some aching loss, something important that had gone missing, but the strange sensation faded as quickly as it had come.

"Spend it well," she advised. After he dressed himself, she bade him a kind goodbye, but as he was climbing over the hill, she stopped him once again. "Oh, Edgar…please, when you see Ainsley, tell her I'm sorry her efforts didn't prove fruitful."

He nodded to her, taking a moment to repeat the words to himself so he wouldn't forget. Edgar couldn't help steal a last glance of Fana as he ascended the hill. With only a week before him, he longed for as much beauty and wonder as he could find, and he was certain that the painfully lovely sight of this woman of the woods, standing so still in the golden falls of light and smiling so sadly, would haunt him until the very end.

Providence

With a sharp gasp, Mag lifted her head from the basin. Water splashed all over her room, and from the corner, Hare broke out of his reverie. He drew to her side as she coughed and sputtered. She wiped her hair back, collecting herself as she did.

"Did it work? Did it speak to you?" he asked urgently. More than just her profits rested on this; Hare's fate hinged completely on the outcome. To his powerful relief, Mag nodded, although she couldn't catch her breath for a while. When she finally replied, it seemed she was so flooded with exhilaration, or relief, perhaps both, that she struggled to form words.

"Get me...go get me that cage." Panting, she pointed a shivering finger at the corner of the room.

Hare looked at her incredulously. "This is no time to be stuffing your face, Mag."

"*Get it for me,*" she snarled, and he rose, not willing to test her.

As he grabbed the cage from the corner, a terrified scrabbling and squeaking rose from within the bars. Mag pulled the cage from him with a greedy grasp and lifted the lid. Her trembling hands dove inside, plucking a mouse up by its tail. She opened her toothy jaws, threw her head back, and dropped the thrashing creature in. In one enormous swallow, the mouse disappeared down her throat, and she reached in for a second and a third, guzzling them down in quick succession. Hare tried not to wrinkle his nose.

"What did it tell you, Mag?" Hare couldn't stand being left in unknowing silence a moment longer.

Mag swallowed her fifth mouse then finally turned her attention to him. "It was merciful," she said, her eyes shining. "It showed me where to go. It's on our side. It wants us to find the revenants."

Hare heaved a great sigh. "This is perfect. I...we're saved." His tongue almost had slipped.

"We are *not* saved; we've just been given a chance. We'll have to act with precision. We must divide our efforts if we're going to succeed. You can still touch the revenants because the curse lingers in your bones—it isn't yet broken. When the surgeon has either died or been consumed, you'll be released from it. When that happens, the revenants will be beyond our grasp. But until that moment, you can still help me get them back. Do you understand what this means?"

"It means we haven't got a lot of time. What should I do?"

"You need to retrieve the stray revenants before the surgeon expires," Mag said, standing up from her seat by the basin. She had procured several more empty ampoules. "Put them back where they belong. The surgeon already has done half the work for us—he's taken three of them."

Mag rushed to the cupboard and pulled out a weathered map from the mess inside it. She hurried back over to the table and spread it out in front of Hare, then lifted a pen from an inkwell.

"Here...here...and here." She marked three locations on the map then slid it over to Hare. "That's where you'll find them. I expect them all secured by the time I get back."

"Get back? What? You're just going to go off on holiday while I do the heavy lifting?" Hare bleated.

Mag rushed over to the closet, where she kept her umbrella and coat. "You'll lift until your arms break if you don't want to spend eternity getting dismantled and put back together again. I believe your father had a penchant for dooming his victims to dissection. I could provide a lovely, poetic punishment for you that's in keeping with that theme. Or perhaps you'd prefer...flames?" His heart skipped a beat at this; Mag's manic energy flashed a bit too brightly for Hare's liking.

"Macabre as ever, Magdalena," he grumbled, trying not to show his discomfort as she wrapped herself in the coat. She seemed to be holding back the urge to smile.

"I prefer to think of it as innovative. Now be swift and be diligent," she directed him, and bustled over to the door. She looked over her shoulder before leaving, her eyes glimmering. "I'm off to the Witches' Wood."

The World

Edgar was rudely awoken from a deep slumber as Ainsley exploded through the front door and into the cottage. The sun had long since set—as Edgar sat up, he realized he had slept through the day. Ainsley landed at the table as he stirred from his pile of blankets near the fireplace. She poured herself a glass of water, drank it down, and breathed out in a huff. Then she filled the glass with ale and repeated the motion.

"Ainsley...what did Fana tell you?" Colleen asked as she came down the hall, but Ainsley kept her eyes fixed on Edgar.

"You. Fana wants you to stay here until after Samhain. She'll talk to you after the festival is over. I suggest you heed her," Ainsley said, then grabbed a hunk of bread from the table and took a huge bite out of it. After she chewed in silence for a moment, she stood up and strode down the hall to the room she shared with Colleen then shut the door. Colleen stared after her then looked back at Edgar with a slightly apologetic shrug. He dropped his eyes, wondering with discontent why Ainsley still seemed angry with him.

Noticing he looked slightly hurt, Colleen drew nearer. "Please don't take her attitude to heart. She's...a bit abrasive, but she means well, really. She's just so furious with the world, and she needs to make sure everyone's aware of it."

Edgar slumped forward, smoothing his rumpled hair, as Colleen took a seat at the table. "She seemed to hate me less before we last parted," he said. "I'd hoped I'd made some progress with her."

"She…" Colleen started, then hesitated. "She saved your life that night. She told me and—"

"We saved each other," Edgar said with a muddled look, and Colleen shook her head. She opened her mouth to speak, hesitating before she continued as if she were second-guessing herself.

"I understand, but with Ainsley, she…there are things you should know. She'll be cross with me for telling you, but I do believe it's for the best. This coven has entrusted me with an honorable task…I record their stories and their spells; I bind them into books; and I preserve their history, so I know much of their way of life and the magic that surrounds them. You've become entangled in this too, so I believe you have a right to know." Colleen collected herself again before she continued. "Do you understand what it means to be a witch, Edgar?"

"I confess myself uninformed, I was unaware that this sort of witchcraft existed until a few days ago, but my assumption is it involves inborn magical talent?" he guessed.

"Yes," she said. "But their gifts come with a price. It all has to do with the origin of witches: in the dark times before the deathless ones, suffering was the norm. Hardships were innumerable. The world was a bleak place, and good people died in droves from plagues, war, and famine. It is said that the first witch, Rhona, after suffering the devastating loss of her family and her clan, traveled across the wide world to seek divine aid. At last, after many toils, the legend tells that she discovered the location of the sacred garden of our Goddess, the World Mother, and broke into it.

"In that sacred place, she boldly awoke the Goddess from her deep slumber to tell her of the agonies that humankind endured. She spoke of so many lives lost and so much tragedy that the Goddess wept to hear of the sorry state her children were in.

The Goddess, however, had previously vowed to leave humanity to its own devices. By her own law, she refused to aid or hinder mortals and didn't intend to break her word.

"In a moment of desperation, Rhona stole the tears from the Goddess's cheeks and drank them. Because of this, in her veins flowed the power of the World Mother, granting her a miraculously long life and the ability to work miracles. She promised upon fear of death to forever use her strength for the betterment of humanity. Mercifully, the Goddess agreed to allow this woman to go free, but as payment for her transgression, she and her daughters would forever have to prove her dedication to humankind."

"Each witch, from the time she is born, has twenty years exactly in which to save three lives. If she succeeds, she will live a blessed life of centuries. However, if she cannot do this before her twentieth birthday, she will perish, not having fulfilled her purpose," Colleen finished, and Ainsley's anger at once made sense to Edgar.

"Those markings on her hand..."

"Exactly. Ainsley has saved only two lives, and her twentieth birthday is on the first day of winter. She's all but given up. She's going to die," Colleen told him, sorrow vivid in her eyes.

In a rush of emotion, Edgar felt a deep sense of camaraderie with Ainsley. The idea that she too had a death sentence to contend with softened the sting of her unfriendliness.

"I understand, now. She thought that by saving my life from the revenants, she could stop her own end from coming. Only she didn't truly save my life—I'm still cursed." Edgar looked at his hands with a frown. "But surely there must be opportunity outside of the Wood? Surely she must still have a chance?"

"Yes, she does. But she refuses to leave the Wood. Most witches go on what they call a pilgrimage, when they venture into the world to do some good, fulfill their duty, and return home. But Ainsley won't go. She despises the world outside of the trees—she feels humanity isn't worth saving. She's disgusted by mankind's potential for cruelty," Colleen admitted, and Edgar at once burned with rage. He felt furious with Ainsley for throwing away her life out of spite. He, who would go to any lengths for a chance at salvation, couldn't abide by such a petty decision.

Colleen saw his look and frowned. "Don't judge her too harshly, Edgar. She's troubled. Please don't condemn her for her blindness. Once you get to know her, you'll realize her love runs deep and her loyalty knows no end. She's the best person I've ever known." Edgar took note of the passion in her voice then looked her over for a moment.

"Forgive me if I'm being intrusive, but I've wondered…" He paused, unsure how to voice his curiosity. Colleen anticipated his question before he could ask it.

"Yes, it is as you think. Our love runs deeper than mere friendship," she answered, unwavering.

"I must say, I'm confused by this…" Edgar started, and Colleen's eyebrows raised in indignation.

"You take issue with our union?" she shot at him, and he drew back.

"You misunderstand me. I don't mean to say I believe it to be wrong. I don't pretend to understand matters of the heart. Love remains a mystery to me, and I'd be an utter fool to blindly disparage something I don't fully comprehend. If love has graced your life, even in a way that seems unusual to me, then I believe that to be fortuitous. I…I daresay I envy you…" he added, the image of Fana leaping, unbidden, into his thoughts.

Colleen gave him a small smile and visibly relaxed. "Why your confusion then?"

"You're not of the Woods, as I understand it. If Ainsley so detests outsiders, how did she come to hold you in such regard?" he asked, and Colleen's smile broadened.

"She didn't always hate the world outside the Wood. There was a time when she was fascinated with it. Instead of studying, Ainsley wandered the outskirts of the forest, always on the look-out for signs of her mother's return. That's how I first came to meet her."

"My family had sent me to live at a small church near the Wood, where my uncle is a pastor. They were concerned for me. They worked as bookbinders, you see, so I'd quickly learned to read and had access to a wealth of reading materials. They believed I had an unhealthy obsession with stories and thought time in the countryside with pious work to occupy my mind would do me well.

"Ainsley used to prowl around the edges of the trees, watching the villagers' comings and goings. We struck up a friendship soon enough, meeting in the woods to escape the notice of others. She wanted to know everything about the world—she loved my stories and I loved telling them. I think she wanted to understand more about Sylvia; a part of her has always felt abandoned, and she needed to know what kind of world had claimed her mother... what might've tempted her to leave her daughters. She didn't know then...she didn't know the real reason behind Sylvia's absence.

"After a year of covertly meeting and avoiding questions from my uncle and Elspeth alike, we at last were able to be honest with each other. For a few months, our relationship remained undiscovered, but we grew careless. My uncle followed me to the woods one day and...and his reaction..."

"What did he do?" Edgar asked, at once very concerned.

Colleen shook her head. "It isn't a time I care to recall. I was subject to some very nasty treatment, suffice to say, and swiftly taken back to the city to my parents. My uncle told them everything, and it was decided that in order to be 'corrected,' I should be married at once to a friend of my father's—a barrister named Donnan Wilson, thirty years my senior. The marriage proceeded as planned, and for six unhappy months I was wife to him. I don't think my father knew what sort of man he truly was when he arranged the match, but I soon found him to be uncommonly cruel. My letters home were always confiscated before I could send them." Colleen's face was grimly blank as she told Edgar this.

"I thought I was fated to live alongside him for the rest of my days," she continued, "but it wasn't so. Ainsley left her home in search of me; she used her every resource, magical and otherwise, to locate me. During this time, she came into contact with the true brutishness of the world. She bore witness to the unspeakable suffering of the denizens of the city. Her grudge began there, I believe—she couldn't forgive the callousness of those who had the power to help others but wouldn't. She couldn't forgive her mother for living in that world, instead of with her in the Wood."

Edgar, who still vividly remembered the deplorable conditions of Edinburgh, again found himself understanding Ainsley's rage.

"When she finally tracked me down, I immediately saw that she had changed. When she heard what I'd been through since our separation, she became even more furious. She confronted my husband, and it wasn't long before things grew violent. In an attempt to light one of her spell papers to keep him from harming us, there was an accident with the gas lamps and a fire broke out. That night, Ainsley helped me escape the fire with her magic, and we were able to return to the Wood. I never knew what became of my husband."

"So it was you Ainsley saved? Yours was the first life?" Edgar said, and Colleen nodded. He paused to think on this. "Who was the second person she saved?"

"Fana," she told him after a short silence.

Edgar's heartbeat quickened at the mention of her name. "How?" he asked, needing to know more.

Colleen gave him a sly smile and shook her head. "Ah, that is her story to tell. Not mine."

He nodded in acceptance of this. After a while longer, Colleen left his side to tend the garden. Edgar sat in quiet contemplation of her words for an hour or so, then lay back down by the fire, determined to get more sleep.

It was the first decent rest he'd had since the death of Mrs. Sheehy, and no one disturbed him for the rest of the night. He awoke the next morning at dawn, feeling groggy but light of heart. A few days were all he had left, but he awaited them with a powerful, bittersweet passion.

His first instinct was to wash, but he surprised himself again. The familiar sense of overpowering anxiety didn't bother him as it usually did. In fact, after he had bathed in the wellspring his body had felt clean, albeit heavy and riddled with aches. When he'd first returned from the pool, Colleen had provided a new set of clothes to replace his ruined ones. Now, as he prepared to discard his old, mangled garments, he fished out the few belongings he had left; chief among them was his pocket watch, now cracked and broken. He regarded it for a moment then stowed it away. As he stretched, looked out the window, and prepared to formulate a plan of where to go, a thought occurred to him.

Fana…she's out there in the meadow. I wonder if…

A voice from down the hall disrupted his temptation.

"I hope you're ready to work. I can't allow you to join us for the festival if you won't work for it. You're going to help Colleen in the garden, and *I'm* going to get the meat." Ainsley's voice cut through the peaceful hum of dawn.

Although Edgar wasn't opposed to work, he felt a touch disappointed. The feeling quickly faded when the true impudent nature of his desire to see Fana became clear to him.

Elspeth and Colleen prepared a hearty breakfast of bacon, eggs, mushrooms, baked beans, and toast. Edgar ate voraciously, abandoning all manners to make way for his wolfish hunger. For some reason, Ainsley seemed pleased by this, and Edgar felt her attitude toward him warm briefly before she set out with her dirk and bow.

Shortly after breakfast, Elspeth's attention became focused on the corner of the room where she began to carry on a conversation with what seemed like thin air.

"Ah, they're preparing for the festival already?" she said, paused, and then continued. "Well, tell Morag I'll be along shortly, won't you? I've got to gather some things first," she paused again, "Thank you, dear." As soon as she left the room, Edgar looked to Ainsley and Colleen with concern.

"Is…Elspeth quite all right? She seems to be…"

"It's just her familiar. You can't see him if he doesn't want you to, is all," Ainsley explained offhandedly. Colleen saw that Edgar remained nonplussed.

"She's bonded with a spirit. He can help her with her magic and offer her soul passage to another place where things aren't as harsh. It's why Elspeth can seem a bit...*odd* from time to time, though. All the travel her soul does between realities loosens her grip on this one."

Edgar accepted this with a slow sort of a nod, and the three of them broke away from the table to begin work. Colleen and Edgar walked side by side into the garden and busied themselves among the vegetables, herbs, and flowers. Exercise in the field was invigorating, and Edgar was quietly pleased with himself for performing the labor. Whenever his back or chest pained him, Colleen encouraged him to rest.

They worked until after lunch, harvesting a magnificent pile of turnips, pumpkins, carrots, potatoes, and fresh herbs. Most of them were to be donated to the commonwealth of the village in preparation for the Samhain feast. After a midday meal of cheese, bread, and pickles, Colleen and Edgar carted most of the food through the village to where the witches and their families were gathering firewood, hauling out long tables, and building a platform for the festival.

Edgar was struck by how beautiful and comfortable the village seemed. Most of the area was protected by a lush canopy of trees, and the pathways that wove between them were mossy and clearly well loved. Because of the leafy ceiling, the village was lit day and night by lanterns of various colors and shapes. Nothing was built in a straight line, and each of the cottages was surrounded by gardens overflowing with life. The entire settlement hummed with magic, and many of the flowers and mushrooms that crowded in on the man-made structures glowed with a wondrous bioluminescence. The smells of cooking were heavy in the air as Edgar and Colleen passed through a small marketplace where many of the witches, their mortal kinfolk, and even a few cats of a peculiar intelligence and awareness were taken aback by Edgar's presence. They were unused to seeing an unfamiliar face among them. As they stopped their wagons to say hello to Colleen and investigate him, he braced himself to endure the same sort of distaste that Ainsley had for him. To his great surprise, however, most of the inhabitants of the Witches' Wood greeted him warmly and were full of questions about news from the outside world.

Under the rain of falling leaves in the spiced autumn air, Colleen and Edgar joined the others in the square. Many of the children were carving faces into turnips and pumpkins, and a large pot of duck sausage stew was bubbling over a fire. Elspeth awaited them there, and she introduced Edgar to the leading members of the coven, all of whom welcomed him. He spoke with hardworking men who were sons, brothers, friends, or husbands to the witches. He met women who were well versed in the ways of magic and had lived for centuries, small girls who were eager for the day when they too could set out on their pilgrimages, and kindly elderly folk who were keen on teaching Edgar cooking and crafting tips.

After several more hours spent helping them with the various festival constructions, preparing food, laughing, and sharing stories with the people from the village, he was overwhelmed by a sense of belonging he'd never before experienced. Many of the people he knew in London always seemed focused on retaining or increasing the apparent importance of their life. After a day in the Wood, Edgar got a vague sense that perhaps such efforts were misguided.

When a young witch cut her finger badly while carving a turnip, Edgar was quick to react. He stitched her up with tools the villagers provided, and after discovering he was a medical expert, many of the other people from the village asked him to look at strange bumps, give advice for chronic pains, or diagnose illnesses that magical cures had no effect on. He did what he could for them, feeling quite proud of his background for the first time since he'd lost his last patient. Out of gratitude, they provided him with a satchel of all the medical and surgical tools and medicines they could find from the village, and Edgar took to carrying it on his person.

Later in the day, after Elspeth gave him a warm cup of chamomile tea and some seed cakes, Edgar felt a bittersweet ache in his heart. He'd never known it was possible to enjoy the company of others this much with so little effort. Some of the younger girls, who were beginning to act playfully shy around him, gifted him with a wreath of woven daisies and ran off shrieking with giggles. As Edgar touched the petals gently, his throat grew tight.

So short a time...if only I hadn't come to Edinburgh... Why did I come to Edinburgh in the first place? What was the reason?

Gusts passed through the trees and whipped through the square, teasing the hems of skirts and bringing with it a collection of dried leaves. Edgar sipped at the remainder of his tea while the chilly wind blew through his hair and made another queer feeling sweep through him. At once he wanted to go into the trees, to explore the hidden green kingdom that belonged to the spirit of the wellspring. He wanted to walk across roadways unused by humans and known to the animals, and glimpse the magic that had gone rightfully undisturbed for so long. Something in that pine-scented breeze called to him, inviting him into the secret place that was forbidden to outsiders.

He slipped off quietly, drawn through the narrow trails into the archways of bark and moss. The earth smelled so fragrantly of rain and plants that he took huge lungfuls of it over and over. Soon the sounds and smells of the village faded, and Edgar was swallowed up by trees and ferns. He felt as though he were in the presence of something holy as he walked among them, lightly touching the trunks with a respectful hand. As Edgar climbed the trail, a spasm of pain shot through his back, and he was forced to sit down for a moment while it passed. His hands were shaking, and a cavernous misery ate away at his chest. These feelings weren't his own, and to his great horror, he heard the far-off weeping of the murdered boy who was eating away at his soul.

His vision blurred, and he blinked madly, but he couldn't regain focus.

Please, no, not here...I have time...I have days...I have a gift from her...

Without warning, the boy appeared before Edgar on the forest path. This time his back was straight and unbroken, but the look on his face flared with malevolence. Upon his head lay a crown that gleamed gold and red in the afternoon light. Edgar couldn't breathe; every time he tried, it got stuck in his throat. Coughing and gasping, he tried to crawl away but couldn't get far. The colors all around seemed to increase in saturation, and Edgar's eyes narrowed against the spinning.

This is my kingdom now.

Hearing the boy's voice in his head, Edgar immediately stood up, though he could hardly endure the pain. The sickening memory of the poisoned wellspring and the way it had transformed Fana into a monster steadied Edgar, and he stood his ground. He shut his eyes and desperately tried to block out the specter's influence. He wouldn't die here only to allow Fana and the people of the Wood to fall back into danger. Without him, Ainsley couldn't bottle the revenant who now stood before him, and it eventually would take over the Wood.

"Get...get *away!*" Edgar hollered, and suddenly the spinning stopped. When he opened his eyes again, the boy was gone. Taking several deep breaths to compose himself, Edgar knew what he had to do. He tore down the trail, his heart racing from fright and anticipation.

It took the better part of an hour for him to find the meadow where Fana's well was, but when he realized it was just ahead, his pace slowed. Entering the meadow uninvited seemed daunting—and seeing Fana again even more so. He swallowed, wiped the sweat from his brow, flattened his hair, and climbed over the hill.

As he entered the meadow, however, he lowered his head. In the center of the clearing was a red-brown fox with two flowering antlers. It looked at Edgar and cocked its head to the side as if confused. He bowed his head in a sign of obeisance, and the fox immediately transformed into the winsome young woman. She looked a bit confused by Edgar's presence but nevertheless spoke kindly to him.

"Didn't Ainsley tell you to wait until after Samhain?" Fana asked.

Edgar clutched his chest. "She did, Miss Fana, but...but something has gone awry. I'm not well. My life is fading, and I fear that if I perish in these woods, you would be corrupted by the revenant's evil, and I could not...I could not bear that."

Fana waved her hand in a calming gesture. "Be calm, Edgar Price. You have your time. Though you might see or hear the spirit, it cannot destroy you until your time has passed. I promise you...I would not take a chance with such things," she assured him, and he relaxed.

After a moment longer of uncomfortable silence, Edgar cleared his throat and scratched his head with embarrassment.

"I'm...I'm sorry to have disturbed you then," he said quietly. "Please forgive my intrusion."

"It's quite all right. This area isn't forbidden. People come here to leave offerings and make wishes." She waved at the trees covered with strips of fabric.

Edgar glanced up at them. "And...anyone can make a wish?"

"Correct," she answered.

Edgar stood, entertaining an idea for a moment. At last he gave an uncertain smile, then shyly tore off a bit of his handkerchief and tied it to a nearby tree, silently making his wish as he did. Fana blinked at him, her cheeks turning pink.

Edgar chanced a nervous glance in her direction. "You can tell what the wish was, can't you?"

"Y-yes, of course I can," she said slowly, pushing her soft, wind-teased hair back from her face, "but it's a very strange wish. I don't think I've ever heard one like it before."

"Was it impudent of me? If so, I apologize."

"No, no. I will grant it. But it is unusual," she said with a laugh, the smallest of lines appearing around her eyes as she did. Edgar's heart surged, and his own smile broadened. "You wish to...to know more about me? What do you want to know?"

"Anything, really. How old are you?"

"Do you mean in this particular lifetime or all my lifetimes?" she asked, and Edgar blinked. He wasn't quite sure what he'd expected, but it wasn't that.

"Erm...both."

"I believe I've seen eighty-four summers in this body, at present," Fana said, grinning to see the small look of shock Edgar couldn't hide in time. "And as for my true age...I couldn't say. There was never a single moment I was born. I was many different souls once—small things. I was part of the animals, the trees, the earth—and as the Wood grew, so did my consciousness. My earliest memories are from a time when mankind was very crude and couldn't speak. But I have died and been reborn many times since then." Her focus grew distant as she sifted through her memories.

"When you say 'died'..."

"This body becomes gravely injured, and I must lay it to rest in the earth for a while to be rejuvenated. But my memories remain," she replied.

Edgar nodded. "So you'll live forever?"

"No. When these Woods are destroyed, so too will I be. It has happened to many of the spirits who have lived on earth. But as long as there's abundant life here, and I'm buried in the place of my birth, I will remain," Fana said with a melancholy grin. She strolled over to the edge of the Well and patted a mossy spot on the ground beside her, indicating that Edgar should join her. Eager to be in her presence longer, he strode over and took a seat, his proximity to her making his heart strain.

"Colleen told me Ainsley saved your life once. What happened, if I may ask?"

She considered his question, appearing pensive. "Hunters from the village outside of the Wood came here one winter, looking for game. I must've looked like just another deer to them. One of their arrows dealt me a serious injury, and I was dying. I couldn't get back to the spring in time to heal myself, and they were gaining on me. Ainsley, too, was hunting that day, and when we crossed paths, she drove them away—frightened them with her magic—and carried me to safety."

Edgar's admiration for Ainsley grew once more, and as he thought on her deed, he noticed the silence was starting to grow awkward. "Um...what is...your favorite thing to eat?" he asked with a lighter tone, and Fana laughed—a sound airy and sweet as flute song—at the sudden change in mood.

"Strawberries," she said, beaming.

"And your favorite time of day?"

"When the sun's just gone down but it's not quite dark yet."

"Can you take the form of any animal?"

"Yes."

"Do *you* have any wishes of your own?" He was so giddy with the momentum of his questions that he didn't anticipate that this might be a sensitive subject. Fana's smile flickered, and her lips parted for a moment as she thought.

"Yes..." was her answer, and she said no more.

Edgar looked away for a moment, feeling clumsy as usual but too invigorated to retreat from her. Normally he wouldn't have attempted to speak to her at all, but with only a little more than a week left, he planned to do everything in his power to live the way he never would have dared to before. Stumbling to think of what to say next, he considered apologizing and letting Fana know that he found it difficult to converse freely with others, but he remembered that she already knew—she knew everything about him.

Edgar sighed. "I envy you, Miss Fana," he said, looking around the meadow and stealing glances at her.

"My apologies. I must seem insensitive, going on about my nearly endless time when you—"

"No, it's not that," he said, stopping her. "It's this meadow and the Wood and the people who live here. It's all just so...wondrous. It hurts to know that it's real, and that I never knew until now, and that I'll lose it so soon," he said, and Fana was at once very attentive.

They sat without speaking for a while. The dragonflies and birds fluttered about the clearing while the hums and chirps of insects filled the silence.

"Come with me," Fana said suddenly, and stood up, offering her hand to Edgar.

His eyebrows rose, but he soon took her hand all the same, and she helped him to his feet. In the few moments that their hands touched, his skin felt electrified, and it remained sensitive even after she'd let go. They set off, Edgar following Fana down many hidden lanes, past a wide river, and finally up a steep sloping pathway.

"Where are we going?"

"I want to show you something. Keep up."

Fana trotted along, hopping over rocks and branches, her movements cervine and nimble. It was a much longer hike than Edgar had expected, and his back began to pain him greatly, but he knew nothing could stop him from following Fana. As the pathway became steeper and the woods thicker, a darkness fell over the woods as a blanket of clouds obscured the sun. The rain started, as it generally did in Scotland, without much warning. It sloshed down the hills in tiny streams, thoroughly soaking Fana and Edgar.

The climb left him breathless, and when a small break in the trees came, he spotted the village below peeking through the trees. It looked like a collection of toys in a child's bedroom. Still Fana continued. The rain reached its heaviest just before Fana and Edgar broke through the trees and onto a ridge that overflowed with grass, ferns, and flowers. Black rocks overlooked the magnificent, dark lochs hundreds of feet below. From this height, the only sounds that could be heard were the rushing of the wind and the voices of birds. In the distance, veils of mist shimmered through arbor-crested mountains that stretched on in untamed expanses. The air was laden with the scents of damp earth and far-off wood smoke from the village fires. Rain fell onto the treetops and the lake waters, moving with the wind and catching the light where it broke through the clouds.

For a moment, Edgar found that he could not draw breath as the world stretched out before him. Faintly, he heard his father's voice telling him he could have any piece of that world that he wished. Fana looked up with a satisfied smile at his dumbstruck expression, and with a mischievous glimmer in her eye, she waved a hand across the view. As soon as she did, the clouds parted as if she'd shooed them away. The sun burst through in a glorious cascade of light, illuminating the lake and turning its black waters to a deep sapphire. The rain shone on the treetops, creating the illusion that they were covered in a film of stars. In the tangle of greenery around Edgar and Fana, butterflies began to recognize that the rain had stopped and bravely ventured out of their hiding places among the ferns. In moments, the air around them flittered with motion and color. In the place where the shroud of rainclouds had been, the pale vapors of a rainbow formed in the air. Edgar's throat ached as tears formed at the sides of his eyes.

"Did...did you make this happen?" he asked.

"Indeed." She grinned up at him, her many cloaks fluttering around her lithe frame.

"Thank you for this, Miss Fana. It's the most perfect gift anyone could've given me. I shall think of this moment when... when the time comes..." Edgar drank in the beauty, desperate to hold on to every last detail.

"Does this truly make you happy?" Fana asked almost cautiously.

Edgar nodded at once. "It makes me remember what it was like to feel whole. What it was like to love the world," he told her, still transfixed by the splendor of the earth and the creatures that lived in its hills and valleys. Without any indication that she was going to do so, Fana took his hand in hers. Edgar looked her way in utter confusion, but she would not let go.

"If you are as taken with this place, as you say, would it bring you joy to see things as they truly are? The way I can see them? Would that frighten you?" she asked in her dreamy, distant way.

Edgar swallowed. He hadn't an inkling what she meant, but he couldn't refuse and risk losing the opportunity. He nodded, and Fana smiled in her usual knowing way. She pulled him to the ground and gestured that he should lie down in the grass.

"You might fall if you're standing. It'll be something of a shock," she explained when he hesitated. "Others have been overwhelmed by it, so prepare yourself." Fana lay down with a few feet between them, still holding tightly to his hand. Suddenly the place where their hands touched grew very warm. The heat spread from Edgar's palm through his arm and the rest of his body, crawling up his neck and into his head.

As it hit his brain, his memories and sense of self grew foggy until he had all but forgotten who he was. For one evanescent moment, he grasped at the ego that was Edgar Winston Price but became powerless as it was wiped clean away. He was merely a point of radiant consciousness. An incredible feeling of lightness coursed through him. It was a surge of glorious emancipation—a moment of pure, tranquil euphoria—as he looked skyward at the rolling clouds.

Then, from below him, Edgar became aware of all the roots of the plants burrowing into the soil and pulling at the water. The awareness spread to the insects and underground mammals. He breathed with them, felt their struggle for survival and the gentle pulses of their lives. He saw in vivid detail how they fit together and complemented one another in an intricate kaleidoscope of consumption and creation. This awareness spread to the plants in the area before shooting up like pillars of light through the trees. The swaying motions of the arbors were a part of him. He felt every vein, every vesicle, every throbbing point of life energy in the hillside and beyond. It was at once mathematical and mystical—a perfectly crafted, infinitely complex design inscribed by the hand of the divine. A sense of jubilance bounded through him, and shock wave upon shock wave of profound understanding struck him. It was not to last, however, and bit by bit, things fell out of his grasp. Everything collapsed in upon itself, his vision becoming smaller and simpler until the threat of recollection of his cramped, single self was imminent. Edgar remembered his name; he remembered his past; and finally he remembered his fate.

At last his eyes worked properly again, and he vigorously blinked. He sat up slowly, drew his hand from Fana's, and leaned into his palms as he tried to comprehend what he'd just experienced. His concept of the universe, which had so recently been rewritten by horror and pain, was now amended by wonder. He looked over at Fana, breathless and shaking at the combined force of the beauty of the world and the beauty of the woman who sat so close to him. Although he wanted so badly to convey the feelings that were cascading through him, he couldn't conceive of words that would do them justice.

Finding himself at a loss, Edgar instead reached toward Fana, offering a shaky hand. She accepted his hand, and read his memories all over again, as he hoped she would, taking particular interest in the present moment and seeing Edgar's thoughts with incandescent understanding.

When it was over, she smiled, her freckled cheeks growing rounder and her eyes shining as their edges crinkled ever so slightly. In that moment, Edgar's chest ached with a most perfect and painful variety of heartbreak.

"So you're not frightened after all," Fana said.

Dead and Gone

The collection of whirling, glittering lights bobbed within Jacob Hare's sights at last. Halation of both flame and filament shone in the distance—he'd be arriving before long. The first of the revenants he sought had taken hold somewhere in that cluster of lights and sat incubating unbeknownst to all but him. Hare planned on harvesting it before it could get too far out of control. As he stared out of the open carriage window, his stomach squirmed with anxiety at the notion of what could befall him if he failed. He fought the urge to shout at the driver to hurry.

A harsh wind blew in and cut right through Hare's clothes, chilling his bones and making him shiver. He longed for the comfort of a fireside and for the ease of mind it used to bring.

So much ventured, just to be free, he thought with torment and sickness at his sorry situation. Freedom was a distant memory, as faded as a name on a tombstone that had long been worn away by so many rainstorms. But he could still recall it, however faintly it lingered in his memory. His youth, which had occurred more than half a century ago, seemed the only gentle time in his life. The cottage near the meadows and woods in Ireland had been his Eden, though it had been by no fault of his that he'd been expelled from it.

Hare shivered again, half from the biting cold and half from the recollection. He put his hands in his armpits and grumbled to himself as he tried to push away thoughts of the day his father had returned to the cottage without warning and stolen him away. Hatred for the murderous man crept up his spine and made his longing for comfort grow ever stronger.

My father, the monster. My father, who strangled the life out of drunken lasses and snapped the bones of children while I was quickening in my mother's womb. She, who helped him do it—lured them in so he could finish the job. May they burn forever. The image of fire flared in his mind again, and he sucked his teeth.

If anyone deserves to burn, it's him. The man who sold my soul to Mag for his own freedom, who chained these devils to me, who took away my right to live...and to die. He drew a shuddering breath and braced himself against tremors. The fact that he had been committing the same crime against others didn't escape him, but Jacob pushed the thought downward in his mind until it made no noise.

He wasn't too far away now. His breath escaped in clouds, stinging his face and causing him to crumple further inward for warmth.

So damn cold...but I'm almost free, he reminded himself. It wouldn't be such a task to reclaim the revenants, and when he did, he could finally rest. *You've been through worse than this, Jacob. This cold isn't anything unusual.*

Yet it was. It was an insidious cold, a cold that crept through his soul and made him dwell on evil things—things he'd shut away and tried to forget—and on people he'd harmed and on screams that he'd evoked in dark places that still rang in his ears. It struck him as odd that these memories should awaken at this, the end of his life—or what he desperately hoped would be the end.

His hand slid up his chest, his fingers worming their way toward a tiny pocket he'd sewn into the lining of his coat. Another chill rocked him as his finger snuck behind the silk and withdrew a gilded locket. Hare pushed on the latch, and the lid sprang open to reveal a lock of hair, earthy brown and tied with a frayed red ribbon. His fingers quivered with the urge to stroke it, but he'd noticed it had grown matted with the oil and dirt of his hands. Hare couldn't bear to watch it deteriorate further—it was all that was left of her. He snapped the locket shut again and returned it to the tiny inner pocket, then bundled his coat tighter against the chill.

Oh, Emily, he thought as he grappled with his misery, *would that I could have kept you better. You were the only person in this filthy world who looked at me without fear or disgust.*

With a mighty exhaling of breath, Hare allowed himself to recall her. The carriage rounded the bend, and the horses pulled him and the driver straight toward the drunken mixture of light and sound.

Hare and Emily had first met on one of the most fetid streets of Edinburgh he knew. She was alone in the alley, peddling buttons out of a box gripped in her bony hands. Hare had stopped at the sight of her, his brain wiped clean of the sordid task he was carrying out. He frequently saw to deeds no one else wanted to do in those days—his indestructible body, ghastly appearance, and stained past made him ideal for such work.

But it all had been forgotten, purged even, when he saw her, standing pearly and meager among the gray, miserable denizens. Too afraid to speak anything more than a few cursory words, he immediately went up and bought all her buttons then took off down the street. Her delighted, breathless look satisfied him all day long.

He returned again and again to that road, buying whatever she had to sell and stumbling through conversations with awkward breaths of laughter. But the attraction was palpable, for the both of them. It was as if they were magnetized to each other, and before long Hare quit his life as a criminal, and they became a pair.

Emily had suffered as the victim of misfortune, just as he had. Her family was eradicated by consumption, and she too had caught the illness, but as fate would have it, she was the only one to survive. Her family's property had been seized since her father owed sizable debts, and she was forced to live on the streets in search of any form of employment she could find.

Hare spent every shilling he had had rescuing her from the misery of the rain-dampened streets of Edinburgh. The plan was perfect and should have worked—he would re-create that Eden from the days before his father had snatched him away. He and Emily were married and bought a humble farm and a plot of land in the green country far from the city. Emily nurtured him in his fits of terror when the revenants tore at his strained mind. She shouldered with him the weight of his eternal life and forced him to think of other, more present things. Emily didn't condemn him for the sins of his father, or even for his own, as the rest of the world did. When she looked at his weathered, eternal face, she didn't see a child born of sin; rather, she only saw Jacob. She took his evil secrets like treasures, as if they were hollow stones to be cracked apart to find the crystals hidden inside. Emily embodied light and forgiveness; she valued change and the chance to reinvent one's self from a fallen state. And so it was that she and Jacob healed each other, mended hurts long since burrowed in their hearts. It was as if they had a hidden world of their own and the rules of it made perfect sense to them both, though no one else alive or otherwise would understand it. Their home was a peculiar one: off-kilter and warped, yet beautiful to the two broken creatures who found safety within its walls.

The first years were as a dream to Hare. The separation from the world he'd known for most of his prolonged life changed him magnificently. He found he could cope with the curse, and it never pulled him into his fits as it once did, though hideous visions filled many of his nights. Being away from the wickedness of the city and the desperate men that haunted its streets was like waking from the poisoned haze of alcoholic drink. It still left a craving, a thirst for the excitement and thrill, for the power and license to focus anger onto living things. But once the craving passed, Hare felt his soul becoming whole again.

He realized during those years that he had forgotten the smell of clean air and the joys that birdsong can stir and the satisfaction at having done honest work and being rewarded for it. He harvested the fruits of the earth, and he and Emily fed their bodies and hearts with things that were good and green and savory.

It taunted him now to remember; all the sensations that reawakened, the gentleness reborn after all this time, a long-coveted love finally found—they now were all ghosts, twirling in the dark when he closed his eyes. Each one of them was sweet and tantalizing; each evoked a deep, aching pain at the idea that they'd once been real, that Hare had once held Emily and seen the sun rise over land that was his alone. Each of these ghosts harmed him more deeply than any of the revenants had. Each one was a memory of a magical country that never could be found again.

Each one was dead and gone.

It was the cold that had wakened him from that dream, cast him from his paradise and back into the wastes of mankind. Cold killed the crops in the field. Cold laid waste to the sheep. Cold threatened Emily, who could still be destroyed, as Hare could not. He had sworn to protect her, and he couldn't break that promise. It would be a betrayal to the only kind bit of luck that life had shown him.

It was thus that Hare returned to the city that winter and visited his old friends. Money had to be earned, no matter which way he did it. Emily begged him not to go, but her health was failing without warmth and food, and he wouldn't allow her to perish in the harsh winter. In the spring he could try to live free of sin again. He carried out the nefarious deeds asked of him without any of his prior detachment. Before, killing someone or pillaging a shop was nothing more than a tiresome chore. He could hardly remember half the names or faces of those he'd brought to ruin.

But that winter, things had changed. There had been three: Royce Baldwin, Fanny Thatcher, Timothy Kemble. Royce had been a corrupt, cruel landlord of many tenements in the city whom Hare had been ordered to destroy in revenge for his unscrupulous manipulation of his tenants. Hare had pushed him from the top of his highest building after pretending to be interested in buying it from him. He couldn't take his eyes off the sight of the man's crumpled body, lying in the street in the rainy night, and stayed watching it for much longer than was sensible.

The woman had died defending her general store from a robbery. Hare had begged his brutish companions to spare her life, but in the end they couldn't risk her going to the police. Hare stayed awake each night the week after her death, troubled by visions of her being strangled to death and later tossed into a shallow grave in the woods. To this day, he still thought of her corpse lying under layers of earth and snow.

It was Timothy's death, however, that disquieted him the most. The man had been a shipper of goods, his services outrageously priced. A businessman had paid Hare two shillings to intimidate him into lowering his costs. Timothy was the sort of man who didn't take kindly to being threatened, however delicately. He'd shot Hare through the gut, then watched in horror as his body repaired itself before his eyes. He'd tried again and again to destroy Hare with the gun, then with a beam of wood, and finally with his bare hands. Hare couldn't bring himself to fight back without understanding why. He fled from that place, leaving Timothy in a panic, and thought that would be the end of it. The following week, however, he received news of the man from his associates. Timothy had killed himself. Hare never found out for certain exactly what had caused him to end his life, but a sneaking suspicion haunted him all the same.

Once he'd earned enough money and stocked up on food and supplies, Hare returned to his frozen garden, feeling hollow and overwrought. Emily's condition hadn't improved since his departure, so to speed her recovery he prepared a feast of beef stew, bread, and milk, then built a roaring fire to warm her. She seemed to regain a little life after that meal, but she still shook with fever. Hare threw more wood on the fire, and she bundled up in the blankets before it. They had fallen asleep then, clinging to each other, Emily shaking with the chill that couldn't be banished from her body.

During the night, the fire Hare had built to warm his wife had grown out of control from the extra fuel he'd piled on, and had escaped the hearth. It spread to the wooden walls, burning quickly through the cabin's thin frame. The wall collapsed, blocking the exit entirely. The air was already so thick with smoke that he couldn't breathe. Emily woke up only long enough to see that this was her time and place of dying. Hare urged her to get to her feet, to try to escape, but she only repeated his name, as if trying to capture his attention. Before she could convey anything more, however, she passed out in his arms, the tears still fresh on her face.

Flames consumed them where they lay cowering, burning them both down to the bones. Only when the house lay in smoldering ashes did Hare's body began to reknit itself. Slowly his charred remains sprouted flesh and organs, and the flow of blood resumed. He was reborn in a pile of Emily's ashes.

From that night onward, Hare's skin no longer would heal properly and had taken on a frightful, waxy look that he couldn't repair by any means he knew. In the aftermath of the fire, he wandered the roads aimlessly, knowing only grief and cursing the world with every step. There was nothing left in this world for him, and he didn't even have the luxury to escape his own life. That was when he'd made the decision to get his freedom, at any cost. That was when he had sought out Mag. He remembered her from their first meeting—when his father had brought him to Scotland, when she'd taken the burden of his father's crimes and laid it onto his innocent shoulders. If she could transfer the curse once, he reasoned that she could do it again.

When the carriage stopped abruptly, the lurching motion shook Hare's morose thoughts loose from his head. He heaved a sigh, patted his pocket where he kept Emily's hair, and straightened his jacket before the driver opened the door. He rumbled out, his nose and fingers already numb with cold.

He paid the driver without looking at him then strode toward the fairground that sprawled before him, purpose in his every step.

Samhain

Ainsley had, at last, made up her mind: she hated Edgar. She'd reached this conclusion as she watched him sitting on the other side of the bonfire while some of the younger witches were fawning over him. Around his neck hung a wreath of flowers and berries, and he was laughing heartily as the girl to his right filled his glass with honey wine for the third time since the festival had started.

Samhain had come at last, marking the end of this year and the beginning of winter. With nightfall the colored lanterns, carved pumpkins, and roaring flame of the bonfire had been ignited. Wine flowed; candied fruits and nuts were passed around; and the sounds of singing and well-loved instruments wafted in the chilly night air. The celebration would continue through the night until sunset the following day. Witches and villagers alike began a dance around the flames. They turned and twisted in wild movements, their bodies lit dramatically in shades of bright orange and black.

Ainsley chomped at a piece of mutton pie, eating it straight out of her hand, and washed it down with a swig of ale. She couldn't draw her eyes away from Edgar and his insufferable behavior. She hated that the others accepted him so easily and that he was allowed to attend the festival at all. This was more than just a celebration; it was a sacred part of their culture. That he should be allowed to tromp in and enjoy select parts of their life without having any understanding or respect for the meaning behind them made her blood itch in her veins.

What a twit. He laughs like a bloody seal, Ainsley thought, sneering in his direction. One of the girls had placed a crown of flowers over his head, and they all erupted into giggles. The sound made her nose scrunch up in disgust. After a moment more of his shameless, drunken flirting, his eyes happened to connect with Ainsley's. She responded to his slack-jawed glance by narrowing her eyes and taking a huge chomp out of her pie. She wouldn't break her gaze, even as he excused himself from where he sat with the young witches and came toward her with a wobbling step. When Edgar took a seat beside Ainsley and greeted her cordially, she snorted at him then proceeded to drink deeply from her mug.

"Enjoying ourselves, are we?" she asked snidely.

"Very much, thank you," Edgar said brightly, with only the very hint of an edge in his voice. He seemed to be growing accustomed to her usual sarcasm, and apparently had chosen to disregard it in this instance. Ainsley endured another gale of vexation and chewed her lip to keep from saying anything.

"Ainsley, I don't know what I've done to make you despise me so, but—"

"That's just it—you have no idea. You have no understanding of what our life is like. You have no understanding of what's going on here," she spat.

Edgar blinked. "I...I thought it was a festival."

"Ach, aye! Well done! Your powers of perception continue to inspire me."

"You know, Ainsley"—Edgar straightened up—"I never thought *I* would say this to another human being, but I'm of the mind that you would benefit from taking things less seriously. You are absolutely no fun. Do you know this?"

Ainsley's jaw fell open, and then she opened and closed her mouth several times, her gray eyes blazing with anger. Edgar hesitated for a moment then put his hand on her shoulder in a gesture of what she assumed was solidarity. She nearly slapped him away, but he smiled so warmly at her that she faltered.

"It's the end of the world for us both," he said gently to her, and her tightly knotted muscles loosened. "If I'm doing something improper, please would you tell me? I recognize my ignorance, and I revile it as much as you do. But seeing as how there's so little time left for both of us, I'd really rather spend it as your friend."

Ainsley stared at him, her mouth still open, as a litany of conflicting emotions shot through her chest. Edgar removed his hand, looking as if the contact was starting to pain him, then left her side without another word. She watched him rejoin his new friends—her old friends—on the other side of the bonfire, and suddenly she felt more alone and helpless than she had in years. Certainly Ainsley was furious, but there was something underneath it that scared her, something that felt both empty and serrated.

The night wore on, and soon the children came by, cheering and screaming and begging for apples and cakes. Ainsley shooed them away as the sound of the Mummers Play rose in the distance. Steaming plates of roast beef were served on long tables, and the luscious victuals of the seasonal feast were laid out, but Ainsley found she wasn't hungry for even a morsel.

The end of the world...

"Somehow I knew I'd find you sitting here being glum," said the only voice Ainsley would welcome at that moment. Colleen's hands pressed on her shoulders, and Ainsley was glad to have her nearby, but her mood didn't change, and she gave no reply. Sensing there was something wrong, Colleen sat down beside her. "Well, maybe not this glum. What's wrong?"

"It's that...that man," she grumbled, and Colleen scoffed.

"Oh, come now. He's not so bad, Ainsley. You said it yourself earlier."

"Bloody Englishman. He said I wasn't any fun. What's he on about? I'm *loads* of fun!" As she spoke, Ainsley could hear the strain in her own voice. Colleen stared at Ainsley, smiling as if she thought this both very humorous and apt. At this, Ainsley desperately tried to remember, as undeniable proof of her jocularity, an instance when she'd landed a successful quip. Her frustration made Colleen's smile grow ever broader, and she blushed with annoyance.

"You have been a shade *tense* recently," Colleen said delicately.

Ainsley crossed her arms over her chest. "Oh, off with you, woman. Leave me be," she growled.

Colleen's eyes narrowed, and she jumped up from the bench in a spritely fashion then moved behind Ainsley. Just as Ainsley was beginning to regret her words, she felt a pair of nimble fingers quickly undo her belt. She cried out as Colleen snatched it away and trotted off toward the woods, cackling with delight.

"You devil! Come back!" Ainsley stood and instantly turned a deep shade of red as her too-large trousers almost slid down. Crying terrible curses at Colleen, she wobbled after her, holding her pants up all the way. Awkwardly she rambled along, following the sound of Colleen's fairylike laughter as she chased her more deeply into the trees.

It was a struggle, but Ainsley eventually caught up with her lover, and when she did, she leapt across the mossy forest carpet and grasped her around the shoulders. Just as she made contact, she tripped over her trousers, and the two of them fell forward, laughing and rolling in the grass. Ainsley kept Colleen pinned to the ground as she extracted the belt from her hands and reassigned it to its proper place.

Colleen giggled, trying to break from Ainsley's grip. "All right, you win, you got me."

"Oh, no, you're not getting away that easily," Ainsley told her with a crooked grin, and tickled her until she was yelping with laughter. When tears formed in Colleen's eyes, Ainsley finally stopped, gazing down at her with a self-satisfied grin.

"Promise to behave now?" she asked.

Colleen's gasps subsided, and giddily she replied, "Not on your life." Before Ainsley could retaliate, Colleen leaned upward and planted a quick kiss on her lips.

All at once, a change flowed through Ainsley. A rush of guilt and clarity hit her with a jarring force, and her eyes welled up. She faced Colleen with no shame; it was safe for her to be open with her.

"I've...I've changed my mind," she murmured, saying it aloud just to affirm the expanding feeling in her chest.

"About what, my love?"

"I'm..." Her throat caught briefly. "I'm going to live."

Colleen's expression of lightheartedness immediately shifted to something vital and dire. She didn't move, however, and lay there staring up at Ainsley with her lips only just parted.

"You're...?"

"I'm not ready to leave you," Ainsley said, touching the side of Colleen's face. "I can't believe I even dreamed it. I've always known our story could never have a happy ending. My life is cursed to be too short or too long. Dying seemed like the easy way out...and I've only just realized how stupid I've been. I'm leaving the Witches' Wood, and I'll save a life, any life I can, and then I'll return to you and savor every precious instant we have left. That's what I want. That's what I choose."

"Ainsley..." Colleen was hardly able to speak. She pulled her in, and they were close and deeply breathing each other's scents and loving each other so fiercely that all else seemed an illusion.

The Coming of the Aos Sí

Fana coursed through the woods like blood through a vein. Her lifeforce streamed with its power, her consciousness split into hundreds of fluttering moths, all dancing around one another and zooming toward the light of the massive bonfire. The flurry of moths burst into the clearing, where the witches were busy dancing, strumming their harps, and making merry.

As the dissembled Fana made her entrance, the music hushed, and the movement of the dance slowed. Before the great roaring flame, the moths gathered into a pillar. Slowly Fana's soul condensed; her consciousness became sharper; her body rebuilt itself. As the cheering started, Fana decided on a whim to keep a single pair of large moth wings on her back for tonight—it seemed appropriate somehow. Immediately she was surrounded by adoring villagers. They swarmed her, alive with loving gestures as they called out her name. Several months had passed since she'd seen many of them. By name she heralded them all, one by one, her velvety wings fluttering on her back as she did.

After the frenetic activity had grown to something of a lull, Fana's eyes scanned the festival area. All the preparations were complete. Tantalizing aromas floated in the air around the feast-heavy tables. A sensation of warmth and calm flowed over her when she saw that everything was in order. Still conversing vaguely with the people about her, she floated through the crowd toward a wooden platform at the other end of the clearing. All the structures were wreathed in garlands of bright-orange leaves and crystalline berries. As she ascended the platform, the crowd celebrated her with their voices again, and she smiled, touched by their affection. After the energy had faded, Fana lifted her arms, and complete silence fell over the clearing. She gazed down at the faces of her beloved kinfolk, letting her life-force seep into the earth below her so she could feel theirs humming before she spoke.

"The hour is almost upon us. The harvest season ends on this wondrous night, and winter will soon come to the Wood. The veil between our world and that of the hidden spirits of old grows thinnest… Shall we invite them in?" Fana asked with a hint of mischievousness.

The eager crowd roared joyously. Fana smiled again, closed her eyes, and began to concentrate. The network of life in the Witches' Wood became clear to her behind her eyelids, and she summoned forth its energy—it vibrated like sound in her fingers. Even the humans, birds, and other animals sensed something sublime and sacred was starting to occur.

From the surrounding trees, a noise rang up, and the revelers were joined by the creatures of the woods, which had been drawn by instinct to this shivering power Fana silently orchestrated. The silhouettes of rabbits, deer, foxes, martens, boars, and owls peeked out from among the trunks. The light of the fire glittered off black eyes that had grouped in the boughs.

Soft and low, Fana began the ancient song to invite the spirits of the old world to come join them around the fire. Her voice grew louder and clearer, and soon it echoed in an unearthly, haunting sound through the woods.

By light of lantern, moon, and flame,
join us at our midnight dance.
The table is laden with fruits of labor and luck,

with the gifts of nature's bounty as your offering.
Cross over the bridge of worlds,
we beseech you, we beseech you.

The spirits of the trees rose first, creaking up out of the branches and floating into the air like luminous mists. Small winged ones peeked out from under the veil then swooped about in midair, their brilliant colors pulsing in the night like fireflies. Large spirits awoke from their slumber in the mounds of earth and lumbered closer to the ethereal dance. The young ones joined them first, the ones who appeared more corporeal and rambunctious. Tiny sprites, fairies, elfish folk, and creatures no human ever had named began their procession through the woods. The people showered them with gifts of food and fond greetings—they had met them before and would meet them again. As Fana observed the scene, she caught a glimpse of Edgar, who stood frozen with shock at the sight of the spirits, his face white and his back pressed to a gnarled oak tree. When the spirit in the tree behind him awoke and drifted out, Edgar dropped to the ground with his hands on his head. Fana fought the urge to laugh, but her song trembled slightly all the same. Soon their clearing and the woods beyond were streaming with the folk of the old world: the Aos Sí.

Fana continued her song until the old ones had heard her—the taller and more graceful beings who watched over the younger spirits and guided them. Her heart overflowed with joy to see them gathered near her again. They had been Fana's friends since the days when the powerful giants and earth weavers had still ruled the land.

Her song faded, and she began to communicate with the nearby spirits through the language that was familiar to them but forgotten to the rest of the world. Reunited, they went about celebrating the night, joyfully partaking of tributes of food and aromatic wines. As the festivities wore on past midnight, Fana's old friends, just as she'd expected, begged her to abandon this world for good and join them on the other side of the veil, in the land of profound wisdom and light. As always, her answer was the same.

"I cannot...not yet. I still have love for this land and its people. I'm not ready to leave them. Not yet."

In the deepest part of the night, the party reached the peak of its fervor. Firelight dancers twirled frenetically in the orange glow, their cries untamed and shrill in the night. Throughout the clearing, drumbeats and the voices of strings roiled, swirling between peals of drunken laughter. Weariness came over Fana, and she stepped away from the riotous crowd. She found a hollow space in a fallen tree that had long since rotted through and grown a soft down of moss and mushrooms. She waved her hand across the air, enchanting the fungi so they glowed and gave her some light to see by, ghostly as it was. Just as she sighed in relaxation, footsteps rustled through the ferns. When she turned to see Edgar shyly approach her, some of the buds on her antlers bloomed.

"Miss Fana, I hope I'm not disturbing you." He greeted her cordially, but Fana noticed he was somewhat bleary with intoxication. The sight amused her, and her heart grew lighter.

"You are not," she replied, curious to see what he might do. When he stayed in his spot across the clearing and stared at her, grasping for words, she moved to the side. "Would you care to join me? I sense there's something on your mind."

"Oh, yes—yes, please." Edgar seemed to remember how to walk and came to sit down beside her. He was silent for a while longer, seemingly grappling for something to say. Fana understood what muddled him so; she experienced his feelings firsthand. This man was an interesting prospect to her, and after so many years of loneliness, the notion of entering into the cycle of infatuation, love, and inevitable heartbreak tempted her. She might've been more inclined had he more than a few days to live.

Poor thing. He seems an earnest creature, and earnestness is rare.

"I apologize. Perhaps I've indulged in too much wine…but I wonder, may I speak freely?" he asked.

"Please do. Speak freely to me whenever you wish," Fana told him with a broadening smile.

"It's just…I'm consumed with thoughts of yesterday evening. That moment…and every moment after, it feels as if you cracked the illusion of a previous reality, and now I'm seeing something entirely different." His fervent speech halted, and he laughed. "I'm sorry, I'm not certain what I mean, but…"

"But…?"

"I have a strong desire to be near you—to talk with you. You make me feel awake," he murmured, facing her with a bashful smile.

Fana's heart stirred with dull emotion—a particular emotion she hadn't felt in ages. Somehow she understood Edgar perfectly and envied him. It had been more than a century since she'd last felt truly awake. She studied him as he trailed off. A hunger for that emotion he spoke of welled up in her, to recapture what had been lost, and she reached out to grab his hand, not simply as a gesture of affection but as a way to experience it firsthand.

Edgar's emotions meshed with hers, and Fana shut her eyes, drinking it in while she could. She opened her eyes again in surprise moments later. The contents of his heart were unexpected to say the least.

Strange…he means almost everything he says. He believes it to his core. His heart is clean too. This affection is unselfish—infatuation devoid of greed. No hidden motive, no desire to win control. He's simply transfixed by my presence.

Fana let go of Edgar's hand to allow herself to feel an organic emotion of her own. It was refreshing to have an experience that belonged just to her. Edgar, however, seemed confused by her erratic action.

She looked up at him with a beguiling grin and laughed. "I see. So this new view of the world fascinates you?"

Edgar blinked back, thrown off by her unbroken gaze. "Yes."

"Is that why your heart is beating so quickly?" she questioned impishly, as she lightly touched his breastbone with the tip of her index finger.

The color in his face deepened in an instant, and his lips parted as if to speak, but he remained silent. Fana's chest lightened even more at his reaction, but then a wash of somberness came over her as she kept her finger on his chest. She pressed her palm to him, and her fingers crept over to the cursed wound. She kept her hand there, gripping his shirt. Edgar laid his hand over hers. Although he trembled ever so slightly, his shyness had dissipated.

"Miss Fana, without a doubt you're the most wondrous creature I've ever encountered. My only wish is to be near you as long as I'm permitted before I'm gone," he told her, that earnestness that Fana prized showing in his expression.

"Are you certain that's what you want?" she asked, her chest tightening with a distant kind of melancholy. "Do you believe that you see me as I truly am? I'm not truly convinced that I'm real anymore."

"What do you mean?"

Suddenly, without forewarning, an earsplitting boom echoed from the bonfire area. Fana and Edgar cringed as a flare of light flashed in the woods, casting long black shadows mixed with angry red light. Fana flew to her feet in an instant, her moth wings propelling her through the night sky. Screams of terror rang out, and by the time she burst through the trees, the festival was in chaos. The Aos Sí were dispersing, fleeing to the safety of their hidden world, while the villagers scattered in panic.

The bonfire blazed unnaturally high once again, singeing the nearby structures. A wild cackling rang out, and the flames rose past the treetops and then were instantly snuffed. In place of the blaze stood a short, bony figure draped in a long black gown. As the figure lifted its head, two huge eyes gleamed out of the darkness, accompanied by a shocking row of teeth bared in a chilling grin. Fana's blood went icy at the sight, but nevertheless she charged forward, drawing the power of the woods into her being and preparing to subdue the uninvited guest.

"Be still, nymph," the intruder commanded, and Fana swelled with rage.

"I know who you are. You are not welcome in these woods. I bid you leave before I must remove you myself, Lunatic Magdalena," Fana barked back, and the monstrous girl's face twisted into a hideous scowl; she clearly despised the title. Fana held her ground, refusing to break eye contact with her. From somewhere close behind her, Edgar ran panting into the clearing. As Magdalena's eyes flashed over to him, her look of ire was replaced with one of mad glee.

"I have no desire to remain in this place. I only came to reclaim my property." She pointed one long, white finger in Edgar's direction, and Fana turned to see him terrified to his core, grasping a nearby tree for support.

Fana stood between them, blocking Edgar from the Lunatic's view. "You've no right to take this man. Leave now, or it will come to blows," she warned, casting a quick glance around to ensure the safety of the villagers.

Faster than Fana could blink, Magdalena's face was inches from hers. She flinched, and the Ophiuchan leaned in close to her neck.

"I was hoping you'd say that."

Fana dipped out of the way just in time, Magdalena's teeth missing her neck by inches. She lunged with swift precision and caught hold of the Lunatic's throat, squeezing tightly and lifting her off her feet. Her legs kicked feebly in the air as Fana held her high. The threat seemed neutralized for a moment, until the creature gave her legs a powerful swing and flipped out of Fana's grasp, landing back on the ground. The two of them stared at each other, fury blazing in their eyes. The witches of the wood began to move in, but Fana held her hands out in a warning motion, not taking her gaze off the woman.

"Keep back!" she commanded, loath to think that any eternal blood could be spilt by the Ophiuchan.

Before the Lunatic could move again, Fana charged forward, channeling all her power into her arms. Magdalena's smile was broader and more crooked than even the surrounding jack-o'-lanterns as she raced heedlessly forward to meet Fana. As they clashed together, Fana was knocked off her feet by the sheer strength of the blow. Shrieking with delight, the Lunatic was upon her in an instant, her hands clamping Fana to the ground, her jaws snapping hungrily at her throat. A bolt of fear shook Fana: she had been unprepared for the ferocity of this assault and long out of the habit of fighting. Gathering her resolve as Magdalena leaned in for a killing bite, Fana shifted her head into the shape of a wolf's and immediately snapped back.

Her razor-sharp teeth connected with the Ophiuchan's shoulder, and the wolf instinct flowed through her. Fana tasted blood and went in for another bite, rending flesh from limb. The Lunatic struggled to remove herself from Fana's clamping jaws and crawled away like a spider fleeing a boot. No more blood flowed from her wound, and her flesh already began to repair itself as she scrambled away.

Fana flipped back over onto her feet, her yellow wolf eyes blazing and snarling at her prey. Her body transformed again, this time into the shape of a massive, ancient deer. Her antlers grew long and sharp, and she took aim at Magdalena, who stood panting by the smoldering ashes of the bonfire. Fana pawed the ground with her hooves then raced at full speed toward the Ophiuchan. Her antlers lowered, ready to skewer her with the almighty force of her charge. Magdalena crouched low to the ground, and when

Fana leaned in to pierce her, the Ophiuchan caught the antlers in her grasp and used the momentum of her advance to flip Fana over. Her hooves clawed the air as she toppled over herself and landed with a heavy force on the other side of the clearing. She groaned, and a gasp went throughout the witches who had stayed to witness the battle. Among them, Ainsley cried out, standing protectively near Edgar and eager to join the fray.

Fana grunted back, refusing the aid of others; she wouldn't endanger anyone's life. She barely had time to get to her feet before Magdalena swept in for another attack, her teeth sinking into Fana's neck. She lowed again, and blood issued forth, then thrashed her antlers and knocked her opponent aside again. The Ophiuchan flew across the clearing and collided with a tree. As Magdalena's frame briefly crumpled, Fana lay flat against the earth and let her body become absorbed by the soil.

She flowed through the life systems of the plants, calling upon their power. Positioning herself below where the Lunatic was trying to regain her footing, Fana commanded the surrounding plant life to spring forward. Soon vines and the start of a sapling sprouted from the earth. Magdalena, not expecting such an attack, quickly noticed that her feet were entirely entangled in flora. She screamed and freed her right ankle from Fana's creeping vines, but soon her left leg was consumed by the bark of the rapidly growing tree. She yowled again into the cold night air, furious and frenzied, as the bark encased her. The tree at last stopped growing, leaving only the Ophiuchan's head and left shoulder exposed. She wriggled in her prison, unable to break free. A flower on a higher branch of the newborn tree began to sprout, and then the bud grew to five feet in diameter. When the pink petals folded away, Fana, returning to the guise of an antlered human, sprang forth from the blossom and landed nimbly on the ground. She grasped her neck where it bled freely but smiled victoriously at her pinioned foe. Magdalena screamed at her, the cords her in neck bulging from the force. She continued to screech, gnash her teeth, and flail her head in pure rage and frustration.

"Silence, Lunatic," Fana commanded, extending her hand as blood dripped from her fingertips. Magdalena stared Fana down, cold fire in her eyes. Fana sensed the true depths of her viciousness just from that hateful glance. "Perhaps I should relight the bonfire right under your feet. How would that be?"

Magdalena's expression shifted from malice to shock, and her mouth fell open. Fana stepped closer, as if approaching a caged bear, but didn't let her triumphant grin fade.

"Perhaps death is too harsh...I've heard you have quite an aversion to being trapped. Tell me, Magdalena, just how many years was the earth your prison?"

As the words rolled off Fana's tongue, Magdalena looked positively electrified with fear. She remained still, her eyes protuberant as she groped for words.

"How did you learn of this?"

"That will matter not when I return you to that sorry state—"

"*No!*" She wailed, all pretense of intimidation gone. She desperately floundered to find the right words. "I'll—I'll leave. I'll leave him be. You can keep your precious surgeon. I won't come back. I swear it."

"You're lying," Fana said lightly, and the tree began to sink into the ground.

The sound the Ophiuchan made was unholy. Fana kept it sinking a moment longer. She had no real intention of actually sealing her in the ground, cruelty was not her path; she only wanted the fear to be real enough to drive her permanently out of the woods. When she grew hysterical, Fana stopped. Magdalena began to weep, though no tears fell from her eyes. In this pitiful state, she looked like a frightened, youthful girl.

"Have mercy," she begged, looking up with urgency at Fana.

"You'll leave at once. If you ever come near to my Wood again, I'll bury you so deep that the next time you see the sun it will be at the world's end," Fana rumbled.

The Ophiuchan responded with a series of spastic nods. "Yes, I promise. You'll never hear from me again," she whispered.

Fana's ire smoothed, and she bade the tree to recede and release its prisoner. She allowed herself a quiet moment of pride as Magdalena sank to the forest floor, whimpering and gripped by tremors. She peered up at Fana from the ground, looking absolutely spectral, after she was fully released and the tree disappeared into the ground.

Fana inched closer and looked down her nose at the monster. "Begone from my sight," she commanded. Her vanquished enemy peered up at her, visibly shaken. Magdalena wavered to her feet, still in a daze, and started to walk past Fana to the exit of the clearing.

She struck so quickly that Fana didn't even see her move. Fingers pierced Fana's flesh at the waist, and she was ripped open, her rib cage split in half.

The Lunatic made a noise like a boiling teakettle, and as that maniacal smile returned to her lips, she tore upward.

Cradle and Grave

Edgar could hardly breathe. Mere minutes before, Fana had been sitting near him, whispering coy words in the dark. Now she lay on the ground, gasping, as blood gushed from her ruptured chest cavity. With a shout of cruel glee, Magdalena bellowed at the witches who hid among the trees, daring them to come and fight.

I have to get over to her. There's still time—I can save her. If the internal injuries aren't too profound, a few rapid sutures... Impelled by his desire to preserve Fana's life, Edgar snatched the satchel and rushed into the clearing without the slightest fear of Magdalena.

The Ophiuchan was more than aware of him, however, and she leapt before him, cutting off his charge. Even as she drew closer, wearing her unhinged, saw-toothed smile, Edgar's only thought was to get past her and repair Fana's body before it was too late. Witches were storming the clearing now, but they were too far away to help. Magdalena bore down on him, ready to strike, when another figure charged forward.

Ainsley slid between the two of them and waved her hands in a strange gesture. As her motions grew wider, the air before her filled with a bright flame. She moved her hands around and through it, as if weaving the flame into existence, all the while muttering furiously under her breath. Magdalena stopped, her eyes fixed on the flame. All around the clearing, other witches began to weave flames in the air, and the Lunatic looked wildly around at the bursts of fire. She gave a covetous glance in Edgar's direction again, then bit down on her lip hard as Ainsley prepared to lob the flame in her direction.

Magdalena turned and ran with unearthly speed, her dark gown fluttering around her legs and her pale face streaking through the woods like a star falling from the sky. Some of the witches trailed after her, but it was clear they could never possibly catch up. The Blight of the Ophiuchans had felled the forest guardian and had escaped alive. As soon as the threat was gone, Edgar sped around Ainsley and flung himself onto his knees beside a gasping Fana.

Her focus seemed far away, as if pain were the only thing she could perceive. Her hands clawed at the dirt beneath her as blood gurgled out of her lips. Edgar quickly assessed the damage, his thoughts moving rapidly and spelling out a procedure in his mind.

This would have easily killed any human within seconds, he marveled as he reached for the satchel. Suddenly a swarm of witches gathered around Fana, all of them crying out and trying to push Edgar out of the way.

"Stop! I can help her!" he shouted.

"Get away from her, you idiot! Don't you dare touch her! We've got to get her to the spring," Ainsley barked at him. "It'll heal her—if we don't get her there soon, she'll die."

"She'll never make it. She's already lost too much blood. Let me work, and I guarantee she'll live long enough to reach the spring."

The witches around him backed away slightly but kept close.

"A-ains...ley," Fana spluttered. "If I die...b...at the Well... p-please...or I'll—"

"Don't try to speak, Miss Fana. It'll make this worse." Edgar removed his coat and unpacked his satchel of tools. "Ainsley, I need light."

The witch blinked at his command then scrawled a seal, the paper becoming brilliantly luminous. It was shocking how quickly the adrenaline had sobered him up, and he faced his patient with a collected head. His movements were practiced and deft. Edgar began to focus, and soon the noise of the angry, frightened witches was drowned out. The tools were crude, but he made the best of them, clearing areas of blood and stitching other structures with a needle. Fana's body was preternaturally resilient, but soon after Edgar began to work on her, she fell unconscious from the pain. Her heart was still beating, though—he could see it. Stitches held together gaping wounds; bones were realigned; her body cavity was resealed. Finally he drew back from her, his hands dripping with blood. After wiping them with a cloth and wrapping Fana in his coat, he plucked her up from the ground.

"Lead me to the Well. Hurry," he commanded Ainsley.

"I'm the one who'll take her there—hands off now," Ainsley growled, and reached out to take Fana from him, but Edgar clutched her tightly.

"I need to be nearby if her condition worsens. Time is precious—arguing could cost her life. Lead me there *now*," Edgar yelled, and though Ainsley bristled, she shot off into the woods. Her pace was difficult to match, but Edgar managed. He knew he had done a shamefully rough job of the surgery, but it was the only way possible in such dire circumstances. His lungs stinging and his legs aching, he followed Ainsley through the woods, not daring to slow down for a moment.

"Keep breathing, Miss Fana," he shouted down to her as he carried her along. She looked like a corpse in his arms and didn't appear to respond, so he shouted it louder. This time she moaned feebly back, and her chest rose ever so slightly.

"Keep up!" Ainsley roared.

They were nearly there. Edgar recognized this part of the woods. He knew the way. Gathering the last of his strength, he rushed past Ainsley and over the hill. The meadow looked so peaceful in the moonlight, but its silence was ripped apart as he charged across the fields of flowers.

In a skidding halt, he arrived at the edge of the Well and gently lowered Fana into the water. She sank into the Well, her ivory skin and still expression making her look like a drowned doll. Her blood soon clouded the water, and she sunk deeper toward the bottom. Edgar's heart leapt in a panic as Ainsley slammed onto her knees beside him.

"I was meant to submerge her, yes? *Yes?*" he asked as Ainsley stared at the pool, breathless and flushed. Fana's body was gone, and the Well was red with blood.

"I-I don't know."

"This will save her, won't it?" He received no response. "Ainsley!"

"*I don't know!*"

Silence fell over them as the water began to clear. The blood dissipated, leaving only the clear water of the Well. Fana had completely vanished. Edgar clutched at his chest, suppressing a sob as a wave of guilt assaulted him. *I've failed again. I've killed another person. I'm no surgeon; I'm a butcher.*

He looked over at Ainsley in horror, and she met his glance, equally shaken.

"She wanted us to bury her," Edgar whispered, his eyes locked with Ainsley's. "What will happen to her if she isn't buried?"

Ainsley swallowed. "She'll cease to be reborn if she isn't buried there, right over there, beneath that flower." She pointed across the clearing to where a wilted white lily sprouted from a mound of earth. "She'll fade from reality, and the Wood will die with her."

"No!" Edgar said hoarsely, running his fingers through his hair and fighting off a storm of anxiety that threatened to crumple him forward. "No, I never intended to harm her. I thought I was helping. I thought—"

"There's still hope." Ainsley rushed over to the flower she had pointed to moments earlier. "It's still alive. It's *her*. It's her soul. If she were gone, it would be gone too. She's still alive. She survived."

"It's…it's *her?* But it looks so weak."

"It's been that way for some time."

"Why?" he wondered aloud, given hope by the knowledge that it still remained.

Before Ainsley could answer, a bubbling came from the Well, and Edgar turned to see Fana float back up from the depths. Her body appeared to be entirely mended, with no sign that she ever was injured, but she remained unconscious. As she rose to the surface, Edgar reached in and gently lifted her from the water.

Ainsley approached and brushed the sopping hair away from Fana's face. "Give her here." She didn't wait for Edgar to surrender the unconscious form. Ainsley plucked her from his arms and carried her across the meadow. Edgar followed on instinct, not daring to believe Fana would recover. Ainsley carried her to a massive tree and ducked into a gap between the roots.

Edgar halted in surprise. Unable to stop himself, he followed. As he approached, he saw a narrow tunnel in the roots, just big enough to squeeze into. Following Ainsley, he pushed through the gap and into the darkness. The tunnel went downward and continued on for some time. Spider webs and tips of roots tickled his hair. After a long stretch, the tunnel sloped upward, and a flight of stairs carved into the ground appeared at the end. A warm light shone from the top of the stairs, and Edgar climbed them with caution. When he came to the top, he found himself inside a massive tree.

The inside had been hollowed out, and a little living space was nestled inside. The entire room was illuminated by phosphorescent mushrooms that gave off a soothing greenish glow. A sleeping area had been carved into one of the walls. The nook was carpeted in moss and flowers, and two curtains spun of spider's silk hung on either side. Ainsley pushed them aside, lowered Fana onto the bed of cushions, and wrapped a doe-fur blanket around her. Her antlers receded into her head, and she was able to lie on the pillows comfortably. Edgar glanced around at the miraculous dwelling, with its collection of rare and peculiar artifacts, bottled wines, jars of honey and pickled vegetables, and rough-hewn wooden furniture.

He stood next to Fana's bedside while Ainsley knelt. Fana seemed to have become thoroughly dry in the last few moments and was beginning to stir from her troubled sleep. At last she opened her round, gray-brown eyes and looked upon her companions.

"Ainsley...Edgar," she said hoarsely, reaching a limp hand to Ainsley's face and letting it fall back at her side. "I was almost lost..."

"That creature is gone. We chased her away—the Wood is safe," Ainsley assured her.

This information seemed to bring peace to Fana, whose face relaxed. "No one was harmed?"

"Not a scratch on any of them," Ainsley said.

With heavy lids, Fana looked toward Edgar, and a small smile spread over her lips. "If it hadn't been for you, I'd surely have perished," she said gratefully.

"If it hadn't been for me, that madwoman never would have come here in the first place." Edgar hung his head. "I endangered everyone. I—"

"Don't blame yourself for the misdeeds of others." Fana held up her hand to stop him, and Edgar didn't wish to argue, no matter how guilty he felt.

"I'll remain here through the night, Fana," Ainsley declared, but Fana shook her head.

"Go back to the village. See that everyone is well. Let them know I am safe, and protect them if danger returns. I'm placing them in your care." Exhausted, Fana shut her eyes and fell into a dreamy lull.

"But you shouldn't be alone after something so awful," Ainsley protested.

Fana hummed in vague assent. After staying silent in thought, she opened her eyes again. "Edgar may stay if he so chooses. Would that ease your mind, Ainsley?"

"*Absolutely not.* I could never leave you in the care of an outsider!" Ainsley cast an irate glance at Edgar.

This seemed to amuse Fana. "Edgar, would you be so kind?" she asked with a delicate grin, and Ainsley's face flushed with anger.

Edgar hated that he could feel how red his own face had grown, but he nodded cordially. "If that is what you wish, Miss Fana, it would be my pleasure," he said humbly, and bowed his head.

Ainsley's eyes narrowed. "That had better be the only pleasure you intend on having for the remainder of the night," she snarled quietly to him, and stood up with her fists balled.

"Please go to them," Fana instructed. Ease their worries."

Ainsley's look softened as she gazed on Fana, and then she left the abode without another word. She left a stone-heavy silence hanging between Edgar and Fana.

"Is there something I can get for you? Tea? It...it doesn't look like you have a kettle. Or a stove. Well, then how about whatever's in this jar? This looks...edible, I think. What *is* this exa—"

"Edgar, come here," Fana beckoned to him sleepily, and he knelt by her bedside. "I want to thank you for what you did for me tonight."

"There's no need for that. You should rest, Miss Fana," he protested, but Fana would hear none of it. "No, I don't want to sleep just yet. I want to grant you another wish," she watched him from where she lay. "Anything you want. If it is in my power, it shall be done."

Taken aback, Edgar hung his head. "I'm...not sure there's anything I'd wish for now, except..."

"What is it? Please don't be shy. Tell me—anything you wish shall be yours." A little more alert now, Fana stared at him as if she were testing him somehow. In times of scrutiny, Edgar always relied on being genuine, so he chose to be completely honest.

"It's...it's probably too much to ask for," he stammered. "I wouldn't want to overstep any boundaries."

Fana's face changed marginally to reveal a jaded expression. "Please. Tell me what you want," she murmured, a little sharper than before.

Edgar swallowed, wringing his hands. "Well, if I'm going to be honest, when we first met...you saw my whole life. Every moment of that. Isn't that so?"

"Yes," Fana replied slowly, her look transforming into one of confusion.

"All my fondest memories, my secrets, the dark things I've kept to myself, and my achievements. You knew me so completely in that moment. What I crave most now is time. Time to experience the things I never thought to do before. You...you've lived for centuries. I wonder...I realize this request is grossly intrusive, but I want to experience your life, as you experienced mine that day." The moment Edgar stopped speaking, he was already steeling himself against her reply. When he braved a glance in Fana's direction, she looked shocked but not angry. The coldness had gone, and her cheeks were tinged with pink.

"It *was* too much to ask," he cast his eyes aside and tried to obscure his face from view with his hand. "Please accept my deepest apologies."

"No," Fana said. "It's a fine wish. But you surprised me. No one has ever asked for such a thing from me. I shall share my memories with you, if that's truly what you want. You might think harshly of me after you've seen them, though. I'm not anything like the women in your society," she admitted, and Edgar grinned back at her.

"And that's precisely why I'm interested," he told her.

It was enough to bring a smile to Fana's face, and she laughed behind her hand. "Very well. Come lie down beside me," she asked of him, and Edgar faltered. Somehow it seemed nearly impossible to do, but his curiosity gave him strength. After a moment, he joined her behind the spider-silk veils. Edgar's heart was hammering again as Fana positioned herself close beside him and grabbed his hand. He couldn't recall ever feeling so anxious, even when he'd assisted in his first operation. Their eyes connected for a long moment, and then a rush in his head blinded him.

Fana's life didn't reveal itself to Edgar in images, the way that Elspeth's power had, instead it came in bursts of illumination. It was a sensation akin to when a friend speaks of something long forgotten, and with the mention of a word, lost memories are instantly reclaimed.

The early days of Fana's life were blurry and dim. Dull notions of thought and self-awareness in near darkness were all that she could remember of that time. She had been born for the first time just after the flower near the Well had first bloomed. She had pushed her way up from the earth as a delicate, fairylike creature. In those days the world was young, and mankind was crude, but she reveled in life. She was the forest, and as the forest grew, so did she.

Hundreds of years passed, and Fana learned from the Wood without ever speaking a word. Instincts guided her, and the animals were her friends. In those days, the Aos Sí populated the green places of the earth in great numbers, and they were drawn to the young forest. Fana learned language and magic from them, as well as how to transform her body into different guises and make plants grow.

As the years slipped past, responsibilities came to her. Humankind had grown in strength and numbers, and it fell upon her to protect the Wood from the worst of them and to share it alongside the best. At the word of the Goddess, she was to guard the race born of the one who had stolen her tears and see that they brought good to the rest of the world.

With each passing century, Fana grew more attached to the witches and their kin. Soon the Aos Sí began to leave her world for the peace of the other side, disturbed by the cruelty and destruction that humanity bred. She was left alone, only to see them when the veil was thinnest, and she ached with loneliness as she watched the lives of those she treasured bloom and die. Only a few lucky witches stood with her through the ages, and with them she shared the burden of eternity. But even they could not live forever. She experienced many deaths of her own, each time returning to the sweet, endless silence of the soil and rising in glorious rebirth as if from a deep sleep. No matter what Fana did in her flashes of life, she couldn't leave the Wood for long and was forever drawn back into that space that was both cradle and grave to her.

She had lost her life three times in battle, twice from betrayal, and once by her own hand after the loss of a beloved witch she had raised as if she were her own child. She had desperately needed the deep rest of death and the healing that only time could bring. Fire killed her another time, and her ashes were buried beneath the miraculous flower. She rose from it half a century later.

It wasn't the pain of death that made that flower wilt over the centuries; the affliction that ate at her was loneliness. Chances had come to her when a soul expressed the wish to shoulder eternity alongside her and protect the Wood in tandem, but each time the bitterness of heartbreak and sorrow shattered her hopes. One man had fooled her, greedy for the power their bond would grant. A woman, who had truly loved her, was murdered by the jealous lover she had spurned in favor of Fana. Once in the guise of a wolf, she and her mate had quarreled, and she had forgotten her strength. Another man had followed through on his promise, but after a hundred years, the weight of eternity had defeated him. He left the Wood, abandoning her, and died alone, far away from their home.

With each passing loss, the flower continued to wilt. After the death of her last mate, she stopped visiting the village. She lost interest in strangers and became wed to her loneliness. Her innate strength nourished her, and she refused to let any human words pierce her heart. Solitude became as sweet as it was bitter.

Memories of powerful emotions, of breathtaking sights, of moments of peace, and trivial things whisked by. Edgar came to know Fana as if he'd been her silent companion these many millennia, feeling everything she felt. There was too much in her head and heart, too many moments blurred by time to experience them all, but most of her miraculous life became known to him.

When the exhilarating, strange experience subsided, and he opened his eyes to face her, he wasn't the same man. The vast timeline of Fana's life made his memories seem like a brief flash in the darkness. He knew her better than he'd ever known himself, and her depth, tenderness, fury, and pain were so astonishing that he struggled not to weep. Feeling small beside her, he reached out to touch the side of her face in a worshipful gesture; words couldn't convey what he felt. Fana's doe eyes opened, and she stared back at him as if apprehensive of what opinion he might've formed. Edgar was powerless but to love her. With careful gentleness, he leaned forward and kissed her forehead.

"Thank you," was all he could manage to whisper.

Fana took his hand again, gave it a brief squeeze, then let her eyelids droop. Soon she fell into dreams, still clinging to his hand and leaning into him. Edgar wasn't far behind her.

Parting Words

When Edgar awoke, he was alone. He sat up in bed, foggy headed and disoriented. There were no windows here; it could have been any time of day. He rose from the pile of blankets and pillows and tried to stand up. As he did, a pain shot through his chest, forcing him to sit back down. He winced, grasping at the wound and hardly daring to breathe for fear it would increase the agony. He endured it, and eventually it passed.

With a staggering step, he followed the tunnel that led back out into the meadow. When he climbed up into the afternoon sunlight, he caught sight of Fana. She sat amid the sea of flowers, strumming a lap harp and singing softly. It was impossible to see any sign that she had been so grievously injured only the night before. Edgar stared at her, another type of pain coming from his chest now, one of deep longing. She was part of him now. And that part was more extensive and meaningful than any other. He yearned to be near her. To be near her was to be whole.

Hearing his footsteps, Fana looked up. With a small smile of greeting, she stowed the harp in one of her voluminous sleeves, where it disappeared, and then she stood and waded through the flowers to reach him. As she grew close, she pulled another object from her sleeve and handed it to him.

"Here," she murmured. Edgar looked down at what she had given him; it was a honeycomb. "Eat. It will restore you."

"Thank you," he said, taking a bite of it. It was overly sweet, but it tasted clean and natural. He already felt his limbs growing stronger. "I feel as if something's gone wrong with me today. This is helping."

As Fana stepped closer to him, he abruptly stopped chewing. After undoing several buttons, she peeled back one of the sides of his shirt, and the two of them fell into a startled silence. The wound had crept all over his chest and was now reaching over his shoulder and down toward his stomach. Black veins coursed through the sickly patches of gray.

"There's not much time left," Fana said simply but with deep sadness in her eyes.

Edgar's appetite completely left him, and he closed his shirt back up. He wanted to hide the abominable sight.

As his head drooped, Fana touched the side of his face. "Edgar, I must ask more of you. I'm sorry. It's a cruel request, but—"

"Anything." He looked up at her fiercely. "I'll do whatever you wish."

Fana, seemingly startled by his willingness to do her bidding, looked him over. "I'm leaving the Wood today. I can only be out of these trees for a short time, but I *must* do this. Magdalena's venture must be put to an end immediately. I'm going to purify the spots where the remaining revenants are, collect their spirits, and put this curse to an end. You deserve to spend the last days of your life in comfort and peace, but I...I need you to come with me. According to what Ainsley told me, you can safely touch them." She slid her hand down to Edgar's and grabbed it.

"Yes," he acquiesced. The possibility of pain and terror was very real, and it frightened him, but the idea of Fana facing those wraiths alone was unacceptable. The idea of leaving her at all was worse. "I'll come along."

"You truly are a good man"—she held his hand a little tighter—"despite what you may believe."

They left the meadow as if it would be forever lost to them thereafter. Fana didn't look back, but knowing her as he did now, Edgar saw the sadness behind her still expression.

The village was in an uproar when they entered it from the forest gate. Within minutes, Fana was swarmed, and she did her best to lay all worries to rest. She floated to the platform at the scene of last night's calamity. Edgar listened in a haze as she told the people of the Witches' Wood why Magdalena had attacked them and what she herself planned on doing about it. Edgar, his thoughts elsewhere, forced himself to take a few more bites of the honeycomb. A voice from the crowd brought him back into the moment.

"I'm coming with you!" Before he lifted his eyes, he knew who had spoken. Ainsley roughed her way through the crowd and to the side of the platform. "I won't let you leave here alone. Let me come, Fana, please."

"I won't be alone. Mr. Price is accompanying me. I'd prefer it if you stayed here, Ainsley. These people may need the skills of your bloodline," Fana said.

"You'll have Elspeth for that," Ainsley called out to the people nearby. "It's because of my mother's decisions that evil was brought to this place—that the revenants exist at all. I only ask for the chance to aid in amending her mistakes. Consider it my pilgrimage."

"I see," Fana mused, somewhat surprised by this claim. "Very well. Your wishes are recognized. You shall join us."

Ainsley thanked Fana with a bow then looked toward Edgar, her eyes afire with challenge.

***

It took the better part of several hours for them to get outfitted and packed for the journey. Fearing something might happen to them while they were away from the Wood, they decided to bring the sealed revenants with them and took great care to ensure they wouldn't be broken or lost. After they loaded their provisions and clothing into a horse-drawn cart, they climbed into it and rode to the edge of the village.

Edgar waited patiently as Fana and Ainsley said their good-byes. Colleen tried her best to hold back her tears, but the notion that she might never see Ainsley again appeared to have broken her. Elspeth appeared slightly pained during the whole event, and her smiles were weak. The group of them approached the cart, still clinging to one another.

"Promise me you're coming back, Ainsley," Edgar heard Colleen say.

"I've told you, woman...I can't promise that," Ainsley grumbled, obviously affected by the situation but too proud to show her feelings. Her face was screwed up in emotion, and she rubbed roughly at one of her eyes.

"Sister, dear, it's quite all right if you need to shed a few tears. No one will think less of you," Elspeth said, but Ainsley only growled back. After bidding her last parting words, she leapt up to the front of the cart, where she grabbed the reins. Edgar helped Fana up into the back of the cart then hopped off to shake hands with Elspeth and Colleen.

"Your kindness has made such a difference to me. I'm afraid this is farewell for good," he told them, a grim smile on his face. Colleen wrapped her arms around him briefly and gave his hand a squeeze—a gesture that made him stutter in embarrassment.

"I hope you fare well, Mr. Price. I'm glad to have met you," Elspeth hummed at him.

The three companions began their journey shortly thereafter, Edgar and Fana waving until their cart disappeared from view. Four quiet hours later, they were about thirty miles out of the forest and on the trail to Edinburgh. Edgar's chest had been both-ering him, and he'd spent most of the time in an agony-induced haze. Fana stared up toward the sky, immersed in thought. She had hidden her antlers and was in the guise of a human, but even so, there was something ethereal about her appearance. Ainsley sang a collection of lively tunes to pass the time, and though her voice wasn't sweet, the robust quality of it was pleasant to Edgar's ears. Long after midday had passed, Ainsley looked back at Fana and Edgar.

"Um, Fana," she called back against the wind as the cart reached the main road. "How exactly are we going to *find* these revenants?"

"I believe they should be in places meaningful to them. They want nothing more than to live again, so they'll cling to the places that make them feel the most alive. I believe that's why the three spirits chose the Wood—they felt traces of Sylvia's curse lingering in that place. Naturally, too, they were drawn to the Well, the center of the forest's power. I have a suspicion they might gravitate toward one another as well. That's why we should investigate places where Edgar has been since the curse came to him."

Ainsley turned to him. "Where were you the night before you came to the Wood?"

"I made an acquaintance in Edinburgh," Edgar replied. "A kind, clever man named Rahul—he was the one who took me to the Wood. He lived and worked at a fair that wasn't too far outside the city, if I recall."

"Could you lead us back there?" Ainsley asked.

"Yes. I'd wager we could get there by nightfall if we rode straight on," he said, and Ainsley seemed to brighten. Edgar directed her toward the All Souls' Fair until the sun sank low on the horizon.

Shortly after moonrise, the hazy lights of the fair cut through the fog. Edgar's mind focused on thoughts of warmth, shelter, and much-needed sleep. He grew restless with anticipation as Ainsley urged the horse on. However, as they approached, Edgar began to get the sense that something was amiss. They were close enough now that the carefree shouts and calliope wails of the fair should be audible in the distance. Edgar strained his ears to listen as the cart trundled on, but only silence prevailed. He thought perhaps they'd somehow taken a wrong turn somewhere when suddenly a halo of the electric lights and flames burned just over the crest of the next hilltop.

Just as Edgar was opening his mouth to alert the others that something might be wrong, they crossed over the top of the hill and it became clear that this wouldn't be necessary. They saw the danger quite clearly for themselves.

All Souls

"What on Earth…" Edgar was the first to speak of the unsettling scene, but Ainsley and Fana weren't listening. Their eyes were fixed forward, gaping and alert. The entirety of the fair was completely still. The merry-go-round did not turn. An oppressive, hollow silence pressed down upon the fairground. The few electric lights flickered eerily, as if the generator they ran on were about to fail. The trio exchanged worried glances. Ainsley brought the horse to a halt, and then they unloaded their weapons, medical tools, and magical implements in case their dreadful, unspoken prediction became a reality. After hitching the horse to a tree and setting the cart out of sight, they walked alongside the fence on foot, only able to see the striped backs of the tents and booths. It was so quiet that the faint crunching noise of their footsteps on the dirt path seemed a racket.

The true hideousness of the situation wasn't clear until they entered the arched gateway of the fair. Fana was the first to stop, and she held her arm back to prevent Ainsley and Edgar from advancing.

Hundreds of human figures stood absolutely still in the night. They were all suspended in motion, as if the world had become an enormous diorama. Each and every person's face and body parts were distorted by a grotesque illusion, as if they were part of a photograph that had been partially burned. Children stood in a line, tossing rings into a game booth, eerie smiles showing beneath a warped, blackened aberration. The rings were hanging in midair, and when Edgar cautiously drew his fingers up to touch one, he found that the image of the ring flickered in time with the electric lights, and his hand passed right through it, but met with an icy chill. Drawing back, Edgar moved his head around, trying to see how the illusion of the burned spots had been accomplished. Ainsley's own expression mirrored his abject confusion—no matter which angle the fairgoers were viewed from, the images remained exactly the same. As they wove between a couple marveling at a fire-breathing performer and a line of guests caught streaming into a theater to see a magic lantern show, Edgar's chest flared up with pain.

"A revenant is causing this, I'm certain," Fana said in a low voice. "Be ready, Ainsley. Edgar, you must find where it has taken root."

He nodded to her then gestured for them to follow. The farther they walked through the lines of games and food stalls, the more frequently the burned spots showed. Edgar was faced with the challenge of having to walk through one that was so large that it barred the way. When he passed through the frigid air, his chest and back split with pain. Ainsley and Fana had to hold him steady as he struggled to catch his breath.

The paths were lined with dancers caught in motion, frozen musicians, and a menagerie of caged animals—wild-eyed bears, giraffes, big cats, and exotic birds. No sound, smell, or touch of wind could be sensed. Edgar drew a sharp breath when he spied a familiar circus wagon, the hatch opened to reveal the interior. A man with a gaudy costume of a spangled oversize turban and azure robes lined with gold sat inside, his hands hovering around a crystal orb. With a small start, Edgar recognized Rahul's handsome, angled face, pulled into an expression of mock concentration. Half of it was blotched away by the dark, burned aberrations. Edgar's stomach flipped to observe that around the edges of the spots were patches of red light that smoldered and glowed like embers. He stood by Rahul for a while, yearning to help him but powerless. Fana and Ainsley approached from behind, drawn by his agitation.

"This is him. This is the man who helped me...Rahul," Edgar explained, incapable of taking his eyes off the unsightly blotches that distorted his face. "We need to do something. We can't leave him like this," he urged, and Fana's expression grew even grimmer.

"The only way to help him is to remove the revenant. Come, let's not tarry." Fana beckoned them all to move on. Edgar followed but kept his gaze locked on Rahul as he left him, his chest tightening with anxiety.

Soon they approached the entrance of a tent that had been badly distorted—tugged and twisted into a peculiar, unreal shape. The letters on the banners and posters that Edgar remembered as being in English now appeared to be utter gibberish. The strange, disjointed lettering had a dizzying effect if he stared at it for too long. Edgar carefully pushed aside the opening of the tent and crept inside the tunnel of cloth. Two electric lights flickered above a thin wooden arched opening that was painted with an exaggerated face of a man, making it appear as if one were entering his mouth. He followed more unintelligible text and arrows into the man's throat, where a shimmering sheet of black light waited. He halted before passing through, Fana and Ainsley on his heels. The tunnel was a vortex, begging him to step forward into its riptide of energy. Dread seized Edgar upon seeing that light, and a nauseating, icy wave flowed through him. A strange whispering echoed in his mind, and he thought he might've heard the distant sounds of crazed laughter, but the sound evaded him when he cocked his head to listen.

"I believe...I believe this is it. The revenant is through here. I can *feel* it somehow, like it's pulling me in." He turned back to his companions. "Once we go through here, I suspect we'll come to where it's rooted."

Ainsley readied her invocation paper and bottle, and then they all passed through the sheet of black light together. At once, the walls were wreathed in flames. Sound returned in a roaring burst, and the three companions were cowed by the cacophony. The heat was so sudden and intense that the three of them huddled together. Edgar and Ainsley coughed and sputtered, blanching under the otherworldly heat, but Fana hauled them forward, and they navigated the twisting corridor of burning cloth. It seemed as if they traveled through the painted mouth over and over—trapped in a loop with no signs of escape. Hurtling through another gateway, they abruptly stood back outside. All came to a disoriented halt and gaped around.

The fair had changed drastically. Electric lights were hung on strings all around them and flickered rapidly in the night. The stars above shifted and turned as if the three of them were inside a bewitched planetarium. The fairgoers, too, had transformed. They were moving and alive now but horribly distorted. Some had warped faces or misaligned bodies, while others were outright monstrous. There were beings made of three human arms, moving along and dancing, one clutched a stick of rock candy, although it possessed no discernable mouth to eat it with. A torso and legs, with two more legs atop its shoulders, trundled by. Other creatures were so malformed they looked to be a cluster of bones and flesh haphazardly smashed together. They all went about joyfully, screaming and cackling, playing games, eating, dancing, and celebrating together. Edgar's mind raced to try to figure out how these cursed beings with such twisted anatomies could possibly be animated, where their internal organs rested and how they functioned. The odor of oily smoke and badly burned food choked the air. At the far end of the fairground, Edgar saw a huge theater that beamed with electric lights of all colors. A lurid, grating sound of off-key music chugged on maniacally within its doors.

Sensing the presence of the revenant within, he bade the others to follow him to the theater. As the three of them started to cross the courtyard, the malformed fairgoers rushed toward them. Edgar and his companions cried out and attempted to get away, but they were soon overtaken. Two women grabbed at Edgar, one neckless, with her head melting into her collarbone and shoulder; the other with a grotesque, smiling visage painted directly onto a smooth, featureless face. Others swarmed them, pulling Fana and Ainsley away from Edgar as they desperately called to each other for help.

The creatures seemed intent on forcing them into their frenetic dance and toward stalls filled with strange, impossible games and waxy-looking food. Edgar struggled with his two captors, but their hands kept grabbing and tugging at him. Soon he was surrounded by more of the female monsters, all of them wrenching him toward the dance and obstructing his movement. A feeling of utmost revulsion at being touched at all—much less by these groping, clawing monstrosities—sent Edgar to a level of psychic agony he'd never before experienced.

Ainsley, whose hands were pinned behind her by a huge, headless, lumbering creature, called out an incantation that created a blinding flash of light. It didn't deter the creatures at all, however, and they merely dragged her onward. Through his streaming eyes, Edgar witnessed a look of complete helplessness fall over Ainsley's face as another fairgoer, this one looking as though it had been partially crushed in a horrible accident, took hold of her leg and yanked at it over and over. On the ground, a torso with two arms, a bald head, a stitched mouth, and white eyes devoid of irises lurched toward her, grabbing her other foot and climbing up her leg. Ainsley let loose a scream that revealed she was as close to the edge of insanity as Edgar was, and tried to kick the abomination away with all her might. Still, it held fast.

Edgar shut his eyes, trying to focus on simply drawing breath and blocking out the sensations. However, he couldn't bear to keep them closed as the strangely soft touch of a hand ran down his face. He opened them to the face of a small girl with dead eyes and a slack smile. She licked at a seven-fingered hand with her gray tongue, then reached up and slid her filthy palm across his cheek. At the touch of the vile creature's saliva moistened fingers, Edgar felt himself losing his tenuous grip on consciousness. Fortunately, the sound of Fana's high-pitched scream from across the courtyard was enough to tear him from his tortured state to look for her.

Fana's head was held in the grasp of a ten-foot-tall, white-fleshed monster with straggly, dingy hair. Its long, bony hands grasped the sides of her face, threatening to twist her neck at any moment. At her feet was a hulking creature with four human legs and a body and face that resembled an anglerfish, complete with spiny teeth and milky eyes. Around her middle she was held by something with skin like liquid tar and hands that looked like a slimy network of pulsing red veins. Together, the viscous creature and the tall one lifted Fana into the air, and Edgar's heart felt as if it might stop. It would surely break her neck; he had to help her.

Edgar fought to get free with a renewed burst of raw strength as Fana squirmed in the creature's grasp, the anglerfish beast opening its jaws wider and wider at her feet. Edgar felt himself breaking free, savagely beating away the grasping female creatures. His surge of violence, however, only made them tear at him more painfully. Edgar nearly freed himself as the anglerfish lowered Fana into its shouting mouth. He dragged his captors along in her direction, but before he could get halfway to her, the abomination had closed its mouth around her, drowning her voice out entirely. Numbly, he heard Ainsley shrieking Fana's name from the other side of the courtyard. Above, the stars whizzed and spun, and Edgar fought the urge to be sick.

Abruptly, a bulging in the anglerfish's side could be seen. Antlers ripped through its flesh, followed by the snapping and gnawing jaws of a wolf. Fana burst through its body, showering the ground with blood as she emerged snarling. The horned wolf charged forth, goring the slimy creature with one brutal swing of her head. A surge of thick black fluid gurgled out of its torn body, and Fana shot toward the tall creature, felling it with a powerful, rearing swipe of her front paws.

She threw back her head and howled in rage, then ripped through the masses of twisted forms on her way to help Ainsley. In Edgar's momentary stunned relief and awe, he had forgotten the creatures around him. Although they had grown still while Fana had made her kills, they now gripped his limbs with a renewed strength. The sudden return of pain made him yell out, and after a few seconds he realized they were all tugging in different directions. The sickening certainty that he was going to be ripped apart struck him as he saw the powerful beast that was Fana slash at the creatures that held Ainsley. They lay in ribbons on the ground in a matter of seconds. Ainsley staggered away, clutching at her chest with eyes unfocused and panicked. Edgar tried to call out to Fana, but the pain was suffocating him.

Just as black was swirling into his eyes, the sound of heavy paws in the dust crashed forward, and a pair of jaws tore the smooth-faced monster's head from its body. Edgar's eyes flooded with spots of light as the creatures loosened their grips in their attempts to scramble away. Fana's claws whistled above him, catching two more beasts. A burst of flame in the corner of his eyes showed that Ainsley had rejoined the fray and was staving off the creatures with her magic. Edgar was thrown to the ground as they fled, but Fana continued to lash out with her claws, growling and wild-eyed with bloodlust. Snarling and spitting, she turned on Edgar. Ainsley hurtled forward, shouting, "Fana, no! Come back to us—that's Edgar!"

Fana's murderous thrashing ceased and her lupine pupils contracted, then focused on Edgar's prostrate form. Ainsley lowered her invocation paper when she saw Fana grow still. The creatures had given up the fight and were scuttling away to safety. Edgar watched Fana's fur transform smoothly into cloth robes, and soon her human shape was nearing him.

"I'm sorry, I lost myself for a moment," she said in a dizzy breath. as she knelt beside him. Her hand on his chest drew Edgar back into reality, and he was able to get a hold over himself. Ainsley joined them, shivering and casting nervous glances toward the spaces between the booths where creatures hung back in the shadows.

"Were either of you injured?" Edgar stammered, scanning both of their forms for wounds or broken bones. Both Fana and Ainsley shook their heads.

For a moment, the three of them could only take slow breaths and hold weakly to one another. They drew inward, their heads together, taking deep solace in each other's presences. "We shouldn't linger," Fana whispered at last. "The longer we're in here, the worse it will become."

In silent agreement Edgar and his companions rose to their feet and Fana led them forward, glaring threateningly at the fairgoers who watched them pass. Edgar, Fana, and Ainsley kicked past the painted doors and into the hall of the theater. The entranceway was plastered with posters depicting fire, images of people burning, and blackened, immolated skeletons in front of a gasping crowd. Inside the lobby, the discordant, jarring music blared even more loudly in their ears, and they crept forward, not willing to draw apart just yet. Edgar kept his eyes forward as they advanced through the second set of doors into a massive circular room.

In the center was a carousel with painted horses and gleaming lights of white, yellow, and red. It spun and churned merrily to the manic sounds of an unhinged calliope. A second, tiny carousel sat perched atop the highest point of the large carousel's peaked roof, this one made of delicate crystals and spinning in the opposite direction. An orange glow burned within the crystals. As soon as Edgar saw the ghostly light behind it, he recognized that tiny carousel for what it was.

"There! That's where the revenant's hiding!" Edgar pointed to the crystal fixture. He would have moved forward at once if something on one of the horses hadn't caught his eye. A man sat on one the wooden steeds. He was fast asleep, his head slumped forward against the metal pole that fixed it to the top, but Edgar recognized him immediately. It was a face he could never forget: Jacob Hare.

"It's him...that's the man who attacked me on the train," Edgar declared, shocked. Fana and Ainsley's attention drew sharply to their bewildered companion. "He's Magdalena's partner—Hare." Fana's eyes narrowed and she looked over Hare with an analyzing stare.

"If he's in league with the Lunatic, perhaps we'd better get him down from there and restrain him somehow," Fana schemed aloud.

"This feels like a trap." Ainsley's gaze shifted to the limp form of the man who had doomed Edgar.

"I think Fana's right, though. He'll be dangerous if he wakes up. We should take this opportunity to apprehend him...but we should proceed with the utmost caution." Edgar looked to Fana and she nodded.

"I'll go. If it's a trap, I can overpower him—of that I'm certain," Fana stated with confidence and Edgar and Ainsley nodded their hesitant approval.

Fana leapt onto the spinning platform and approached him on wobbly legs. She was only a few feet away when she came to a stop, her eyes focused on an animal near her.

"Well, how...how charming," she said dreamily as she stroked the neck of a wooden deer. "It looks...just like I do." She let out an uncharacteristically girlish giggle.

"Miss Fana?" Edgar called to her, confused, but she seemed enthralled with the wooden deer.

When the stag descended, Fana swung a leg over its back and climbed onto the dipping-and-rising seat. She laughed in delight, a soft and gentle sound, then clung to the pole, a smile breezing over her face before she laid her head against the metal. Her long lashes drooped, and then she fell into a drowsy state, completely ignoring the cries of Ainsley and Edgar.

Ainsley rushed forward and attempted to climb onto the platform.

Edgar stopped her. "Think about what you're doing," he warned.

Ainsley seemed to heed him, then looked back at Fana. "Aye, you're right—I'll use a spell," she suggested, and readied a strip of invocation paper. Before she could prick her finger with her ring, her hands dropped, and her stare became fixed on the spinning animals.

"Ainsley, focus." Edgar touched her shoulder, but her eyes were already glazing over.

"It's—it's just so damn…" she murmured, then drifted forward.

Edgar tried to stop her, but he was weak from pain, and Ainsley was determined. She leapt up on the platform toward a wooden tiger, threw her hands around its neck, and laid her head between its ears. Edgar rushed after her and was trying to pull her off it when a heaviness came over his eyes. His balance wavered, and a feeling of rosy well-being washed through him.

The lights and mirrors flashed brighter in his eyes, and his chest felt as if something tiny were hopping inside it. A hazy smile came to his lips, and he heard himself laugh, drowsy and satisfied, amid the mad sounds of the calliope.

Ainsley and Fana look to be in good health. This is a perfectly lovely place to relax for a moment… Things needn't be rushed. We've all the time in the world.

Edgar stumbled about, feeling light and carefree, when his gaze happened upon a rooster among the other animals. It made him break into little chuckles to see such a funny animal among a collection of mighty beasts, and he found himself drawn to it. The longer he looked at it, the more humorous it seemed, and soon tears streaked down his face. Edgar was on top of it in moments, his heart fluttering at the whirling sensation. He felt simply blissful, and it wasn't long before his eyelids shut comfortably, and he was swallowed in the euphoria.

Time lost its meaning. Had he been here ages or simply a few seconds? Edgar couldn't tell. Colors and lights swirled past behind his eyelids as the haunting music streamed through him.

How did I come to be in this place?

"It doesn't matter now," a mild, male voice answered his thoughts. The words dragged a bit, but the sound was pleasant, as if someone were murmuring to him while he was drowsing off.

"I see…quite right." Edgar sighed, the turning and bobbing delighting him further. "I should like to stay a little while longer, in that case."

"Stay forever."

"Well, thank you, good fellow. Perhaps I shall take you up on that. I haven't felt this wonderful since—since I was…" A sharp pain split through him, from his chest to his spine, and a brief flood of despair and horror disrupted his sense of calm.

Edgar opened his eyes blearily. A man he didn't recognize stood beside him, smiling.

"Hush now," the stranger soothed him. "Forget all about that. Don't turn from paradise—embrace it. There's nothing but pain out there."

"I s-see…I…" Edgar muttered, but when the man touched his shoulder, the white-hot pain lit up inside him again. Wide-eyed, Edgar reeled backward, catching a glimpse in the mirror of a pale boy wearing a crown. Edgar leapt off the rooster, trying to escape the ghastly child, but when he turned, there was no sign of him.

"Get back on. Enjoy the ride," the man urged Edgar before he could even collect his thoughts. Lucidity was returning, and with it came alarm. He scrambled back from the lanky, scruffy man, and in one loping movement, he sprang off the spinning platform.

"Stay back," Edgar shouted at the man, whom he now guessed to be the revenant's spectral manifestation. With a flash of mirror light, the revenant stood before him on the ground.

"Why? Why would you want to live in the outside world? I've created one that's much, much better. Stay here. Forget all about the cruel things that happened out there," the revenant pleaded.

"I'm going to fix it all," Edgar assured him. "Don't worry. Just let us go, and we'll put you back to rest. There's nothing left for you here, and the peace you'll find will be much deeper than anything you'll find here.

The man's face darkened. "We're all going to stay right here," he replied, his friendly tone had turned to a warning murmur.

With a great creaking noise, the beasts on the carousel thrashed about, shaking their shackles loose and tearing free of their poles. Ainsley, Hare, and Fana were hurled off the backs of the creatures they rode, landing in three separate heaps, still unconscious. The beasts, now appearing as flesh, fur, and bone, prowled toward Edgar.

Clamping jaws, stomping hooves, swiping claws, and drilling beaks assaulted him at once. In less than a minute, Edgar was tattered and bloody. An alligator snapped at his leg; the roar of a leopard boomed in his ear; a bull charged by, horns lowered and gleaming. It was all Edgar could do to stay on his feet. As a black bear swiped a fearsome paw at him, nearly taking his head off, one of the animals in the corner caught his attention. A Pegasus stomped and champed near the wall of the chamber that housed the carousel, and Edgar was seized with a manic plan that he immediately reasoned was his only viable option.

He rushed forward, winding behind it and lodging his foot in the saddle. The beast flailed about and beat its wings, but Edgar held firm to the saddle and eventually yanked his way upward. As he clung to the saddle with all the strength his strained arms could muster, the bottom of his stomach dropped out when the winged horse launched into the air, just as he hoped it would, trying to throw him. The farther up it went, the more violent its movements became, until it was high above the carousel. Edgar had to act now or risk falling to his death.

When he leapt, his entire body seized with fear, but his aim was true. He landed with a thud upon the top of the roof of the carousel and rolled over onto his back, groaning. The apparatus spun twice as fast now, and he had to lay flat to avoid being thrown off.

Edgar heaved one arm in front of the other and dragged himself forward, all the while the spinning scrambled his innards. His mind felt as if it were being pulled out of his skull by the sheer gravitational force, and his shaking hands betrayed him— he let go for a split second and launched backward. Yelping, he latched on, eyes watering.

One hand. Then the other. Each inch felt as if he were dragging an anchor behind him, but he strained forward, focusing on each individual, impossible movement. He could see the shimmering light whirling in the crystal. He lurched forward again, letting out an almighty roar of frustration. It teased him from two arm lengths away.

With a rush of wind, the Pegasus dove at him again, and Edgar felt the tip of its hooves just graze his back in a ripping burst of pain.

I can't make it…

He shut his eyes, feeling the blast of air as the winged beast plunged toward him again. It connected with the canvas top seven feet beside him, tearing a hole clean through it. As the whinnying creature blasted back and prepared to perform another lethal dive, Edgar threw his arm forward and yanked upward with all his remaining strength. Sweating and extending his arm as far as it could go, his quaking fingers touched the edge of the crystal. The force of its spinning smashed into them and his hand ricocheted back. Agony shot fissures through his finger bones—a broken window, a shattered pane of red-and-white stained glass—but Edgar held fast. Drawing in a huge breath and releasing it in a bellow, Edgar pulled his whole body forward. He threw his arms around the madly spinning crystal carousel statue and strained to rip it out. Hope fueled him; if he could just pry it loose, it might make the nightmare end. When the gleaming fixture began to crack and come free at last, he tossed it over the side of the carousel with a straining heave.

A tinkling of broken glass informed Edgar that the infernal object had been destroyed upon impact. At once, the hideous spinning slowed. In a heart-rending hush, all the snarls and roaring below fell into sudden silence. In the next instant, all that could be heard was a clattering of heavy wooden bodies on stone. Consumed by tremors, Edgar slid down the top, his head still spinning. As he tried to climb over the railing and grasp a pole that would help him get down, his dizziness made him slip.

He landed hard on his feet and crumpled to his knees, cringing in pain. The wild animals had frozen back into their wooden shapes and lay fallen around the room. Only a few feet away, a tiny orange flame pulsed above the shattered remains of the crystal carousel. Edgar forced himself to stand back up then limped over to where Ainsley lay.

"Wake up!" he cried, shaking her violently. "You need to seal it! *Wake up!*"

No matter how much he tried to rouse her, she wouldn't stir. The orange flame grew higher still, the sound of raging wind emanating from it. Panicked, Edgar fished a bottle out of Ainsley's rucksack and hobbled over to where the spirit fire was growing.

He was just a few feet away when the flame shot all the way toward the ceiling. Edgar cringed from the heat and squinted as visions formed inside the wall of fire. It was the entire fair, all jumbled together and weirdly warped, flaming and horrendous.

The acrid smell of smoke assaulted him, and the dying whine of the calliope flared up. In the center of the flame, images of mangled horses, colored lights, and distorted fairgoers surrounded the spirit of the lanky man, who stood unstable and wreathed in fire. It was at once a kaleidoscope of suffering and forced merriment, of the final cries of badly kept beasts and of laughs of mockery, and of exaggerated, painted grins and candied apples fallen to the dirt.

"You had to spoil everything, didn't you? You had to ruin it," the revenant yelled over the maddening sounds. Edgar struggled to get closer, his hand shielding his eyes. "It was perfect before you came in—before those two murderers came in—and destroyed everything. It was paradise; I was whole back then. It was a perfect world."

"You aren't remembering it properly!" Edgar called into the conflagration, feeling a strange, surging empathy with the tortured spirit. Something about his timbre and words drilled into Edgar's core and resonated there. "That world was just as flawed before. There's no such thing as paradise."

The flames subsided somewhat, and the man's form became clearer. His eyes looked hollow, and his mouth was slack.

"No paradise? Nowhere at all?"

"No," Edgar replied. "There's cruelty everywhere. And it can happen to anyone…for no reason at all."

"If that's the way it is…if that's how it is…" The revenant shuddered, and the flames died down to a soft halo around his body. The music had all but faded. "Then I don't want it at all. It's not worth it. It's all for nothing." The spirit wheezed as he began to shrink. The flame sank to Edgar's knee, now so small that it could have fit in a teacup. Edgar knelt beside it and caught it inside the bottle. He scooped it up, and just as he placed the cork over it, the carousel's lights flickered, and then the entire building flickered. Finally the scene disappeared altogether, like smoke melting into invisibility.

Edgar, Ainsley, and Fana were lying at the edge of the fairground beside a line of crates. In the distance people streamed by, laughing gaily and carrying on. They had spontaneously unfrozen and seemed oblivious that anything had been wrong at all. Edgar glanced at the fluttering, bottled flame in his palm. Looking into it made him feel an insurmountable despair, though he couldn't exactly find a particular reason why this was so.

Suddenly an arm wrapped around his neck, and the bottle rolled from his hands. Edgar cried out, his eyes rolling back to catch a blurred glimpse of Hare's maniacal snarl. Though exhaustion racked his body, the adrenaline from his encounter with the animals still coursed through him. He reacted quickly, throwing Hare backward to the ground. The two grappled in the dust, Edgar's hands seeking Hare's throat.

"It's mine! Just let me have it. You're dead anyway!" Hare grunted at him, and an inferno of anger erupted in Edgar's chest. It was unlike any rage he'd ever experienced. In that moment, he understood what hate meant—never before had he wanted to utterly destroy a person so much as then. The deep resentment Edgar still harbored for his father was innocuous compared to what he felt for Hare at that instant. Emotion burst forth from him in the form of a ferocious scream.

Edgar lifted Hare from the ground and charged forward with him until he slammed against the crates. Hare toppled over them, and Edgar sprang after him, hidden from view behind the wall of supplies. As Hare sank downward, his face to the ground, Edgar leapt on top of him. With a fury that burned endlessly and uncontrollably; he grabbed Hare by the back of the head and slammed his skull onto the hard-packed dirt until blood mixed with dust.

"*You bastard! You filthy piece of degenerate waste!*" Edgar shouted as he rhythmically broke the fiend's skull. When Hare lay still on the ground, drawing in a slow guttural breath through a smashed jaw and nose, Edgar groped for something—anything—that he could use to further harm him. His hands found the satchel of medical supplies he wore at his side, and he reached with shaking hands and withdrew a surgery knife. With a snarl, he plunged it into Hare's back, right where his heart should have been.

"You leapt from the train and broke your neck. You shouldn't be alive...you shouldn't be alive," Edgar heaved, sweat pouring from his forehead. After pulling the knife from Hare's back, he rolled the man over. Hare was laughing, blood trickling from his wide-open forehead, over his crumpled face, and into his mouth.

"It must be a...ruddy...miracle..." Hare spluttered, flecks of blood and spittle flying from his bone-shredded lips as he did. Edgar bared his teeth and shouted again, pushing the blade to Hare's throat. He gave out a wheezing laugh again, as if he found Edgar's suffering and fury humorous and feeble.

"You mock me. You mock a man whom you've doomed to be utterly destroyed...utterly defiled," Edgar hissed at him, his voice strained and hoarse. "You took my life from me. You took everything. You made me—my flesh, my soul—into a *product* for your witch, and now you lie there and you laugh."

This only succeeded in making Hare laugh more boisterously. Edgar's blood boiled within his veins as tears stung his eyes.

"Of all the self-important little shits I've met...do you really think you're the only person in the world who's ever been hurt?" Hare gurgled up at him through a malicious smile.

The very last of Edgar's restraint snapped. Bellowing with wrath, he hacked away at Hare's throat. All surgical precision was abandoned, yet his knowledge informed him in exacting, cold detail of where and how to cut. Muscles, tendons, cartilage, and bone were ripped apart by hands that had been trained for much more benevolent purposes. With savage gratification, Edgar grasped Hare by the top of his gray hair and tore his head loose from his body, the man's mouth caught halfway between a snarl and a smile.

He held up the dripping, severed head—his ghastly prize—and stared into Hare's eyes. They still moved about; they still could see. Just as he was growing entranced with what he had done, footfalls behind him interrupted his visceral satisfaction.

Fana stood watching him, the bottle in her hands, her face carefully blank.

Sunken

In the black expanse of midnight, Magdalena spied a distant pond. Its dark waters were glossed with moonlight, and the twinkling caught her eye from where she walked on the roadway. She stopped as soon as she found it, a dull, tired relief sweeping through her. She stalked off the path and through the trees that lined it, stepping up to the bank and looking inward. An icy film had begun to form over the surface of the pond.

Magdalena didn't hesitate before plunging into the pool. The thin sheet of ice cracked apart, and she sank, far deeper than she imagined it could go. Her skirts billowed out around her, and she opened her eyes to the stinging temperature of the pond. Being completely submerged helped create the connection between her and the Cold Voice. It usually came to her in times when she was cut off from the rest of the world, deprived from stimulation. That was how it had first come to her, when she was buried deep within the earth, unable to move or breathe. Since then, that was how she continued to find it.

Willing it to speak, she shut her eyes again and let her body float. She felt no misgivings this time—she knew it was going to support her. The sting of cold became numbness, and the sounds faded farther away. From out of the eerie tranquility of drowning without the threat of death, the voice split through her head. It sounded to her like roaring wind, cracking stone, and the rumble of a quake. It rose to meet her this time, eager to communicate.

The nymph still lives.

The voice was silent for a moment as if it sensed Magdalena's frustration and embarrassment at having failed at her task.

They have fled the Wood. They have your chattel and your associate. Another revenant already has been seized.

Rage thundered through Magdalena's chest, and her lips pulled back. She had a strong distaste for failure; it wasn't a condition she'd ever grown accustomed to. She allowed an inquisitive feeling to come to the forefront of her mind, appealing to the Cold Voice for advice.

Find them.

Images of the fair she'd sent Hare to streamed through her mind, flowing into her from the Cold Voice. So he was still there. Magdalena resolved to do as it said, communicating her intent to the Voice, and prepared to break the connection, but a feeling of dread betrayed a thought she was trying to suppress.

The Cold Voice rang in her head one final time. *There may yet be a way to achieve your goal, even if you fail to procure the seventh revenant. I will show you if it comes to that. For now, find them.*

With the feeling of being released from a great pressure, she felt the Cold Voice leave. Magdalena's eyes snapped open, and she kicked upward toward the surface. After she crawled out of the water, it took a moment for her to expel the water from her lungs. When her airway was clear once again, she sat in the ice-beaded grass, her breath rising in clouds toward the patches of stars. The first snow of the season started shortly after, fluttering in delicate flakes that caught on Magdalena's eyelashes and in her wild dark hair. As she sat waiting for a light to come down the lonely road, she tried to remember what the true pain of cold was like when she was human. Though hours passed before her reveries were broken when an unlucky carriage approached, she was still unable to recall it.

Warden

Edgar regarded the three uneasy people crowding around the bound man. Inside the cramped space of Rahul's carnival wagon, it was hard to move and breathe, but all eyes were focused on Hare. The criminal was whole again, his body and head rejoined. Theories as to how this miracle had been scientifically accomplished argued loudly in Edgar's mind, and he could hardly focus for the cacophony they made. Ainsley voiced her opinion that they should keep Hare in two parts lest he try to escape, but eventually the group overruled her—they needed to be able to speak to him. For a while after they'd put him back together, he'd put up a struggle. However, he no longer fought against the cords around him or the gag in his mouth.

Edgar's chest heaved as Hare stared up at him with malice. It wasn't long ago that he had stood bound and powerless at Hare's hand. Now that the situations were reversed, he certainly reveled in the victory, though he couldn't ignore the revolting fact that his clothes were soaked in Hare's blood.

Rahul, who kept to the back, looked the most uncomfortable out of them all. He had nearly run away when they had come asking for help with a still-blinking, severed head in hand, but after a hurried explanation and a fair amount of begging, he had reluctantly agreed to let them keep their prisoner secret in his wagon for the time being.

Fana was the first to break the tension. She floated forward, her nose high and her features cold, and knelt beside Hare. His breathing grew ragged as she lifted her hands and undid the gag around his mouth. "Be still," she told him as he gasped for air and leaned back from her. "I only mean to question you at this time. Will you comply?"

"What do you intend to do with me?" he said, throwing a question back at her.

Fana blinked patiently. "That all depends, Jacob. Are you not aware that your actions are unforgiveable? Working with Magdalena, dooming other innocent victims... Do you wish to atone for what you've done?"

"Not a bit. I'd let all of you *and* the bloody world burn if I had the chance," he growled back, and Fana's eyebrows rose.

"How dare you speak that way to—" Ainsley snarled, but Fana held her hand up to silence her.

"What were you doing there in the revenant's hiding spot?"

"Same as you," he grumbled in a defeated sort of way, as if his thin loyalty to Magdalena had been trumped by his own exhaustion and distaste for the whole affair. "Trying to bottle the thing up and take it away from here."

"And what did you want with it?"

"I want nothing to do with the devils. It's Mag who's after them," he spat. "I was the one who paid her to detach them from me. I only wanted to be free of them."

"Ah, yes, buying your freedom by dooming others. Sounds familiar somehow," Edgar hissed, and Fana again looked backward at him with a stern glance. Hare didn't look toward Edgar, but his face seemed to harden.

"And where do they come into Magdalena's designs? Why does she crave them so?" Fana questioned.

Hare hesitated for a moment. He paused, looking as if he were weighing the consequences of answering honestly. "Revenge," he finally croaked out, his lips trembling in rage. "She's been after it for centuries, or God knows how much longer. The others like her—the ones who buried her after she rebelled—she's got them locked up in this...this cellar of hers. Pits in the ground, and they're down there, screaming day and night from the things she does to them. You've never imagined such cruelty—she utterly destroys them, body and mind. But it's never enough for her. She wants them to suffer constantly, without rest. The way she suffered. She wanted seven revenants...one for each of them, so they never would have a moment of peace again."

Hare spilled the information as if disgorging a sickness from inside him, and the weight of understanding passed over the four listeners. Rahul looked shaken—though he'd claimed to have prior knowledge of the secret, arcane network that passed silently through his world, Edgar guessed he had a dearth of face-to-face contact with it.

"I begged her to take the revenants away, the way my father had done. He couldn't bear the agony either, so he passed them on to me. Left me to shoulder his burden while he escaped to death. And I've suffered for more than sixty years. I'm tired. I only want to die. That's all I want." He shuddered, hanging his head so his face was obscured.

Ainsley tensed up after Hare fell silent. "This—this is what my mother did. This is why she was sent away, isn't it, Fana?" Her voice trembled. She looked ashamed, a hand covering her lips as if she regretted every word she'd ever shouted defending her mother's actions. Fana looked her way with sympathy.

Hare's gaze rose to meet Ainsley's, fire burning in his eyes. "Well, how's that for a bleeding coincidence?" he snarled. "Your mother was the witch who cast the curse? And did she ever regret it? Did she? Or does seeing me this way make you feel like a crowd cheering at an execution? Are you here to make sure her good work doesn't go to waste?"

"I haven't seen her since I was an infant," was all Ainsley could say. It was clear something had changed inside her, but she hadn't had time to digest it yet. This seemed to quiet Hare's rage for the moment.

"If death is what you want, then I shall oblige you," Fana sounded almost disappointed, and Hare looked up at her with wild eyes.

"You don't get it, do you? If I fail Mag—if I don't give her the payment we agreed on, she won't let me die. She'll keep me down there with the others, and I'll be torn apart. She'll make it so I can never die—I know she will. That's why I have to get them. I *have* to give her what she wants. Unless…" Hare looked at Edgar, who could feel the blood draining from his already-white face, turning it even paler. "There's nothing you can do to save yourself, boy. It'll eat you up in a few days and take your soul with it. But if you die before…if you kill yourself before it consumes you, I'll be free of the curse. The spirit will have fully detached; your soul will be saved; and I'll be able to die. You're dead anyway—let me be free of her in the process. We can both do it—we can die tonight." He was positively manic with exhilaration by the time he stopped raving.

Edgar's blood ran cold at the sight of him. Even so, he said, "My soul can be saved?"

"Yes, yes! I've seen it—we kept a man prisoner, waiting for the revenant to consume him, but we didn't watch him closely enough. He killed himself—went mad from terror and ended it all. Bit his tongue off. The revenant never manifested; it couldn't get enough strength. Please. Please…I beg you," Hare groveled. "I can't go to her…I just can't. You don't know what she's capable of."

"There's another way for us to save you from her and free the revenants as well," Fana said abruptly before Edgar could even consider Hare's words. "Don't you realize they suffer even more than you do, Jacob? They're trapped in this world, thirsting for life, devouring all they can get, with no hope of ever returning to it."

Hare turned his moistened eyes to her. "There's another way…?"

"We kill Magdalena. We release her prisoners, purify the revenants, and give you the fate you desire and deserve," Fana said solemnly.

Hare gaped at her. "That's not possible. She can't be killed."

"Of course she can. Nothing is truly immortal, not even the Goddess herself," Fana replied. "Ophiuchans perish under flame. It takes hours, sometimes even days, but eventually it destroys them."

Hare's eyes darkened at this statement, and he fell into a contemplative silence. "She has to die then. She's never done a good thing for this world. I'll help you if you agree to protect me."

Fana looked at him skeptically. "What could you possibly offer us?"

"I know where they are—the last two revenants. She showed me. I can take you to them," he told her in a hurried voice, and Fana's silence indicated that she was considering his offer.

"Very well, but you'll still be treated as our captive. If by the end of this disaster you've helped us sufficiently, I'll reward you a quick death," Fana finally said with cold sincerity.

Hare seemed to see the real prowess behind her beguiling exterior for the first time and gave a shallow nod to show that he understood.

"Then we should get going immediately," Ainsley piped up, all fire and smoke once again. "Magdalena will be after them too, and we've got to get there before her. And Edgar's time is running out."

"That's an excellent idea! You should leave at once!" Rahul suggested from the back of the wagon, sounding overeager.

"Look at the state I'm in," Edgar rebutted, gesturing to himself. He was covered in various wounds from his clash with the revenant and was drenched in Hare's blood. "I can't go on. I need a while to rest."

Ainsley's brow pinched, and Rahul deflated. Everyone could see there was no other suitable option. "All right, one day. But we leave all the earlier the next morning," she bargained. Edgar acquiesced with an exhausted nod.

"So, ah... you're just inviting yourselves to stay *here*? To keep *him* in *here*?" Rahul asked nervously.

"We can keep him in our cart if it will ease your mind," Fana offered. "I'll stay and watch him there. I don't require sleep."

"I, however, would prefer a bed," Ainsley said without any qualms about imposing on the already overgenerous Rahul. He softened at the notion and gave a withered grin.

"Well, for you I shall have to make an exception. I can't turn away a lady as lovely as you, my dear," he said smoothly, and Ainsley looked as if she were fighting the urge to glare at him. "Mr. Price can sleep here as well, if he so desires. I'll stay with some associates tonight."

"Thank you again, dear man," Edgar told him, placing a hand on his shoulder.

Rahul shrugged and offered his careless grin. "It's nothing, but do try not to touch anything if you can help it, and forgive me if I keep my distance. I've no interest in getting involved with the reality of dark magic and curses. I'll stick to illusions, if you don't mind."

He waved to them and was off. Soon after, Fana bade Edgar and Ainsley good night before she took her leave with Hare in tow. After he left the cart briefly to change into a fresh pair of clothes, a fleeting pang of worry came over Edgar as he thought of the two leaving together, but it was quickly smothered by the reality that if anyone on the earth could protect herself, it was Fana.

Still, once Edgar and Ainsley settled into their respective corners of the wagon and blew out the lamps, he found himself dwelling on the woman of the woods. The restlessness he felt wasn't so much anxiety regarding Fana's safety as it was a longing for her presence. The memory of her lying beside him the night before was almost excruciating as Edgar finally dropped into a deep, restorative sleep.

***

Though his mind was refreshed upon waking, his body seemed to have worsened. True soreness had sunken in while he slept, and the throbbing of his chest wound was impossible to ignore. Edgar sat up, breathing through his teeth and grimacing. With shivering fingers he pried open the buttons on his shirt to examine the wound. It had spread across the expanse of his chest and was creeping over his stomach. The edges were the same sickening gray-purple of decayed flesh, while the center was black and oozing with a thick, dark substance that smelled like blood but looked like watery tar. Breathing through the pain, Edgar cleaned the wound with his handkerchief. All the while, he thought longingly of hot water and soap and how unlikely he was to find them anywhere nearby.

It's coming on faster than Fana expected. There won't be enough time...I need more time, he thought, as he stumbled over to the little window and stared out. He felt a fluttering pressure inside his chest, as if the revenant were quickening there like a fetus in a womb. *By tomorrow I could be gone.*

Edgar sat back down at the small table Rahul kept in the middle of the wagon. Ainsley was snoring peacefully in the cot, oblivious to his grim musings. As Edgar rationalized the situation, he came to a quiet, almost diagnostic conclusion that made the pit of his stomach ache with a dull pain.

There's not going to be a tomorrow. My body won't hold out long enough for us to get to the other revenants. Arcane malady or not, I've seen enough patients close to death to understand that. My life must end tonight. "So this is it, then," he mumbled to himself, his hand shaking at the thought. "My last day."

How should I spend it? he wondered vaguely, the roiling in his gut increasing.

The answer came to him with ease. It came as a melancholy, beautiful ache that spread across him. He knew what he wanted from his final hours or rather whom he wanted to spend them with. As he took a few minutes to ponder the particulars, a quaint notion occurred to him. He decided cheerfulness would suit his end better than gloom.

Edgar rose from the table and exited the wagon without waking Ainsley. The fair stood tranquil in the morning, lacking the frenzy and clamor of the night. People milled about or lay relaxing on whatever bit of unused paraphernalia was most comfortable. After asking a few of the sleepy fair workers about where he might find Rahul, Edgar sought out his friend, who apparently had found refuge in the spirit-medium sisters' tent. It didn't take him long to cross the fairground to where their tent was pitched, and as he approached, Edgar saw that Rahul was already awake. He held a steaming cup of tea and was sipping it. When he saw Edgar approach, a cynical smile spread across his face.

"I'm beginning to know that look very well," Rahul purred, before taking a long drink of his spicy-smelling tea.

Suddenly self-conscious, Edgar stopped in midstep. "And what look might that be?"

"Ah, that would be your signature 'I'm about to ask for a favor, Rahul' look. I don't expect I would even need to be a mentalist to see it coming." Rahul showed his teeth in a knowing grin, and Edgar hung his head.

"How transparent of me," he grumbled.

Rahul laughed, downed the rest of his tea, then stood up and drew closer to Edgar. "So this is how it is to be? The ever-obliging Rahul constantly coming to the aid of a very needy medical man? Is that my only worth to you, Mr. Price?" he snickered, and Edgar turned a delicate shade of pink. Rahul let him stand speechless for a moment then laughed again, this time louder. "Oh, please, don't look so miserable. I've never seen a man as miserable as you, and my livelihood chiefly concerns manipulating the bereaved. I only wanted to torment you a bit as retribution for the favor I no doubt will be granting you soon."

He stopped to observe Edgar, reading his face as one might peruse a book. Rahul's expression changed from mirthful to taken aback.

"Ah. I've seen that look before too." His voice was considerably softer. "So this is something of a last request, I take it?"

"I suppose you could call it that." Edgar shrugged, endeavoring to smile.

"Well, *that* I wouldn't dream of refusing. Come, let's hear this plan of yours," Rahul said.

Edgar told him what he intended to accomplish by the end of the afternoon, and Rahul promised it would be simple to acquire what he needed. The two men traveled between the various tents, shelters, and caravans, visiting Rahul's friends and collecting the necessary items. After the sun had reached its highest point, they took a short break to share a meal of bread and cheese in the courtyard. The two talked and laughed as if this were an ordinary day. Edgar got the notion that Rahul was doing this on his behalf, knowing he didn't want to spend his final hours of life preoccupied with thoughts of death.

As the sun sank lower, they returned to Rahul's wagon with their collection of goods and arranged them on the table inside. They took some time to prepare the food, and by three o'clock, they had created a lovely, inviting tea spread. Edgar and Rahul took a step back to admire their work.

"Well, that's quite pretty. I say she'll be impressed," Rahul said with a sigh.

"I do hope so. I've never actually invited a lady to tea before today. I'm not certain how one should proceed," Edgar said doubtfully, though it was difficult for him to be nervous about anything at this point.

Rahul raised an eyebrow at him then nodded as if deciding to keep his thoughts to himself. "Well, I shall go tell her that her presence is requested, as one last gesture to my friend, whom I knew for so short a time." He touched Edgar on the shoulder. "I thought you should know that I received a message yesterday from my mother. My cousin's health is improving. It seems she'll survive the infection." Edgar smiled broadly at the news, and Rahul matched his grin. "They'll be returning home to India soon. It's all thanks to you."

"You say 'they' as if you won't be going with them."

"Ah, I can't bear to leave this gloomy country. Not yet. Something about it holds on to me and refuses to let go. Perhaps I will be free of her one day, but dear Caledonia still keeps me in her arms for now," he said with an air of romance. He and Edgar shared a glance for a moment longer, and then Rahul stepped toward the door. "So I won't see you after this, will I?"

"I believe this is goodbye." Edgar kept that thin smile on.

"I hope there will be peace for you, Mr. Price." Rahul spoke with such kindness and understanding that Edgar's heart ached. The surgeon's smile flickered, and something caught in his throat. After this, they uttered a few more cursory words of farewell, and Rahul was gone.

Awaiting Fana, Edgar flattened his coat and tightened his cravat as the minutes ticked by. Instinct had him constantly reaching for his pocket watch, only to find time and again that it was still broken.

At last the door creaked opened and she entered, looking willowy and drowsy as always. Edgar felt a strange buoyancy in his chest as he rose at once and guided her to the table, which was set with a full tea spread. Although she was fully in the guise of a woman, without any trace of her antlers or the flowers that bloomed upon them, he still saw magic in her every movement. Edgar took care not to touch her—he didn't wish for her to know his plans at this time.

"Well, look at this! What have I done to merit such a treat?" she asked in her bell-like tone. Edgar smiled, flustered as he joined her. He filled her cup, his heart still pattering.

"No particular reason. I only thought it would be a pleasant way to spend the afternoon," he lied. He covertly reached for the table behind him, building up to his surprise. "I also procured a small gift." He revealed a jar of a cheerful red substance and set it on the table. "You said strawberries are your favorite, so I hope this will please you even more. It's called jam."

Fana laughed, but her eyes were kind. She obviously was touched by what he'd done for her, but something had tickled her as well.

"You know they make preserves in the Witches' Wood too," she said with a giggle.

Edgar fumbled in embarrassment. "O-of course they do. I...I should have known that. It's...oh, dear..."

"Please don't fret. This is lovely. I can't tell you how happy I am. This is exactly the sort of thing I love best. Thank you."

Edgar's shame shifted to quiet, nervous glee. Soon they sat and the quivering atmosphere between them grew peaceful, and they fell easily into talk as they sipped their tea. Rahul had helped him find a savory assortment of things to enjoy; among them were smoked salmon, cucumber sandwiches, scones, and sugared tarts. Fana had a great interest in experiences outside of her world, and they discussed the marvels of the various countries Edgar knew of.

She was fascinated by the existence of steam engines, pyramids, and expeditions that spanned seas. Caught up on talk of countries of ice, jungle, and sand, Fana then spoke of the things she always had longed to do, as did Edgar. She confided that she had long harbored a desire to fly in a hot air balloon, which she'd first learned about from the memories of a Frenchman nearly a century ago. Edgar, too, mentioned that he had often thought of visiting Chicago after hearing such marvelous accounts of the World's Fair some two years prior. Their daydreams grew to be rather extravagant, and soon they playfully indulged in plans to actually travel to these places together and experience the wonders of the world. Now that his life was coming to an end, Edgar, although it was foolish, felt this was the closest he would ever get to actually going on such adventures, and it soothed him in a strange sort of way.

All too quickly, the sky began to smolder with color as the light grew dimmer, and still they murmured and hummed away. It was effortless to share long hours with a person from whom Edgar could keep no secrets. The world seemed to grow still as he listened to her lilting voice and took in the heart-stopping image of her face stained red by the fading sun. A sad, painful urge overtook him, and he couldn't help reach for her hand in the final poignant silence that fell between them. He stopped before their skin touched, fearing what she would say if she knew he planned to die in so short a time.

"Miss Fana, I..." He stopped as her eyes grew wide. Suddenly he had no inkling of what he had so powerfully wished to say to her only moments before. "I want to thank you for spending this time with me. It means a great deal."

"Of course. But tell me, Edgar, why do you look so troubled?"

Edgar looked at her with his lips trembling, and just as he began to speak, an image in the reflection of the windowpane made him choke. The crown-adorned child stood directly behind him. Edgar spun around, his heart pumping madly, expecting to see the demonic boy breathing down his neck. However, he only caught sight of empty air, and it left a pit in his stomach.

"Edgar?"

"I'm...I'm dreadfully sorry, Miss Fana. I just remembered something that I forgot to do. Won't you please excuse me?" He tried to remain airy, but something in the way his voice shook betrayed him. He fled the wagon before Fana could object, though, looking back, Edgar could see that she tracked him with a disturbed gaze that suggested she sensed deception.

The heavy rhythm of his pulse banged in his ears as he crossed the fairgrounds. The dewy smells of evening tickled his nose. The twinkling of lights that gleamed in the red dusk and the festive sounds of the crowd made the pain in Edgar's chest grow more intense.

Oh, God, not yet.

It had to be done. The twinge in his body was growing unbearable. Something next to his heart was pounding inside his chest now. There was no escaping this—best to do it while he was still sane and coherent. There was no knowing how the coming terror might warp his decisions. He stopped in his frantic search for a method, breathless as he clutched his breast.

Edgar reached to his belt where he wore the satchel and found the hilt of a scalpel. He let his hand rest there a moment, not daring to look at the instrument. Biting down hard on his lip, he willed himself to grab it.

After several minutes of watching the ember sun and trying to muster his courage, he found he had none left. Choking back a sob, he closed the satchel and resumed his march. He had to find Ainsley.

It was just after dark when he located her. She was sitting with a rowdy group of men in an area at the back of the fairground that was protected by a canvas ceiling, creating a sort of cave. She was involved in—and looked to be winning—a raucous card game. A dirty bottle of Scotch sat half defeated at her ankle. Too distraught for manners, Edgar pushed past the shouting throng and touched Ainsley on the shoulder. She batted his hand away without really looking at him.

"Away with ye. I'm mopping the floor with these hooligans!" she chortled, her accent intensified by the drink, and the rest of the group roared with laughter and playful insults.

"Ach, the mouth on this one! Reminds me of my departed mum, she does."

"I know a bluff when I see one, lassie!"

"Aye, yous had better focus or I'll have ye for all yer worth! There ye are, ya manky mongrels," Ainsley cried, ignoring Edgar as she slammed down her hand to a chorus of disbelieving groans.

"It's rather important that I get a word, Ainsley," Edgar pressed.

"Away with ye, I sa—" Ainsley looked up and finally saw his face. Her grin waned, and she set her hand of cards down on the board that was an excuse for a table. "I'll have to leave you here, boys, cough up my winnings," she said, her accent growing less pronounced.

After settling the last of her wagers, Ainsley followed Edgar's lead away from the cluster of men. She asked after Edgar several times, but he wouldn't answer her until they were well out of anyone's earshot. At last he faced her, his eyes hollow. Edgar found that he couldn't ask her what was pressing on his mind and instead retreated into something safer.

"I notice you've thrown your distaste for outsiders to the wind," he said a bit snidely, and Ainsley's face pinched.

"It was only a means to pass the time. They're all still scum, if you ask me," she said, but her voice lacked the scathing disgust she usually employed. While discomfort showed on her face, she apparently chose to turn her gaze on Edgar rather than face it. "Never mind about that. What's this nonsense I heard from Rahul? What are you trying to do with Fana? I won't allow you to court her as if she's some silly lass from one of your society balls. She's our guardian, the soul of our land, not some plaything to be won over with lies and cloying remarks. No matter how pure you think your intentions may be, you can never be her warden. If you don't leave her be, I'll have to—"

"Warden?" Edgar interrupted, discarding the acid remark he'd been formulating while listening to Ainsley's tirade.

Ainsley stopped, her mouth still open. After squinting at him, she appeared to regret having spoken on the topic. "Never you mind. You have something to discuss with me?"

"No, tell me what that is," he pushed, but Ainsley's brow furrowed in anger.

"What did you come and bother me for, Edgar? Out with it," she said firmly.

Edgar scowled. He supposed it didn't matter what a warden was. Steeling himself against the raging anxiety in his gut, he took a deep breath. "I need you to do something very important for me," he said with a shudder. Ainsley's expression didn't change as she waited for him to supply her with the request. "I can't allow myself to live past tonight. The spirit is consuming me. I can feel it. If I'm not destroyed before it succeeds, I can't predict what sort of danger will arise. My life must end. Tonight. Right now."

"But we need you to get the other revenants. You can't just back out now, not after everything—that's right cowardly," Ainsley protested, her anger growing hotter.

"Ainsley, I'm going to *become* another revenant before long. You and Fana are strong enough on your own. Use Hare if you have to. It cannot be me." Edgar's chest was heaving.

Ainsley faced him with an undercurrent of sorrow beneath her rage. "Fine then...do it. I don't know what you're blathering to me for. You don't need my permission," she seethed.

Edgar's eyes watered before he could get a hold over his misery. "I'm not asking for your permission...I'm asking for your help," he said with a quavering voice.

Ainsley couldn't mask the electric anguish that shot through her face. She blinked, her lips growing thinner. "No," she flatly replied.

"Please, Ainsley," he pleaded, blinking furiously so his tears wouldn't fall.

"*No*," she persisted, refusing to meet his eye. "You're a surgeon. You know where to cut."

"Goddamn it. I'm terrified. I don't want to die alone. Please help me," Edgar barked, a tear finally slipping from his eye. She paled at his words and finally looked into his eyes. "You kill almost every day," he reminded her. "You're good at it. You can do it quickly."

For a long moment, Ainsley considered his request then looked at the back of her hand, gazing at the incomplete set of tattoos. "I can't, Edgar. I left my home so I could save a life, not end yours. I can't do this... Ask Fana. She'll help you. I believe she had meant to be the one to do it," she said with an air of finality, and before he could argue, she stalked away from him.

As Edgar watched her go, he saw her dabbing at her eyes. His body went slightly numb as she disappeared into the crowd of fairgoers. Like sudden lightning, his chest seized up in pain again, he leaned forward and gasped. Then came a sensation of a pair of small hands attempting to pry open his chest from the inside out. His rib cage creaked, sending a bolt of white terror through him. The urgency of the moment propelled him past his doubts, and he left to search for Fana. He fled to Rahul's wagon, his mind rattling with fear, only to find it empty.

She must've gone back to Hare, he thought wildly, then resumed his run. The sun had gone now. Edgar hurried past the gates of the fair and down the dirt path. The cart was where they had left it, out of sight between the fence and the edge of the woods. In its bed, among their belongings, he saw Hare sitting up and watching the sky change from red to black. He was still bound, and anchored to the cart itself for good measure. As he glanced at Edgar, who was stumbling along the path, a strange blankness came over his face.

"So this is it then?" he called to Edgar as he wheezed past the cart. Fana was nowhere in sight. Hare grew intense with excitement, his eyes fixed on Edgar as he tried to walk past without saying a word to him. "This is the moment? Running off to die in the woods like a dog? Well, hurry it up! Hurry! Soon you'll be free, and then so will I!"

The sound of Hare's strained cries followed him as he plunged into the trees. He guessed in his panic that if Fana wasn't guarding Hare, she might be taking refuge in the woods, where she felt most comfortable. It was long past dark, and the wound on Edgar's chest was issuing more black blood before he realized he'd made the wrong choice. Panting and unable to continue, he found a small clearing and sat in the moss to catch his breath. The pain intensified so much that he lay on the ground before slowly passing out.

Edgar was brought back to consciousness with a shake and opened his eyes to see Fana's gentle face and flowered antlers, backed by the cold glory of the stars. She knelt beside him and leaned over his chest, her hand cupping the side of his face. As clarity returned to him, the contact they shared allowed Fana to understand his thoughts. Edgar stared up at her with watering eyes and a pounding heart, silently begging her to be the one to guide him to death. Her face went through a visible change.

"Are you certain?" she whispered, and Edgar reached up to grab her hand.

"What choice do I have?" He tried to laugh, but it came out sounding close to a sob. Fana closed her eyes and held his hand tightly, pressing it to her chest for a moment. With care, she lay down beside him, her antlers sinking into the moss and grass between them. A surprise rocked through Edgar as she took him into her arms very gently and held him there for a long time. His jagged fear eased ever so slightly. After a moment, he held to her as well and inhaled the freesia-like scent that hung around her. Her presence was intoxicating, and though Edgar wanted nothing more than to surrender to it, the silence between them had lasted too long.

"Miss Fana…what are you…how are you going to…?"

"Hush, dear one," she hummed to him, her warm breath on his ear. "You needn't be afraid. Fall back to sleep…I will do it then. You'll feel no pain." Though she seemed to be doing her best to comfort him, he noticed a note of deep sorrow in her voice. He pulled her closer and quivered, his eyes welling up.

"Th-thank you," he whispered back. After thinking for a moment, he ventured another question. "Fana, you've died before. What will it be like?"

She opened her eyes, and Edgar saw from her expression that she wanted so desperately to lie to him. She thought for a long time, her lips parting and shutting a few times, before she finally spoke. "The words you gave your last patient are what comes to mind: 'It'll be even quicker than dreaming.' There's no reason for fear, I assure you. Death is...quiet," she said, and held him a bit tighter.

This far from eased Edgar's mind, though he knew it should have. He was raging inside, rejecting this quiet swiftness with all his being. An insurmountable craving for experience clanged through him. This hungering demanded that he stay and take everything he could get: emotion and sensation, passion and anguish, violence and beauty. Chief among these urgent desires was to remain with Fana for just a bit longer. To be near her was to live as Edgar never had imagined, and he refused to fade away when she still burned so brightly with life in his arms. Sensing the surge in him, Fana drew back a fraction. Edgar's tears flowed freely now, and he gripped the back of her robes until his knuckles ached.

"No..." he said in a ragged breath. "No, not yet. I need more time."

"Edgar..."

"Please. Please. You did it before..I saw it when you showed me your life. You took something of mine—a memory of something. I beseech you once more. I need just a little more time," he said, his grip tightening around her shoulders.

Fana broke free and sat up, peering down at him. "If I do this, your mind could be fractured."

"I don't care. I just need to live a little longer. I can't leave you yet," he begged, and sat up to face her.

She leaned toward him, looking deeply into his eyes and searching as if the truth were hidden somewhere inside them. Edgar reached up with a shaky hand, hesitant to touch her, yet aching to do so. She didn't flinch when he wove his fingers into her hair and gripped her softly behind her ear. He inched forward ever so slightly, burning to get closer yet terrified of overstepping his bounds. Fana, too, drifted closer, with restraint pulling her backward and desire beckoning her forward. In the midst of their hesitance, the dynamic between them changed in a sudden, simultaneous moment of liberation.

With trembling softness, Edgar touched his lips to hers. Fana pressed back, her hand sliding down his shoulder and gripping his arm. She kissed him once more with intense passion before pulling away, leaving Edgar's lips tingling and his heart yearning for more. His breathing was audible as he opened his eyes and scanned her face.

"Let me live," he pleaded, and by the way her eyes brimmed with sadness, he knew she would comply.

"Which memory would you have me take?" she asked in a grave voice. Edgar paused. He was unsure of what he could stand to lose. Fana waited while he thought but eventually brought up a suggestion. "I've seen your whole life...wouldn't you like to live without the memory of that terrible day of profound loss? Of your father?"

Edgar's body at once felt rigid, and his face turned stony as soon as she'd said it. His heart nearly seized up, and his breathing grew even shorter. "Out of the question," he stated, blood pounding in his ears.

Fana looked genuinely confused. "Why ever not?" she questioned. "To be free of the weight, even for a few days...I should think it would be a good thing."

Edgar's frown deepened. "That day—what my father did—it made me who I am. It formed me. It taught me what this world is truly like, and that's a lesson I do not wish to forget. That pain *is* who I am. If you take it away..." He trailed off.

For a few moments, Fana couldn't reply and instead watched him with poignant sadness. "Do you not think of yourself as anything more than a victim?" she said at last.

Edgar's anger spiked again. He gathered the fabric of his coat in his palm and squeezed. "It's my decision isn't it?" he asked, dodging the question. "I'd like you to take all the memories I don't need. Everything unimportant that happened before I came to Scotland. Give me as much time as possible. Just leave the entirety of my education, my apprenticeship, my career, and that day. I must retain my skills. Everything else is of little consequence."

"Edgar, you would remove all the pleasant memories from your life in favor of keeping something so awful?" she protested.

"It's what I choose. I understand what I'm doing." His expression was so resolute and stern that Fana at last gave in.

"I must warn you…you're going to be very disoriented. It might even drive you to madness. Are you ready for that possibility?" As she laid her hand on his chest, Edgar felt a static-electric buzz.

"I'm willing to take that chance to be with you a little longer, Miss Fana," he said, confidently resolute.

Fana smiled sadly then shut her eyes. Her hand searched under his shirt and found the raw epicenter of pain in his chest. She pressed down, and a spasm crossed Edgar's back, feeling like broken bones grating across one another. The electrical buzz grew stronger, and Fana took a deep breath.

"Think carefully on the times you'd like to forfeit, Edgar. Hold them in your mind," she murmured, sounding increasingly more grieved.

Edgar did as told, recalling his trip to Lyon several years ago, long nights spent with novels he was engrossed in, and girls he had dreamed of but never managed to speak to. He had almost no time to grieve for the lifetime he was about to lose. It slid from him too easily. Fana absorbed it through her hands, through which a healing energy flowed. Soon the pain eased, and Edgar's harried breathing became pacified. As she finished pilfering his mind, he stared up at the sky, his pulse spiking again. A rush of anxiety rocked him, and he sat up, shivering.

"Fana...Fana....something's happened to me. I..." he stuttered, panic raging through him until she took him in her arms again and soothed him until he was calm.

Once the greater part of his anxiety had lessened, she explained what she had done and what he had lost. The explanation both comforted and disturbed him. The knowledge of what had occurred helped him regain control, but he felt as if he'd been emptied. He held close to Fana. Her warmth and gentleness was all there was in the world at that moment.

"So now your time is extended once more," she told him, stroking the back of his head. "Will you still help us capture the revenants?"

"I'll go wherever you are. I'll do whatever you ask of me," he breathed into her shoulder.

Fana drew away, overwhelmed by his fervent emotions. Edgar pulled back too, breathing more deeply. Until that moment, he hadn't appreciated how wonderful it was to simply exist without agony racking his body. As his thoughts reorganized themselves and he grew accustomed to the hollow feeling his stolen memories had left behind, he was reminded of Ainsley's words. *Warden...what did she mean by that?*

Fana, who was still gripping his hand, suddenly pulled back. She looked at him with deep shock. "What were you thinking just then? Who told you of that?" she asked with a serious note that rocked Edgar. He sat stunned for a moment before answering.

"It was Ainsley. She said I could never be a warden, so I should leave you be...I was only wondering what it meant."

Fana's face grew uncharacteristically cold. "She had no right to mention such a thing," she muttered, and suddenly he realized Fana had kept something from him when she had shared her memories—something of great importance and great pain to her.

Edgar chanced a searching glance. "I'm sorry. I don't mean to pry. Why is it of such a sensitive nature? I wish to understand you better."

Fana gave him a hard look. However, she could not hold it for long, and when she dropped her eyes, he noticed a deep hurt on her face that she could no longer conceal. "You saw what I've been through," she whispered. "Those people I trusted. They all pledged to be a warden to me and my Wood, but none of them fulfilled their promises. They abandoned me; they weren't strong enough. They couldn't be trusted."

"Do you mean they broke your heart?"

"It's deeper than that, Edgar." She finally sounded aggrieved again. "When a creature pledges to be a warden to a spirit like me, it's not a simple gesture of affection. It runs deeper than any human connection you can imagine. It's a duty to share the same soul, the same life-force. They all became part of me, part of the land I'm anchored to. Whosoever undertakes that oath dies and is reborn as a spirit of the Wood. Their sole duty in existence is to watch over me and our land. We were bound by fathomless love and devotion. And each time one of them was destroyed, so was a part of me. I've been torn apart by fate. I wanted to bury that part of myself forever and never think on it again. That's why Ainsley should have kept it to herself."

Though Fana's voice was controlled and her demeanor calm, her misery was apparent. Edgar couldn't hide his excitement at learning this new information; he felt he understood her more deeply than even she could guess.

"Fana," he began breathlessly, "if I may be so bold…your fear and sadness are familiar to me. Though I might not have felt it as powerfully as you do, it's the very same breed of misery. We're both creatures of heavy misfortune. We've both had our hearts smashed to pieces. I know what it is to…to hide from what we most desire. To deny ourselves joy out of fear of loss. To not be able to live without being haunted by what has been. But I know that is not permanent—I have seen men and women with grave injuries make a full recovery. It's possible. If you would allow me a chance…"

"Edgar, stop." Fana's voice trembled, and she couldn't meet his eye.

"You are ineffably wise and strong, and you deserve to attain what you desire. I felt your loneliness. I felt that pain when I looked into your heart. I could—"

"You could what?" she blazed, suddenly all fury. "You speak to me of liberating oneself from pain as if it's another procedure you might perform. You, who cannot bear to part with your own sorrows. You...a perpetual victim by your own choice."

She stood up, glaring down at him. Fana had lost all her softness and had become the wild, untamed creature that remembered the earth before men had changed it.

"You can't begin to understand what you're speaking about. You're a mere child. What? You believed you were created only to love me? To be the antidote to my poisoned soul? That somehow you're special and different from all the rest? That *you* alone can heal me?" she raged, tears spouting from her eyes.

Although Fana's words rattled Edgar, he wouldn't let them crush him. He stood up, anger and passion burning in his heart. "I wouldn't presume something so arrogant. Perhaps I might've once, but no longer," he hissed at her. Though he was taller, her prowess made him feel as though he were shrinking. However, he refused to relent. "I'm aware of why you act this way, because it's what ails me as well. I share your disease. I'm not the remedy to your pain, but I can help you search for it. You and your world give me purpose and hope. You've made me aware of the life I should have led. I have no qualms devoting myself to you. You can have every part of me. Let me stand beside you. Let me love you, Fana."

Fana's tears flowed more rapidly, but her face only became sterner. "Your words are false. You only seek a way to preserve your life through me. You don't understand how deep a sacrifice you would have to make...or the meaning of eternity. There is no real love in your heart."

Although she spoke these words harshly, it was apparent to Edgar that she was crushing her own hope by saying them aloud, rather than seeking to dismiss his feelings.

"Touch me." He extended his hand to her, keeping his eyes loving. "Look into my heart and tell me that what I've said to you doesn't match how I feel. If what you find there falls anything short of genuine, I will never speak of this again."

He held his hand out until his arm ached as Fana looked him over with varying degrees of terror and yearning. Her hand trembled forward after a moment, seeking to make contact with his, but before they could connect, she drew it back to her chest. She hung her head for a moment, her expression becoming blank again. Fana's back straightened, and she turned away from Edgar. Without saying another word she drifted back into the woods.

It was a very long time before Edgar was able to let his hand fall.

Contract

With bared teeth, Hare had watched the surgeon wander off into the woods. He trembled in anticipation—it wouldn't be much longer now. If only he could get free of his binds, it could all end tonight. He could finally be rid of his life. No more threat, no more terror. Just silence.

Wiggling his feet and shifting about, he peered at his dismal surroundings. Though there was little chance of rain, the cold bit right through him. As he squirmed again in a futile attempt to get comfortable, footsteps alerted him to another person approaching. The first sign he saw of the stranger was the glowing, red crescent on the cigar in his mouth. He walked, seemingly aimlessly, down the dirt road toward the cart. After a few moments, he stopped and stared at Hare. The man, who was at least six and a half feet tall and heavily muscled, raised his hand in greeting. Hare, without the use of his arms, decided after a tense moment to merely nod in the stranger's direction.

A long, uncomfortable pause took hold. The man wouldn't break eye contact, and a blooming nervousness crept up on Hare. The man strode forward, approached without saying a word, climbed up into the cart, and took a seat beside him. Bristling with uneasiness, Hare chanced a look at his uninvited companion. He was completely bald, save for a walrus mustache on his upper lip. A series of intricate tattoos covered his arms: thorny roses, coiling snakes, Queen Victoria's solemn face, pierced and bleeding hearts, a snarling lion, and other more crudely wrought designs. He wore a black leotard that led Hare to believe he was part of a strongman act at the fair, but perhaps the strangest thing about him was what he wore pinned to one of the straps of his garment.

Glittering on his chest was a gaudy pewter brooch in the shape of a Green Man's face, studded with fake emeralds. They formed the leaves that ringed his face like a beard, and the pewter swirls were wrought into a slightly ominous countenance. The dark-red eyes of the thing seemed to catch the light of the man's cigar. Hare could scarcely think of anything to say to this peculiar fellow, so they simply sat in silence while the strongman puffed away on his cigar.

Nearly ten minutes passed before he looked over with smoke streaming out from under his bushy mustache and spoke to Hare.

"Fancy a smoke?" he mumbled, and offered Hare a cigar.

Puzzled as to where he'd produced it from, Hare declined with a grunt. The strongman shrugged and went back to happily puffing away. After almost half an hour, Hare couldn't resist the urge to speak to him.

"I'm sorry, mate, but I must ask you," Hare started awkwardly, still trying to avoid eye contact. "Why are you wearing that curious article?"

"I should think it would be obvious. I am employed at the fair," he said with a sniff.

Hare let his mouth hang open for a bit before pursuing the conversation further. "I mean that…brooch."

The man glanced down at his wooly chest, where the object sparkled in the moonlight. A grim look washed over his face, and he let out a long sigh that was clouded with smoke. "It's a very complicated explanation. I hardly think you would be interested."

Hare shrugged after another pause. "I think I'd prefer it to silence if you insist on staying here." He made no bother at being amiable.

The strongman sniffed again as a tormented look seized him. "My name is Alexander McNair. I was born outside Glasgow and spent my boyhood on a pig farm with my father, Georg—"

"I'm sorry, but what has all this got to do with your taste in jewelry?" Hare asked.

Alexander gave him a look that was both ferocious and hollow, which silenced Hare for the time being. "I first came upon this brooch on the day my father was killed," he continued. "I found him in the pen among the hogs, half eaten and covered in filth. This brooch was in his hand...I believe he fell into the pen and was knocked unconscious when he spotted it among the animals and attempted to recover it from the sty."

Hare blinked up at him. "That's a bunch of bollocks, mate. Hogs don't eat men." He wanted to laugh, but Alexander remained serious.

"They most certainly do, given the opportunity. I'm a first-hand witness to it. Now kindly let me continue," he huffed. "I kept the brooch, which he died trying to attain. I wore it continuously in memory of my late father. It has been an object of great curiosity since then, and I'm quite convinced it has been touched by the Devil himself. Allow me to explain: after my father's death, I sold my inherited land for a pittance and went to work in a textile mill in Glasgow. On my third day, the man who worked beside me became momentarily distracted by the brooch—a mishap that caused him to be pulled into the machinery. First he lost his arm, then moments later his life." Hare's look remained skeptical, but Alexander was unfazed.

"Disturbed by the memories of his demise," he continued, "I left that factory for more ambitious prospects. I invested all my remaining money into purchasing a millinery shop, intent on making my fortune in the world of hats and other splendid outfitting necessities. I hired an up-and-coming hatter who had enjoyed success in his field for the past five years. When he came to work for me, he couldn't resist commenting on the brooch every time he saw it. Soon he became obsessed with the object, wishing to buy it from me for increasingly large sums of money. I, of course, refused, and this was the beginning of a long series of quarrels between us."

"You're barking, mate." Hare turned away, but the strongman held his hand up.

"Allow me to continue," Alexander said in a deep rumble. "The man's aggravated condition worsened with every hat he produced. Soon he was gripped with tremors and raving fits, always returning to the subject of the brooch and relentlessly harassing me to part with it. Pushed to his wit's end, he set fire to my millinery shop in an act of spite and hatred, then disappeared. I lost everything I had at the infernal will of this accursed brooch."

"I hardly think that piece of junk is to blame," Hare started with raised eyebrows, but a stern look from Alexander halted his speech.

"Desperate, I took a job with a traveling circus that passed through town. I started as a stable boy, but through sheer gumption I became a knife-throwing expert. During this period in my life, I became amorously involved with many of the lady performers, including one Monique Delacroix, my partner in the throwing act. We would take turns aiming for one another, you see." Alexander went on as if Hare hadn't spoken at all.

"What in the—"

Alexander stopped him once again. "Kindly let me continue. After several years, Monique got wise to my philandering, and I became privy to the fact that she was plotting to kill me out of jealousy. Being of a despairing nature, I had no plans to stop her. On the night I was intended to die, however, something went wrong in the act. As she was preparing to throw, she slipped and her heart was pierced by one of her own knives. She died instantly. My associates tried to convince me her error was due to her distressed state, but I know differently. This brooch caught the light at the precise moment. It threw her off and caused her untimely death."

"I honestly don't understand how you could come to that conclusion."

"*Kindly let me continue,*" Alexander repeated in a tone that was only marginally harsher than before. "Of course, I could no longer bear to stay in that circus, so I abandoned it. I followed a friend of mine to the All Souls' Fair, where I trained for a number of years to become its resident strongman. During this period I tried to rid myself of the accursed thing several times, but each time I tried to take it off or leave it unattended in my dressing room, some bit of misfortune would soon arise. An accompanying accident always occurred: gravely injured trapeze artists, a catastrophic lightning storm that caused widespread property damage, a disastrous vat of porridge that gave an unforgettable bout of violent illness to the fair workers, among other misfortunes. One night, as I merely *flipped the clasp*, the glittering of its stones frightened my beloved cat, Timbles, into fleeing. I never saw him again.

"Powerless to help myself, I took up drinking, gambling, and other sinful practices. As I mentioned, my nature has always been despairing. Then, something peculiar happened one year ago on this very day," he said mysteriously, and Hare's eyebrows perked up.

"Is that the truth now?"

"Ah…no. It wasn't this very day, but it was certainly within a few weeks." Alexander shrugged and moved on. "I decided that I no longer had an interest in living and sought to take my own life. That night I put a revolver to my head and said my prayers, and as I was looking down through my tears, the awful vision of that brooch gleamed up at me from above the very heart it had broken. I went to remove it for a final time and happened to prick my finger on the pin. In a recoiling movement of pain, I accidentally fired the gun.

It pierced the wall of the tent and shot the lion tamer dead. The brooch had taken another life." Alexander sighed.

Hare stared at him with his eyebrows still raised, but the man's seriousness never faltered. "And a year later you're *still* carrying the damn thing around? Why have you never tried to destroy it?"

"I'm too frightened to do so."

As Hare thought of this, something began to nag at him. "And the leotard it's pinned to? Do you ever…?"

"It stays on my person day and night, my good man," he said with yet another sniff, avoiding Hare's eye. "It isn't easy, but I must bear this burden for the good of the world. My life and countless others' have been already been ruined by it—I cannot let it curse another."

Hare couldn't think of much to say to the man after this. The weighty silence hung between them once again. After a minute of mulling over the man's bizarre tale—which he wasn't entirely sure he believed—he realized he felt very disquieted. That brooch, Hare was certain, had nothing at all to do with the man's poor circumstances, but he recognized the suffering it caused him. For the first time in many years, he felt truly sorry for another human being. The least he could do was ease his mind by removing the offending object from his life.

"Look here," he started up again with a shrug. "What if you gave it to me? You've borne it long enough. Pass it along to another. I'm willing to do that for you."

At hearing this, Alexander gave him a dumbfounded stare. He didn't break his gaze for over a minute, and soon his face was slick with tears. "How could I ask such a thing of another man?" he finally said.

"I'm a rotten fellow," Hare grumbled, embarrassed to look him in the eye. "Whatever it brings to me, I most likely deserve."

"A…chance at redemption?"

"Sure, something like that. Here, pin it on me." Hare's hands were bound behind his back, so he gestured with his chin.

"If I remove it, there's no telling what disaster could arise," Alexander said in a husky, quivering voice.

"Have courage, man," Hare whispered, certain nothing would happen.

Sobbing quietly, Alexander removed the brooch with shaky hands and pinned it to Hare's shirt. After Alexander patted him, he turned away, sobbed once more, then became strangely stoic. He looked back down at Hare for a moment more and finally seemed to notice he was tied to the cart. Alexander looked away from Hare with a blank gaze.

Hare expected the awkward quiet between them to continue, but less than a minute later, the strongman got up without another word and left him behind. Hare peered after him with his lips slightly parted in dull surprise. Shaking his head, he found he didn't have the energy to give the curious incident much more thought.

The moon rose higher, and Hare waited. He still felt the weight of his own very real curse on his body—the surgeon wasn't dead yet. Groaning with displeasure, Hare shifted in his bonds.

What's taking so long? he wondered.

In the distance, something rustled in the overgrowth of the woods. Someone was coming his way.

That blasted nymph is back, he thought with disdain. Her persistence at guarding him irritated him to his core. He turned his face toward the sound and motion and tried to think of something needling to say upon her arrival. All thoughts of colorful language, however, faded in one stomach-wrenching instant. The jolt of panic at recognizing who was coming toward him was enough to make him gasp and choke for air.

Magdalena had found him. She crept toward him, smiling like a jackal. When she lifted a hand and waved, he saw the ghost of a bloodstain clinging to her corpse-white flesh.

"No..." He shuddered as tears sprang to his eyes.

"Jacob, at last," she purred. With a light step, she hopped into the cart and sat across from him. "You appear to be in a spot of bother, my friend."

"M-Mag...how on earth did you find me?" he sputtered.

Mag's smiled widened. "I sent you here in the first place. Don't you recall? Or has our time apart left your grip on reality further fractured?" she asked, cocking her head a bit.

Hare couldn't bring himself to answer and instead swallowed thickly as sweat beaded on his brow. Instead of keeping her attention focused on him, Mag rifled through the cart.

"What are you doing?"

"Where are they? You were apprehended by the nymph and my surgeon, weren't you? This is her cart, is it not? Where are they? The revenants," she hissed.

Hare had to struggle to overcome his panic and answer her. "Uh, they—she took them. The red-haired witch keeps them with her. She doesn't want to risk losing them," he stammered.

Mag swore, bit her lip, then quickly reevaluated something. "And the surgeon? Where is he?"

"Nearly dead. Shouldn't make it past morning," Hare replied.

Mag's wild eyes darted around as she thought, chewing on her bony finger all the while. Eventually her gaze flashed on him again, and to his great horror, he saw anger there. "How could you allow this to happen? You said this would be simple. You said you could handle this," she growled, but never lost her smile.

At the sight of her teeth, Hare at last cracked. He bubbled over with tears as panic rampaged through him. It was over. He had been so close to freedom. And now she would destroy him as slowly as she could. She would find a way.

Mag seemed surprised at his tears but almost pleasantly so. Her grin widened even more, and she put a cold hand to his face. Her caress awakened goose bumps on his flesh, and he let out a whimper.

"Jacob…" She sighed, keeping her eyes fixed on him and still stroking the side of his face. "Poor Jacob. Tell me something…" She leaned closer and breathed in his ear. "Why did you enter this contract with me if you knew you couldn't follow through on the terms? Why would you do that to yourself?"

"I was desperate!" The scream escaped his throat, and he cringed again.

Mag shook her head and finally leaned away from him. "No. Your father was desperate. You've just been foolish. Don't grieve just yet, Jacob. There's still time to make this right. I pity you. I want to help you, but I dare not face the nymph without a plan again… She's too fearsome, even for me. It's too great a risk." Her face went stony. Hare often saw her fade into some dark memory or madness, and this was just such a moment, but as usual it passed. "What have you told them?"

"Nothing," he instantly lied. "I haven't breathed a word. But they want me to show them where the next one is. I told them I would take them there tomorrow, but they don't know, Mag, they don't know where it is. I swear it. I swear."

"Hush, I need a moment," she said, and put her fingers to her lips. Soon her eyebrows rose. "I believe I can make this work. Hare, I want you to pretend I was never here. Take them to the next revenant tomorrow."

"What?"

"Do exactly as I say," she instructed. "Listen now—I have much to tell you. If you're able to assist me, there may be hope for you yet."

Long Since Buried

Rain never bothered Magdalena; at that moment, she barely felt the downpour that smashed down on her head. The streetlamps were foggy ghosts lining the cobbled roads and shimmering through the curtain of water. It was well past midnight, and the roads were entirely deserted, even in the center of Edinburgh. In the shadow of the university museum, Magdalena pressed her back to the black stone of the building and peered at the great doorway beyond a nearby iron gate. Behind those walls—the boundaries of the Anatomical Museum at the University of Edinburgh—stood three towering stories filled with bones, painted models, and pieces of dried human and animal parts. As Magdalena waited, she whispered the skipping-rope rhyme she'd heard the children sing in the streets decades ago.

"Up the close and down the stair, in the house with Burke and Hare...Burke's the butcher; Hare's the thief, Knox the boy that buys the beef."

She smirked as she cast her pale-blue eyes toward the windows. Indeed the bones of the very butcher in question lay behind that gate and, beside them, the vengeful spirit of a man he'd killed. With the thief's son arriving soon, Magdalena delighted in the macabre reunion that was mere hours away.

Hare will lead the nymph and her pet witch through these gates. I can kill her if she doesn't know I'm coming. Then I'll reap the rewards of their risks.

Magdalena paced and anxiously wrung her wrists. Everything she desired in this world was at stake. The outcome of this night would determine whether her long, torturous journey could at last come to its just conclusion.

If it were all to slip away now, I don't think I could bear it. Her thoughts clattered too loudly in her head. The fact that Hare had allowed her scheme to come this close to failing was unacceptable. Her centuries-old grudge had almost been settled. Justice would come to the Ophiuchans, who had robbed her of her humanity and her clarity of mind. She bit her lip, pausing to consider.

I suppose they're not entirely to blame, in all fairness, for that particular bit of misfortune. The fault also belongs to Father.

He had indeed been the one who had summoned the ancient order to Magdalena's bedside when she had fallen ill, long ago in the days when the plague had still raged through Vienna. The same malady that had claimed her mother had crept in on her. Her memory of those days was so foggy—she could only recall extreme heat, pain, hellish dreams, and her father's maniacal grieving. After her mother had died, he had sworn to keep Magdalena safe for all time but soon broke his promise. His pain compelled him to ask a favor from the order of the Ophiuchans.

In that century, the Germanic clan of Ophiuchans had settled in the mountains, living in caverns or hollows and hunting the wild beasts or occasional hapless travelers of that lonely wilderness. They kept to themselves and, to occupy their time, pursued such scholarly or leisurely activities as they saw fit. But after several years of harsh winters, hunger drove them toward the farms and towns of men.

This was when Magdalena's father, Lord Magnus Köhler, first came to meet Ulrich, the elder of that clan. The Ophiuchan, seeking a way to avoid trouble for both humans and his people, came in secret to consult with Magnus. As a lord of a prosperous state, Magnus formed a pact with Ulrich, offering live animals and a small territory of land in exchange for protection from invaders or criminals. This bargain created a harmonious bond between the clan and the state for many years. Magdalena, unaware of his true nature, had watched the fearful-looking Ulrich's comings and goings throughout her youth. Ulrich, too, had watched her as she had matured.

That night, as Magdalena's life was slipping away, her father called upon the deathless elder of the Ophiuchans, begging for a chance to save her life by letting her join their order. Although Ulrich was reluctant to share the precious blood of the Divine Serpent with anyone, he greatly desired Magnus's wide estate and power. At last he agreed, and a deal was struck.

Seven tall, pallid figures had slipped quietly into Magdalena's bedchamber and disturbed her from her fever dream. The burst of fear that flowed through her after seeing their faces remained vivid in her mind. Two women pulled her up and held her steady. Erminhilt, fair and tall, pulled back her arms. Ingvildr, ever frozen in the body of a withered crone, held Magdalena's mouth open. Ulrich approached, grim faced, stern, and flanked by three other Ophiuchan men. Another Ophiuchan female, black of hair and sharp of feature, drew nearer with a tarnished iron goblet in her hands. Magdalena had at last cried out in fright when she caught sight of the dark-red liquid in the cup.

"Thank you, Rúna. Now, Alaric, Eadwulf, Wildad… Begin the rite." Ulrich spoke in a rumble, and the three men at his sides began to chant in barely audible, murmuring voices.

Magdalena's eyes rapidly scanned their faces, looking for anyone she could appeal to for help; two of the men were daunting and gray with harsh expressions, but Alaric looked to be only several years older than herself. She cried out to him to no avail and was far too weak with fever to struggle against the grip of the cursed women's arms. As Ulrich approached with the goblet in his hands, Magdalena had caught sight of her father watching horror stricken from the back of the room.

She'd hardly had time to draw breath as the goblet touched her lips and overflowed with the blood of the Divine Serpent. It poured down her throat, tasting bitterly of rusty metal and thick mud. The last thing she could clearly remember was Ulrich's cold face with its dark curtains of hair staring down at her. Then everything flared white.

Her heart stopped almost instantaneously, and her throat felt as if it were being corroded by acid. Magdalena lay gripped in agony but totally paralyzed, the torment and terror building inside her having no outlet for escape. This sensation built to a blaring roar of excruciating torture, lasting for seven days and nights. All Magdalena knew then was blinding flashes of pain, wild movement, sounds that ripped at her ears, and an urgent hunger that could not be sated. Halfway through the hallucinatory ordeal, she started to come back to the world, but only with the most primal and raw of senses: need for consumption, struggle, flight, resistance. When the blinding white faded, she began to perceive reality with a startling precision. Everything felt razor sharp and explosively loud.

She had been in the cellar when she'd awoken, bound with chains. Focusing, Magdalena ripped herself free, marveling briefly at her own strength, and hurried up the stairs.

As she staggered through the halls, calling for help, with shock she discovered the grisly remains of every human being and animal in the sprawling estate, including her father, who had tried so desperately to save her. The Ophiuchans awaited her in the courtyard, standing vigil over the half-gnawed bodies of all those she'd ever known or cared for: sundered kitchen maids, stableboys in a grisly heap, bloodied tutors, and ladies-in-waiting with huge strips of flesh missing from their pretty faces. The Ophiuchans told her what had become of them. Magdalena had slaughtered and consumed every last one in her primal compulsion for living flesh. She fell weakly beside the corpse of her father, whose throat had been torn out. The grinning crone, Ingvildr, approached her and warily tried to put a comforting hand on her back as she offered her a cage of live frogs and rats. The Ophiuchans had simply expected her to join their ranks that night—to continue living with them in that desecrated, hollow place that was once her home. They were to be her new family for all the ages. In a fit of fury, Magdalena slapped the cage out of the crone's hands and fled to the mountains.

Since that moment, rage was all she had known.

I never desired this half life—this great emptiness, she thought with disgust. *Ever dying, never whole. My body is cursed with this unholy blood—constantly caught in a cycle of destruction and rebirth, feeding off the living, surviving on time stolen from others. Death would have been a kindness. Father and Ulrich…they are to blame for everything…*

The flood of memories engulfed her, and she let them come. She so often ruminated upon them, going over the details and events endlessly in her mind. She reminded herself of every injustice daily, stoking the fires behind every cruelty ever visited upon her. Nothing was ever forgotten and certainly wasn't forgiven. She despised everything about them—their callousness, their greed, their haughty superiority, their self-serving wickedness. Magdalena refused to believe that they hadn't known what the transformation would do to her. They had planned for her to annihilate everyone around her—to keep her isolated and in pain. Ulrich wanted her broken so he and his clan could recast her as one of them. But he had never expected her to be so strong.

After her transformation from a rosy-cheeked girl of fourteen to the monstrous creature she had become, Magdalena swore that she would destroy every last one of the elders who had done this to her. She hid in the icy mountains as she adjusted to her new self, but eventually the attempts of the other Ophiuchans to find her there drove her away. She left her hiding spot in Austria on foot, searching for more information about her condition. In the far reaches of Russia she found her answers in the form of another clan of Ophiuchans. It was there she first learned that flame was the only way to kill her kind. She soon left them, continuing southward. Finding food wasn't a challenge for her; no matter where she went, the sight of a young girl wandering alone never failed to lure unsavory people intent on harming her. She played into their schemes just long enough to get them alone; most of them didn't even realize anything was wrong until they saw the dangerous glitter of teeth.

For one hundred long, trying years, Magdalena roamed southward through Asia, and eventually made her way back to Europe, learning to control her new strength and absorbing all the knowledge she could. Her hunger for flesh was insatiable and she killed indiscriminately, both for nourishment and out of frustration. Even during those formative years, she knew she would need to become unimaginably strong, cunning, and learned if she wanted to exact the revenge that was her very reason of existence. After a century of preparation and study, she returned to her father's estate in Vienna on the anniversary of the night of her ruination.

Upon her arrival in the deep of night, she was pleased to see that Ulrich and his clan hadn't made use of the cellar for much else than keeping old bits of furniture, supplies, and tools tucked away. First she slid her supplies through the barred grate, and then she crept through, breaking her bones as she forced herself through the tiny space. After an hour, her body reset itself and she got to work. She drained the wine kegs and filled them with any stored fuel she could find. The Ophiuchans were in the habit of studying late into their sleepless nights, so it proved to be an easy task.

When her trap had been set, she waited by the stairs in the pitch dark of the cellar. She sat poised with the harpoon she'd brought, ready for the first victim to wander in. It so happened that it was Alaric, the golden-haired creature disguised as a youth. Just as he bent down to dig through a box of shut-away treasures, Magdalena pierced the back of his head with the harpoon. She knew it would disable him long enough to apprehend him; she'd tested it on herself to be sure.

One by one they fell to her, and one by one she chained and gagged them in the cellar. She waited until each one awoke and became aware that they were about to perish. After enjoying their muffled pleas for a time, Magdalena closed the barred metal gate, set her deathly devices aflame, and watched, her eyes brimming with relief and satisfaction as they immolated and then burned alive. Their jaws still champed in agony long after they'd been reduced to thin, charred corpses. When they were still, Magdalena believed she was at last free and spent several days sleeping in her old bed and trying to forget all else.

After three days of dozing, she awoke to a sickeningly familiar sight. The door swung open, and all seven of the elders, looking entirely unscathed, drifted into her room. Magdalena made a mad dash for the window, but they caught her before she could leap. She apparently hadn't burned them long enough; they'd survived the blaze.

Magdalena didn't give in without a fight. She'd succeeded in tearing Eadwulf's arms from his body and beheading Rúna before Ulrich caught her. She clashed with him, fighting for her very life, but he overpowered her in the end.

For several long nights, Magdalena sat in darkness as they discussed her fate in the estate above. The laws of their order prevented them from taking the life of another Ophiuchan, even one who had attempted to destroy them—it was a crime to waste any of the Divine Serpent's blood.

At last they arrived at a solution: they decided to bury Magdalena so deep in the earth that she would have no chance of seeing the light of day again. They would keep her alive, her holy blood and flesh preserved if they ever required it, but permanently trapped. It was the only way they could feel safe. They explained this to her as if they felt true remorse for their decision.

How clearly Magdalena could still see that gaping gash in the ground as they pushed her in. It felt as if she'd fallen for miles, plummeting downward into the hungry darkness. From the moment she slammed into the bottom of the pit, she knew her bones had been shattered. They'd hardly had time to reset themselves in the proper position before the burial began. Within minutes she felt it: the rhythmic slap of soil on her back.

Her cries for mercy, muffled and choked by dirt, still rang in her ears. She still felt her hands clawing madly at the sides of the pit while they threw more soil on top of her. Not even an hour had passed before she was completely encased in the ground. From there, the pressure around her only increased. The more she struggled, the more filth crept down her throat. The urge to cough and expel the obstruction was constant and maddening, but there was nowhere for it to go. Still the pressure and weight increased.

Every time Magdalena thought it couldn't get any more agonizing, it worsened tenfold. For the first few days, as she endured the overwhelming physical pain and mental anguish, she grew increasingly certain that the Ophiuchans would return for her—that they just wanted to scare her badly enough to earn her obedience. She bargained silently with them, her tears soaking the crushing earth. But they never came.

Even now, as she stood in the Edinburgh rain, revisiting that dark memory, tears stung at her eyes.

Time had no meaning deep in the earth. There was only a suffering so heightened that Magdalena's only resource was to try to disassociate completely from her consciousness. Sleep wasn't something that came to her often, and her hunger for living flesh grew ever more acute. She hoped with a fierce, frantic passion it was possible for an Ophiuchan to die from starvation, but after the first several years, she abandoned that prospect. After ten years, her sanity had all but faded. For fifty years she remained in that prison of absolute darkness and pain—crushed, unmoving, starving, alone, suffocated, and in total blackness.

Then one day, amid the depths of her misery, something changed. In the soundlessness of the deep place, something whispered. At first Magdalena thought it was her own madness growing beyond all control, but after she spent an unimaginably long time straining to hear it, it sounded louder. A voice was speaking to her, seemingly coming from the earth itself. All she could do was listen for it and become more attuned to hearing the words it tried so desperately to breathe to her. As frustration drove her deeper into lunacy, it became a sort of torture unto itself until one jarring, life-changing moment.

Without warning or reason, the whisper that had been so quiet and distant became louder than a peal of thunder. She never would forget the first words the Cold Voice had spoken to her. The sheer force of it almost split her head apart.

Let me in.

Yes! she had wanted to scream. The voice was neither male nor female; it was instead the voice of grinding stones, of beastly roars, of crashing water. It was ancient beyond anything else in this world, harsh and untamable. Magdalena's willingness to allow it to communicate with her had opened a pathway between them. From that moment on, more words and more strength seeped into her from the source of the Cold Voice. Although it never answered her when she asked what it wanted or what it was, it gave her direction. She had long forgotten which way was up: gravity had no meaning when pressure crushed in from every angle. The voice guided her hands and feet; her already unnaturally strong Ophiuchan limbs surged with power from this outside source. Magdalena surrendered to the voice as if possessed, allowing it to conduct her upward, inching herself closer to the surface by piercing through the packed earth and pushing herself up. It was two years of near-constant effort before she finally broke the surface.

The feeling of ripping her way out of her subterranean prison was akin to being born again. After finally expelling all the dirt from her airway, she lay gasping on the ground. The images of the stars and moon beaming back were so bright she felt they would blind her. The Cold Voice had been silent while Magdalena gathered her strength bit by painful bit; she began with the insects and worms she could find near her breached grave, then climbed the trees to find birds. Soon she hunted the villagers in the nearby hamlet, glutting on fresh, living meat and blood to her sanguine heart's content. Freedom had set her madness loose, and she carved a trail of carnage through the land as she went.

It took her nearly a month to find her way back to the Cold Voice through submerging herself in freezing water, but when she did, the voice had more instructions for her. It led her to study dark magic, pointed her toward the tomes and scrolls that detailed true power, and to open her abominable boutique in Edinburgh. Her goal was simple then: to kill as many Ophiuchans as possible. She would only be satisfied when the earth was rid of all but seven of them; they would have a more specific punishment. Death was too good for them.

She hunted down her own kind, whether or not they had previously offended her. She needed practice for hunting the elders who had trapped her. Her rage, unquenchable bloodlust, and unrestrained sadism became known throughout the world, earning her the moniker of "the Lunatic Magdalena." The elders knew she had risen and was coming for them. Magdalena wanted them to know; the terror they felt at being hunted was part of their punishment. Several times they attempted to track her down and stop her before she caught them, but the Cold Voice always alerted her and led her to safety. Soon she learned the art of bewitching her shop so it was only accessible by a select few, and she could rest easy for a time.

At last the voice whispered to her that she was ready. It led her to the elders when they were separated and vulnerable, and one by one, Magdalena succeeded in capturing them all. She placed them each in their own personal, abysmal oubliette in the basement of her shop. Her punishments for them were varied—through experimentation and interrogation, she spent years carefully discovering what each of her captives feared and reviled most. Then she brought all their nightmares to reality. But no matter how they suffered at her hand, no matter how they begged, it never satisfied her. Her wrath could never be put to sleep, and her despair remained severe as ever. Nothing could soothe the suffering they'd subjected her to, not even after all these years.

In the midst of her doubtful frustration, the strange case of the younger Mr. Hare had presented itself. When he had arrived on her doorstep begging for help, she couldn't stop herself from smiling broadly. She marveled at the fact that she hadn't thought of using him before—after all, it was she who had transferred the revenants from father to son to begin with. It was the perfect solution: eternal torment. No rest. No escape. Perhaps then the elders would truly know what they had done to her...perhaps then her aching heart could start to heal.

But not if the revenants are allowed to slip away. Seven souls for seven elders. If it is incomplete, then all this has been for nothing. I cannot fail...not when I've come this far.

She looked up at the anatomical museum's windows once more. Everything would be decided here. As if her thoughts had triggered it, a noise of wooden wheels on cobblestones creaked in the distance. Hare had done his work: they were here. Slinking among the shadows, Magdalena crept out of sight as the cart groaned through the rain and came to a halt in front of the museum's entrance. She crouched in a corner, hugging herself and burying her head between her knees as she sent her thoughts into the abyss.

If you're listening, please do what you can. You have brought me to this. Do not let it be for naught. Please.

The Tunnel of Bones

"Stop here," Ainsley heard Hare rasp as the horse clopped its way in front of the black iron gate. "In there...it's in there, I'm certain." He pointed through the wet and the dark to a doorway. Ainsley's brow knitted, and her head clouded with doubt. She pushed her wet curls out of her face after she pulled the cart to a halt. As she went about hitching the horse up, Fana and Edgar slowly undid Hare's bonds, watching him closely as they did. Once he was free, Ainsley grabbed her crossbow and bolts from the cart.

Her confusion at Edgar's sudden recovery had filled her with a host of mixed feelings, none of which she wished to acknowledge at this time. She wanted to focus on only one thing: capturing the remaining two revenants so she could be free to search for a life to save. The world outside the Wood was just as cruel as she'd remembered; she didn't think it would be too difficult to be of help to someone, especially in this filthy city of stone and mortar. However, although she found it a bit hard to swallow, the outside had some good in it too; the friends she had made last night at the card table had shown her something of that. She shouldered these thoughts and gazed over the anatomical museum at the university, which Hare had led them to. Now that they'd finally arrived, Ainsley's trepidation intensified.

Without pausing, she marched up to the gate, quickly wrote a seal on the damp paper in her pocket, and threw it against the locked gate. The paper singed; the iron glowed a hot red; and moments later it sprang open. She pushed it aside gruffly and moved on to unlocking the main door, while Edgar, Fana, and Hare followed her through the gate.

While she was working on the second spell, she glanced back at her company. She was sure now that it was more than just her imagination: Edgar and Fana were acting strangely around each other. Not only that, but he also seemed even quieter and more peculiar than usual—at times his eyes would unfocus and his breath would grow short, as if a sudden fear or confusion had gripped him. As a low burn of anger coursed through her chest, she tried not to think of what Edgar had done and why he was still alive. Fana never made this many exceptions for one human life. Never.

Fighting the urge to glare at him, she finished writing the spell and the door sprang open. They all gathered close to one another as they stared into the yawning entrance of the museum. Even in the dark, the outlines of massive skeletons and ghostly reflections on glass were visible. Fear nagged at Ainsley, so she threw her shoulders back and puffed her chest out to mask it.

"Let's go," she whispered, and pushed forward before the rest of them could budge. The first sight that greeted her was a massive pair of elephant skeletons that stood like sentries on either side of the door. Ainsley stepped past them, her eyes studying the bones. The deeper she plunged into the cavernous hall, the thicker the silence and darkness became. As the hair on the back of her neck prickled, she became certain a malicious spirit resided in these halls.

"Where is it?" Fana whispered behind her as they all shuffled in and Hare closed the door behind them.

"Above, on the top floor," Hare breathed. "I can feel it. It's Joseph, the miller. He was the first victim."

As if speaking the name of the spirit had invoked its presence, a muttering stirred up from the edges of the museum among the displays of bones, body parts, and dried tissue. Ainsley felt a sudden shift in the atmosphere; it was almost magnetic in its force and seemed to press in on them from all sides. Each one of them felt it, making them cry out softly and stumble. The world around them began to warp, as if they were looking at it through curved glass.

Inside the display cases, the bits of preserved flesh shifted slightly, as though they were gradually coming back to life. A skinless man's fingers began to twitch. A low rattle went through a set of hand bones. In a jar, a long-dead heart gave a twinge, as if trying to remember how to beat. Close to Ainsley's shoulder, a head that had been cut into in order to show a cross-section slowly twisted toward her, its mouth opening wider and the eyelid rising upward. Ainsley bit her tongue to stop the bile rising in her throat, then fixed her eyes on the staircase at the end of the room.

"Hurry! Don't look at them. Just keep going!" she commanded her horror-struck companions as she led the charge across the display hall. As Ainsley pounded forward, panes of glass broke near her, and skeletons shivered into motion. Jawbones clacked against skulls, and dry joints creaked as she made it to the first step. After throwing a quick glance backward to make sure everyone was still close behind, she raced up the staircase. Ainsley readied another sheet of invocation paper as she flew up the stairs and onto the second floor. Edgar came up panting behind her, clutching his chest.

She turned back to him with blazing eyes. "Can you see where it's hiding? Can you feel it?" She predicted it would be only moments until the dead things started crawling around in this room too.

With a bleary gaze, Edgar studied the room. "Th-there," he gasped, pointing to a marble statue depicting the bust of a man. The pedestal it stood upon was flanked by two more elephant skeletons, and the floor around it was littered with the skulls of lions. Above it hung the bones of something that looked to Ainsley like a sea monster. "Right in the center of the statue."

Ainsley nodded, and before Edgar could say anything more, she rushed toward the statue. Warily she held out her hands as she advanced, reaching toward the statue's chest. Instead of meeting with hard stone, her hands passed through a veil of what felt like static electricity. She continued, walking through it entirely. Inside this space, the view was completely different. Although this room also contained the dissected remains of deceased things, the specimens were as tall as trees. These ghastly objects were very much alive and oozed fluid as they pressed up against the glass. Inside jars clouded with formalin, fetuses and severed hands struggled against their entrapments. Edgar and Fana passed through the barrier and joined Ainsley in this nightmarish realm. They huddled close to one another, gazing up at the towering skeletons around them.

Moments later, Hare also stepped through into the revenant's hiding place, and the environment around them changed yet again. The shelves in the back of the room issued lines of smoke, and embers flared. Less than a minute later, flames burst up. Out of the corner of her eye, Ainsley saw Hare cringe at the sight of them.

There was fire at the fair too, she thought. *That murdering dog is afraid of fire. Perhaps the revenants' hiding places reflect what we least want to see.*

Suddenly the floor shook, and a red light sprang up in the stairwell across the room, as if someone had lit a colored gaslight. The wall to Ainsley's left crumbled away as a hole began to appear. A tunnel was forming out of the wall, the interior lined entirely with bones. As she stared into it, transfixed, her chest tightened, and an overwhelming sense of dread filled her. The rumbling increased, and Ainsley whipped around to see another tunnel open up in the opposite wall.

"Keep going ahead," Hare's voice was quavering as he tried to keep his balance. "He's up there." He pointed to the stairwell that was drenched in red light.

Ainsley took a wide step backward, knocking into Edgar and Hare. With quivering hands she reached for her crossbow and readied it with a crank. Something was coming down the first tunnel—something with a heavy step and four paws.

"Ainsley, no," Fana warned, but Ainsley held her ground. Fana stepped closer to her and reached to touch her shoulder, as if to give her command more weight. Ainsley shook it off, still aiming into the tunnel.

"Something's coming. I won't stand here and let us get mauled," she muttered, keeping her finger on the trigger and stepping closer. "Go on if you have to."

"Ainsley, the revenant isn't that way." Edgar warned her.

Abruptly, it appeared. A beast, massive and covered in shaggy hair, loomed out of the shadows. It slunk low like a wolf, with the long body and needle fangs of a weasel, and the heavily muscled girth of a bear. It bared its fangs and let out a threatening growl. As its black eyes gleamed in the lowlights, Ainsley gritted her teeth.

I've killed thousands of beasts in the Wood. I can kill you too.

She strode forward, her fear giving way to her anger. Ainsley lifted her crossbow and fired directly into the beast's neck. Although the bolt hit its mark, the creature did little more than shudder. Then, in a flash, it turned tail and raced back into the darkness of the tunnel. Ainsley's fury built, and she cursed herself for not slaying it in one shot.

"It's gone, we have to move ahead," Edgar tried to persuade her, but she before she could stop herself, her hunter's instincts overtook her body. Ainsley raced down the tunnel after the beast. Her companions' cries of protest were far away now. Though the blackness swallowed them, she still heard its huge paws slapping on the bones that made up the floor of the tunnel. Ainsley, only stopping to reload her crossbow, fired bolt after bolt as quickly as she could manage, hearing some of them hit the creature. The beast never slowed, though, and didn't seem the least bit perturbed by her assault. She continued after it, her stamina fading with every step. With each gasp of air, her frustration spiked. The beast was *mocking* her, and she'd be damned if she let it get away.

In the darkness, Ainsley felt hunks of its fur beneath her feet. It was shedding or molting, which spurred Ainsley to quicken her pace to keep up. That meant the beast was weakening; she was sure of it. A low red light lit the tunnel, and she finally saw the hulking mass of the animal. Her presumption was correct: parts of its fur and skin were falling off, and patches of bone showed through the tufts of fur.

As Ainsley loaded another bolt with a wrenching of the crank, she aimed for the back of its head, the animal came to a slow halt in front of her. Her charge stopped too, and as its body twisted around, more and more of its fur fell off. When it turned to face her, Ainsley's stomach did a sick flip, and her knees nearly buckled. Its face had changed; it now had the visage of a woman whom she'd only ever seen in a drawing. It was her mother, Sylvia, who stared back at her, placid and dead eyed.

Ainsley's breath caught in her throat, and the arm holding the crossbow dropped in a feeble motion. As the beast's body continued to stretch, almost all the fur dropped away, revealing a strangely shaped mass of bones with her mother's face and a mane of red hair at the top. Ainsley's eyes streamed, overwrought by the violated image of her mother, and with an unwavering hand, she aimed for the center of its forehead. As the bolt connected, the face simply smiled back at her, the eyes still lightless and unseeing. The creature whipped around again and continued down the tunnel. Furious and sick to her stomach, Ainsley ripped after it with a war cry reverberating in her throat.

I'll get it; I'll hunt it down...I won't stop chasing it until it's completely destroyed. I'll die before I let it get away, she thought as blood pounded in her ears. The red light grew brighter as she followed the twisting tunnel. It seemed to have no end. The farther she ran, the more power this place seemed to have over her mind and body. It fed her rage and piqued her confusion. All thoughts of her companions had left her entirely. As Ainsley hurtled forward, the beast spoke to her, its voice mimicking a human's but lacking something vital.

"Oh...oh...Ainsley," the creature called out as it clattered over the bones. It no longer had front paws, but two skeletal arms that ended in blades like scythes. "What a mess you've made."

"*I've* made?" she raged back, gasping for air, at once bizarrely convinced it was her mother speaking. "You did this, *you!* You cursed him in the first place. You brought this pain on all of us!"

"I punished the unjust. I gave him what he deserved," the beast shouted back, with a soulless fury that bit into Ainsley's heart. "Isn't that what you always say? Never let them get away with anything?"

"I'll rip you apart piece by *bloody piece!*" Ainsley shrieked, holstering her crossbow behind her back and splattering a seal of blood over an invocation paper. It incinerated as she tossed it at the monster. The flames enveloped the beast, but it gave no sign that it was suffering. Instead it laughed, its voice shifting and changing until it became eerily familiar. Ainsley staggered backward as the flames died away, and the creature trundled to a halt and turned to face her again.

What looked back at her was different yet again: it was her own face smiling back at her. Filled with wild rage, Ainsley drew her hunter's knife from her belt and raced forward. She leapt for the beast, catching it round the neck and pulling herself upward over its bones. She madly hacked and stabbed at its visage, trying to slice the likeness of her own face off the abomination. With each plunge of the knife, however, its laughter only grew louder, and the creature itself swelled bigger. Ainsley was thrown from its back and hit the ground hard. She gasped and rolled out of the way just in time to avoid getting pierced by one of its sickle-like legs.

Ainsley was back on her feet after only a moment, and in a blind rage she slung every harmful spell she could think of at the creature. Nothing would faze it, though, and Ainsley realized too late that her attacks actually were feeding it, making it stronger. Stumbling back from the beast, she pressed her back to the wall. The creature moved in on her, holding an arm on either side of her body.

A rushing sound of flapping cloths thundered down the tunnel. Fana erupted from the darkness. Before the monster could turn to see her, Fana skidded forward, grabbed one of its arms, and ripped it out of its socket. After tossing it aside with disgust, she extended a hand to Ainsley and helped her away from the beast. Fana looked icily down Ainsley as she pulled her to safety.

"Fana, I'm sorry—I don't know how to kill it. I thought it…" she stammered while trying to placate her.

"It *can't* be killed," Fana dismissed her. "It's a distraction, Ainsley."

"But we can't just *leave* it!" Ainsley protested, still under the influence of the beast. It baited her anger and will, but Ainsley then deflated under Fana's irate glare. She felt as if she were emerging from out of a dream at that moment. "C-can we?"

Without answering or letting go of Ainsley's hand, Fana pulled her back down the tunnel, away from the beast. As Fana led her away into the darkness, Ainsley kept her eyes fixed on the creature. It didn't appear to want to pursue them but merely stood undulating and laughing while mocking her with her own grin. Ainsley tried to swallow the last of her fury as they fled, but it was still impossible, so instead she channeled it into her motivation to trap the revenant.

After an anguished run through the tunnels, Fana and Ainsley burst back into the central room to find Hare and Edgar trapped in a ring of fire. Above them, the ceiling was dripping with a noxious waxy substance that was melting a collection of bones beneath it. Ainsley pierced her finger once again then smeared a spell across the paper. It produced a powerful gust of wind that reduced the wall of flames just long enough for Hare and Edgar to leap to safety.

"Keep your focus," Fana hissed at all of them. "This place will addle your mind…try to bewitch you. Remember what we're here for."

Only after Fana had made her point did Ainsley begin to even guess that the revenant had ensnared her and manipulated her thoughts. Blinking, she followed Fana across the floor of rattling bones and bursts of flame. They traversed between the towering shelves until the stairwell was in view. They all pounded up the steps, drenched in the red glow of the unseen gas lamp. With every step, the oppressive force that pushed in on them intensified.

As they entered the room at the top of the stairs, Ainsley heard Edgar gasp and saw him visibly shudder. It was a lecture theater—round with walls lined high with benches and a metallic table fixed into the center. It took Ainsley only a moment to gather from Edgar's reaction and the objects around her that human corpses were publicly dissected here. In the center of the theater, on top of a table, was an upright glass case. It housed the complete skeleton of a man, but in stark contrast to the bones of the lower levels, it remained entirely still behind the plate of glass.

Their footsteps echoed loudly as they crept across the room to where the skeleton stood. Cautiously, Ainsley edged up to it and peered down at the plaque attached to the glass. The words WILLIAM BURKE were etched upon its surface. As they all drew in close to read it and Hare began to shiver, a breath on the back of Ainsley's neck made her glance back, and when she did, she let out a high-pitched yelp.

Behind the four of them stood another figure: a man whose neck was bruised and face discolored from rot and trauma. They all leapt away, making noises of fright and revulsion as what Ainsley immediately knew was the manifestation of Joseph, the revenant, swayed in place with wide eyes and a snarl on his lips. He was dark haired and dressed in a frayed shirt, dingy trousers, and a pair of suspenders. He stood short, with a compact build and an unkempt shadow around his chin. A dangerous gleam in his eye pronounced him as the sort of man whose temper should not be trifled with.

"Get back—stay away from me!" Hare whined like a wounded dog; clearly deeply shaken by the revenant's presence. The spirit's eyes flicked to him, baring its teeth. The revenant growled, beast-like, as he advanced. Hare froze, unable to move in time. To everyone's shock, however, Joseph only shoved Hare aside to move toward the bones in the glass case.

Joseph threw his head back, and a tortured cry issued from his crumpled throat. In a blur of movement, he was standing beside the dissection table. He continued to scream, a sound that rattled everyone's eardrums. As the revenant bellowed, he violently slammed his fists against the glass case as if he were trying to shatter it.

"Degenerate scum—depraved cretin, murdering piece of *filth*!" Joseph shouted at the bones, pounding the case over and over. "I'll peel your flesh from your bones. I'll gut you. I'll make you watch your innards burn!"

From there the revenant's curses blared out even more ferociously. Obscenities vicious and foul burst out of the entity's mouth. He raved at the bones inside the case, promising acts of violence and violation against the man they had belonged to. The revenant's bellowed words were more than simple vulgarities. They had a palpable heft to them, the sheer malice they contained a tangible force that was enough to stun even Ainsley, who was momentarily frozen under the weight of their belligerence. She could only stand there, watching him senselessly beat his fists against a glass case that would not break.

On the floor beside her, Edgar was moaning and clutching his chest as tears streamed from his eyes. Overcome with horror, Hare knelt, his fingers woven into his white hair as a look of abject helplessness washed over his face. Fana was the only one among them who seemed to be able to resist the spirit's ferocity, which felt to Ainsley like pulsing waves of intense heat.

Fana struggled to her feet with her hand shading her eyes. She took a heavy step toward the dissecting table and reached out as if to stop the spirit, but he turned his gaze on her and began to scream again.

"Don't try to stop me! If you can't see that he's done wrong, then you can't see at all!" he spat at Fana, his eyes bulging from his skull. "He can't get away with it! They cut him up once—that wasn't enough. I'll slice into this maggot for the rest of eternity for what he did. I was coming home! I had the ring she wanted. She was going to say yes! *He stole everything from us!*" the revenant shrieked, and the force blew Fana off her feet. She fell and lay cringing on the floor. Ainsley too endured the wave of pain from the sound, and when she opened her watering eyes, something in the skeleton caught her attention: a faint glint came from its left eye socket. As her hand moved to grasp a piece of invocation paper, Hare shivered up to face the revenant.

"Listen! Listen to me! I'm sorry, but you're dead, Joseph. It's over. Burke and my father—they did what they did, and yes, you died hard. There's nothing more can be done. I can't change the past, and you've damn sure hurt me long enough. Let's end this. It's time go to your rest—"

The revenant turned his attention away from Fana and flew on Hare in a matter of seconds. As the spirit latched on to him, they both burst into flames. Hare screamed as his flesh seared under the intense heat.

"*How dare you?*" Joseph raged as the fire engulfed both of them. "You repugnant excuse for a man! You think you can doom others then act as if your wounds are the only ones that bleed? You are mistaken—you deserve not a shred of pity. Your agony has not yet even *begun*. I will see to that!"

The fire burned intensely, and then Joseph himself became the embodiment of the conflagration. A heavy, greasy smoke filled the theater, and Hare howled until his flesh had become so black that he couldn't make a sound. Ainsley fought back the urge to be sick as she hurriedly pulled her thoughts together. Edgar was still quivering in pain on the floor, but he was the only one who could touch the revenant's anchor. After crawling over to him and ducking under the waves of intense heat, Ainsley threw her arms around Edgar and hauled him up onto her shoulder.

"No, p-please..." he wheezed, clearly riddled with agony. Ainsley bit her lip and ignored him. As she lifted him to his feet, Edgar made a sound akin to those of many of the animals she had killed—a sound they only made moments before death.

"Hold fast, Edgar. It's almost over. You're almost through this," she called over the crackling flames. Hare had almost been reduced to bones now, and Joseph drew back upon seeing that his victim was no longer suffering.

"No, not yet! I could kill you a thousand times, and it wouldn't be enough. Come back, you swine. Come back!" the revenant roared as more flames issued from his mouth. In a powerful, vaulting motion Ainsley managed to get herself and Edgar onto the dissecting table. Edgar screamed so loudly that it got the revenant's attention. Panicked, Ainsley held a trembling Edgar tightly to her side as she punched through the glass in a single motion. It slashed her knuckles and hand, but it was broken at last.

"*Get away from there!*" Joseph screamed, rushing toward Ainsley and Edgar. As the spirit approached them, the heat from his body shocked them. Both Ainsley and Edgar reeled from the sting of burns. Joseph appeared moments away from bursting into flame and engulfing them, as he had to the smoldering pile of bones that was now Hare.

"Edgar, grab the ring—look there, in the skull's eye," Ainsley winced, shaking him.

Edgar couldn't move. Snarling in desperation and feeling her skin sizzle, Ainsley took hold of Edgar's hand with her bloodied one and shoved it through the hole in the glass. She used his fingers to dive into the skeleton's eye socket and fish out a diamond ring that was glowing white. Though Edgar's hand touched it, its proximity filled Ainsley's fingers with molten-hot pain, and she let the ring drop to the ground. Just as they both buckled under the heat, Fana rushed over and smashed the ring with her boot heel. In tandem, Ainsley and Edgar toppled from the table, and for a long while, Ainsley fought just to stay conscious.

She heard Fana struggling with the newly released revenant and felt Edgar tremble beside her, but little else penetrated the thickness of pain. When the worst of the cruel sensation had passed, Ainsley labored to prop herself up on an elbow and assess the scene.

It was quiet now. The theater had lost its warped quality and now looked tranquil. Fana slumped against the charred dissection table and held a jar with a white flame encased in it. She panted, her eyes unfocused, like a cornered beast, her attention clearly elsewhere. Behind her, Hare's body was slowly regenerating. Ainsley could tell he'd gotten his lungs back when a sick coughing sound echoed through the theater. Still shaken and wiping the tears from his cheeks, Edgar sat up beside her. Apparently the pain had stopped, but it looked to have left him utterly dazed.

Fana quavered upward to her feet, set the jar holding the revenant and her satchel on the table, and fluttered over to Edgar's side. She smoothed his hair and looked him over with concern. Soon Ainsley felt very uncomfortable, as she sat so close by.

"Edgar, you aren't hurt, are you? The burns?" Fana scanned his person, and then, seeing Ainsley, blushed slightly and moved to attend to her as well.

"I think the injuries are shallow...for both of us," Edgar replied on Ainsley's behalf. "My pain faded almost immediately after the revenant was sealed."

"We've done it then," Fana breathed with relief before taking Edgar's and Ainsley's hands in each of her own. "Only one revenant remains."

Ainsley frowned. The tender way the woman of the woods looked upon Edgar was impossible to dismiss. She feigned a smile then carefully got to her feet.

Behind them, Hare had completely reformed and was sitting up, clutching his chest. His face looked even grayer and waxier than usual, and nothing of his general rebelliousness remained. Ainsley pitied him as much as she despised him. As if guided by some strange force, she crossed the room and offered him her cloak as an emotion very much like disgusted guilt filled her. For a moment Hare surveyed it with hollow eyes, then took from her and wrapped it about himself. Evidently, he was too defeated to object.

Eventually he rose and stumbled around the room, wobbling in place until he wandered to the table in the center and used it to brace himself. Hare's face revealed just how thoroughly disturbed he was, and Ainsley suddenly felt indecent watching him. She turned her eyes away only to find that Edgar and Fana were still embarrassingly close together and talking in hushed voices. The surgeon mumbled—his words low and panicked—something that sounded to Ainsley like, "I can't remember...I can't remember where I...why I..." over and over while Fana tried to hush him. Her frustration built, and she merely sat in place and mulled in her shock. The spirits they had encountered before Joseph had certainly unsettled her, but this one in particular made her chest feel unbearably tight. Images of the beast in its tunnel of bones haunted her as she sat on the hardwood floor.

It got away…I let it get away. I feel as if…as if something inside me will never truly be complete until I've destroyed that thing. And I'll never get another chance to do so.

Unable to face her own thoughts anymore, Ainsley decided they had spent more than enough time in this glorified mausoleum. She got back to her feet and swiveled around with her hands across her chest.

"We should leave before…" Her words faded as a violent shock jolted through her. "Where's Hare? Where are the revenants?"

He was indeed nowhere to be found. The jar and the rabbit-hide pouch full of Fana's things, including each of the revenants, were missing, along with him. Edgar and Fana leapt to their feet and frantically peered around to see if they were mistaken. Welling with panic, Ainsley leapt down the stairs and into the display hall on the second floor.

With a ghastly grimace, Hare awaited them in front of one of the huge windows at the end of the hall. Though his stance was threatening, his eyes were full of anxiety. Fana's pouch was clasped in his shivering hands.

"What the hell d'you think you're doing with that?" Ainsley demanded, as Edgar and Fana pounded down the stairs and came to a halt behind her.

"I'm sorry." He shrugged and turned his face downward. A strange, quivering smile flickered onto his lips, and his eyes grew even wilder.

Fana and Ainsley cautiously crept toward him, ready to spring if necessary. With her attention focused on Hare, Ainsley was shocked by a silky murmur that flowed out of the darkness behind her.

"Stay where you are."

Ainsley and Fana whipped around. The face nestled among the darkness sent a cold rush to Ainsley's core. The Lunatic had found them. Ainsley's heart seized as she saw that Magdalena had

Edgar in her grasp. One hand clutched his throat, while the other held both of his wrists behind his back. "This can end peacefully, if you so desire."

"Get your hands off him." Ainsley tried to advance on her, but Magdalena immediately seized Edgar so tightly that his face contorted.

"Another step and I'll rip him in half," Magdalena said calmly.

Ainsley and Fana shared an identical glance of stunned confusion. Fana swallowed. "You won't harm him—you need him. If you walk away now, I won't bury you alive. This will be your final warning, Blight."

Magdalena cocked her head to the side and smiled like the edge of a knife. "Ah, yes, wonderful effort, but that threat grows tiresome. You hold no sway over the earth here, nymph," the Ophiuchan chuckled. "This isn't your precious forest—the soil here has been dead for many hundreds of years. You couldn't command it, not if everything in your world depended on it. And as for him"—she squeezed Edgar again—"he's disposable. True, I plan on using him, but I have other ways of achieving what I want. He means nothing to me."

"You're bluffing," Ainsley growled.

"Care to test that theory, witch?" Magdalena's huge mouth opened in wicked delight, her threat puncturing Ainsley's courage. She was indeed too volatile to experiment with. Magdalena shuffled along the wall and closer to the window, where Hare stood waiting for her. Fana, who stood nearer to Hare, flashed her eyes in his direction. Ainsley guessed by her expression that she was considering making a rush for him and the revenants.

Fana, however, grew momentarily pensive. "Jacob," she called in a pleading tone.

Magdalena stopped moving and squeezed at Edgar's throat again. Ainsley poised herself to leap to Fana's aid at any moment. Hare, whose grin had entirely faded, tried to avoid looking over at

Fana. He seemed to be afraid that by giving her his attention, he would be defying his mistress. However, when she called to him again, Hare slowly turned toward Fana.

"Bring them to me. We can help you, Jacob. We can stop her together. Just don't do this...please," Fana said calmly.

Hare's face pinched in a look of torment. Magdalena stopped moving completely, her eyes flitting madly between the two of them. The fact that she no longer commanded the room's full attention obviously made her nervous. Hare licked his lips, and his gaze fell to the floor. His mouth pulled and stretched, but he couldn't answer. His gaze lifted back to Fana, and he took a long breath.

"*Hare!*" Magdalena screamed at him, her bright-blue eyes ablaze.

In an instant, his head snapped toward the Ophiuchan, and his face grew stony. Ainsley knew it was over then. "I'm sorry," he muttered, then moved toward Magdalena. She too crept closer to him and the window, and though Magdalena's anger had abated somewhat, Ainsley felt more threatened than ever. Fana's face clouded as Hare and the Ophiuchan drew nearer. Ainsley had known Fana a long time, and could tell that she was still weighing her options. Though it was almost physically painful to remain inactive, she waited for Fana to make the opening gambit.

"I cannot let you do this," Fana said at last and strode forward to intercept Hare with controlled poise. The Ophiuchan's hand flew to Edgar's throat, and her fingers dug into his flesh. He choked, and his eyes grew wide.

"I'll tear his windpipe out," Magdalena snarled.

Fana halted again, her face flushing paler.

"F-fana..." Edgar coughed through the creature's viselike grip. "I'm...dead anyway. Get the revenants. Don't let her win." His voice was hoarse and sputtering, but he forced the words out.

Magdalena's mouth grew to a thin line, and before he could say another word, her grip tightened. In a mere instant, as Fana lunged to stop her, he passed out. Fana halted and her eyes widened. Ainsley's heart smashed against her ribs; Fana still wasn't taking action, and she couldn't take this any longer.

"He's right, Fana!" she hollered. "He's going to die either way!"

"I…" Fana shuddered, her eyes huge and glued to Magdalena. "I can't." She sounded as if she could hardly believe her own words. Ainsley's brow furrowed, bewildered, as Magdalena tossed her head back and burst into high, cold laughter.

"Oh, how could I have missed it?" Magdalena cackled, her eyes alight with fierce delight. "Oh dear, you can't be serious. Could my little nymph be in love? How wonderfully tragic."

Ainsley's frustration suddenly snapped. She grabbed her crossbow and loaded a bolt. She was almost quick enough, but Magdalena's keen senses surpassed hers. With a disorienting speed, Magdalena leapt out of the way and slung Edgar's limp form over her shoulder. Fana at last rushed forward, but Magdalena was already halfway across the room. She darted over to Hare, snatched the pouch from his hands, and without a moment's hesitation, went careening for the window. Magdalena hit it with her shoulder, and it shattered on contact. As she leapt into the night, shards of glass shredded her once-pristine taffeta gown and she dropped out of sight in an instant.

"*Mag*! Don't leave me here!" Hare yelped. He made to run after her, but Ainsley wouldn't allow it. She let loose another bolt, and it sunk into his calf, rendering him momentarily immobile. She was on him in seconds, pinning him to the floor with her knees.

"*You filthy bastard, we would've helped you!*" she howled down at him as her hand crushed his neck in a motion of rage.

Fana fluttered over to the window, her boots crunching the broken glass. She threw her head back, but just as feathers began to sprout from her arms, she stopped. Ainsley couldn't contain herself. The more she throttled Hare, the more her anger impaired her judgment.

"You've destroyed everything we've worked for! For nothing! *Nothing*!" Ainsley screeched, tossing aside her crossbow and pulling out a slip of paper.

"She would've *tortured* me!" Hare wheezed.

"You don't yet know torture... I'll make you pray to your false God that Magdalena had taken you—if you can even form words," Ainsley seethed.

With a quick stab, blood once again flowed from her finger, and with precision, she wrote out a seal. Her stomach churned as she stained the paper with the symbols, and though her throat caught with guilt as she did it, she wouldn't let Hare walk away from this day unpunished.

"Wh-what are you doing? Stop!" he whispered, trying to crawl away from under her weight. Ainsley kept him pinned with her knee as she finished the seal. She was trembling with rage, her chest jittering with the compulsion to harm him so deeply that he would never recover. The foulness of injustice clouded her judgment, and she hissed the words that would ignite her spell.

"*Spirits of the sacred flame, rise. O eternal fire, I invoke thee.*" The seals glowed brilliantly and began to smolder. "You're going to burn for the rest of your miserable existence, Hare," Ainsley shouted, as the ward paper smoked furiously then burst into flame.

Once the paper flared away, only the seals remained floating in air, crackling with fire. A bead of sweat rolled down her forehead as she used her hands to contain the force of the spell she commanded. With a great deal of effort, she pushed it closer to Hare's chest. He screamed at the sight of it, though Ainsley knew that his fear, no matter how deep, wasn't enough to match the punishment that was about to descend on him.

"*Ainsley, no!*" Fana yelped from behind. She sounded so thoroughly terrified that Ainsley lost focus and the spell dissipated. Ainsley took a moment to catch her breath, and though her entire body shook with wrath, she looked back and caught Fana's eye. The timeless nymph's eyes betrayed fear, not anger, and as soon as she connected with her gaze, Ainsley came to grim realization that, had she successfully cursed Hare to burn forever, any hope of life in the Witches' Wood would have been lost to her forever. She would have suffered the same fate as her mother.

Ainsley lost all strength. Defeated, Hare easily threw her off him. She toppled over as he wriggled away. He hurtled toward the window, and Fana dove to stop him. She made a grab for him, but he dipped out of the way just in time; in the moment that she stumbled after missing him, Hare jumped headfirst through the window. Ainsley heard the sickening thud as he hit the ground.

As Fana regained her balance, she cast a glance back at Ainsley. She tried to apologize to Fana, but her words were stuck in her chest, and she merely released an anguished breath. Fana's eyes sharpened, and she immediately took the form of an owl, her body melting and shrinking into the feathered creature faster than Ainsley had ever seen her transform. With a flap of her massive wings, she soared through the window and left Ainsley crouching in the desolate museum hall. Stunned, Ainsley could do nothing but glance about at the macabre collection that surrounded her. She'd never known anything like the despair and shame that ripped through her during those long, torturous moments as she waited for Fana to return.

She'll catch him. She's fast... Perhaps she'll catch them both. This isn't over...not yet...

As the moments dripped past, the last vestiges of hope disintegrated in Ainsley's chest and she knew she was lying to herself. No amount of surprise shook her when Fana swooped back into the room half an hour later. The owl's feathers ruffled then slowly bloomed outward before the shape of a woman reformed. Ainsley looked into Fana's eyes, noted the tears that welled there, and hung her head.

A Legacy of Burdens

The horse refused to take another step. The exhausted, obstinate creature stood firmly in the square. Fana eased herself down as Ainsley tried to urge the beast onward. The woman of the woods drifted away from the side of the cart, feeling as if a massive weight lay upon her shoulders. She came to rest by a black column that rose high above the grassy square, then leaned against the stone as she looked blankly to the sky. Daybreak would be on them in a little less than an hour.

"Move, you bloody lummox. *Move,*" Ainsley grunted, yanking the reins to no avail.

"Ainsley, it's no use," Fana called from where she sat. "He's been walking all day and night. He needs to rest."

Ainsley's expression darkened, but eventually she removed the horse's harness and prepared some food for it. The two of them had scoured the city through the night, desperate to find even a trace of the Lunatic, Hare, or Edgar. The hopelessness of the situation was beginning to overwhelm them.

Fana sighed, her chest aching with raw misery. *How could I have been so careless? How could I let this come to be?* She wanted to be back in her pool, assimilated with the woods. She longed for the green nourishment of the forest and the safety of being spread throughout it. Bearing the millstone of her concentrated soul for so long was too difficult. She sometimes wondered how the witches could stand being alive for so long, permanently trapped inside their own heads.

"Well, should we leave him then? Go on foot?" Ainsley glanced at Fana, her voice high and urgent, her eyes frantic, as if she dare not accept the possibility that they had failed.

Fana's tired gaze connected with hers, and she slowly shook her head.

"Well, what are we going to do, Fana? There can't be much time left. That devil has probably—"

"Ainsley, it's done with. We've lost them. Magdalena has claimed the revenants. We can't stop her now." Fana was shocked to hear her voice warble as she spoke. She fought off tears, trying not to think of Edgar. She had let him slip away—along with the rarity of his devotion, his honesty, and the purity in his heart. Fana couldn't bring herself to touch him the last time they were alone together, to understand the truth behind his feelings. So she had endeavored to deny them, to convince herself that they were inauthentic, that his judgment was altered by the approach of death. She cringed under the realization that she had lost him due to stubbornness and fear, lost him to her careless faults, lost him to Magdalena. At this moment, the grief over the loss of that beautiful potential pained her more deeply than any other injury of her past.

"Fana, you know this isn't over yet," Ainsley protested as she hurried to the nymph's side and took her hand.

"In all likelihood, Edgar is doomed. Even if we do manage to locate them, the revenant will have consumed him already. And there's no hope of being able to find the last one without him." Fana laid out the bleak facts one by one, watching Ainsley's face grow more ashen with every word.

Ainsley opened her mouth as if to challenge her further, but after a moment's silence she deflated with a breath and sank down next to Fana. They sat in silence for a long while, watching traces of light creep over the horizon.

"How did it all go so wrong?" Ainsley whispered, sounding as if she wanted to get up the energy to be agitated but could not find it. "This is all my mother's fault. Why did she have to do it in the first place? She cursed that murderer, and now we're all paying the price. She couldn't just let him go—she had to keep the pain alive, and throw everything away to make that happen. She damned herself; she damned Hare; and she damned us. She *knew* what she was doing. She knew she'd be banished from the Wood. She knew…"

Ainsley's tirade grew weaker until she fell quiet. She shut her eyes and took a shuddering breath, her streams of untamed red hair obscuring her face.

"No…maybe that's not it, after all," Ainsley said in a small voice. Fana looked over at her, deeply concerned. "I can't keep blaming the past for everything that goes wrong. If I hadn't leapt on Hare—if I hadn't lost my focus in there, Edgar would still be with us, and we'd still have the revenants. All these things—so many things—were lost because I just wouldn't see. I share the blame."

Fana's heart ached even more to see Ainsley in such a state, and she reached over to grab her shoulder. Sharing a long, miserable look, they clung lightly to each other, as if they were the only things keeping each other anchored to the ground.

Before Fana could be entirely swept away by the emptiness of her heart, Ainsley spoke again. "We never should have left the Wood. We weren't made for this side of the world. We owe nothing to this place—these people. Let the spirits take them… Let the Lunatic have her way. We should go back to where we belong," Ainsley suggested in a voice that wasn't her own.

The strange lack of life in her voice disturbed Fana deeply, and her grip on the young witch's shoulder grew tighter. The fire within her—the fire inherited from her mother Sylvia that had stoked her with rage and reckless confidence and passion—had all but been snuffed out. To see her so anguished left Fana repulsed, and her eyes dropped to the ground. As a sick sensation spread through her, she realized it wasn't just because of Ainsley. She had come to revile herself as well.

Neither Ainsley nor Sylvia is fully responsible for this. I've been cowardly. I've been cold, foolish. I've been so frightened of pain that I've detached from this world I swore to love and protect. We've come to this because of my urge to retreat into what felt comfortable and safe to me. Edgar could have been saved—I could've made him my warden. I won't make another mistake so costly... I won't leave a legacy of burdens as Sylvia did. I won't hide this time.

Fana stood, her body shivering with nervous rejuvenation. Ainsley looked up to her, surprised at her sudden movement.

"You're right about one thing, Ainsley," she began, her voice trembling. "We weren't made for this place. But even though we don't easily fit into this world, it doesn't mean we'll flee from it. I now see the pattern of my errors, and I seek to put an end to it. Forgive my weakness, dear one," she said, a grim but determined energy filling her.

Ainsley stared at her, clearly surprised at her abrupt shift in attitude. "But you said yourself that we have no hope of finding them."

"I remain convinced that we can't discover where Magdalena is *now*, but I forgot to consider the fact that we know where she will *be*," Fana felt inspiration beginning to blossom. "She won't let that last revenant stay free. Though we can't easily get into where it's rooted without Edgar's guidance, if we can find the place it poisons, surely Magdalena will be drawn there as well. If we can get to her, we can use to her to find Edgar—he might still be alive. We can still stop her."

"Do you honestly think that will work?" Ainsley's pained visage was colored with a tinge of hope.

Fana hesitated as she weighed their chances. "No. It's essentially impossible," she admitted, but a dauntless smile crept onto her face nonetheless. "Still, I must try. If there's a chance to save the revenants...to...to save Edgar, I must try."

"Save Edgar?" Ainsley echoed. "But his fate is sealed. Either way, he...no, you can't mean—"

"I do," Fana assured her. Shock flooded Ainsley's expression, but the jangling of her emotions seemed to bring life back into her.

"Will you stay, Ainsley?" Fana asked, her heart filling with mingled measures of hope and trepidation.

Ainsley stood and took a small step forward. Fana knew at once from the look in her eyes that, though she was still mired in the weight of her confusion, the rekindling of that ever-present flame was already underway.

At the End

"Hurry, Hare. Put him in the trap we built for the others."

"Don't make me go back there, Mag, I beg of you."

The pair of agitated voices brought Edgar back from the darkness. As he listened to their argument, he fought off the instinct to open his eyes or move an inch.

"Are you not aware of how close we are to losing everything? I need to get to the church this instant, and I haven't eaten yet. I'll need my strength," Magdalena hissed at him, panic behind her fury.

"Please...I never want to go down there again. I'll go to the church first. I'll meet you there. If they show up, I'll handle it. Please."

Hare's fragile timbre sent a shock through Edgar. Magdalena fell quiet at this. Edgar could feel that he was sitting, propped up against a wall. It was quiet and he felt no touch of wind on him, which led him to believe they were indoors, but nothing else was clear. Wanting to assess the situation further, he remained still.

"Have it your way then. Do you know the way?" The frustration and resignation in her voice suggested a desire to bypass the argument to save time.

"Saint Cuthbert, wasn't it?"

"Yes. Now fetch the ampoule. If needs be, collect it without me. I'll join you shortly," Magdalena directed him.

After some shuffling sounds, a door opened and shut. Footsteps crossed the room, and Edgar couldn't help jump as he felt

Magdalena's cold hands on him. His eyes snapped open to see her ghostly-white skin and huge eyes only a foot from his face. She smiled at the sight of his shock.

"Ha-ha, good morning," she purred, lifting Edgar up and onto his feet as if he were a mere child. They were in the same shop she'd brought him to before.

"Wh-what's happening?"

"We've established that you cannot behave as a polite guest, so I'm going to escort you to a more fitting location," Magdalena said conversationally, gripping Edgar's upper arm. His eyes flashed to the door, and she shook her head. "Ah, not this time, Mr. Price. We've arrived at the end, I'm afraid."

Edgar pulled away from her, his stomach sick with fright and his chest feeling as if it were ripping apart, but she was too powerful for him to overcome. The Lunatic yanked him across the shop and to a door in the back—the door Hare always looked upon with such dread.

Edgar choked under a wave of aversion. "Where are we going? What's back there?" he demanded in a panicked voice.

Magdalena remained silent as she wrenched it open to reveal a set of stairs that led both up and down. They made the turn to descend, traversing a dank stairwell. As they went deeper, a hideous smell of stale blood, rotting flesh, mold, and filth filled the air. He tried to struggle against her to make the way as difficult as possible. As he fought, he fell in a painful tangle. Instead of waiting for him to get up again, Magdalena dragged him down the rest of the stairs. He thrashed to get away as they came to a heavy wooden door at the bottom of the staircase. Magdalena lifted a ring of keys from a nail near the door and unlocked it.

A gaping dark space lay beyond the door. As the noise of the creaking hinge echoed in the space beyond, a blood-curdling scream rang out from the end of the cavernous corridor. The voice was frantic, shrieking in German. It sounded to Edgar as if someone were pleading. As more moans and weeping echoed in the hall, Magdalena restrained a grin. She wrenched Edgar inside and heaved the wooden door shut behind them.

The Lunatic barked a harsh command in German at the chorus of wailing voices, and one by one, they fell quiet. A trembling silence filled the chamber as Magdalena fumbled about in the black room. A match flame flared up, and the hiss of gas sounded. The Ophiuchan lit the lamps, revealing a wide room made of metal and brick. A way's off, Edgar spotted an open doorway. Through it, at the far end of the dungeon-like space, were seven pits—he guessed them to be oubliettes. From inside those deep pits, sobbing and shuddering gasps rose into the air. His stomach lurched at the thought of who—or what—might be down there. A metal ladder in the corner explained how Magdalena accessed her victims.

Lining the walls were wooden shelves and tables, all stocked with a most unusually cruel and diverse array of tools. A few of them he recognized from the dissection theaters and hospital rooms, the others from museums. Their purpose was clear. Next to the shelves sat a row of Medieval torture devices: an iron maiden, a rack, a Judas Cradle. Other malevolent devices cluttered every inch of the space, stained with evidence of frequent barbarism. Edgar froze, transfixed in horror by a figure that dangled from a wooden beam. The man was stark naked, suspended above a pit by chains wrapped around his wrists. A metal mask that formed a grotesque visage of an animal covered his face, barring speech and digging into his skull with spikes, though no blood flowed from the wounds.

It took him only a moment to realize this man wasn't human but an Ophiuchan like Magdalena. He could see his face through the metal bands of mask; his eyes, huge and glassy, rolled about, peering back down at Edgar. Decades of endless misery stared down at him. His flesh was whiter than paper, and judging from how grotesquely emaciated he was, the Ophiuchan hadn't eaten in years. With a frightful yelp, Edgar scrambled to his feet and raced for the door, but Magdalena caught him before he could even touch the handle. Terror swarmed through him, but a vaguely pitying look came over Magdalena's face as she saw his reaction.

"Ah, there, there...don't worry, *liebchen*. These aren't intended for you. Though you have caused me great distress, you aren't deserving of such torment. I daresay you've had to contend with enough already."

The softness in her voice made Edgar's insides squirm. The hanging Ophiuchan's haunted eyes never strayed from Edgar. Magdalena fluttered over and locked the door, blocking her captives from Edgar's view.

"Why have you brought me here then?" Edgar said, fighting off another wave of panic.

Magdalena pointed to a corner of the room, to a crate about seven feet in height and width, with a small latched door. She grabbed a candlestick from one of the tables and forced Edgar over to the box. With a quick hand, she undid the latch and pushed him inside.

As candlelight illuminated the cramped space, Edgar took a sharp breath to see the interior of the crate was made entirely of mirrors. Reflections of himself repeated into eternity. The vision of the flickering flame, multiplied hundreds of thousands of times, made him feel as though he were surrounded by a universe of dying stars. Magdalena commanded Edgar to sit in the center of the crate before setting the candle down beside him.

"What is this?" he asked, looking about the crate.

"Mirrors are one of the few things that keep revenants contained. Once it consumes you, it'll be trapped in here until I collect it—they cannot bear the sight of themselves."

"And what...what was all that back there? Who are those people?" Edgar dared ask as she stood above him.

With an unreadable expression, Magdalena considered his question for a moment. "Wretched things that are getting what they deserve," she finally said. "I plan on serving them final justice very soon. In fact, I have you to thank for that, in part."

Edgar blinked as he started to piece together everything in his mind. "That's really what this is all for?" he asked in a disbelieving tone. "You're using me…you're removing the revenants from Hare so you can attach them to those creatures in there? That's why I'm going to die?"

"Ah, how astute of you," Magdalena sounded mildly impressed. "Hare told you, didn't he? Yes. This is the only way I can ensure their eternal suffering. The revenants will be fed, fully realized, and full of rage. They'll never allow their victims a moment's peace, and I'll never let these horrid creatures die. Seven spirits for seven sinners," she sang the last five words like a child's doggerel, which made Edgar's neck prickle unpleasantly.

"Who could possibly deserve such a thing?" Edgar said before he could stop himself.

Magdalena's face turned grim as she gazed down at him with contempt. "Have you never felt the sting of true cruelty? How have you lived in this filthy world this long and never been exposed to it?"

"I have," Edgar replied, hatred running through him like poison.

"And if you could, would you arrange for that wrongdoer to understand the pain they caused? Wouldn't you impose it on them tenfold, since they're apparently so ignorant of the devastation they've caused?" Magdalena's voice trembled as she stared deeply into Edgar's eyes.

For a moment their eyes connected as Edgar imagined a scenario in which his father would be held accountable for his brutal actions. Even through his desperation, the thought filled his chest with a visceral pleasure. As altruism and instinct battled within him, he found he couldn't answer her one way or the other.

As Magdalena seemed to sense his aroused sense of vengeance, her eyes widened. "I'll kill him for you, if it's any consolation. Whoever made you feel this way, I'll find him and give him what he deserves. Consider it a trade for your sacrifice," she offered, as if she were extending some act of great kindness to a kindred spirit.

Edgar swallowed, simultaneously fascinated and disgusted by the Ophiuchan. "He's already dead," he answered, his voice ashen.

"What a pity," Magdalena groaned, and sunk down beside him, her gown pooling around her. She surveyed him as the candle sputtered between them. "You poor, miserable, dear thing," she muttered, sounding truly sympathetic as she studied Edgar's face in detail. She leaned in closer to him—so close he could see the sharpness of the teeth that filled her wide mouth and the orange light reflected in her massive eyes. "I'm sorry it had to be you...I truly am. But if it brings you any comfort, know that the pain will end very quickly. Soon there will be nothing but deep quiet...eternal peace." Her mouth flickered into a strange sort of smile then fell again.

Tears sprang to Edgar's eyes as Magdalena reached toward his chest.

"Let's see how long you've got," she said. She reached for the buttons on his shirt—her hands were as cold, pale, and delicate as a porcelain doll's. Although Edgar cringed instinctively, he couldn't escape her. With agonizing slowness, she dispatched with the garment, and with each graze of her icy flesh, bile rose higher in his throat. She peeled his shirt away and lifted it off his body. As she leaned over his naked torso, her eyes narrowed.

"The nymph has touched you—but her work has only delayed the inevitable," Magdalena surmised as she inspected the putrid wound on Edgar's breast. "A day longer...perhaps even tonight."

Edgar paled at hearing this, and his expression shifted to one of utter hopelessness. Noticing this, Magdalena drew closer to him, her expression verging on condolence.

"I *am* sorry, Mr. Price," she repeated in a voice that was nearly human. Despite everything, he found himself believing her. Those revolting, perfect doll hands cupped the side of his face as she loomed over his retreating form. Her eyes fixed on him, and she stared more and more intently at him. In silent horror, Edgar marveled at how young she appeared. Her body was lithe in the way only an adolescent's could be. She still had the wide eyes, the apple-like cheeks, the flat chest. Her features were untouched by the hardness of age—she was a child on the cusp of a maturity that would never come.

The powerful emotion that swelled behind her expression grew to an apex. Then it began to transform. Her face became drawn, and her lips parted. All the humanity in her expression faded, something base and ravenous taking its place.

Edgar's heart pumped madly as Magdalena pushed him farther downward until he lay supine. Her hand slid from his cheek to the soft spot between his neck and chin. As she pressed down lightly, Edgar's blood pulsed against her clammy fingertips. He let out a meager noise of protest as she hovered forward until her cold, dry breath stroked his cheek.

His body shook with tremors as Magdalena's lips made contact with his neck. Everything inside him was screaming to push her off and make a run for it, but there would be no use trying to fight her inhuman strength. In mere seconds, she could break him to pieces if she so desired and leave him in supreme agony during his final hours.

Magdalena's lips parted, still stuck to his flesh, and her teeth pierced the skin of his neck. Edgar let out a faint cry as they dug deeper. The pain was all-encompassing, the terror insurmountable. He writhed under her as she slurped from the gash in animalistic pleasure. As her hunger threatened to overtake her, her jaw clenched, and she tore herself away, her chest heaving. Her face was smeared with blood, and it dripped from between her teeth. Edgar's heart pounded wildly as her hands pushed him down again.

She lunged forward once more, this time aiming for something less lethal. Her teeth pierced his chest on the side that remained unsullied by the revenant. Edgar screamed this time; the sound was so loud it reverberated in the chamber. Instead of merely drinking from the wound she had opened in him, Magdalena bit deeper until she had torn away a hunk of his chest. She pulled upward, chewing Edgar's still-warm flesh with her mouth open, a look of deep epicurean satisfaction washing over her. Edgar's screams faded to rhythmic, catching gasps. His tremors grew more violent as she dropped downward again to take one final drink of the blood that flowed freely from the shallow hole in his chest.

Catching her breath, Magdalena regained her composure. She drew a handkerchief from her pocket and wiped her mouth clean. A faint stain remained on her blanched skin as she stared down at Edgar as if he were a remaining morsel of cake that she was convincing herself not to wolf down.

"Forgive me," she said in a throaty voice after a long silence.

Without another word, Magdalena turned away, candle in hand, and stooped to leave through the crate's low door. Before she departed, she hesitated then set the candle back down and slid it in his direction. Saying no more, she slipped out and shut the door behind her. Edgar heard the clicking lock of the latch. He lay in a heap, wincing as he tried to stop the bleeding with his discarded shirt. He was faced with innumerable reflections of himself, defeated and slick with blood. For a long while, all he was able to do was stare at the sorry images and ruminate.

How did it ever come to this? he thought miserably. He sifted through his memories, trying to find the point where everything had gone so wrong.

It's because I came to Edinburgh. Why did I ever come to Edinburgh? It all began on the train…and before that Mrs. Sheehy…and be-

fore that…before that… Edgar's breath shortened even more. There were great gaping holes in his memory. All that remained were fragmented images of events, with no understanding of how he'd arrived at any of them.

I am…part of the Membership of the Royal College of Surgeons. I…where was I before school? Before the apprenticeship? Where was I raised? I gave those moments to Fana, didn't I?

Edgar's eyes widened when he recognized again that most of his life was missing. The myriad reflections of the husk of a man whom he hardly recognized terrified him.

No, I remember. I was a boy once. I was running in green fields, somewhere near a lake. I was carefree and happy once. I remember my mother. I remember my father. My dear sister. I remember the world when it was yet unspoiled. And then….

Edgar breathed heavily through his teeth as he thought of his father's face and the emptiness that had been behind his eyes. These memories in particular were so clear to him. They were the only things he could truly recall with any great clarity. The devastating day when everything had changed; when he had changed from an innocent, inquisitive boy to a fearful creature marred by evil. The day his mother had drowned sweet Ella in a fit of sorrow and hopelessness. He despised her for it, but he couldn't entirely blame her. She had been ill and unable to control herself. She had tried to get help, but no one would give it to her. But his father—Edgar could heartily blame him. He had denied her the care she needed. He had ignored her pain and allowed the situation to worsen. And then he'd murdered his wife; he'd known what he was doing. It hadn't been madness on his end; it had been malcontent retaliation.

And what was it that pushed him to attempt to end my life too? Pity? Grief? As Edgar closed his eyes, he saw the look on his father's face as it appeared when he had tried to quash the first life he'd created. *I wish he'd succeeded*, he thought ruefully.

It still seemed so clear to him—that image remained while all other memories had been lost to him. Edgar saw it all so vividly now. His father's corpse lying broken in the courtyard. The still form of his mother wrapped around the body of his sister. These evil visions consumed him, and soon he began to await death with some amount of eagerness. The end of all things painful.

And the end of Fana too...oh, Fana. Oh, love...oh, light, where are you now? he thought with a powerful yearning to hold her one final time. The sweet memory of the single kiss they'd shared haunted him in that mirrored box. He clung to that and the innumerable golden images of the wonderful, sad life she'd led. Those he could remember. Those remained. As the candle dripped down farther, the pain grew such that he was beginning to fade into unconsciousness. Edgar continued to stare into the blurry eternity created by the mirrors.

All of a sudden, something at the very edge of one of the reflections disturbed him from his brooding. He sat up as best he could to get a better look at a dark shape coming closer to him in the reflection. Edgar turned back to look at the direction it appeared to be advancing from, but it wasn't in the mirrors behind him, nor to the sides. It only came from the front.

It took mere moments for Edgar to realize who was coming for him. The figure crawled toward him, throwing one arm in front of the other as he laboriously dragged himself forward. The golden crown, set with diamonds and emeralds, sat crooked atop his sandy hair.

Strangely, Edgar felt no fear, only a vast numbness of acceptance. The hellish child came forth out of the mirror, passing through the pane as if it were water rather than glass. Then he was there with Edgar in the dim light. Only the candle stood between them. Edgar sat up with a wince, his chest flaring up in pain.

"The time has come, hasn't it?" Edgar's voice sounded thin in his ears. The boy stopped crawling and looked up to him. His blue eyes appeared clearer, and he seemed more aware of Edgar. During the pause, Edgar thought to say a bit more to the child. "Well, I'm ready. You can take me now."

The ghostly boy didn't budge; he merely stared at him with a mixture of curiosity and aversion. Edgar blinked, uncertain what to do next but unwilling to fight the revenant off any longer.

"Can't you speak?" Edgar asked in a whisper as he observed him. Although some of the ire left the boy's face, his eyes remained fixed on his prey. When the silence grew unbearable, Edgar tried again. "Why...why have you got that crown?"

The spirit drew back, apparently puzzled by Edgar's attempt to communicate with him. The boy didn't open his mouth, but Edgar heard his words all the same. It was as if the wind itself were speaking for him.

Because I am a lost prince.

"A prince?" Edgar raised a brow. "Who are you exactly?"

I don't know. I can't remember much. Not even my name, the wind carrying his voice said. The boy's eyes stayed glued to Edgar, never blinking, never shifting.

"Well, what *do* you remember?" Edgar pushed further, at once very curious. The spirit was silent for a long time and grew so perfectly still that Edgar thought he might disappear again.

Eventually, however, he answered in a meek tone, *I remember dying.*

Edgar drew a short breath.

My grandmother stopped to stay at a boardinghouse...a house owned by two men. She drank something to ease the pain in her legs. She took too much and died in the night. I couldn't scream; I couldn't speak—I was mute in life. I couldn't tell anyone what had happened. I went and found the proprietor, a man called Hare, and when he saw what had transpired, he looked so happy. He sat down next to her body and beckoned me over. Then he picked me up and laid me over his knee and kept pushing me until my spine snapped. I couldn't make a sound—I just kept looking up at his face until the light faded. That's what I remember.

Edgar could scarcely breathe when he heard this. The boy's blue eyes bore into him, and he pulled himself toward Edgar again, his lame legs sliding on the floor of the crate.

This is why I've got to do this, mister. There was a mistake...I wasn't supposed to die. Now I've been given a chance to live again, and I shall make the best of it. I shall reclaim my kingdom.

"Your kingdom?" Edgar inquired.

Yes. My grandmother always told me I was the lost prince of a nation to the east. She told me this every night before we slept—it was to remind me that good things were coming soon. Every day was hard. We didn't have much food, and Gran was always sick, but we kept going on. I knew we had to. We had to save up enough to get back to my kingdom. They were all going to welcome me home—I just had to wait. Gran promised me every night. But that man ruined everything. He robbed me of my birthright. I'm going to return and get what is mine. I'm sorry I have do this, but I'm a prince, and you're just a man. I'm more important than you'll ever be. It just makes sense.

Edgar's face fell as the boy pulled himself ever closer. "My child, there never was any kingdom," he told him, his eyes full of sympathy.

The boy stopped crawling, an ugly look of anger darkening his face. *Liar! How dare you say such a thing?* he snarled.

Edgar shook his head. "I'm sorry. What your grandmother told you—those were just pretty lies meant to give you hope," he continued. The boy finally looked away, gazing to the side in a moment of doubt. "Think about it. No one ever came looking for you. Your grandmother was of mundane lineage, yes? Did she ever tell you the name of the kingdom or why you were in Scotland in the first place?"

No, no, no! You're a liar, an awful liar!

"I understand—many of us were told the same sort of false-hoods when we were children. But the truth is that we are owed nothing when we come into the world. There is only what lies before us...only hope that we shall build a life that has more empathy than indifference in it. But tragedy can take any of us and for no reason at all. It took you. And for that I'm truly sorry. It took me as well," Edgar finished, the lump still rising in his throat.

The child's face fell, and huge tears dribbled down his cheeks. *No...this cannot be... I was supposed to be a king...*

"So was I," Edgar stated plainly, and the boy looked up again. "So were all of us. We were all promised kingdoms of our own, and we came to believe we deserved them. The whole world lay before our feet, and we could've had any part of it. But dark things came, and they stole our chances from us and wounded us in places they knew could never heal. They left us wondering how something so profoundly beautiful could also be unspeakably cruel."

There has to be a kingdom... There simply must be...

"I'm sorry, but there is no kingdom waiting for you. Kingdoms belong only to those who create them, brick by brick. We build our own destinies. Nothing is ever achieved from misery, no matter how patient it may be," Edgar said.

In steady streams, tears flowed out of the boy's blue eyes. Slowly he advanced on Edgar, a combination of rage and despair on his face. Edgar made no movement to avoid him. The boy pulled himself closer and reached out as if wanting an embrace. Edgar took the spirit in his arms, though it instilled great fear and pain in him.

The boy felt like flame against his breast. Edgar gasped and nearly passed out again from the searing contact. The child was sinking into Edgar's chest now, into his body.

This is it. It's ending. It'll all be over soon.

The boy had completely disappeared inside him, and as soon as Edgar could no longer feel the weight of the boy on him, his eyes snapped open. The pain had stopped entirely, leaving only a feeling of great, trembling weakness, but he had life in him yet.

Carefully he sat up and looked himself over. The longer he sat there, the more awake and alert he felt. Something jolted through his limbs, as if electric wires were buzzing under his skin. Edgar stood, since he suddenly found sitting to be impossible. He paced around the box, circling the candlestick. Then he crouched beside the door and tested it. It seemed to be locked tightly and didn't give at all. At once, Edgar was possessed by a strange hope that he should get away from this place. He knew then that he couldn't accept this fate; he would fight to the very last.

Rearing back, he threw his weight into the door again and again. The mirrors began to splinter. The more he heaved against the door, the more it cracked and sent splinters slicing into him. The pain, however, no longer seemed to faze him. With one last mighty heave, he broke through the door and into the dark room beyond.

Panting, he rushed to the door that led to the oubliettes, but it was latched too tightly to get through, and the door was made of iron. Without the key, he had no hope of freeing the imprisoned Ophiuchans. He made a quick search for it but found nothing. When he ran toward the exit, he also found it to be locked. This door, however, was made of wood.

Edgar doubled back to the table that held Magdalena's set of instruments. Breathing heavily, he ran his fingers over them. He lifted an ax and a saw from the table then turned his eyes to the door.

Aegri Somnia

Sunset had come, and Hare still had not caught sight of Mag. The graveyard outside the Gothic steeples of Saint Cuthbert grew misty and pale in the fading light. The shadows stretched over the mossy, moldering stones, casting the names of so many forgotten men, women, and children into darkness. Hare shifted in place, blinking up at the dingy yellow sky through the alders that protected the resting place of the dead. The trees hissed and breathed in the gusts as if whispering of a storm to come.

Hare rocked on his heels, growing more impatient by the moment. Perhaps it was time to act without her—isn't that what she'd told him to do? In hours, the surgeon would be dead and the curse broken. Then Hare would be powerless to collect the revenant, and the invisible gate that led to its hiding place would be impossible to find.

The crunching of leaves alerted him to someone's approach. "Mag," he said as he turned, her presence alleviating the heavy feeling in his chest. "What kept you?"

The Ophiuchan shook her head as she continued down the path to join him. Clearly she had no intention of answering him. Her focus flitted all over the churchyard; she seemed even more frantic than usual. At last her eyes fell upon Hare, stopping for a moment at his chest.

"What is this preposterous bauble you've been wearing?" she asked, touching the brooch the strongman Alexander had passed along to him. Its green face caught the light, and the red eyes seemed even more curious in the fading light of day.

He cast a glance downward; he'd quite forgotten it had been there at all. "A bit of trash some drunk at the fair gave me. What does it matter?" he retorted.

Mag looked at it with vague dislike. "I hate the sight of it," she answered, then turned her attention back to the aged head-stones. "Were you able to locate the revenant?"

"There." Hare pointed to an obelisk-like grave a few paces off. "It's in there."

"Strange. I feel very little of its presence. It seems to be for-saking the world around it entirely," Mag observed.

Hare nodded. "It's a quiet one… That's what worries me," he murmured, keeping his eyes on the stone. The entrance to its hiding place looked to him like a clear cluster of prisms twisting around, creating a rift in reality. "I don't know about this, Mag. This feels wrong to me. Especially wrong." He wasn't sure why he voiced his concerns to her or what he intended to accomplish by doing so.

Mag's irritation flared, just as he'd expected. "You're losing your courage *now?* You're mere hours away from freedom; you have just one task left. We were so lucky that the surgeon lived, that we have him. If you collect this revenant successfully, you'll be free to go. You'll never see me again," she urged with a crazed sort of fer-vency, obviously frightened of losing everything she desired.

Hare licked his lips, unsure what to say. *We've come this far, might as well see it through, give her what she wants.* "All right," he said. "I'm going in then."

"And I shall stay here. If the nymph comes poking around, I'll be ready to stop her," Mag assured him, and Hare nodded again.

With a final nod, Hare stepped up to the warping stone with determination. Before he slipped through into the revenant's domain, he cast a look back at her. For a moment their gaze connected and a miserable camaraderie hovered between them. Hare turned away and stepped through to the other side.

At once, everything became bright crystal and glass. Hare stood in a garden of glittering rocks, all cut into ornate shapes to mimic flowers, trees, ferns, and grasses. Snow covered the ground in a blinding, white coat. The grave markers, which had been stone moments before, now appeared to be cut from an extraordinarily brilliant crystalline substance. The sky was completely clouded over, but the crystals still flashed and sparkled. Before him the church loomed, although its surface had transformed into ivory, silver, and pearls.

In this glass garden, everything was perfectly still. Nothing moved. Hare found it difficult to draw a full breath in such resounding quiet. Not the slightest breeze blew as he took a few careful steps forward, mesmerized by the refracting light in each of the individual crystal leaves on the trees. He half expected something to burst out from behind a corner and attack him as he made his way up to the doors of the church. However, nothing but his light footfalls disturbed the stillness. Hare hesitated then pushed open the huge double doors.

They creaked loudly as they came apart, showing the way into the church's main chamber. Beveled plaster ceilings and stone archways lined the massive hall, but this no longer was Saint Cuthbert's. The interior held none of the white, glowing splendor of the glass garden. Although it was dismal and dark inside, the walls were graced with innumerable stained-glass windows that burned brightly with the same glaring intensity as the outdoors. They depicted the stories and trials of various martyrs: a woman awaiting lions in the arena, angels descending as a man knelt before the executioner's blade, another man tied to a wooden pole as he sunk into a deep pool of water. The pews were crowded with statues, each in the shape of a man or woman. Invariably their faces were stricken by grief, and their attention was focused on the windows. As Hare continued warily down the aisle, he realized the images of the suffering and sanctified were unknown to him; they were stories he'd never been told. However, when he approached the image of a woman being strangled by two men, he stopped as a jolt of nausea assailed him. He swallowed thickly and continued forward.

It's in here somewhere. Just look for the shining thing and break it.

As he advanced, the soft sounds of mourning echoed from the beveled ceilings. Hare's movement slowed. He kept an eye on the statues, feeling threatened by them, but the longer he went on, the more he became convinced that they weren't going to spring to life. At the very end of the church, past the pulpit, a massive stained-glass window glowed brighter and with more concentrated color than all the rest.

It depicted a woman in a flowing white gown. She stood with her golden hair cascading behind her, but her eyes were shut as if in sleep or perhaps death. Above her head, a bright star streamed light onto the patch of leaves and thorns among which she stood. At her feet bloomed a single red rose with petals redder than blood. The light that glowed from behind the flower made it appear to be aflame.

Hare's eyes were drawn to the rose and the shimmering incandescence behind it, and at once he knew. That was where the revenant's essence hid. As he grew nearer, he recognized the smooth features, pale countenance, and doleful eyes of the woman in the window as one of the revenants. It was Margery, the final victim. The discovery of her body stashed under the bed of the lodging house had brought an end to his father's spree of murders.

It was very difficult to look away from her face. As he grew close enough to smash the pane, the image of Margery began to move. As if a raindrop were sliding down the glass, a single tear rolled down her painted cheek. Hare stopped in place as her eyes opened, the pupils staring down at him in judgment.

With a ghostly burst of mist, the image of Margery issued forth from the window. She was blaring with bright color and light, and left behind an empty space that showed only the thornbush and the rose. The specter billowed forth, transforming into a corporeal, human shape. She eased to a stop before him, her blue eyes staring deeply into his with a searching, cold glance.

"Why have you disturbed the sanctity of this place?" her harrowed voice whispered.

Hare stared her down, not daring to flinch. "Begging your pardon, miss," his voice husky in his ears, "but I must take you away from here."

Margery's eyes narrowed, and she remained still, the plumes of mist still curling between the beams of light that streamed from her form. "Why would you have me leave this hallowed hall? Here I am eternal. Do you see them?" She pointed at the white statues, and Hare nodded. "They are the mourners. They weep for me. They weep for all the lost ones. It is a compassion, a kindness, that never ceases. They grieve for all of us—the lost, the forgotten, the broken."

Uncertain how to proceed, Hare swallowed once more. Margery floated around to his side, keeping her eyes trained on his.

"Here I am respected. I'm safe. Here I will never change; I will never fade. Why would you remove me from my sanctum, when your father put me here in the first place? Am I not deserving of protection? Would you deny me that?" she pushed, cocking her head to the side, her golden locks spilling over her shoulders.

Hare didn't know how to answer her. "This isn't real peace," he finally said, but Margery only raised an eyebrow. She seemed to ponder his statement as she continued toward the wall. With a soft wave of her hand, she beckoned for him to follow. Hers was such a gentle and haunting nature that Hare found it difficult to resist. He cast a glance back at the rose that seemed to simply burn with color and decided that entertaining this miserable soul for a few moments before she was trapped again would do no harm.

He followed Margery to the wall. Where there should have been an elaborately painted window, there was only blank stone. She looked back up at him with her sharp blue eyes, and her lips parted.

"I wonder, what is the reason you seek to destroy my haven?" she chanced.

Something about her was hypnotic and beguiling, and Hare found himself speaking the truth before he could stop himself. "I need to take you away from here, give you back to the one I sold you to."

"And why? What will you gain?"

"Freedom. Peace. The right to my own death," he said, the words leaping to his lips.

Margery's face changed ever so slightly to reveal a look of subtle satisfaction. "What if I could offer you something even better?" she was almost exhilarated.

Hare was at once skeptical, but Margery continued despite his look of distrust.

"Death is devoid of feeling. You've been miserable for so long. Would you not say you deserve something more? Such as everlasting contentment?" Her words were as musical as they were enticing.

Despite his resolve to resist, Hare was intrigued enough to question further. "What are you talking about?"

"A chance to put down that heavy burden. To release the weight of these years of pain," she said in a near whisper. With a puff of mist, Margery waved her billowing sleeve over the blank stone wall, and when the curtain of fabric and vapor was swept away, a brilliant image shone there.

A collection of jewel-bright panels of glass depicted a set of images that made Hare's heart leap. It was him—his story spelled out on the wall. Panels showed segments of his life: the cottage in Ireland, his toils in Edinburgh, the home he'd made with Emily. Centered above them was a circular set of panels around an image of an open grave under a red sky. In each of the five sections was a portrait of each of the people who had blocked Hare on his journey to freedom: the surgeon, the witch, the Lunatic, the woman of the woods, and himself. His own portrait showed himself wreathed in flames and looking up with an expression of terrified anguish, begging for salvation. Although the sight of it repulsed him, he couldn't tear his eyes away from its flaring colors. They were all so vibrant that they pained his eyes—reds that were as smoldering coals, rich purples soaked with life, blues that seared like sunlight. The hues all refracted, piercing through him and entrancing him all at once. He continued to stare until the area behind his eyes ached with a stinging pain and he was finally forced to look away.

"What is this vile thing?" he demanded in a throaty tone.

Margery looked at him as if he should already know the answer. "It's you. Everything you carry. I've projected it there for you to see. Your story could be made beautiful too. And forever the mourners would cry for you, Jacob. They would lament your loss, feel for you so that you won't have to any longer. If you leave me undisturbed in this place, you can leave this sanctum with nothing but an eternal moment of bliss. I can give you that," she whispered, taking his hand. Her touch felt like polished stone on a winter's day.

Hare swallowed, glancing back at the gorgeously grotesque images. "You're saying I would forget it all?"

"Everything. You would be cast from this place, unable to see or feel anything more than the moment of your choosing. Choose a memory, choose an instant, and I will make it last forever. It is all you will ever know. Let me keep the rest of them. Let others grieve for you, as you deserve to be grieved over. You have endured so much. It can end here." Margery's grip on Hare's hand grew tighter. His mouth grew dry at the very prospect.

"How can I trust you?"

She shook her head solemnly. "I have no way of proving myself. But that creature out there who waits for you—you *know* she is cruel. Even if you do her bidding, there's still a chance she'll tear you to pieces. You could be free—this very instant. No need for risks."

Hare's chest swelled with the hope of this possibility. His hand instinctively searched for the tiny metal locket that held Emily's strand of hair. He squeezed it, thinking of what it would be like to hold her again. To be convinced that she still lived. What did it matter that it wasn't reality as long as it felt authentic?

"A-any memory I choose?" he asked in a quavering voice, seriously considering the specter's proposal. She nodded, never blinking once.

Hare's mind wandered into the past. *Why shouldn't I just stay there with her? Why not live in that perfect moment? Something so lovely should be eternal, shouldn't it? What obligation do I have to Mag, to this world?*

His hand held tighter to the case in his coat lining. Fragments of Emily were all he had left. All he wanted was to have her whole and happy again, even if it was just the ghost of a memory.

That's a type of freedom all in itself, he told himself, and the decision was made. He faced Margery with a trembling lip.

"Yes," he agreed. "Yes, take it. Take it all. Leave me with only this one summer afternoon, when the sun was low and—"

"You needn't speak it aloud. Just think on it, and you'll be there. Thank you, Mr. Hare. I'm glad this can be our long-awaited farewell," Margery told him, releasing his hand.

Hare's heart hammered in his chest as she lifted her pale fingers, reaching for him. As her fingers lightly pressed his forehead, he shut his eyes. The weight was already slipping from his shoulders and his weary mind as a haziness worked its way up from the back of his mind.

Emily, his heart whispered, *I'll be home soon.*

The Promise of Hope

The burst of energy that came with the exhilaration of escape carried Edgar only so far. His arms shook, and his muscles felt limp from the heavy work he'd done cutting through the wooden door. He had burst from Magdalena's dungeon, through her shop, and into the street with an unnatural, forced, fierceness that felt as though it had come from a dose of drugs. Emancipation from that subterranean hell evoked the most elated, frenetic rush that he'd ever experienced. Once the adrenaline had worn off, however, and his legs had grown weary from miles of fleeing, something else took its place.

Edgar's back and chest were screaming, and the wounds on his neck and breast still bled. He barreled down the streets through the lines of posh citizens. Last time he'd walked these streets, he'd looked just like any of these gentlemen strutting down the avenue with their identical black suits and bowler hats. Now he was so disheveled, battered, bloodied, and wide-eyed that he appeared almost dangerous. A few ladies cringed at his appearance, thinking him to be a madman filled with a sudden passion to run about the streets. But Edgar paid them no attention. The mannerisms of polite society, which he'd worshiped for most of his life, had all but been torn out from him.

With his memory shattered and his body failing, one thing consumed his thoughts. He needed to get to the final revenant before Magdalena did. Only hours were left before he would be gone—the spirit had nested inside him and had begun to consume him. He felt this as a corroding, pulsing ache deep within his chest. There was still one useful thing he could do with his life, and he wasn't going to leave this world quietly until it was done.

His mad gallop eventually slowed, and he collapsed next to a massive Gothic fountain in the middle of a stretch of lush gardens. From where he sat panting, he saw Edinburgh Castle looming above the city. The splash of the water behind him cooled his panic marginally, and he took the time to catch his breath. His chest felt as if it had been hollowed out, and when he pulled his stained shirt aside to check the state of things, he saw that the mark had changed to an inky black and now spread all the way down his torso. The entry point of the revenant had become dry and burnt, almost like charcoal.

Edgar let out a moan and let his head roll back. As he did, a trickle of something leaked unexpectedly from his eye, and he wiped at it, thinking it was a rogue tear. He was shocked to see a blackish-red substance on the back of his hand. Edgar's breathing was labored, and he felt as though he might collapse.

Not yet…not yet… He waged a war inside his head as he tried to lift himself from the side of the fountain. He strained but couldn't get to his feet. Images of his father leaping to his death, of Ella's limp form, of his mother's corpse lying in bed came to him in whirling waves, churning like the hoop of a spinning wheel. Fana's prediction about his mental stability was coming to fruition.

This is all I have left? This is what I chose to keep? What a fool I am. Which lovely things did I trade away so these nightmares could keep me company as I fade? I could've had so much more, but instead I chose this hell.

Edgar looked up at the clouds. They were cast in pale yellow from the sinking sun, and a chill had started to go through the air. The feeling of turning hollow increased, and he was possessed by the notion that his rib cage might implode at any moment. As his vision blurred and his eyes grew heavy, hopelessness again overtook him. He kept his eyes fixed upward, wanting to see nothing but the clean, unstained expanse of the sky. As he stared at the far-off clouds and silhouettes of birds, a vision entered his eyes that at first he took to be a hallucination of the revenant's design.

It was a great barn owl, too large to be natural. Edgar was captivated by its exquisite form, but his eyes opened wider when a peculiar detail stirred him. The owl had antlers. Hardly daring to believe it might be true, the shock was enough to bring Edgar to his feet at last.

"*Fana! Fana!*" he cried upward at the bird. He was certain that the few people who were strolling through the park would think he was utterly deranged. At any rate, many of them hurried away from the vicinity. The bird regarded him instantly then did a quick swoop in midair to double back toward him. It descended toward him in a manic flapping of wings. Feathers shot off from its body and filled the air around it until a cyclone of them wrapped around it. The swarm of feathers grew to more than five feet high, and when they began to fall, Fana stood before him, tears brimming in her brown eyes.

"Edgar? You're alive?" she said in a strangled voice, taking in the sight of him.

They stood in shock for a moment longer before rushing to each other. They met in a tearful embrace, laughing in giddy disbelief. Edgar's strength suddenly gave out again, and they sank to the ground together.

"Fana, is it really you? Is this truly real?" Edgar murmured, gripping her tightly as his fingers wove through her hair. "My dearest wish was to see you one last time. I only wanted to hold you once more," he said, pressing into her shoulder. "Why in heaven's name are you here?"

"I was flying about the city, looking for Magdalena...looking for the last revenant. I never thought I would see you alive again."

Fana broke away to stroke his face. Edgar's heart jittered when he saw the tearful relief in her eyes. As she touched him, he knew she was soaking up his memories and feelings and was now aware of what he had been through. From the way her expression morphed into one of acute, pained affection, Edgar could tell she finally recognized the depth of what he felt for her. A few tears rolled out of her eyes, and she held him closely again. His heart overflowed with bittersweet joy. It was a blessing beyond anything he could have dreamed of to be with her once again, to have her nearby at the hour of his destruction. How could he be frightened or despairing when she would be the one to guide him?

"I'm...I'm so sorry, Edgar," Fana said. "I've been utterly unreasonable. When I thought we'd lost you forever...I can't describe the remorse. To think I'd let you disappear from this world because of my cowardice and distrust—it felt as if I were watching the whole Wood burn. I became so cold to you, and I pushed you away, and it almost cost me everything. Please forgive me. I can't bear to lose you again. If you...if—"

"Miss Fana, what are you saying?"

"I could end this curse in you," she said softly, touching the spot on his chest that had appeared as burnt flesh. "The revenant can't survive if you fall to death before it can consume you, and that's what would happen if you were to become the warden of my Wood. Death and resurrection."

Edgar's chest filled with a sort of hope that hurt to even endure. He blinked away a few more tears while gripping Fana more tightly.

"But it isn't...it isn't an easy existence, Edgar. You expressed the desire before, but I lack the means to explain how much of a sacrifice it would be. The life eternal is nothing to be desired... and what I offer you can hardly be called a life in itself. You would be responsible for much, for the well-being and protection of many. You would lose the singularity of your soul—never truly be *just* yourself again; you would share your life with me and everything in the Wood. It's the heaviest of burdens to bear, and more than likely our story will end with grief...but I believe there's no worthier candidate than the man who sits before me. If you can forgive me, if you are willing to take up this burden—"

"Fana, there could be nothing in this world awful enough to keep me from you," Edgar told her with a heart so full it nearly drove away the pain.

Fana let out a little joyful laugh. She pulled him to her once more and pressed her lips to his. The euphoria of that moment and the promise of a future full of lifetimes with this wondrous spirit banished all of Edgar's suffering for a moment.

Fana leaned away from him but still gripped his arm tightly. "We must return to the Wood at once, before the spirit takes you. The spring is the only place where the ritual can occur. I can fly us there; I believe there will be time enough," she urged him, and Edgar was moments away from agreeing when something stopped him. Fana noted the hesitance on his face and looked as if she were afraid that his promise had been empty.

Edgar soothed away her anxiousness with a comforting hand. "There are things left undone," he murmured to her. "I can't let the final revenant fall to Magdalena. There's no hope of my capturing it if I don't have the curse."

"Edgar, no. Your revenant will overtake you before we can find the last one. You have but hours to live." She shook her head in fright. "It is regrettable, but—"

"I know where it is—just over there." He pointed toward a tower in the distance. "Saint Cuthbert's Church. I heard Magdalena and Hare speaking of it. I am capable of this; I have to try. My strength left me prior to now, but the hope you brought me has given me more. Fana, be my guide. I am weak, but with you beside me, I feel certain we can get to it before Magdalena does."

Fana's expression grew grave, and he knew she couldn't deny it was the right thing to do.

"Yes. I will help you. But what of Ainsley? We need her. She's still searching the city—"

"No, there isn't time. We must go at once," Edgar told her in a firm voice.

Fana considered him for a moment. Knowing the risks, she finally assented with a nod. After she helped Edgar to his feet, the two moved through the gathering dusk toward the steeple in the distance, drawing on each other's presence for courage.

Salvation

Magdalena pulled in a sharp breath as Hare stumbled back through the invisible gate. He was expelled from the veil as if pushed and had fallen down, making no effort to rise. She hastened to his side, dropping beside him and grabbing him by the shoulders.

"Hare! Hare!" she hissed, shaking him vigorously. "What happened?"

The man's eyes were open, and he stared blankly forward, blinking every so often. His jaw was slack and his face appeared to be at peace, but he made no response. It was as if he couldn't see her at all. Magdalena drew back for moment, dread coursing through her, followed by a fierce realization that he had failed. She smashed him against the ground over and over while shouting his name, but he all he did was blink lazily.

"Damn you!" she spat, panic hammering within her. She cast a look toward the area where she knew the gate was. There was no chance of removing the revenant herself. With growing anguish, she continued to thrash Hare about. Her chest tightened, and tears of frustration stung her eyes as the reality of the situation sunk in.

"No...no, no, no! It can't end this way! This all can't be for nothing! Hare, wake up! *Wake up!*" she shrieked, digging her fingers into his flesh. Even with the spots of blood staining his shirt, Hare lay still.

The revenant has done something to him. There could be time to fix this. Yes, I have to fix it. This isn't over yet.

With fiendish strength, Magdalena hoisted Hare over her shoulder and tore through the graveyard. She sped across the city, bowling over anyone who got in her way with her inhuman strength and speed, trampling them under her child-like feet as she rushed by. Her home was far from the church, but her limbs, fed by the blood of the Divine Serpent, did not tire. The moon had risen by the time she threw open her front door with a bang and exploded into the shop. She tossed Hare to the floor before frantically digging through her belongings.

So the revenant used dark magic to put him in this state. I'll do the same to get him out! she thought maniacally, plucking a bottle filled with a thick black substance out of a pile on a shelf. She wrenched Hare's mouth open and dumped the contents down his throat. He swallowed it all but made no movement. Magdalena watched him, her panic and paranoia growing with each aggravated breath. She tried reciting ancient chants, stabbing him with a curse-breaking dagger, burning bundles of sacred plants that could call back the soul, but nothing worked. She wasted countless precious ingredients on him, but nothing would bring Hare back to consciousness. Fighting back tears, Magdalena bit her bottom lip hard. She couldn't accept that she had lost. Not when they were this close.

The Scroll of the Silent, of course! she thought, as a bolt of inspiration struck her upon remembering one of her more esoteric, but potent, artifacts. Magdalena sped from the room at a blinding pace and hurtled down the stairs in search of it. She came to a violent halt, however, when she saw that the door to the basement had been laid to waste. Nearly falling to her knees, she numbly advanced toward the pile of splinters, touching them briefly to see whether they were in fact real.

No... A wave of acute shock smacked her square in the gut, and she took a rattling breath. Kicking aside the destroyed remains, Magdalena burst into the room, already knowing what she would find. Then, at last, her knees gave out when she saw the hole smashed into the mirror trap. The surgeon was gone.

Magdalena fell forward onto her elbows and shook in silence for a long time, her eyes bulging from her head as she tried to piece together how she had lost everything in so short a time. Moment by moment, crushing disappointment, wrath, and feelings of powerlessness collided inside her. These emotions became so great that she could hardly breathe. The feeling pushed itself into her mind until she finally broke. Magdalena threw her head back and let out a scream that shook the dungeon.

The tension in her mind blared intolerably and finally snapped. She lost control of herself. Hardly conscious of her own actions, she rolled about on the stone floor, screeching and wailing. She lurched to her feet, tears spilling down her face, and lashed out at her tools and instruments, sending them flying off the tables and shelves. They fell to the floor with such noise that it sent the prisoners in the next room into an uproar. Their delirious begging began anew.

The reminder of the presence of the heinous creatures in the next chamber pushed Magdalena even further past her breaking point. She ripped the door off the wall and hurled it at Ulrich, who hung from the rafters, howling behind his humiliating mask. It struck his arm and broke it, twisting the bones so that he hung at an unnatural angle. Her fury was such that she spat threats and taunts at him in the old tongue.

"You'll never be free of me; you'll never get out of here. Losing the revenants means nothing—I still have you. Hope is dead, and you will never be. I will never forget what you did!" She ripped at him with her nails and teeth until he was reduced to a few shreds of meat that fell in wet pulpy clumps to the bottom of his oubliette. She didn't flinch at his destruction, his body would, of course, reform later.

Even after all that, Magdalena's ire had not been assuaged. Instead, it only grew hotter and more agonizing.

She threw herself against the wall, ceaselessly bellowing and destroying anything she came near. She tore out clumps of her own hair, which came free with bits of her scalp. Scratching great bloody lines down her face, she whipped upstairs to her private chamber.

Without hesitation, Magdalena ripped into her treasures. She smashed delicate things to the ground, their shattering feeding her pain. She tore her paintings to shreds, ripped her bed into a flurry of feathers, reduced her letters to scraps, crushed jewels under her feet, and hurled her chandelier against the wall, where it exploded like fireworks spun of glass. The hysteric fit lasted until she had decimated every last thing she loved. Blinded by her rage, she hardly perceived a moment of the devastation she had wrought. Finally she came back to her senses moments after she smashed her beautiful, beloved cello over her knee.

She slumped forward, holding the remains of the instrument in her palms and breathing raggedly. For a split second, she remembered all the gorgeous songs it had sung under her fingers over the last century, and she stopped breathing altogether. Tears flowed down her pale cheeks, and she softly wept, tossing the broken cello aside with disgust and hiding her face in her bony hands. She fell over, curling into a ball and moaning. As her hands filled with tears, she choked on the salty liquid, cursing the world and everyone in it.

You cruel, cruel God. You torture me. You let me believe I could bring those devils justice, but you snatched it from me at the last moment. I am the most wretched of all beings. I was born to suffer under your wicked designs. I never wanted any of this. I curse you, malicious hoarder of kindness, you who dispense luck to the undeserving. Curse you, curse you! There is no God, there is only—

Magdalena!

The Cold Voice erupted in her head so loudly that Magdalena shrieked, gripping her skull for fear it would shatter.

Come to your senses!

She sat up whimpering, looking around with wild, protruding eyes. "Yes, yes...help me, exalted one. Everything has gone awry. Everything has been ruined. Hare failed, a-and I—"

Silence, the Cold Voice commanded, and she shut her quivering lips. *There is another way. A way that will help us both. Will you do as I bid?*

"Anything, lord of my life, anything," Magdalena whispered.

Send the transgressors, the ones who buried you, to me. Let me take them. Their souls will nourish me for eternity, and their minds will shatter in my realm. No being, mortal or otherwise, can bear to look upon my kingdom. They will be trapped for all time.

"Yes," Magdalena agreed huskily, her broken heart soothed. "Yes, that is what they deserve. I will give them to you, Lord. That pleases me more than you can know. How shall I proceed?"

Attend me carefully. The curse of William Hare was born of the stone the witch used, but the spirits themselves are anchored to the coffins she crafted, the Cold Voice boomed in Magdalena's head. *Gather them now.*

She took a sharp breath in and rifled among the wreckage of her possessions until she found the box where she'd stored the tiny set of coffins. They were discovered many decades ago by a group of boys who were hunting rabbits atop Arthur's Seat, the massive hill that overshadowed Edinburgh. Inside were a set of carved figurines, their eyes open—showing that they still lived on in the state between life and death, tied to William Hare. Once there were most likely seventeen, but only eight survived. They came into the possession of a wealthy collector of rare artifacts, but in 1845 he put them in an antiquities auction. The Cold Voice instructed Magdalena to take them up, so she sought them out and purchased them. They had remained in her possession ever since. The witch Sylvia Allaway had created them, one for each of Burke and Hare's victims, and buried them in a shallow cave on Arthur's Seat. They served as a memorial to—and also an anchor for—each of those tormented souls.

Take them and climb to the burial hill, the Cold Voice said, and Magdalena saw Arthur's Seat in her mind. *The veil is thin there. It will be the only place their souls can reach me. Take the revenants who survived. Take the transgressors. Take the coffins.*

Flashes of arcane symbols and sets of wicked ingredients burst into Magdalena's head. Information surged through her, electrifying her brain so fervently that she shut her eyes against the pain and whimpered. The images were burned into her memory—she could not forget them.

Draw them in the blood of the witch who cast the curse.

"My lord, that's impossible!" Magdalena objected, as a spike of fear ran through her. "That woman disappeared into the wilds and hasn't been heard from in years. I won't be able to—"

Her daughter. The young witch the nymph brought with her. It is the same blood. Find her... She is near.

Magdalena hastily agreed, and more flashes of information seared behind her eyelids. She gritted her teeth as the rest of the ritual unfolded in her head. She was to light a fire with the sacred ingredients in the middle of the rings of the witch's blood. She was to place the coffins around it then incinerate the revenants. This would open the gate. The final step was to throw the witch onto the pyre. Her blood mixed with the flames would allow the Cold Voice to claim the Ophiuchans for eternity.

When the flashes subsided, Magdalena slumped backward, a soft, crazed laugh shuddering in the back of her throat. This was redemption. The Cold Voice had saved her again. It had drawn her from the darkness, given her hope.

"I shall do this, my lord. I shall repay your kindness, gift you these tributes. Thank you, merciful one. Bless your endless love," she whispered in rapture. The tears that streamed down her cheeks were now ones of gratitude.

Magdalena stood up and stepped forward with purpose, her feet shifting through the broken bits of glass, splintered wood, and torn fabric. At last, she knew what it felt like to be bathed in the grace of salvation.

To Life Eternal

Edgar and Fana stumbled through the graveyard at Saint Cuthbert's. Edgar's lips became a thin line as he squinted in the gloom of the dark churchyard. He came to a swift halt when he spotted the gate to the revenant's hiding place among the headstones.

"We've found it," he whispered to Fana, whom he still leaned on for support. Fana's expression was anxious. He bit his bottom lip, dread and courage battling for dominance in his chest, and gently broke away from her, taking the first few steps toward the gate.

Fana started to follow him, but he turned back and shook his head.

"You should stay behind. I won't stand a chance if Magdalena tries an ambush—you're the only one strong enough to stop her," Edgar explained.

Fana paled at the suggestion. "Edgar, I cannot allow you to proceed alone. The revenant could destroy you in seconds. Besides, what if she already waits for you inside?" Edgar shook his head yet again.

"I have a feeling she would've avoided this one. Take a look around—there's no evidence of the revenant's curse. It doesn't want to be found. I don't think Magdalena would've risked it."

Fana's complexion grew ever whiter. "And you would wander blindly where the Lunatic would dare not go?" Fana's voice ran shrill in Edgar's ears, as if the mere thought of losing him caused her distress.

He laid his palm on her shoulder in a gesture of reassurance. "Hare and I are the only ones who can do this," he reminded her, and her look of chagrin faded slightly. "Trust in me. If I cannot succeed in this final task, I cannot confidently join you as warden of the Wood. It will take but an instant."

Although Fana still appeared apprehensive, she gave a begrudging nod and took a few paces back. Edgar drew a deep breath and squared his body at the gate. Limping under the spreading pain in his shoulder, he dragged himself to the torn spot in reality. With a clenched jaw, he took one large step through the glinting barrier and emerged into the revenant's domain.

A garden of shimmering crystal surrounded him. Edgar blinked at his surroundings for a mere moment, on high alert for any form of danger. When he couldn't find any evidence of a threat, he marched toward the entrance of the massive ivory church. Summoning all his remaining strength, he pushed the double doors aside and entered the church with unabashed bravery.

The second he did, he saw the revenant, an angelic woman in a white dress, standing there, awaiting his arrival. When Edgar laid eyes upon her, the pain in his core flared up, and he fought back tears. With his shirt still hanging open and loose, he noticed the burnt spot spreading on his chest. It singed into him like fire eating through wood, leaving his flesh split and cracked. Groaning against the molten pain, Edgar forced his legs to keep going. At the end of the aisle, he saw a stained-glass window depicting a single red rose in a garden of thorns. A star flashed high above it. A glaring, pulsing light of deep ruby shone behind the image of the flower, and at once Edgar saw his target. He kept his eyes fixed on the rose, knowing he must destroy it to remove the dark spirit who nested here.

The slog forward was torturous, and the spirit's eerie blue eyes never strayed from Edgar's face, though he endeavored to ignore her altogether. He urged himself to keep going, throwing one heavy leg in front of the other. He no longer could ignore the pain in his chest, and tears flooded from his eyes in response to it.

Keep going. Almost there. Just…a bit more…not long now, his thoughts tried to scream over the horrendous pain that sawed through him. He lurched straight past the spirit, refusing to acknowledge her with even a glance out of the corner of his eye. Still, Edgar felt her turn to watch him continue, her face deadly serious. As he stood beside her, the wound spread at an alarming rate. It crawled over his shoulder and down his left arm, rendering it useless. Although Edgar moaned and his head grew dizzy, he wouldn't allow himself to stop.

"The pain can end right now, you know," the spirit said, dulcet and sympathetic. "I can stop it, and you can go back to a time when everything was still wholesome and kind."

Edgar cringed, blocking out her words as he kept moving. The farther he moved away from her, the less the agony affected him. It was as if his brain were so used to it now that it stopped registering it. With a heaving chest, he pushed past the pulpit.

"Edgar, it doesn't have to be this difficult. You can stop everything now. You can return to those green hills, to the lakeside when the world was yours! You can still have your kingdom!" The revenant's voice had taken on a frantic timbre.

Nearly there, Edgar bellowed in frustration. His legs wouldn't go faster; his body shook so violently he was afraid his strength might give out at the last second. Fifteen feet away… twelve feet…

"Edgar, you can see your sister again! You can have Ella back! *Ella! Alive and well again!*" the revenant called out, crying herself hoarse.

Edgar dropped his head, sweat pouring down his forehead. Ten feet away.

As he lifted his face to the stained-glass rose, something to the side of it caught his attention. A window of the most delicate stained glass pulsed with the light from the garden outside. Edgar started as he saw what he reasoned must be the story of Hare's life told in exquisite shards of glass. A farmhouse, a gray city, Hare crowded by the spectral forms of the revenants, the face of a young woman, the reaching claws of Magdalena, and finally Hare's image seemingly asleep on a white plinth. Just as Edgar tried to piece together the meaning behind the window, something beside it distracted him.

Directly next to it stood another set of glass panels with an eerily familiar set of faces. Hare, Ainsley, Fana, Magdalena.... and himself, depicted as having been buried under the earth. The sight of himself, rendered in glass and trapped in darkness, forced him to turn back in to defiantly face the spirit at last.

"*Edgar, you could have the whole world!*" she wailed, her eyes pleading to him.

Edgar bared his teeth, his face slick with sweat and tears. "No!" he growled, looking the spirit straight in the eyes at last. "No, I don't want that anymore! I want to be free of those memories. I want what is real—what is yet to come!"

At his final rejection, the revenant's hair flew upward, and her eyes became grotesquely wide. She opened her mouth to reveal a dark, slimy tunnel of a throat that impossibly seemed to be larger inside than out, and let loose a scream that shattered all the windows behind her and made the marble mourners crumble to powder. Mingling with her shriek, a thundering sound reverberated throughout the sanctum. It sounded as if the earth were splitting, and the entire church shook violently. From the ground, vines and thorny tendrils of hard crystal blossomed upward. They took hold of Edgar's legs and crawled up over his hips.

"*I tried to save you! I offered you deliverance!*" her voice resounded with unholy wrath.

Edgar yelped as the crystal encased him. The pane with the rose was just out of reach. He was stuck, frozen in the crystal's massive strength. He dropped his head, stunned that he had come so far only to fail here. As he stared with hollow horror at the refracted light that shone from the diamond-bright stones around him, a realization crept into his mind.

Why, it's not crystal at all... It's...it's only glass!

With this understanding, Edgar was reinvigorated. With a strenuous heave and squirm, he wriggled inside the cask surrounding him. The more he believed it to be fragile, the more it gave way. With a final push, it shattered as if it were but a thin film of ice, and Edgar sprang forward.

He sprinted the remaining few feet, the sound growing so awful that his eardrums were on the verge of rupturing. Edgar launched himself forward, fist first, and felt his knuckles collide with the surface of the glass. The shards cut into him, but the tinkling of that broken rose was the sweetest, most musical sound he'd ever heard. As it shattered, everything around him exploded in a storm of broken glass and ruined stone. The shards whirled past him, shooting forward in the direction in which he had thrown his punch. As they rocketed past, many cut into his flesh.

By the time the glass storm had disappeared, Edgar dropped to the floor, bleeding from head to foot. The graveyard materialized around him again, but he could only stare up at the sky, frozen in horror. He heard Fana shouting and vaguely saw her race forward to bottle the defeated revenant. As she rushed to his side after securing the spirit, Edgar felt the curse creep all the way down his left arm. When Fana lifted him, cradling him in her embrace, his blackened, charred arm broke off and disintegrated like a used-up log in a fireplace. Fana wailed, holding his shivering, shredded body closely as his blood stained her robes.

He was moments from fading away as she gently laid him down in the grass. When she stepped back, black feathers erupted outward, and she assumed the form of a raven that was easily seven feet in height. The huge bird grasped Edgar in its talons as if he were a mouse, and with a whipping of wind, they shot upward into the night. Before he passed out, he caught a glimpse of an orange moon and a sky spattered with frosty stars.

***

On the other side of the darkness of sleep, the comforting sight of the Witches' Wood greeted him. He lay in the meadow by the Clootie Well as Fana looked over him with concern. Fana woke him with a soft stroke against the side of his face. Some of Edgar's lacerations had been mended, which he attributed to Fana's magic, though he was sure death was only minutes away. The place where his arm had once been attached suffered a deep, throbbing ache that verged on numbness. It was already past midnight, and the world seemed to hum with quiet and peace. It was such a stark difference that Edgar was grasped by the delusion that he somehow had already died. Fana was saying something to him, but he couldn't make out her words. The burned spot was creeping toward his heart.

"Edgar! Can you hear me?" At once her voice was clear to him, and his gaze focused on her. She looked as if she were whirling with terror. It was the most harried Edgar had ever seen her, and he clumsily reached out to comfort her but was too disoriented to know how.

"Fana..." He tried to speak but found he could only let out a weak breath of air. He was sure one of his lungs already had been reduced to ash.

"Are you ready to die, Edgar? Are you ready?" Fana's voice was rife with panic, and tears spilled from her eyes. She grabbed his hand and squeezed. He hesitated for a second then gave a weak nod.

Fana picked him up tenderly and brought him to the side of the Well. She dipped him in the shallows of the water, the coldness of it simultaneously stinging and soothing him. Their gaze connected a moment longer, all else besides Fana appearing hazy. A spasm of utmost misery crossed her face and she shut her eyes tightly, two tears pushed from the corners of her eyes. She labored to take a steadying breath, then lifted her hand back in preparation to fulfill her grim pledge.

Fana's hand protruded long and assumed again the talon of the raven. With her claws flashing onyx and opal, Fana cut across his throat and gashed it open. Throbbing, ripping pain bit into Edgar and he tried to gasp in vain. He heard her give a recoiling sob seconds before she dropped him into the pool. Edgar's blood pumped out in torturous bursts into the water as he sank toward the bottom. He counted the pulses as his life ebbed away. In the last seconds he could remember, he saw the boy again. He drifted upward and away from Edgar, as if he had been released from an embrace. The crown slipped off his head and sank toward the bottom of the spring. Their gaze connected, and in one last moment of mercy, Edgar thought he saw a hint of peace in his eyes.

In half a minute more, Edgar too was gone.

Out of the void, memories began to burn brightly. They were primal things, things unrelated to mankind. They were ancient histories of stone and fire, events that had been coded into the earth, miracles that ran rich with the essence of life itself. There were flashes of a network of roots, all stemming from a tree that gave life. Then there were memories of the soil, of the things that grew within that. All the little lives that had sprouted from it and returned to it in death. Seeds, bones, insects, wood. The sublime struggle of growth and decay, eating into each other ceaselessly. The pale imprint of a billion consciousnesses, both complex and crude, all swarming together, consuming one another, assimilating and developing into a grand, infinite wonder. The momentum of entropy ate through these memories, speeding them toward something divine.

Animals and birds, fish and spiders—everything they had seen or done—glowed vivid in the void. Then came Fana. Her awareness of the world had been small at first, unknowing and untamed. The story of her maturity, the process that had taken place over thousands of years, blinked by in a pulse of light and emotion. And as this played out, all the lost memories of Edgar's life also returned to him.

He viewed the story of his own life as if understanding it from the outside. Sights both wondrous and cruel flowed back into him, though they were apart from him now. He was detached from the power that those memories once had over him. And the tale of Edgar Winston Price was complete, unbroken and whole. His story had lived inside Fana, and through her, he reclaimed the narrative of his own life, which had now become synonymous with the millions of lives that belonged to the Wood.

For a moment longer, Edgar remained in that tranquil state, safe and separate from his memories, existing only as a point of understanding and awareness. In that realm, a peace ran deeper than time itself. Coursing with the life of all creation, Edgar stood outside the world of pain and the brutality of the physical. But even in this state of ecstasy, he knew he couldn't remain there for long and willingly merged back with the persona he had gained at birth. When they came together, he still felt that magnificent connection with the web of lives and memories that were part of the Wood. As his body and garments repaired themselves in the miraculous waters of the Well, he knew this connection never would be severed as long as he remained in this form.

At the bottom of the pool, Edgar became whole again. He appeared as he had before the curse had corrupted him, down to the last stitch of his trousers. His body was finally free of pain, and a power unlike anything he'd ever experienced pulsed inside him, radiating from his core. The poisoned spirit had been released. His eyes opened again to the light of the moon, and he rose to the surface of the pool. As he broke the surface and waded out of the cold waters, feeling the drops roll down his hair and face, Fana awaited him with open arms.

They were drawn to each other and soon joined in an embrace. They had become as one, divided into two parts and flooded with euphoric relief. Edgar understood everything inside Fana's heart and mind, and he knew she possessed the same awareness of him. There was no need for words any longer, not with this pathway formed between them. As they held each other tightly, buds on the verge of blooming opened throughout the meadow. Edgar knew this without having to lift his eyes to see them.

In the meadow and in the trees, plant life sprouted and grew, blossoming and pouring heavy fragrance into the air. Fana laughed with elated joy and broke away from him, spinning around as the grass reached upward from beneath her feet. The lily flower that was the center of all her being had transformed from a wilted, tattered ghost to a healthy, buoyant, perfect bloom. Fana laughed louder and louder, the trees rising as they grew. Leaves and petals swirled about in the air, and she joined them in a spinning sort of dance. Edgar waded through the sea of expanding life and took her by the hands, beaming at her. Soon they would be flying back on Fana's wings to Edinburgh to bring Ainsley home, but for now they reveled in everything they had gained. As they held each other, leaning into a blissful kiss and sinking to the grass together, he knew the deep peace he had found in this sacred place never would leave him again.

Blood of the Witch

Ainsley paced the street outside the fence of the Palace of Holyroodhouse, the residence of royals. It was already past midnight, and she had worked herself into a frenzy of worry. Fana had agreed to meet her there at nightfall, no matter the situation. Ainsley had waited for hours, hoping the woman of the woods might at last show herself, but she had grown sick with the notion that something awful had happened. Her own search for any sign of the final revenant or Magdalena the Lunatic had proved fruitless.

Perhaps I should go looking for her, she thought as she chewed her lip, still pacing. *But where would I look? She could be anywhere. What if Fana comes looking for me here and I'm nowhere to be found? I don't know my way around this bloody pile of rock and brick they call a city...I...*

The buzzing of her thoughts quieted as a light flashed in her periphery. Ainsley's head whipped around. The light had come from the great peak in the distance—the massive hill called Arthur's Seat. Ainsley stared in the direction from which it had come, wondering if it had just been a trick of the light or perhaps a quick flash of lightning, and then it flared up again.

It was a shimmering curtain of color and light, looking as if it were woven of green fire. It swam and swayed in waves, hovering over the crest of Arthur's Seat. Ribbons of purple and blue surged through it. Ainsley's breath caught in her throat. She was rendered motionless as she took in the sight of the celestial miracle that looked as if the heavens themselves had donned an ethereal robe dotted with stars. Dread gripped her as much as wonder. These lights clearly hadn't appeared on their own—something had summoned them there.

She felt compelled to charge up to them, knowing that whatever had created them was linked to their dealings with the revenants. She hesitated, however, as she thought over the possibilities.

It could be a sign of the final revenant. Or it could be Fana. She could be signaling for me to come to her. A way to find me. But it could also be Magdalena...

Unable to stand idle for any longer, Ainsley took off down the lane and made for the craggy meadows that sloped upward to the peak. She ran until she was breathless, drawn forth by the green fire in the sky.

A student of the hunt, Ainsley scaled the steep hills and rough pathways of the hillside with ease. Her only thought was to reach the peak, and even after miles of vigorous activity, her determination wasn't shaken. She climbed through clouds of mist so thick that they obscured the rest of the world for minutes at a time, but she always rose through to the sight of the glorious vision. The closer she grew to the sublime veil that hung before the stars, however, the more apprehensive she became. Innately she sensed this was a place of deep magic. A vestige of mystery clung to these hills that looked over the dark lochs and meadows of Holyrood Park, as if the imprints of happenings nefarious and sacred had been etched into the earth. As the way became steeper and more treacherous, Ainsley's worries turned inward.

Until a few moments before, she had been stewing over her deep hatred of the Lunatic and her own willingness to search for the final spirit. Anger had driven her up the hill and had driven her thus far. As she mentally prepared herself for a fight should one await her at the peak, she felt daunted by a sense of emptiness.

Ainsley was strangely reminded of the rabbit she had freed, how she hadn't been able to kill that day. Where there was usually confidence and a cold readiness to struggle for what she wanted, Ainsley only felt doubt.

The existence of witches…we're granted nearly eternal life only if we prove to the Goddess that we exist to preserve life, not destroy it. Have I been so caught up emulating my mother and defending her ways that I've lost sight of my purpose?

The wind was vicious this far up the peak, and her flame burst of hair whipped around her face as her breath grew thin. Though she could hardly see, the moonlight shone upon her hand as she lifted it to her eyes. The two markings sat side by side, devoid of the third, which would allow her to live past the coming solstice. Clenching her fist, she dropped it to her side and cast away her troubled thoughts, fixing her attention on reaching the source of the weird lights.

The peak was approaching fast, and even from a distance, Ainsley saw strange dark structures laid on the top, silhouetted against the sky. Another fogbank swallowed her, making her heart thump against her ribs. She drew her dagger in one hand—the invocation papers she had brought to Edinburgh were dwindling faster than she had anticipated. Scaling the crags, she took a final deep breath as she hoisted herself over the rocky bank and up to the peak. In the eerie green light, Ainsley at last made out what the shapes were.

In the center of the narrow, rocky peak stood an unlit pyre. Around it, seven stakes had been driven into the ground, and to each of the poles an Ophiuchan was bound. They were tightly wrapped to the poles with heavy ropes and gagged so they couldn't make a sound. Nearest to her, an old woman, who looked immeasurably weak and tired, rolled her head to the side to gaze at her. At once, all seven turned their eyes upon Ainsley and began to make muffled noises of imploring distress. A man with dark curtains of hair strained to speak to her through his gag, but he couldn't convey any meaning. As she scanned the line of Ophiuchans, including weeping women and a hysterical yellow-haired youth, her heart leapt slightly as she spotted the bottled revenants lying in a pile, along with a set of tiny coffins a few feet from the pyre. Her first instinct was to grab them and run, but her eyes kept flashing around in search of Magdalena.

"I thought you'd be pleased by my aurora," came the Lunatic's delighted, unsettling sing-song voice from behind the pyre. She stepped out with an almost childlike playfulness, her monstrous teeth glinting at Ainsley. The witch smiled and raised her dagger to Magdalena, taking control over her fear and letting her hunter's instincts guide her.

"Lovely work, yes. I had a feeling it was you," Ainsley said in a low growl, not allowing her smile to fade. She and Magdalena drew closer. Their eyes were locked, their expressions growing more strained. The tension amplified so much that Ainsley felt she might let out a shout to relieve it.

"Yet…you still came. Drawn to the place where your mother completed the curse…the reason we're all standing here today. Come to clean up her mess?" Magdalena said, still poised and ready to spring.

Fury shot through Ainsley, and she sheathed her knife and pricked her finger in one swift move. Magdalena charged at her, but before she could make it, Ainsley's hands exploded with fire. She let the flames curl about her fingers, commanding them with prowess.

"*I came to watch you burn!*" she bellowed, weaving the flames so that they flew at Magdalena in a funnel of bright light.

The Ophiuchan sidestepped out of the way and continued to rush at Ainsley, her fingers spread and her jaw open wide, ready to sink her teeth into the witch's neck. Ainsley shoved her down at the precise moment, using Magdalena's momentum to send her to the ground.

In an instant, Magdalena was back on her feet and had just enough time to dodge another wave of flames. She dipped in and out of Ainsley's reach, toying with her as the witch burnt through strip after strip of invocation paper. Ainsley howled in rage, her mind clouded by frustration. Magdalena was simply too fast, and Ainsley didn't have time to calculate another plan. If she let up for even a moment, the Ophiuchan would tear out her throat.

The more Magdalena danced, the more aggressive Ainsley became. She was spitting with fury, lobbing as much fire as she could. Some singed the sides of Magdalena's gown, and one grazed her face, but none of them struck her squarely. Ainsley lashed out further, urging herself to become more accurate and to focus her power toward one section of Magdalena's body. All she needed was one clear shot. If Magdalena could be stunned, Ainsley could roast her alive atop the pyre for as long as it took. She could end her for all time.

As Magdalena leapt back again, Ainsley conjured a globe of flame so large that she could scarcely hold it. When she hurled it at the Ophiuchan, a primal scream escaped her throat and sweat poured down her forehead. Magdalena dropped to the ground as the flames sailed straight over her and burst onto the pyre, which burst ablaze in moments; the fire's flickering orange glow illuminated the top of the peak. The wind was so strong it nearly knocked Ainsley off her feet in the moment it took her to recover, and the sound of it tearing at the roaring pyre was like a death rattle.

Silhouetted by the flames, Magdalena scrambled backward. She flashed her sideways grin in Ainsley's direction, her jet-black hair fluttering around her face.

"Do you think she would be proud, witch? To see you undoing her work?" Magdalena shouted over the whistling wind.

Ainsley gritted her teeth, her fingers itching to draw another slip of paper. She glared at Magdalena, waiting for the perfect opportunity while trying to block out her words. "Keep your mouth shut and fight!" she screamed. As she wiped the sweat off her forehead, the blood from her finger dripped down her face.

"Oh, I see," Magdalena yelled with a chirp of delight. "I understand now! She doesn't even know who you really are, does she? She never returned to meet you after you'd grown. Isn't that right?" Magdalena degraded into a shrieking sort of laughter that drove into Ainsley's core.

Again Ainsley tried to block out the sound but found herself twirling her hands about, creating a small but powerfully charged sphere of flames. She wove it with all the remnants of magic she could feel in the air around her, pouring every ounce of her skill and experience into that single spell. As Magdalena continued to laugh, Ainsley leapt forward and shot the sphere straight at the Ophiuchan's head. It connected with Magdalena's face and knocked her off her feet.

Ainsley let free visceral war cry and charged over to examine her handiwork. Magdalena's face had been burnt away, and only a circle of ash and crispy, destroyed shapes remained. With a sneering smile, Ainsley spat on her still form then marched over to where the bottled revenants lay.

Glowing with pride, she stooped down to examine them, already imagining what it would be like to tell Fana that she had redeemed herself and saved them all. Just as she laid her hands on the bottles, however, a slender, child-like but horrendously powerful arm curled around her neck. Ainsley struggled to look back, her eyes popping in terror. Magdalena's burnt face stared back her. The skin was blackened to ash and her mouth was gone, showing only those hideous teeth and huge, white, lidless eyes staring out at her from the charred remains of the Lunatic's countenance. Ainsley tried to cry out, but no air could pass through her throat. Tears stung her eyes as the flesh on Magdalena's face slowly reconstructed itself. It had mended just enough for Ainsley to see the Lunatic's triumphant smile before her grip squeezed her consciousness completely away.

Ashes, Ashes

Fana's flight path changed as soon as she caught sight of the aurora swirling around Arthur's Seat. Her raven feet held tighter to Edgar's shoulders as they continued on, joined by an innate sense that they were needed there. Beguiling as those lights were, they were aware that danger awaited them beneath those curtains of shimmering green. Thinking in tandem, Fana and Edgar swooped lower, taking note of a great fire that was burning atop the peak and circled by dark posts. Just as they were coming in closer to the craggy plateau, a rock launched past Edgar and struck Fana's wing. She immediately spun out of control, and they plummeted to the earth.

Edgar landed hard on his feet, immediately collapsing as Fana crashed a few feet away from him. As she struck the ground, she burst into feathers, and when they flooded past her, she was again in her human form, wincing and clutching her arm. Edgar was just getting past the worst of the pain and trying to rise to his feet as Magdalena strolled toward him, backlit by the blazing pyre.

"E-edgar...Fana...you...came," a weak voice mumbled from his side, and Edgar whipped his head around to see Ainsley lying wan and bound a few feet away. She looked as if she were fighting to stay conscious, and a gash in the side of her neck bled freely.

"I had an inkling you might join me for the celebration," Magdalena said with a spritely wickedness as she looked down at Fana from her spot by the pyre, then turned her gaze to Edgar. "But you, now *there's* a surprise! And...and my, how you've changed, Mr. Price. I must express my gratitude to you both—you do keep things so interesting. I was afraid this was going to be too easy," she chortled a bit to herself, then sauntered around the hilltop, gazing at the macabre scene she'd created with a look of satisfaction. Around the pyre elaborate, arcane symbols had been painted in fresh blood, glistening in the firelight. Eight circles of wicked design ringed the ground around the pyre; in the middle of each one lay one of the tiny coffins. As Magdalena tiptoed between the carefully painted lines to where the pyre stood, Edgar moved to Ainsley's side and helped her up, pulling a handkerchief from his pocket and pressing it to the wound on her neck.

"What have you done?" Fana demanded of Magdalena, clenching her fists and taking in the sight of the restrained Ophiuchans. "What is the meaning of this?'

"Wait and see," Magdalena hinted playfully, collecting the pile of bottled revenants from the ground.

Edgar grew tense, desperate to rush for the revenants but unwilling to recklessly approach the Lunatic. Gently, Magdalena laid the bottles in the center of the pyre, her fingertips blackening as they were eaten by the flames. She pulled them away, wincing as the bottles began to heat up.

"Magdalena, I command you to remove them at once. This could turn disastrous—this magic is too powerful for any of us to control." Fana's voice thrummed with worry.

Magdalena cackled in disbelief that this nymph would dare give her any order. "Are you laboring under the delusion that I care about such things?" she spat at her, that cruel smile still splitting her face. "If my meddling brings about catastrophe, then I welcome it!"

She puffed out her chest and stared at Fana. Just as the hatred between them was about to boil over to violence, the fire behind her rose high and the wailing of five tortured voices rose from the flames.

They grew higher and burned purple as tormented sounds resonated from the bottles. Edgar and Fana moved to stop Magdalena, but halted when they beheld what was transpiring above the flames. Geometric patterns of light and color spread out in the air. It was as if space had begun to fold in on itself, starting as two segments, then folding into four, then multiplying in a horribly intensifying speed. As reality folded away, it revealed a black void, ringed by the shifting and swirling patterns that were as hideous as they were stunning.

The pit itself was sickening to behold in its nothingness. It was the antithesis of all that existed, ever hungering, ever destroying but unable to satiate its hunger. This gateway to a hellish emptiness spread out until it was about twenty feet long, the patterns churning around its border. As Edgar and Fana gaped in terror, Magdalena's cries grew crazed with delight. She leapt in exaltation, as if she were in the midst of a great burst of holy ecstasy. Ainsley clung to Edgar's side, and for the first time since he'd known her, she was paralyzed with fear.

"Yes, oh, brilliant lord! Yes, oh, bringer of justice! I can hear you so clearly now!" Magdalena shrieked upward to seemingly no one, tears of joy running down her paper-white face. She was practically dancing with ebullience. "I shall give her unto to you. She will burn first, and then I'll send these wretches along to your eternal embrace!"

Magdalena turned and fixed her gaze on Ainsley, her icy blue eyes possessed with a humming insanity. She prowled toward her, her hands stretched outward as she cast a side glance to Fana, daring her to try to interfere. Edgar stood in front of Ainsley, firmly committed to protecting her, though he couldn't imagine how he could face this hurricane of a woman and prevail. The witch had lost too much blood to get to her feet, though she still held fast to Edgar's legs as she struggled to stay awake.

Fana hurtled toward them with dire speed. Magdalena seemed to anticipate the attack, and caught her by the shoulders.

Fana pushed forward, her arms widening and elongating as she did. Her body sprouted fur and lengthened as she assumed the form of a huge wolf. She bore down on Magdalena with paws flexing as white teeth flashed. She lunged, snapping at the Ophiuchan's throat. Magdalena didn't stop laughing, dodging just out of reach with each clamp of Fana's jaws; the Lunatic seemed to enjoy watching her struggle.

Edgar doubled back as fast as he could, pulling the dirk from Ainsley's belt and cutting her arms loose of the ropes that bound them. She moaned a little noise of gratitude as he helped her to her feet, leaning against him for balance.

Magdalena at last grew tired of tormenting Fana and pushed her to the ground. The wolf frantically rolled onto its back as Magdalena sprang to her feet. She shot past Fana, bashing Edgar aside and lifting Ainsley from the ground with her iron grip. As Magdalena brought her toward the pyre, Fana righted herself and leapt into the air.

She grew long and scaly and transformed into a monstrous blue-black serpent as she flew forward. Her coiling body was instantly ten feet long, and her head resembled an adder's. With a striking bite, her fangs pierced Magdalena's shoulder. The frenzied Ophiuchan let out an earsplitting cry as the motion rocked Ainsley from her arms. Fana drew her backward, pulling Magdalena into her coils and squeezing to immobilize her. Edgar ran for Ainsley again, though she appeared to be gaining more strength by the moment. The adrenaline coursing through her seemed to revitalize her, and by the time Edgar was at her side, she had risen to her feet, though she still struggled to keep her balance. He reached out to help her when a moan from one of the poles stirred him.

A hoarse, papery, pleading sound begged for Edgar's attention. He looked up to see a pair of eyes he recognized—he was fairly certain it was the same Ophiuchan man who'd been suspended above the oubliette. He appeared as a withered wraith, his marble-like eyes rolling around in a skull that was stretched with leathery skin.

"Ainsley!" Edgar called to her as he started toward the Ophiuchan. "If we release them, perhaps they could—"

"Are you mad? They'll eat us alive!" Ainsley managed to scream back, shooting Edgar a warning glance. "We have to—"

"*Get away from them!*" Magdalena's voice carried over the fierce wind. With a violent thrashing, she fought off Fana's constricting grasp and scuttled away before her serpent's strike could pull her back. She barreled toward Edgar and Ainsley, but inspiration struck Edgar before she could reach them. He leapt backward and made it to the pyre's side, raising the knife above the bottled revenants. The flames stung his hands, but he endured the pain with watering eyes.

"Don't come any closer or I'll smash them!" he threatened.

"N-no…" Magdalena halted, her look of frenzied energy devolving into ashen fright. "No, the fire will—" She bit her tongue, looking sick that she'd already said too much.

Edgar bit his lip against the pain. "Stay where you are," he warned, edging his hand out of the heat just a margin.

Fana was rearing up behind Magdalena, her forked tongue flitting out as a hiss rattled in her throat. Magdalena's face contorted into an ugly snarl, her lip curling and twitching. "You will not take this from me…not when I've come this far. They…*deserve this*," she growled at him, each word dripping with malice.

"Magdalena," Edgar said, the threat and violence in his heart slowly transforming to sympathy. "They committed a horrible crime. They did the unforgivable—that, I cannot deny. But you've answered their cruelty with more cruelty. Keeping that pain alive through their suffering…it won't save you. You could be free from this. You could leave here now and never think on any of it again."

Fana's serpentine form drew back, her liquid amber eyes fixed on Edgar. Ainsley looked at Edgar with an intense gaze, as if horrified by the very idea that they would let Magdalena walk free. Edgar's words enraged Magdalena so much that tears of pure loathing and ire fell from her eyes as she bared her teeth at him, breathing heavily through her nose.

"You ignorant, pathetic child," she seethed at Edgar, tears of desperation pouring out. "You've no concept of the depth of my pain. You've lived unscathed. *You all have!*" she screeched at everyone surrounding her. "This isn't some slight I can merely ignore. This kind of mark does not *fade*—these monsters *ruined me*. I can't look upon anything beautiful in this world without feeling the sting of my wounds. All things in my life have been touched by their evil; nothing has been left unbroken by their crimes. There is no abandoning this sort of tragedy; there is only retribution. And it must be served. It *must*." Magdalena wept with frustration, reaching out in a plaintive gesture toward the revenants.

"You had an eternity!" Edgar felt that passion behind his words grow. "You had power, life unending, limitless possibilities. And you chose destruction and violence.every step of the way. You nurtured this grudge from the start; you kept it alive and fed it until it consumed you in turn. You obsessed over it, allowed it to become your only reason for existence. You stopped living after they hurt you—by *choice*, you kept yourself in that hell where they put you. You're the one who destroyed your ability to love the world, Magdalena, not them," Edgar said, speaking from deep within his heart. He believed and understood these words more powerfully than she could ever know; they weren't solely for her benefit.

Magdalena howled at him, her piercing eyes fixed on him, burning with hatred and misery. She could no longer bear to stand idly and listen to him. She belted forward, her hands grasping for his throat with the intent to tear it out.

Just as Fana struck out again and missed, Edgar smashed the knife down on the bottles, crushing them with the hilt of the dagger. When the glass shattered, the five spirits escaped into the flames, and the wailing ceased. Magdalena reached to throttle Edgar, but Fana struck again and caught her by the leg. The Lunatic was thrown to the ground, howling like an animal and beating the rocks with her fists so hard that they cracked under her force. All the while, her murderous gaze never strayed from Edgar.

The revenants circled in the purple flames for a moment more. Their witchy hues faded by the second, the holy fire cleansing them of their evil. One by one, they rose as wispy clusters among the smoke and disappeared into the sky, finally freed from their torment.

Magdalena grew silent as she watched them fly away. Soundlessly, reality began to fold outward again. The void sealed itself back up, and the fractal patterns faded, as if they had only ever been a mirage. Magdalena's wails cut through the voice of the wind. She rolled on the ground, her leg still clamped in Fana's jaws, beating her fists and weeping like a child. Her cries came in rhythmic bursts, and she tore at anything she could get her hands on—grass, soil, stone.

"I'll kill you all. I'll kill every last one of you!" she bellowed, pointing an accusatory finger at Edgar and Ainsley. Before anyone could react, Magdalena twisted around and seized the trunk of her own thigh. Ripping at the fabric of her gown, she drove her razor fingers through her pallid flesh, took hold of the now-exposed bone, and snapped it as easily as if it were a twig. With a lurch forward, she tore away from her own leg, the flesh easily separating and freeing her from Fana's grasp. The maimed, rabid creature shot forward, crawling on her belly at a furious speed toward Edgar, who barely had time to lift the knife in retaliation. She grabbed on to his legs, tearing at the flesh with her razor-sharp nails as her eyes bulged. Edgar's feeble knife blows did nothing to faze her. She was going to shred him to bits within seconds.

Fana shed her scales and sprinted forward in human form. She wrenched Magdalena off Edgar, and both she and the Lunatic tumbled to the ground, their hands reaching to rip at eyes, throats, and stomachs.

Fana was atop her for a moment and craned her antlered head back to look at Edgar. "Go now. Free the Ophiuchans! We have no hope without them!"

Though it split his heart with worry, he trusted Fana's orders and bolted toward the first pole. Struggling to stay conscious, Ainsley dizzily staggered to the other side of the peak, taking ragged breaths and used her remaining few strips of papers to free the captives. She used the blood from her neck wound to write spells that cut the ropes with sharp blades made from wind.

The sight of her prisoners being freed sent Magdalena into an apoplectic fit. With her leg already reforming, she hobbled after Ainsley in a last-ditch effort to stop her, but Fana grabbed her again.

"Fana, keep her contained! We need time!" Ainsley wheezed as the first Ophiuchan, a black-haired woman, dropped to the ground, groaning and stretching her limbs.

Fana hurled the Lunatic backward and took the few moments during which Magdalena stumbled to transform into a cave lioness. Lithe and powerful, she stood imposing before the Lunatic, her eyes like molten gold. She prowled around Magdalena, pushing her back from where Edgar stood freeing his second Ophiuchan.

"You...you arrogant, nasty little cheat," Magdalena spat, as she tried to break past Fana's dangerous pacing. "You, who have known only love and adoration. Do you honestly think you'll be the one to stop me? Do you know how many have tried but were ruined by my hand? You might have destroyed my designs, but don't think for an instant that you'll get away with this."

She grew quiet and still for a moment, keeping her eyes locked on Fana's in an unwavering stare. They were both frozen for some time, but Magdalena could keep her anguish in no longer and snapped once again.

"*All of you will lie in ashes by morning!*" she roared, rushing at Fana.

The cave lioness leapt to meet her, her claws extended and fangs flashing. The two creatures crashed into each other like a massive wave smashing into a cliffside. Fana's claws tore at Magdalena's gown, slicing deep gashes into her. The Ophiuchan held fast, absorbing the blow. She caught Fana by the throat and kept her back before shoving her hand deep into her gut. When Magdalena ripped her hand out, a fountain of blood shot out with it. She dropped the groaning feline to the ground and bounded over her shivering form. Edgar, who had just freed his fourth Ophiuchan, turned back in horror. He had sensed the trauma done to his love, their connected souls enduring the same injury. He knew the rushing, paralyzing pain that enveloped her, even if he didn't physically feel it.

Fana slowly reassumed her human shape. She lay shivering on the ground, clutching her midsection and moaning. Edgar rushed toward her, but the Lunatic caught him before he could reach her. She grabbed him by the throat and held him high above her, watching his life ebb away with a sadistic satisfaction. As he choked for breath, she marched him toward the pyre, intent on throwing him onto it.

Magdalena's myopic focus on destroying Edgar burned so intense, however, that she didn't notice that Ainsley had freed the last of the Ophiuchans. The pale, phantom creatures were all getting to their feet, sharing glances of wrath and the rush of emancipation. They strode around Magdalena in a ring, closing in step by step, their eyes hungry and mouths open. She saw them only a second too late.

She turned, dropping Edgar to the ground as they all closed in on her. She let out a little cry, holding herself and whimpering.

With a look of shock and fascination from outside the ghostly ring, Ainsley watched as Magdalena tried pathetically to

fight them. Even in their intensely weakened states, seven Ophiuchans could easily overpower one. All seven took hold of her,
grabbing her arms, legs, and shoulders. Together they lifted her
above their heads as she howled and wriggled, all of them emitting low, giddy laughs of disbelief and exhilaration.

Magdalena had been rendered speechless—she merely
bubbled into tears as they marched her toward the pyre. Edgar
crawled away from them, still frightened of the deathly, skeletal
creatures. Just as Magdalena loosed her death cry and the Ophiuchans leaned back to hurl her into the flames, a voice rang out.

"Stop! I beg you, stop!"

Edgar could hardly believe his ears: it was Ainsley who had
spoken. The Ophiuchans' eyes all looked upon her as if she were
an insect that had dared address them. Magdalena still whimpered, rapidly looking from the pyre, to Ainsley, and back to the
Ophiuchans, who held her next to the flames.

"As I helped free you from this monster, will you hear my
humble request?" Ainsley, brash and bold as she was, had a tremble in her voice as she spoke to the tall, spectral Ophiuchans. They
whispered among themselves for a few moments, and the Ophiuchan with the dark curtains of hair and the eyes Edgar recognized stepped forward from the throng.

"We shall hear you," he said in a voice that was as arid as sand.

Ainsley swallowed, clearly stricken with the fear. Edgar
feared that this creature might be possessed by the urge to consume her at any moment. She lowered her head and flaming hair
in a sign of obeisance before she spoke again.

"Oh, undying one, I beseech you. This whole disaster began
with my mother and a criminal who committed an unspeakable
act. She punished him, seeking to bring justice to a man who had
walked free from his evil deeds. The result couldn't have been further from justice. Because of my mother's thirst for his suffering,
so many, living and deceased, were left haunted by an evil that

should have long been laid to rest. No good came of her cruelty," Ainsley said timidly, growing ever more anxious by the look of impatience on the Ophiuchan's gaunt face.

"This devil did the same to you," she continued. "Magdalena wanted to punish you for what you did to her. You know firsthand how wrong this was. I have seen this pattern of atrocity repaying atrocity, and it only spreads pain. It never just ends with a single punishment; the cycle feeds itself. You can't get your time back; you can never be whole again after such evil has entered your life…but you can be merciful to those who've wronged you. And there is hope beyond that mercy. There's power in it."

"What are you asking of us, child of Goddess? Speak clearly," the Ophiuchan breathed at her, narrowing his moon-like eyes.

Ainsley was silent for a few moments, her mouth hanging open, looking as if words fought to leave the tip of her tongue. "Let this creature live. Is it not part of your laws that you are not to spill the blood of the Divine Serpent? It yet flows through her cursed veins. Forgive her. Do what you will to her, treat her with fair retaliation, but let her live. Give her another chance," Ainsley pleaded on Magdalena's behalf.

The Lunatic stopped fighting and stared at Ainsley, her face betraying pure shock. Magdalena's tears continued to flow down her face, but she was stricken in a way that rendered her completely motionless.

"She is, regrettably, correct, Ulrich," one of the female Ophiuchans said, though she did so with hesitant distaste. "Her flesh is our flesh."

Ulrich looked for a long time at Ainsley, then back to Magdalena, who lay, stunned and pathetic, above the heads and at the mercy of those she had terrorized countless times.

"Is it your desire to live beyond this night, o blight of our race? Do you yet wish to continue, knowing that we do not intend to forgive you as easily as this child has?" Ulrich asked Magdalena in a deep, threatening tone.

Magdalena was paralyzed, but after a moment she numbly nodded. "Y-yes...I want to live," she shuddered, crying harder than ever. "I want to live! *I want to live!*" she kept repeating until she was screaming it.

"Silence, blight!" Ulrich shouted over her, and Magdalena fell back into her whimpering. "Very well. It shall be so. You are pardoned from death but not forgiven. Your path to redemption will be a miserable one, Magdalena Köhler," Ulrich announced, and the others murmured their agreement.

For a moment longer, the Ophiuchans regarded Ainsley and Edgar, neither of whom dared to move an inch. Edgar ached to run to Fana, but he knew it could be suicide to make a sudden movement in the presence of these starved creatures. At last they turned from them and began their slow departure. They marched silently down the side of Arthur's Seat like the strangest of funeral processions, carrying Magdalena above them. Their blank, white faces moved against the mountain like a slow shower of meteors in a black sky. When they were at a sufficient distance, Edgar sprang from where he stood to scoop up Fana.

As he cradled her, she smiled up at him in relief, touching the side of his face with tenderness. Before either could speak, Ainsley made a small sound of sudden emotion as she held her hand out. A golden light shone upon the back of her hand, and she regarded it with tear-filled eyes.

"I—I saved Magdalena..." she said, as if she were just realizing what she had done. "I saved her life...I've done it. I'm going to live! Fana, I'm going to live! Fa—Fana..." Her triumphant words died almost as soon as they came. She hurtled to Fana's side, holding her close.

"Ainsley, I'm overjoyed," Fana breathed weakly, looking up at Ainsley with glowing pride. A spot of blood lay upon her lips as she reached up to touch her face in a loving gesture.

"Edgar, she's hurt!" Ainsley yelped, a little shadow of her trademark rage trying to flare up but instead lapsing into horror. "You can help her. You're a surgeon! Fix her like you did before!"

Edgar opened his mouth to say something, his Adam's apple quivering. He already had seen the wound in Fana's belly. His trained eye knew there was nothing he could do, even if he had a full operating room and a team of assistants at his disposal. Seeing the hollow look on his face, Ainsley opened her mouth in what promised to be a shout, but nothing came out. In the weak light of a sky that was preparing for morning, Fana's smile was easy to see.

"Ainsley, it's going to be all right," she said softly.

Ainsley blinked away angry tears. "No, we've got to get you away from here. We can still make it. The Wood isn't that far. We can—"

"Not this time, I'm afraid..." Fana gasped, her eyes shining with radiant love for them both. "I've died enough times to know when the moment has come for me again. And it has indeed come," she said, struggling to keep her cheerful smile.

Edgar's eyes stung at the sight of her, and he couldn't stop his face from pulling into a grimace as he endured a jagged paroxysm of sorrow. He could do nothing but hold her a little more tightly as she shook in his arms.

"Edgar...you know what to do." Fana nestled her head in the crook of his arm and rested it there for a moment, savoring her last moments of comfort and warmth. "Bury me under the lily. Stand guard over my grave."

"Fana, no..." Ainsley moaned, running her fingers through Fana's soft brown hair. "We need you. We all need you so badly."

"Edgar is your warden now. Teach him. Help him...guide him so he will know how to protect you all, dearest one," Fana replied, her breathing growing more ragged. "Will you do this? Will you learn to love him as you love me?"

Tears shining on her cheeks, Ainsley looked up begrudgingly at Edgar and nodded. "I will, Fana," she said, her head bowed.

Fana's tranquil smile returned. She looked up at Edgar and stared into his watery eyes. Her peacefulness faded for a moment, and her lips quivered. He recognized sharp fear in her eyes— death was moments away, and she struggled to cling to life, but something else was frightening her.

"It might be a half a century or longer before I see you again," she whispered, holding tightly to his shirt. "Edgar...Edgar, my love, I'm so afraid...I'm so afraid you won't be there when I rise. I'm so frightened you'll disappear." Her words became more slurred by the moment. "Promise me, please...promise me I'll see you at the end of this long darkness."

Edgar leaned down, fighting off the tears for her sake, as he kissed her lips for the final time. When he drew backward, he looked deeply into her eyes. "My dear Fana, it will not be a long darkness. It will be...it will be as if you hadn't slept at all, and when you wake...when you wake, I will be there waiting for you."

Fana smiled once more. The peace of it reached her eyes just before the light faded from them altogether. Her lids closed, and she fell softly against Edgar, her body going limp. For a very long time, Edgar and Ainsley held her in their arms. She still felt so warm.

At long last, the sun crept over the ocean inlet and bathed everything in warm, gentle light. The lochs and sea became bright liquid silver in its radiance. The heat of it touched the two weary souls, reaching into them and, however feebly, soothing their broken hearts.

What Became of Jacob Hare

A man lay motionless on the floor of a shop with no name. His eyes stared blankly up at the ceiling. Although he was surrounded by the wreckage of things once loved, he took no notice of it. There was no way he could have known that, moments earlier, the final spirit that had haunted him for most of his life had been thrown into fire, cleansing it and releasing him from his curse for all time.

He could not have known, for his mind no longer perceived the world he belonged to; rather, it was consumed by a single fraction of a single instance of happiness that had occurred decades ago. The sun and the moon rolled by, chasing each other in their eternal pursuit but still he did not move.

In the early hours of the morning, almost a week later, Hare's body, no longer preserved by the curse, could not go on living without sustenance.

Jacob Hare quietly died on the floor of that shop among the glittering, broken things that never would be seen by any living thing again. In the moments before each coming darkness of night, a ray of withering sunlight shines through a crack in the wall, catching the green fire and coal-bright eyes of the curious ornament pinned to his coat. His bones still remain there, the skeleton's hand lying over his chest, eternally protecting his dead lover's lock of hair.

Where Love Waits

Inspired to weed the garden, Colleen rose early. After a quick breakfast and a spot of tea, she marched outside into the mist of the pale morning. Breathing deeply of the dewy vapors in the air, she set to work among the pumpkins and potatoes, singing a cheerful little tune Ainsley had taught her some years ago.

Not long into her work, her heart was stirred by an approaching noise. Colleen stood and harkened to it, facing the dirt path. Surely enough, it became louder by the moment. Wooden wheels ground over the dirt. Colleen grew breathless for a moment as the clop of hooves also came through the mists. She rushed to the gate and stared with a fluttering heart down the path.

The first thing she saw through the shroud of fog was her hair, radiant as a torch in the evening. Colleen flew past the gate, unable to stop herself from laughing in relief as she hurried to the arms she had longed for during the unbearable absence.

Ainsley leapt off the cart and greeted her with a smile, wide and clear. Colleen sprang onto her, holding her so tightly that Ainsley groaned under the pressure. Soon they were both laughing, staring happily at each other's faces as if to ascertain that they really had been reunited. After the initial joyous burst had passed, a question hovered in Colleen's mind. Ainsley must have guessed it from the look of concern on her face.

With another knowing grin, Ainsley grabbed her lover's hand and held their clasped fingers upward. There, as clear as a summer morning, was the answer to the weighty query that had tortured Colleen these last few sleepless nights.

"I've done it," Ainsley said at last, letting joy show like sunshine on her face as Colleen searched for words worthy enough to express what was in her heart. When she could not do anything but stammer, Ainsley let out a great, loud laugh and lifted her upward. They spun around for a moment, Colleen consumed with giggles before Ainsley brought her back down and grasped her tightly. Colleen buried her face in her love's chest, her tears of relief soaking Ainsley's tunic.

"Ay, hout na!" Ainsley cried teasingly. "My dear, bonnie love, if you keep that up, you're going to ruin my clothes."

Colleen looked up, wiping away her tears and laughing once more. In an instant, Colleen saw past the happiness at their reunion and noticed something troubled Ainsley. Her disposition had changed: it had become much more muted and vulnerable since they'd last seen each other. This sent a wave of disquiet through Colleen, and she couldn't help ask after it.

"Who was it? Who did you save?" she questioned at last, as she held fast to her arms, refusing to let Ainsley go. The witch's expression darkened slightly, though her smile didn't entirely fade. When she didn't answer, Colleen grew even more apprehensive. "Ainsley?"

"Come now. We'd better go inside. Elspeth should hear this too," Ainsley said in a comforting voice. She quickly took care of the horse and cart then led Colleen with an arm wrapped around her shoulders.

Before they could make it to the door, Elspeth burst out in a flurry and made for Ainsley, throwing herself around both her and Colleen. "Oh, dear sister!" she cried. "You're alive! My familiar came to tell me. He just now returned; he said you were coming. He told me you—"

She grabbed Ainsley's hand to see for herself then looked up at her, beaming tearfully. They made their way inside the cottage, and Elspeth and Colleen hurriedly put together a meal. As she sat in the comfort of the home she had missed so powerfully, enjoying with gratitude the food given to her, her heart swelled and twinged all at once. Why had she needed to leave this place to understand that this was where love had waited for her all along? Too proud to cry or express her overflowing affection, she set her tea down and looked across the table at her family.

"I hate that I must tell you this, but I don't come with just good news to share. Fana is...Fana is gone," she croaked, and watched with a sinking heart as a numb wave of grief crossed their faces.

"Ainsley...how?" Colleen pressed.

"It was Magdalena. Fana died fighting for us," her voice dreary and husky. Colleen and Elspeth shared a look of pain. "And it was...it was Magdalena's life I saved," she admitted, keeping her head held high and enduring their expressions of horrified confusion. "I suppose I'd better start from the beginning..."

Ainsley paused in thought then reached into her pocket. She withdrew a small drawstring bag, opened it, and extracted the eight miniature coffins that she'd collected before they left. After laying them out, she shared with Elspeth and Colleen everything that had transpired since she had left the Wood, and at last grim understanding came to their faces. Their happiness was certainly dampened, but something strong bonded them while they sat together in silence and solidarity.

Elspeth was the first to break the strange, sacred silence that had come over them. "What will you do with these?" She gestured to the coffins and their eerie wooden occupants. "This is all that survives of Mother's curse. Will you keep them? Destroy them?"

Ainsley thought over Elspeth's question for a moment then shook her head. "No. I think we should let them go. Their power is all but depleted, so they can bring the world no further harm. Here they'll only serve as a sad reminder. There will be someone who'll find meaning in them, out there. It's time to move past this," Ainsley said with a sigh.

Elspeth nodded. "I do believe you're right, sister. Well, now, you should get some rest, my dear. I'll go tell the coven about…what happened," she said with a note of tenderness in her voice, then floated over and kissed Ainsley's forehead lightly. As she gathered her things and made for the door, she held the handle and stopped. She looked back at her sister, her eyes watering again. "Oh, Ainsley. I can hardly yet dare to believe. You're… you're going to live. You're going to stay with me forever." Ainsley smiled at her, her eyes aching with tears.

Without another word, Elspeth left, and Colleen and Ainsley sat in comfortable silence for a while. Eventually Colleen rose to refill Ainsley's cup with tea.

"You…you *are* going to live," she said quietly, as if the fact were just sinking in.

"I most certainly am." Ainsley took Colleen's hand and held it. "I'm going to be here from now on. We're going to have Sunday mornings together. We're going to have festivals. We're going to spend every rainy night shivering in our room, and watch countless sunsets, and eat good meals, and argue over silly things until we can't remember why they seemed important to begin with. We're going to do it all."

Colleen smiled, but it wasn't as broad as Ainsley might've hoped.

Ainsley's face fell. "What's wrong?"

"Nothing! Nothing. I couldn't be happier. It's just…." She slowed then looked Ainsley straight in the eyes. "You *are* going to live. Forever, essentially, like Elspeth said. And I won't. I'm just—I'm afraid that… Will you still love me when I'm wrinkled and gray and horrible?"

Ainsley pulled Colleen in close. She gave her a reassuring kiss and a smile so wide it nearly hurt. "My darling, I'll love you *especially* when you're old and gray and horrible. In fact, the more horrible, the better!" she joked, and Colleen laughed, some of her nerves assuaged. Ainsley grew serious again, her smile bittersweet. "I told you before...our story has to end one day. And it'll break me apart when it does. But it's certainly a story worth telling. And I'm going to be there for every last moment of it."

The Kingdom

Fana lay buried. It was done. Edgar sat beside the place where she had been committed to the earth, resting in unimaginable peace. Ever so delicately, he grazed the petals of the pale lily that grew over her grave. It still bloomed fuller than ever, nearly luminescent with life. He was struck by a strange urge to cry and smile all at once, and after a moment of quiet, he decided on the smile.

Just days ago, she had been dancing in this meadow, unbridled joy on her face as flowers sprang up around her delicate feet. Edgar's heart ached as he recalled the beauty of that scene and saw the evidence of her miraculous spirit still growing around him in such splendor.

He stood up, wishing to walk amid the sea of flowers and ferns. As his hands grazed them, the life inside each of them felt electric under his touch—he was so intimately connected to them now. He meandered to the Well and stared into its blue-green depths. While he studied it, a glint caught his eye. Kneeling to get a better look, he noted with a small laugh of shock that his pocket watch lay sunken in the sediment.

It must've fallen as I was dying, he guessed. It was still frozen at the time when it had been smashed and would remain there for as long as it existed. Edgar thought about diving in and removing it, but it suddenly seemed important that it stay and become part of this place. He wanted a piece of himself to remain here.

As he gazed at the water, he noticed his reflection. The same face still peered back at him, but it lacked that hollow misery that he had glimpsed in the window of the Great Northern Hospital in what seemed like another lifetime. He stepped back from the Well, looking again at Fana's grave.

He shivered to think that she had just been in the sunlight and now lay so still in the darkness...that she was gone.

No, not gone. Not for long, he reminded himself, and the hurt softened slightly. *My dear Fana...eaten again by the soil. Spread throughout this hallowed place, invigorating the trees, flowing through its waters, sighing in the wind. And slowly you will come together again, and I will draw you up, resurrected from the earth, whole again.*

Though it was enough to know this, he sat by her again, wanting to be as close as he could for a while longer before she dispersed. It would be immeasurably difficult to forget all he had seen and to lay his fury and melancholy to rest. His eyes had witnessed such savagery, such obscenity. He was certain that for the duration of his life—which would be much longer than he ever anticipated—he could never truly forget those gruesome sights. Many years would pass before those fractured parts of his soul would stop aching, but the promise of healing was certain. Tragedy had dug deeply into him and torn nearly everything out of him, but like Fana, he would be whole again one day.

As he and Ainsley had brought Fana's body home in the cart, a realization had come over him. There was no sense in ceaselessly dwelling on those noxious memories and reopening his wounds. He no longer had the desire or willingness to give those things more power than he absolutely had to. He refused to feed his demons and vowed to rid himself of them for good one day. The time for doubt had passed; the time for action had at last begun.

A little yellow dandelion sprout stood by his hand. Edgar touched it lightly and felt that same electric pulse. Following a peculiar inspiration, he willed life into the tiny thing, and his eyes widened as it began to change. It took most of his concentration, but after a few minutes, the petals curled in on themselves, growing tightly in their case of leaves, then burst forth with white seeds. Amazed, he plucked it. With a gentle breath, he blew the puff away from the head, quietly wishing for this tranquility to last. The wind carried the seeds all over the glorious meadow, where they would no doubt find root in the fertile ground.

So this is part of being a warden then. I too hold some sway over these little miracles, Edgar marveled, feeling an overwhelming sense of gratitude and exhilaration. How fortunate he was to be able to live in this Wood; to reside among the worthy, hardworking folk who populated its glades and clearings; and to bear witness to every spectacular, mysterious part of it. Truly he was the luckiest of men to be able to walk the pathways of this glorious green kingdom.

So I found a kingdom after all. Though it's certainly not the one I expected, I wouldn't change a thing. It's so much grander to be a part of a kingdom than it is to have just one lonely piece of the world.

He thought of the poor, sorrowful, broken boy who could never speak, the one who'd been his companion and the resident of his very bones for a time. Something inside him felt he owed it to the child, who had been the undeserving victim of such an evil fate, to pour as much love and light into the Wood as he could. It could never truly make amends for what the boy had lost, and he might never know of Edgar's actions, but he was moved to do it all the same. Here Edgar could be a part of something important, something vital, and though the miracles he could create now were small, he knew they eventually might grow to touch the lives of everyone who surrounded him.

Yes, I will do this for you too, Fana. For all of you. I will do it because I have to…and because I want to. And perhaps the more love I give this kingdom, the sooner I shall see you again. Perhaps.

Author's Note

The inspiration for this novel first came to me while I was studying abroad in Edinburgh in 2010. The curious set of the miniature coffins discovered by a group of boys atop Arthur's Seat in 1836 was on display at the National Museum of Edinburgh. After seeing them, and reading about their possible meaning as effigies to the Burke and Hare victims, I couldn't get them out of my head. Long after I'd left, the memory of those tiny coffins haunted me, along with other chilling and fascinating tales I'd heard in Edinburgh.

The story developed over three years, and in 2013 I began to write *The Resurrectionist* as a way of solving the mystery of the coffins in my own way—in a sense, I simply needed to lay my own curiosity to rest. Though this book is a work of fantasy and I've clearly taken wide liberties with the historical material, many of the settings and elements are based in fact.

From 1828–29, Irish immigrants William Burke and William Hare were responsible for the murders of sixteen people in Edinburgh. Their methods generally involved luring a victim to Hare's boardinghouse, where they plied them heavily with alcohol before suffocating them. They were motivated by greed, selling the corpses of their victims to a local surgeon, Robert Knox. Each victim was publicly dissected, and Dr. Knox is largely thought to be complicit in the crimes.

During their ten-month killing spree, William Hare's common-law wife, Margaret Laird, was pregnant with their child. Hare was pardoned for his crimes due to his confession and condemnation of his accomplice Burke, who was hanged and publicly dissected as punishment. Burke's skeleton was set up for display at the Anatomical Museum at the University of Edinburgh and can still be viewed there at the time of this writing.

After being pardoned, Hare, Margaret, and their infant are thought to have escaped to Ireland. It also has been rumored that William Hare was thrown into a lime pit and subsequently suffered blindness before becoming a beggar.

The victims I focus on in this novel are Mary Paterson (also known as Mary Mitchell), Effie, Ann McDougal, James Wilson, Joseph, Margery Campbell (also known as Margaret Docherty), and a mute boy whose name is unknown. Joseph, the first victim, was a miller who was afflicted with fever before Burke and Hare suffocated him. Mary Paterson was believed to have been a prostitute. Effie worked as a cinder gatherer—one who sold oddments in the street. James Wilson, locally known as "Daft Jamie," was a well-known, beloved man with mental disabilities who often was seen entertaining in the streets. Ann McDougal was a relative of Burke's wife, and was lured in by the pair. The mute boy arrived at Hare's boardinghouse with his grandmother, who may have died due to an overdose of pain-killers. After she passed away, the pair murdered the boy too, and diverging from their previous M.O., they supposedly killed the child by breaking his back. Margery met Burke by chance and was murdered after he convinced her that they might be related and asked her back to the house. A couple, Ann and James Gray, lodgers at the boardinghouse, discovered Margery's body, which led to the exposure of the crimes.

The uproar over the Burke and Hare murders raised public awareness about the necessity for cadavers in the medical research community. They also contributed to the passing of the Anatomy

Act 1832, which significantly curbed the trade of illegally obtained corpses in Britain.

The Caledonian Hotel and Saint Cuthbert's Church are real locations in Edinburgh, as was the Great Northern Hospital in London. Clootie Wells also exist in numbers throughout Scotland and Ireland. These are thought to be magical pools guarded and inhabited by a nature spirit or goddess. People make pilgrimages to the Wells, tying bits of cloth from their clothing to tree branches in hopes of getting wishes granted. Clootie Wells are thought to be places of both healing and recovery.

Acknowledgements

I must acknowledge, with great gratitude, Dr. Eric Schroeder of UC Davis, who introduced me to not only the story of Burke and Hare, but to Scotland itself during a study abroad program. Thank you to my friends and family who read, re-read, and re-re-read the manuscript through all of its many transformations—your patience, feedback, and creative nurturing were invaluable. Thank you so much to Charlie Franco of Montag Press, to editor John Rak, and to Mateus Roberts for the incredible cover art. Finally, to my wonderful editor and dear friend Angela Brown, thank you from the bottom of my heart. This book lives because of you.

A. R. Meyering is a native of Los Angeles, California and a graduate student studying philosophy. In the past, she has worked as an English teacher in a small town in Kumamoto Prefecture, Japan. Her dark fantasy novel *Unreal City* won a Literary Classics International Book Award gold medal for YA horror and a Moonbeam Award bronze medal in YA horror. While doing her undergrad in English she studied abroad in Edinburgh, focusing on Scottish occult literature and folklore.

Made in the USA
Columbia, SC
22 October 2020